NOV - - 2018

Song of the Dryad

Song of the Dryad

Natalia Leigh

Song of the Dryad

Natalia Leigh

Enchanted Ink Publishing

Enchanted Ink Publishing
PO Box 620652
Littleton CO, 80162

First Edition: October 2018

ISBNs: 978-1-7326782-2-4

Printed in the United States of America
Library of Congress Control Number: 2018956341

To Greg,

For showing me magic in the mundane.

PROLOGUE

Charlotte Barclay stopped trick-or-treating the year she turned nine.

It was a sharp October night, the kind that meant winter was on its way, and she could see her breath as she followed the other children from house to house in her rural neighborhood. The oak trees stretching overhead were tall and dark, casting moving shadows through the yellow porch-light haze. One girl wore a fairy costume, with a pink dress and big glittering wings, and Charlotte felt it necessary to point out that fairies didn't wear sparkly pink dresses—they mostly wore leaves and flowers and sometimes even acorns on their heads. The girl was devastated, and when Dad asked Charlotte why she'd said such things, she replied simply, "Because it's true."

She'd always been able to see things, like the winged creatures that flitted through the shade in late summer and the tiny man in tatters that pulled weeds from the flowerbeds once the sun went down. Charlotte spent more time with the fairies than she did with her human friends, and some of her favorite memories were of adventures in the garden and stringing flower crowns with pixies that could fit in the palm of her hand. She told her parents and grandparents about them, of course, but they just smiled and laughed and ruffled her hair. No one else could see the fairies, and Charlotte had no idea why.

Charlotte's pillowcase was weighed down with silver-foiled candies when one of the neighbor boys stole a chocolate bar before she could stop him.

"That's mine!" she yelled. The boy took off running into the trees, his laughter ringing out in the dark, and Charlotte followed him. She crashed through the underbrush in her heavy black boots, the ones Dad made her wear so that her feet wouldn't get cold, and whooped triumphantly when the boy tripped and fell to the forest floor.

"Loser," she said as he gathered himself up and brushed damp leaves from his hands.

"Weirdo," he said back, sticking out his tongue.

Charlotte ignored him. She knelt down to grab the candy bar he'd dropped, and when she looked up, her breath hitched.

What she saw was big and naked and hunched in the rotting underbrush. It was crouched low behind the trunk of a wide tree. It had the body of a man, sickly gray skin, and the horned head of a goat.

The creature turned its head toward Charlotte, and its glowing eyes paralyzed her where she stood. It held something pale and round in its clawed hands, and stringy flesh slopped from its mouth as it incessantly chewed.

The creature swallowed, and its hairy lips pulled back in a grim smile.

Charlotte screamed. The boy scrambled away from her, hands over ears, and ran back the way they'd come. Charlotte wanted to run, but she couldn't move. The creature reached toward her, its claws cutting through the inky dark, and she squeezed her eyes closed.

"Charlotte?" came Dad's voice through the shadows. "Charlotte!" He crashed through the trees behind her and swept her up into his arms. "Baby, what's wrong?" he asked, wiping tears from her cheeks.

"It's there," she cried, pointing at the creature, which had risen up onto two legs and now towered over them. It tipped its head from side to side, glowing eyes rolling as other creatures howled in the treetops.

"What is?" Dad asked, turning around.

"The beast!" Charlotte wailed, and then buried her face in his jacket and sobbed. She plugged her ears, trying to drown out the sound of screaming in the treetops.

Dad carried her all the way home.

She stopped going into the woods after that. Eight years later, she'd almost convinced herself it had never happened.

Almost.

CHAPTER ONE

A pounding headache pulsed behind Charlotte's eyes, and teaching violin lessons wasn't doing anything to ease the pain. Her student drew his bow across the strings, and his violin let out a high-pitched squeal.

"Tomas, your bow is slipping again," she told him, then reached out to move the bow back to where it belonged, between the bridge and the fingerboard. Tomas tried again, and this time the string sang out a pleasant sound. "Much better," Charlotte said, pressing her fingertips to her aching temple. "Let's start from the top."

She'd been teaching violin lessons for the last few years, hoping to save up money for college. She enjoyed it most of the time, but some days were more difficult than others.

After a last squeaky version of "Twinkle, Twinkle, Little Star," Charlotte helped Tomas pack up his violin and walked him out into the music store to find his mom. Apart from Freddy, the purple-haired girl sitting behind the register, and a family looking at an expensive keyboard, Mélodie was empty.

"Is your mom picking you up today? Or your dad?" Charlotte asked.

"I think my brother is coming for me," Tomas said, banging his violin case against his thigh. Charlotte tried not to let him see her grimace.

Right on cue, the door swung open and a boy stepped in. He looked familiar, but Charlotte couldn't figure out where she'd seen him before. School, probably, but he wasn't in her grade. When he saw Charlotte and Tomas, he smiled.

"Sorry I'm late," he said, pushing the mop of brown hair off his forehead. His nose and cheeks were red from the cold. "Mom is busy tonight, and I almost forgot I had to pick him up. How did it go today?" He put an arm around his brother's shoulders.

Tomas just shrugged.

"It went well," Charlotte answered for him. "Just remember to keep that bow straight while you're practicing, okay, Tomas? Don't let it slip around too much."

"Hear that, bud?" Tomas's brother asked. "Keep that bow straight." He ruffled Tomas's hair and laughed. "Oh, I'm supposed to pay you, aren't I?" He dug in his pocket for his wallet and handed Charlotte a wrinkled ten-dollar bill. When Charlotte reached for it, she noticed that he was wearing a braided bracelet with a Celtic charm hanging from it—a three-sided knot made with one continuous line.

"It's actually twenty dollars," she said, offering the boy a small smile.

"Oh, shit." He opened up his wallet again, but there was only a movie ticket stub and a few dollar bills inside. "I'm so sorry. All I've got is the ten and"—he counted the crinkled dollar bills—"three ones."

"Don't worry about it. Your mom can square up with me on Tuesday." Charlotte pocketed the crinkled bill, trying not to let it bother her. She hated asking people for more money. "And, Tomas, when you're practicing this weekend, remember to keep your shoulders back, elbow up. It'll help your bow not slide around."

"Okay," Tomas said, tugging on his brother's hand.

"Thanks," the boy said, allowing Tomas to pull him toward the door. "I'll make sure he practices. Have a great night!"

"You too," Charlotte said, waving goodbye. She watched the two boys push through the door and step out into the September evening, and then she walked back through the music store and into the small room in the back that she rented out to teach lessons. There were posters on the walls of happy children holding instruments and grinning at their sheet music. An old CD player sat on a table in the corner, and Charlotte removed the *Suzuki Beginner's Violin* CD that she used to help students when she didn't feel like playing her violin for them over and over again. That would wear down her bow and the strings, and she couldn't afford to keep replacing everything.

After putting her teaching materials away, Charlotte pulled her violin case out from under a chair and ran a hand across its textured surface. She flipped the silver buckles and pushed the lid open. Inside, her violin sat snugly in its velvet-lined cavern. The wood was smooth and polished to a shine; Charlotte made sure to clean it with a soft cloth after each use. She had an old violin sitting in her closet at home, but for Christmas last year, Grandma gave her a brand-new violin, saying she'd need it for classes at the Bellini Institute. Charlotte's heart raced just thinking about it.

The Bellini Institute was a prestigious university that only the most talented young musicians, artists, and dancers got admitted to. Charlotte's audition was next September, so she still had a good deal of time to practice, which she certainly needed.

Charlotte tightened up her bow and spread her audition piece across two stands. It was "Chaconne" by Tomaso Antonio Vitali, and she would need to memorize the nine-minute piece in its entirety, but tonight she wanted to focus on the technical, tricky sections.

She rosined up her bow, and the violin strings sang out in clear voices as she tuned them and started to play. The calloused tips of her fingers danced across the strings, familiar with this piece they had played hundreds of times. But they still weren't good enough. Her fingers needed to be more precise, her notes clearer. She played harder, her brow creasing as she played through a technical section that required advanced shifting. Rosin rose in puffs around her as she pulled the bow across the strings and drew out the note with a slow, thick vibrato.

Her music filled the tiny practice room, echoing off the walls and ceiling. Out of the corner of her eye, Charlotte saw someone peek in the practice room window, hesitate, and then slip by. That small distraction caused her to play a note a bit too flat, and she exhaled quickly in frustration. She'd been playing for seven years, since she was in fifth grade, and tiny technical screw-ups like that shouldn't have been a problem anymore. If she didn't get into Bellini because of a simple note error, she'd never forgive herself.

Charlotte finished the piece and then spent the next hour tackling the sections that had been giving her trouble. Her head still throbbed with pressure, but she gritted her teeth against it. She had these headaches so often that she'd learned how to push through the pain. She was about to play the entire piece a third time when someone knocked quietly at the door.

"Come in!" she yelled, lowering her violin.

Freddy poked her purple head inside and smiled. "Sounds amazing," she said. "You're going to get into Bellini for sure."

Charlotte laughed and shook her head. That's what everyone told her, that she would get in for sure, but no one really knew, and while she appreciated their support, she didn't find it very realistic. Nobody realized just how difficult Bellini was to get into, and pretending otherwise wouldn't help.

"I've got to close early tonight. Aspen is taking me out to dinner." Freddy's pale cheeks warmed with pink, and Charlotte smiled.

"Where's she taking you?"

"Don't know," Freddy said, crossing her arms and leaning on the doorjamb. "Down to Denver, maybe. Don't get me wrong, your dad's restaurant is awesome, but tonight is special, so we want to make a date of it."

Charlotte laughed as she put her violin away. "How long have you been together now?"

"One year as of . . ." Freddy looked down at her watch. "As of five hours from now." She grinned, and the ring in her lip flashed.

"That's awesome," Charlotte said, but the words lacked enthusiasm.

Freddy picked up on it right away. "Don't worry about it, girl. The right guy will show up eventually. Just do you, and he'll show up when it's time."

"Thanks," Charlotte said, slinging the strap of her violin case across her shoulder. "I should be thankful, right? I've got all this free time to practice my violin."

"That's the spirit." Freddy slapped Charlotte on the back as she walked by. It sent another wave of pain through her head, and she bit back a miserable groan. "I'll see you Tuesday." Freddy waved goodbye as Charlotte stepped outside into the chilly September air.

It was a blustery evening, and Charlotte pulled her hood up over her brown curls as she walked across the city center, lovingly dubbed the Oval by locals. It was nearly October now, and the air was fresh and cold, marking the end of summer and the beginning of winter.

It was only six o'clock, but the sun was starting to set, and it would be dark in another hour. The air had the distinct smell of cold and dry leaves. Charlotte smiled. She hoped it would snow soon.

She walked past the Mapleton City Park, where children bundled in jackets could usually be found playing on the swings and calling out to one another in joyous voices, but tonight it was abandoned, and the swings creaked on their old chains. Her scuffed boots clicked on the cobblestone as she followed the sidewalk around the park and toward the bus stop. There was no one else waiting, so she took a seat on the wooden bench and blew warm air onto her fingers.

The bus was ten minutes late, as usual. The driver was a kind old man who always wore a fishing hat decorated with shiny lures, and he often got so distracted talking to people at the bus stops that he didn't get anywhere on time.

"Evening, Miss Charlotte," he said as Charlotte climbed aboard and swiped her bus pass.

She gave him a gentle smile and went to find a window seat. There were a few other people on the bus, the same ones she saw every Thursday, but no one looked up or even seemed to notice that she was there. They mostly stared at their phones or slumped against the cold windows, perfectly content with ignoring each other.

The bus creaked, and then it lurched forward and was on its way. Charlotte held her violin case in her lap, careful not to jostle it on the bumpy ride home. As soon as they were out of the city, oak trees started to flash by the window.

Mapleton had once been covered in thousands of oak trees, but over the years a few hundred acres had been cleared, and what remained of the oak forest, called the Greenwood, was all up north. That was where Charlotte's family lived, in a little cottage surrounded by trees and animals and creatures with rose-petal dresses and translucent wings, but Charlotte didn't like to think about those.

The bus hissed to a halt at a four-way stop, and Charlotte wiped the condensation off her window to peer at two men putting up a sign on the edge of the road. Both the sign and their work truck had the same two words printed in black: Nolan Enterprises.

Charlotte frowned. People had been trying to build in the Greenwood for years, but the city kept shutting them down. Seemed like the city had finally caved and sold, and Charlotte shook her head at the idea of it. The Greenwood was older than anyone in this city, older than the city itself, but it was only a matter of time before some businessman decided to level it and build a car dealership or something equally offensive. She rolled her eyes so hard that they may very well have gotten stuck in the back of her head.

As the bus passed by, she spotted a lone deer standing in the darkening shadows. It had a glorious set of antlers and a coat of honey-brown, and Charlotte thought it strange that the men and their truck hadn't frightened it away. It turned its head and met Charlotte's eyes, and for a moment they watched each other.

The bus heaved, shattering the magic of the moment. The deer dashed away into the trees, and Charlotte slumped back against her seat.

Her stop was coming up next, so she reached up and pulled the cord for a stop, even though the driver knew that she got off at the same place every day.

"You have a good evening," the old man said, tipping his fishing hat to her.

"You, too," she said, raising a hand to wave. Then the doors slid closed, and she turned and started the long trek up the gravel road toward home.

"Chaconne" was stuck in her head, so she hummed it to herself as she walked. But as she neared home, a different sound caught her attention.

Her boots were loud on the gravel road, so she stopped walking and tipped her head to one side. At first, all she could hear was the wind and the rustling leaves overhead, but then she heard something else.

It was faint music, carried on the wind from far off, and it made her think of summer and daisies and dancing in warm rain. Her arms prickled with goose bumps, and her heart raced. She strained harder to hear the music and looked around for its source, but she couldn't see anything in the dark except the many trunks of old oak trees that lined the road.

The music spun around her, and Charlotte realized suddenly what it must be. She remembered delicate wings and floating lights and tatters on a tiny man, and she shut the memories down as quickly as they surfaced, a throb of pain bursting through her head as she did so. She pulled her attention away from the music and the moving shadows in the forest, and with her head bowed she continued home, leaving the music to play for some other passerby unaware of its origin.

※

"I'm home!" Charlotte called out as she walked through the front door. It was toasty warm inside, and she could smell freshly baked banana bread wafting out of the kitchen. She pulled her feet out of her boots and slid across the hardwood floor to her bedroom, where she dropped off her violin case and backpack before going in search of food and family.

When she walked into the kitchen, her grandma already had a slice of bread waiting on the table.

"Welcome home," Grandma said. She wore a green apron with red toadstools on it, and her long gray hair was pulled back in a braid. Her glasses were bright blue, and pale pink nail polish completed her funky look.

"Sit, sit. Dinner is almost ready."

Charlotte did as she was told, then slathered up her banana bread with jam before taking a bite. She pulled her feet up under her, sitting like she did as a child when she wasn't tall enough to see over the table.

"Are Mom and Dad home?" she asked around another bite of bread.

"Your dad is working late, and your mom has been in her studio since this afternoon. She's got that big showcase coming up at the end of November." Grandma nodded toward the closed door in the hallway, where soft orange light seeped through the cracks around the frame.

Dad had a restaurant in town, the Blue Moose, and he'd often come home late with flakes of oregano in his hair, but Mom was an artist and spent most of her time locked away in her studio, painting or sculpting or staring thoughtfully out the window into the garden.

Grandma hummed to herself as she served up the veggie chili into two big bowls, then took off her apron and sat down at the table. Charlotte had to sneak a few shakes of salt into her chili when Grandma wasn't looking, lest she risk greatly offending her.

"So, what new experience did you have today?" Grandma asked, her eyes shining behind her bright glasses.

Charlotte sat back and thought about it. She massaged her temple mindlessly, despite knowing it would do nothing to ease her headache. "Well, I met someone new today," she said after a minute and described the boy with the Celtic knot on his bracelet.

"A Celtic knot?" Grandma asked. "Seems like an interesting boy. Might be someone you should get to know." She wiggled her silver eyebrows, and Charlotte laughed.

"I didn't even catch his name. It was just a random thing."

"No such thing," Grandma said. "Everyone you meet, you meet for a reason." She took a slurp of chili and smiled. "I'd bet you'll see that boy again. One way or another."

Just then the door creaked open in the hall.

"I'm home!" Dad called out and appeared around the corner. His curly brown hair was fluffed up, which meant he'd probably spent a good portion of the day running his hands through it. It must have been a rough day.

"Welcome home," Charlotte said, standing to give him a hug. He was tall and thin, but his chest and arms were strong around her. "Long day?"

"Very. It was one thing after another. Maybe I should retire."

"Yeah, right," Charlotte said. He loved the Blue Moose—he probably wouldn't retire until he was dead.

Dad hung his jacket up in the hall closet and removed his boots, then stretched his arms and yawned. "Where's Emily?"

"Studio," Grandma said. "She's been at it since this afternoon."

"Hopefully she had a breakthrough. She's been frustrated lately."

"Are you going to go get her?" Charlotte asked hopefully. She never liked to interrupt Mom's studio time, but it was fine if Dad did it.

"Nah, if she's on a roll, I want to let her work. Besides, I'm exhausted. I'm going to shower and wash the basil out of my hair." He bent over and kissed Charlotte on the forehead before walking down the hall to his bedroom.

Charlotte helped Grandma clean up the kitchen and made herself a mug of herbal tea. It wouldn't help her headache, nothing seemed to, but something warm to drink always calmed her down in the evenings. She headed toward her room, pausing outside Mom's studio door.

The light was on, and a yellow haze leaked out from around the door. Charlotte reached for the doorknob but hesitated. She pictured Mom hunched over the desk, brush in hand as she brought worlds to life on canvas. The showcase was in November, but she'd said just that morning that there was still much work to do. So, with a sigh, Charlotte dropped her hand and stepped away. She'd see Mom tomorrow, but tonight she'd let her work.

CHAPTER TWO

The next morning, Charlotte squinted her eyes open and groaned, still groggy from her headache the night before. The sun slept in late at this time of year, so it no longer slipped through the curtains to wake her up in the mornings. She'd have to start setting an alarm again—what a drag.

She sat up in bed and stretched her arms overhead, glad to feel that her headache had diminished to no more than a gentle throb along her temples. She reached for the frankincense oil on her bedside table and massaged a bit into the back of her neck. It never made the pain go away, but sometimes it eased her suffering, if only a little.

The headaches had started when she was ten, and no drug, herb, or aromatherapy technique did anything to ease them. Doctors had turned her away with shrugged shoulders and mumbled replies: they had no idea what was wrong with her. Countless brain scans later, and they still had no answers—all of her results came back normal. Charlotte had an idea about what might be causing these headaches, but she never spoke her suspicions out loud.

Charlotte barely had enough time to scarf down a piece of toast and a bowl of oatmeal before she had to run out the door. Mom's studio door was still closed, and Charlotte didn't have time to stop in and say good morning. She was probably going to miss the bus as it was, and saying hello to Mom always had the potential to turn into long conversations about dreams or artwork or whatever else Mom was thinking about at the time. Charlotte didn't have the time to spare.

She hurried out the front door, and her feet slid out from under her the moment they hit the porch. She fell right on her butt in the doorway, shock giving way to frustration when she saw mud tracked all over the porch.

"Stupid raccoons," she mumbled to herself as she climbed to her feet, but she didn't mean it. She'd watched the raccoon family all summer and had become rather fond of them. They seemed smart and curious, and she could spend an hour staring out her window watching them hunt for berries along the edge of the Greenwood. She assumed it was the raccoons that walked all over the porch at night with their muddy paws. Either way, now she had to go back inside and change into a clean pair of pants, so she would definitely be late to class. Pre-Calc was just going to have to wait.

❧

Charlotte had no qualms about being late for math class, but she'd never been late for orchestra. The orchestra director, Mr. Hamilton, was extremely strict about punctuality. If you were late, you didn't get to play.

"Don't slide into your notes," Mr. Hamilton said to the class, waving his hand to cut them off. "They have to be heard clearly by someone in the back of the auditorium. What have I told you a hundred times? Anyone?"

"Don't throw a hand grenade on your instrument," a few of the students recited together.

"Exactly!" Mr. Hamilton jumped up, waving his baton at his students. "Don't let your fingers explode all over the strings. Play carefully. Technically. Now, let's run through measures one hundred through one hundred fifteen. First violins, start us off."

Charlotte tucked her violin under her chin and readied her bow on the strings, eyes trained on Mr. Hamilton to give them the downbeat. She was the section leader of the first violins, so she sat immediately to Mr. Hamilton's left in the front row. She could hear the students behind her readying their instruments as her stand partner/best friend, Melanie Miyake, drew in a breath. Mr. Hamilton counted them off, and the room filled with the sound of violins.

The viola section butchered the last five measures, and Mr. Hamilton spent the rest of the class drilling them over and over.

"How is the piece coming along for Bellini?" Melanie asked when class was over and they were packing up.

Charlotte shrugged. "I've been working on it, but there are still some sections that I'm struggling through. My fingers don't feel fast enough."

"You should come see me if you're struggling," Mr. Hamilton said, clearly eavesdropping as he walked by. "I'm free during office hours if you need help." He popped Charlotte on the head with a folder full of sheet music before disappearing into his office.

"Teacher's pet," Melanie grumbled, and they both laughed.

They made their way toward the lunch room, fighting the crowds and groups of kids that stopped in the hallways to say hello to their friends. Charlotte held her breath in the gym hallway, or else the stench of sweat would have ruined her appetite.

She hadn't had time to pack a lunch that morning, so she got stuck purchasing one. The only plant-based option was a wilted salad that looked well past its expiration date with a few wrinkled cherry tomatoes and an Italian dressing, but it would have to do. She and Melanie usually liked to eat outside on the school patio, but the sky had been growing dark all morning and had finally let loose with an onslaught of rain. They decided to hide out in the orchestra room instead, and they giggled and gossiped while Mr. Hamilton sang along to some horrible '80s song in his office.

"So," Melanie said, her glossed lips turning up into a sly smile as she scooped a dumpling out of her bento box. "Marco asked for my number yesterday."

"Oh my God!" Charlotte said, and in her excitement a tomato slid off her fork and rolled across the floor, gathering lint and dust as it went.

Melanie pushed a lock of silky black hair behind her ear and smiled. "Yeah, and he texted me last night. We've been talking all day." Melanie pulled out her phone and handed it over.

Charlotte read quickly through their exchange of flirty messages and tried to ignore the jealousy she felt. Melanie had no lack of suitors and hadn't ever gone to a school dance without a date. Charlotte, on the other hand, hadn't even been on a real date, and the closest her lips had ever come to a boy was in fifth grade during a round of truth or dare under the slides on the playground. She'd been dared to kiss a boy on the cheek and had felt a rush of excitement and guilt after grazing her lips across his salty skin. He'd wiped it off with an air of disgust, and Charlotte had shrunk under the laughter of the other girls and boys.

"Do you think he'll ask you out?" Charlotte asked, handing the phone back.

"I hope so," Melanie said. "And if he doesn't, maybe I'll ask him." She winked and then dissolved into laughter.

Charlotte laughed along, but under her happy smile was the looming question: When will it be my turn?

After lunch, Charlotte and Melanie headed to their junior English class. Charlotte sat in the second row by the window, which was nice because she could stare outside when class got dull. Today, though, they were studying Shakespeare's *A Midsummer Night's Dream*, which Charlotte was enjoying. Learning Shakespearean language had been a struggle at first, but after getting a basic handle on the slang, she'd started to enjoy his work.

She took off her coat and slid her violin under the table, then took out her book and binder. She hummed the Vitali piece to herself, her calloused fingertips tapping out the complicated rhythm on her book of Shakespeare's works.

From where she sat, she had a perfect view into the main student parking lot, where cars zipped into parking spaces and students ran across the wet, glistening asphalt to escape the downpour. Charlotte rested her head on her hand, and as she stared outside, she spotted someone who looked vaguely familiar.

He wore a black hoodie and carried a large art bag slung over one shoulder. Intrigued, Charlotte narrowed her eyes as she watched him ride his skateboard across the busy parking lot and up onto the wet sidewalk. When he paused to pick up his board, his hood slipped back and Charlotte got a glimpse of his face. She recognized him right away—he was the boy from the music store. She must have seen him around school before, but she couldn't recall his name or remember ever having a class with him. Maybe he was a senior?

Charlotte watched him from the window and wondered what kind of artwork he was carrying around in his bag. Did he paint? Sketch? Use charcoal or acrylic? Thanks to Mom, Charlotte knew a thing or two about the process. When she was young, she used to curl up in a chair in Mom's studio and watch her work, sometimes for hours on end. She loved the patient precision of it, the unyielding focus and the small wrinkle her mom would get between her eyes while she worked. Charlotte had tried her hand at art, but it never felt right. She would struggle for hours on one painting, trying to make it look the way it did in her head, but it never turned out the way she wanted. Art became a sore spot for Charlotte, and that was about the same time she first picked up the violin. After discovering her love for music, she stopped pushing herself to be an artist. She had notes and phrases and the glorious harmonies of strings playing in tune—charcoal was useless to her now.

The boy took the stairs to the front doors two at a time, splashed through a deep puddle, and then was lost in a sea of faces.

"Settle down, people," the teacher said from the front of the room. "Let's open up to Act 3. Who can tell me a bit about what happens in this act?"

Charlotte pulled her gaze reluctantly away from the window and raised her hand.

❧

Halfway through AP Biology later that day, Charlotte looked up from her study of plant cells to see a student come through the door with a red note. The other students looked up as well, everyone curious and hopeful. Red notes meant student dismissal, so whoever it belonged to would get to pack up and leave class.

Charlotte looked back down at the diagram she was working on. She hated biology and couldn't figure out why she'd thought an AP class was the smart way to go. She'd picked her classes back before she was certain that she wanted to attend Bellini, and now it felt like a painful, useless class. Once she graduated next year, she'd never have to look at a nucleus again.

"Ms. Barclay," the teacher said, and Charlotte looked up. "You're dismissed. Make sure to finish those diagrams for our next class."

Confused, Charlotte slowly put away her books and binders and zipped up her backpack. Why would she receive a dismissal slip? She'd only ever received a red note one time, and that was in her freshman year when her dad picked her up early to take her to an orthodontist appointment. Yippee. But she had no reason to receive one today.

Charlotte took the red note from her teacher and saw Dad's signature in the lower right corner. *Why is he here?* she wondered. It was a Friday, so he should have been at the Moose preparing for the dinner rush.

She left class and headed down the long hallway toward the main staircase. The walls were lined with neon club posters that screamed at her to JOIN THEATER TODAY or COSPLAYERS UNITE. She ignored them all, kept her eyes forward when she passed a couple making out against the lockers, and finally descended the main staircase to find her dad waiting outside the administrative office.

"Hey, Dad," Charlotte said to his back. He turned around, and she knew from the look on his face that something was wrong. "What is it?" she asked, bracing herself for the worst.

His forehead was creased, and the wrinkles around his eyes were deep and dark. "It's your mom."

CHAPTER THREE

Charlotte didn't panic. Ever.

When she was young, she'd watched Melanie break her arm falling off the swings and had remained perfectly calm while walking her to the nurse's office. Dad cut the tip of his finger chopping onions for dinner one night, and Charlotte had fetched a towel to hold on the gushing wound while she called 911 with the other hand. When bad things happened, she tended to get extremely calm.

Now she sat quietly in her dad's truck, staring out the window and watching the small town of Mapleton flash by. The rain poured down in sheets, and Charlotte followed the windshield wipers with her eyes as they traced an arc across the glass. She'd been silent since Dad told her the news.

Mom was missing. The last anyone had seen of her was yesterday afternoon, and she hadn't been heard from since.

"Did you see her last night when you got home from school?" Dad asked, desperation in his voice.

"No." Charlotte shook her head. "Her door was closed. I thought she was just working late."

"That's what we all thought," Dad said. His hands were tight on the steering wheel, and there was tension along his jaw.

They sped through two lights and across the intersection onto Old Hickory Road. It was a steady incline up to their house, and the road was wet and muddy from all the rain. Lesser vehicles may have faltered, but

Dad's truck growled all the way up the hill. Gravel crunched under the truck tires as they drove up the long driveway to the house.

Charlotte was surprised to see a patrol car parked outside when they got home. The officer, a woman with straw-yellow hair pulled into a low ponytail, stood at the door, talking to Grandma. Dad put the truck in park and jumped out so fast that he forgot to put on the emergency brake.

Charlotte slid across the seat and pushed the emergency brake down with her foot, moving slowly and methodically.

She climbed out of the truck, fetched her backpack and violin, and then walked across the browning grass to join the others at the front door. She was rain-soaked by the time she stepped up on the covered porch.

"This is so unlike her," Grandma was saying. "Something's wrong. She wouldn't just leave like this." She had her long gray hair hanging loose and her bright blue glasses pushed up on top of her head.

"What's the protocol here?" Dad asked, shaking rain from his windbreaker.

Charlotte looked at the officer's name tag. It read BECK.

"I'll need to file a report first. I need a physical description of Emily, as well as information regarding when she was last seen. A photo, too, if you have it. If she's still missing after twenty-four hours, we'll take the next step." The officer caught Charlotte's eye and gave her a quick smile.

Dad invited Officer Beck inside, and Charlotte sat with them in the kitchen after grabbing a picture of Mom out of the photo album on the coffee table. She handed the photo to Officer Beck and watched her slide it carefully inside the pocket of her jacket. Grandma put the kettle on for tea while Officer Beck pulled out a pen and pad of paper. Dad gave the officer a description of Mom, down to the blanket of freckles across her pale shoulders.

"Has Emily been known to disappear from time to time?" Officer Beck asked, and Dad shook his head.

"No, not without telling someone where she's going." He ran his thumb across his lower lip and then began tapping out a nervous rhythm on the table with his fingers.

The officer turned to Charlotte. "When was the last time you saw your mom?"

Charlotte took a steadying breath before she spoke. "Yesterday morning, before I left for school."

"What did you talk about? Anything out of the ordinary?" She smiled when Grandma brought three cups of tea to the table, but she didn't drink any of it—some people didn't like to see dandelions floating in their teacup.

Charlotte shook her head, trying to remember everything she and Mom had talked about.

"I'm not sure," she began.

"Take your time," Dad said, reaching over to take Charlotte's hand.

"Anything you remember could be of help to us," the officer said, pen and paper in hand.

Charlotte sat back in her chair and looked down at her hands. The tips of the fingers on her left hand were calloused from her violin strings, and she ran her thumb gently across their rough texture as she thought back to the last conversation she had with her mom.

Mom had come into the kitchen wearing her silk kimono robe, the deep green one that looked so beautiful on her. She had her blond hair pulled back in a messy braid, and a few tendrils hung down around her face. Charlotte pictured the way she'd sunk into the chair across the table and pulled one of her long legs up to her chest. She'd rested her chin on one pale kneecap and smiled, and Charlotte had immediately asked her what was wrong.

Mom had laughed, and the sound was rich and beautiful. "What do you mean? I'm just looking at you."

"No, you're smiling at me. Usually you don't smile until after you've had your coffee."

"Well, I had a good dream." Mom stretched her arms overhead, and the kimono sleeves slipped down, revealing the colorful dragon tattoo that curled around her forearm. "I dreamed that I was dancing barefoot in the Greenwood, wearing my wedding dress while a choir of bluebirds sang for me." She closed her eyes and swayed back and forth.

"I love you," Charlotte said, "but I think you're crazy."

Mom sat back in the creaky kitchen chair and smiled. "You and everyone else, love."

Charlotte stood to leave for school, and Mom reached out to catch her arm as she passed.

"It's cold out today," Mom said. "Want to wear my scarf? The red looks so nice against your dark hair."

"It gives my hair static," Charlotte said, gently pulling away. "Thanks though. I've gotta go or I'm gonna be late." She knelt down and gave her mom a hug, and that was the last she saw of her.

Remembering all of this, Charlotte relayed it back to the officer with as much detail as she could. Hearing it, Dad smiled. The officer scribbled everything down on her pad of paper and got up from the table and asked to look around the house. Dad got up to show her around, and Grandma went back to the kitchen.

Grandma had been a bustler for as long as Charlotte could remember. Anytime she was upset or stressed out, she would flit from room to room in the house, tidying and straightening up. Now she grabbed a plant-fiber sponge from under the sink and started to scrub the front of the fridge. The fridge wasn't even dirty, but she scrubbed it until she was panting from the effort.

"Grandma," Charlotte said gently, "it's clean."

"I know, I know." Grandma tossed the sponge into the sink. "I'm going to go fold the laundry." She walked across the kitchen into the laundry room, the scent of lavender oil trailing after her.

After walking through the house and into Mom's studio, Dad and the officer went outside to check the doors and windows for any sign of "forced entry," as Officer Beck called it. Charlotte stayed at the table and traced a whorl in the wood with her finger while she waited. She listened to the rain pelting down on the roof and striking the window panes. *Mom loves rain*, she thought.

"This is a good start," the officer said as she finished up the initial search and pushed through the screen door with Dad in her wake. Her boots left muddy footprints on the hardwood floor, and her rain jacket dripped as she stood in the entryway. "I'm going to take this report back to the station, and then I'll be in contact about the next step."

"How long will that take?" Dad asked.

"Not long, Mr. Barclay. If Emily still hasn't shown up by tomorrow, then I'll get my team out here."

Dad didn't look entirely pleased with having to wait, but he narrowed his eyes and gave the officer a firm nod. He walked her to the door, thanked her, and then closed it behind her. Charlotte stayed seated at the table until she heard the patrol car pull away down the gravel drive. She listened to Dad slump up against the front door, and then she stood up and walked slowly across the kitchen and down the hall to stand at the threshold of Mom's studio.

The door was sitting open, and the lamp on Mom's desk was turned on low, filling the room with warm yellow light. Charlotte stepped inside, her socks whispering over the fluffy rug that Mom kept on the floor. After closing the door, she stepped up to Mom's desk and looked down at her workspace. Mom had been working on a new watercolor painting, but she hadn't gotten very far. Her paints were dried up in their tray, and her brush had fallen on the floor. Charlotte bent down to retrieve it, and as she stood back up she caught a glimpse of color outside.

It was a flash of red fabric, as bright against the dreary forest as fresh blood over white teeth. In an instant the color was gone, swallowed up by the Greenwood. Charlotte rushed to the window and shoved it open, then stuck her head outside.

"Mom!" she yelled, but the rain was coming down so hard that it washed away her voice. Charlotte didn't even take the time to put on her boots before she crawled out the window into the pouring rain.

"Mom!" she yelled as her feet landed in the mud below the window. "Mom!" Charlotte pushed her dark curls away from her face and pulled up her hood to shield her eyes from the pouring rain. She set off across the yard, the grass slippery beneath her feet. She pushed past the old tree swing Grandpa had repaired for her and started up the embankment behind the house. It was steep and the rain had turned everything to mud, and Charlotte had to use the trees as leverage as she climbed. She tipped her head back and looked up the hill, and around the trunk of an old oak, she saw the flash of fabric again. This time she recognized it—Mom's red scarf.

"Mom!" she yelled. "Slow down!" She struggled the rest of the way up the hill, ran across the abandoned hiking trail, and ventured deeper into the Greenwood, wincing in pain as she stumbled over rocks and twigs that lay concealed in the mud.

Charlotte kept her eyes forward, trying not to let her gaze or mind wander. She'd seen things in these trees that no one else could see or understand, and she didn't want to risk seeing them again. If she just kept her eyes forward and her mind focused, she could grab Mom and get out of here.

She scrubbed a hand across her face, trying to wipe the rainwater out of her eyes. She was following an old game trail through the trees, and for a moment she paused and glanced back the way she'd come. The Greenwood was dense and dark, and Charlotte had already gone so far into the trees that she was unable to see her home from here. Her heart thumped hard, fear starting to tingle across her skin.

"Mom!" she yelled again, wondering if she should turn back. Then, just up ahead, she saw the flash of red fabric. "Stop this!" she screamed into the rain, continuing down the game trail despite the instincts telling her to turn back. Up ahead, two trees tangled together in an embrace, and Charlotte had to squeeze between their trunks and push branches away from her face as she slipped through. She felt suddenly on the verge of tears when she looked up and saw her mom's red scarf lying on the ground. It was spread out in the mud in the center of what looked to be five tall standing stones, and sitting beside it was one of Mom's favorite sandals. White-gray fog hung low around the standing stones, and the sight of it gave Charlotte goose bumps. She moved forward cautiously, wondering what kind of trick this was. Something felt familiar about this place, but she couldn't figure out why.

The stones were much taller than she was, despite being broken off in places and eroded by Colorado's mountain weather. Each had a niche carved into its belly, as if some small statue or ornament was supposed to be displayed there, but they were all empty. Some of the stones were even tagged with graffiti, though it was old and faded.

"Mom?" Charlotte called out softly as she walked into the clearing. A ring of red-and-white mushrooms sprouted up from the forest floor, forming a perfect circle in the center of the five crumbling standing stones, and the articles of clothing lay in the circle of fungi. Some small voice in Charlotte's head told her to be wary of this place, but she pushed it away, irritated that her childish fears still had so much control over her. Charlotte stepped into the ring of toadstools and bent down to gather up Mom's belongings.

The sounds of the forest fell away around her and the rain stopped in an instant. The grass beneath Charlotte's feet, previously brown and littered with wet leaves, was now thick and green. The sound of rain beating the canopy of leaves overhead had been replaced by the singing of birds. She looked up and had to catch her breath.

Wherever she was now, it sure wasn't the Greenwood.

CHAPTER FOUR

A clump of long, damp curls had fallen into Charlotte's eyes, and she pushed it away with trembling fingers. She stood very still, her heart beating hard and fast. She moved only her eyes, afraid to shift from the spot where she stood.

The five standing stones still loomed over her, but now they gleamed in the yellow sunlight that shone through the leaves overhead. A warm breeze blew through the trees, making the tall grass around Charlotte's knees sing.

That's not right, Charlotte thought, finally turning her head to look around. Just a moment ago she'd been running through a muddy forest that looked on fire with autumn colors. Now, the air smelled like summer. Strange, beautiful plants grew around her in abundance. They had stems the creamy color of pearls and flowers that grew like tufts of cotton candy. The trees grew tall and twisted, their trunks bending and twining together. Their leaves were the size of Charlotte's hands and greener than grass in early spring.

Oh my God, Charlotte thought, her fingertips tingling. *Where am I?*

Mom's damp scarf caught the breeze and flickered across Charlotte's vision, reminding her what she'd been doing in the forest in the first place. She'd been chasing Mom, or so she'd thought. She held her mom's sandal in her other hand and realized for the first time how strange it was that there was only one. Why would Mom run into the Greenwood without a shoe on her left foot? Or had she simply dropped it? But why would she wear her sandals into the forest in the first place? None of this made sense. And where had the rain gone? Charlotte tipped her head back, but all she saw overhead were leaves and snippets of a blue sky.

Maybe this was a dream. She'd been exhausted and suffering from such a horrible headache the night before that it would make sense she was having vivid dreams. Sometimes herbal tea gave her strange dreams, too.

Something moved in the trees behind her, and Charlotte whirled around. Three pairs of eyes blinked out at her from the leaves, and she let out a squeal of surprise.

"What do you want?" she demanded, holding out Mom's sandal like a club. It was a flimsy, pathetic thing, but it was better than nothing.

The three pairs of eyes disappeared, and what sounded like a skirmish took place in the bushes. Voices argued in hushed tones, and then a small man came hurtling out of the bushes as if he'd been pushed.

Charlotte let out a scream, and the tiny man did the same, but he held a spear instead of a shoe. It was about half Charlotte's height and tipped with a point that gleamed in the sunlight streaming through the leaves overhead. He pointed it at her with shaking hands.

"C-c-come with us," he said in a surprisingly high-pitched voice.

"No," Charlotte said, still wielding Mom's shoe.

The small man glanced over his shoulder, back at the bush where two pairs of eyes had reappeared.

"Whatifshewon'tgo?" he asked the others in such a quick voice that Charlotte struggled to understand him. The others responded, but Charlotte couldn't tell what they said. They started to argue again, giving Charlotte a moment to try to figure out exactly what she was looking at.

The man wore a green tunic and tan cloth pants that were tucked into tall, soft-looking boots. He wore a green cap and had sun-weathered skin. He couldn't have stood any higher than Charlotte's waist.

What is he? she wondered.

The arguing stopped abruptly, and the man turned back around, lowering his spear. "Please," he said in a kinder voice, "will you come with us? She's waiting for you."

"Who is?" Charlotte asked. She slowly lowered the shoe and narrowed her eyes.

The man blushed and a smile flickered across his face. "Our lady waits for you, and we are to take you to her."

"Where am I? How did I get here?"

"Through the portal, of course," the tiny man said, as if it were the most normal thing in the world. He gestured to the ring of standing stones with the tip of his spear, and Charlotte stepped back.

"I'm looking for my mom," Charlotte said. "Do you know anything about that?"

"Our lady will explain everything," he said.

Charlotte's heart raced. Did he know where Mom was? Was he the one who took her? She felt like throwing the shoe at him but resisted. If he knew where Mom was, then she needed him to take her there.

"Okay," she said, "but no funny business." She shook the shoe at him threateningly, and he nodded.

"No funny business," he agreed. The bushes rustled behind him and two more men stepped out. They were the same height and wore the same clothes, but their faces were very different. One had a large nose and small eyes, and the other looked like a young man, his skin still smooth and untouched by time. They each carried a spear, which Charlotte kept a close eye on.

"You go first," she said, stepping back.

The men looked at each other as if trying to decide if they'd allow it, and then the younger one shrugged and gave Charlotte a smile. "Very well. Let's go!"

He led the way through the trees, whacking bushes and branches out of the way as he went, and the older men sighed in exasperation but followed him anyway.

Charlotte watched them go, wondering if this was a bad idea. She looked around at the strange forest and the mysterious standing stones, and got the feeling that perhaps this wasn't a dream after all.

They led her out of the forest and into the sun. It was warm on her skin, pleasant, but not too hot. Her jeans and sweatshirt felt too heavy suddenly, still dripping with rainwater. Charlotte lifted a hand to shield her eyes from the sun and squinted. Then she stopped walking.

Across a field of shimmering yellow grass was a tree of unbelievable size. It stood so tall that half of it was concealed in clouds. Its branches reached so long and wide that the shadows they cast must have covered miles of grassland. Stretching out around the tree was a village straight out of a fairy tale. The tiny houses had thatched roofs, and smoke curled from the chimneys, despite the heat of the day. A sparkling blue river cut through the valley, and a creaky wooden water mill made lazy circles around and around. It was as if Charlotte had fallen back in time.

"Hurry up, now," one of the small men said, and then rolled his eyes when Charlotte wielded the sandal at him. She followed along behind them, her head on a swivel as she tried to take everything in. The dirt beneath her feet gave way to a path laid with tiny flat stones that sparkled in the sunlight. They looked like flakes of silver, but they shone in rainbow hues when the sun hit them.

The path cut through the valley of yellow grass, and Charlotte reached out to trail her fingers over it as she walked. The soft tufts on top felt like the silky hair at the end of a cat's tail.

The village in the distance grew larger as Charlotte followed after the men in her muddy socks. She hesitated at an idyllic arched wooden bridge that stretched out over the slow-moving river below, and was startled when the youngest of her three escorts doubled back and took her hand in his.

"Come," he said. "We don't bite." Though unsure of it all, Charlotte allowed him to lead her across the bridge and into the village. The path turned to cobblestone, and Charlotte winced as she caught her toe on a rough stone. She regretted not putting on her boots.

The deeper into the village they walked, the more Charlotte seemed to draw attention from the others. One woman stopped watering her plants to watch Charlotte walk by, and a group of men smoking long pipes fell silent as their eyes followed Charlotte's movements. One of the old men blew out a long stream of gray smoke, and it smelled like burned cherries and musky incense. Charlotte waved the smoke out of her face and coughed.

"Hurry up," one of the men called from up ahead. "She won't wait all day."

Charlotte's young escort pulled on her hand and she let him tug her along. She glanced over her shoulder and was surprised to find a group of the small creatures following her. They paused and turned away when she looked over her shoulder, but she could hear their soft-soled shoes on the cobblestones again when she looked away.

The three men led her across a square with a sparkling fountain, and then they stepped up in front of the enormous tree.

"What is this?" Charlotte asked, gazing up at the branches that towered over them.

"The Great Tree," the oldest man replied, his wrinkled face cracking open with a smile. A group of curious onlookers had gathered at the base of the tree, and the three men waved everyone out of the way.

"Move it, move it," they said, thumping their spears on the cobblestone.

The onlookers whispered and pointed, but they moved out of the way to allow Charlotte and her escorts to pass.

"You're a rare sight here," the youngest of the guards said to Charlotte.

"Where are we?" Charlotte asked, getting a nervous tingle in her belly.

"Lyra," the young man said. "It's the domain of our good lady."

Lyra? she thought. *Where the heck am I?*

Charlotte tipped her head back. Thousands of leaves rustled overhead, the sheer size and volume of them making it sound like a waterfall about to crash down and sweep everyone away. Something shimmery caught Charlotte's eye, and she watched as three tiny, winged creatures rode a falling leaf safely to the ground, their wings sparkling in the sunlight. The leaf alighted gently in the grass, and the tiny creatures fluttered into the air, twirling on the warm breeze before flying away.

Charlotte had her fair share of vivid dreams, but this felt different. Those shimmering wings—she'd seen them before, in the back garden when the summer flowers grew tall and bloomed in bursts of color. It had been years, and despite her greatest attempts, she'd never been able to wipe the images from her mind.

One of the men stepped up to the tree, calling Charlotte's attention away from her distant memories.

Carved into the trunk of the Great Tree were tall double doors painted in shimmering gold and silver. They must have been twenty feet tall and made of solid wood, and the great silver handles were in the shape of a stag's head, antlers and all.

The man knocked hard on the door and then stood back.

"Just wait," the young one whispered to Charlotte. "You're going to love her."

The door began to creak open, and with a mighty groan it swung outward to admit Charlotte and her escorts. It took four small men to push each door open, and they stepped aside and watched Charlotte with curious eyes as she walked through the doorway.

A warm breeze rustled her hair as she stepped into the room, which was full of natural sunlight that streamed in through stained-glass windows. The tree was hollow inside, and birds flew over Charlotte's head. It smelled of the forest after a rain storm, and of the humid butterfly pavilion that she used to take field trips to as a child. Soft moss carpeted the ground beneath her feet, and mushrooms sprouted up from it in colorful bunches. Everywhere she looked there were plants. They grew from the ground and spider-webbed across the sides of the tree, covering every surface in greenery. And in the center of the room, most awe-inspiring of all, was a throne made of branches and leaves, and sitting upon it was a woman with a head of antlers that were draped in moss and garlands of flowers.

"Welcome," she said softly and blinked her impossibly wide, round brown eyes. Her lips turned up into a smile. "I'm so glad to see you. I've been awaiting your arrival." She lifted one hand, and a songbird fluttered out of the warm air to land on her finger. The woman stroked the bird's head and whispered something to it that made the bird sing.

"H-how did you know I was coming?" Charlotte asked, finding it difficult not to stumble over her words.

"Because I sent the oak men to fetch you," the woman said. She cast a kind look to the small man standing at Charlotte's side, and he removed his cap and blushed.

"For what?" Charlotte asked. She looked over her shoulder at the eight small men closing the giant doors behind her. "And where am I?"

The woman narrowed her round eyes and cocked her head to one side. She studied Charlotte for a long time and then stood from her throne, her golden hair swishing past her waist as she did so. The bird on her finger flew away and was lost among the greenery.

"What do you know of us?" the woman asked.

"Is this a dream?" Charlotte asked, though she feared she already knew the answer.

The woman shook her head, and her massive antlers cast moving shadows over her shoulders. Charlotte felt a familiar fear grip her stomach and twist it painfully. At this point she'd typically push her memories of the creatures she saw as a child down and away and would instantly feel a headache throb behind her eyes. She couldn't push the images away this time, though, because they were standing right in front of her.

"Where do you think you are?" the woman asked, her tone growing impatient.

"I don't know," Charlotte whispered, her nerves starting to fray. She'd only made it this far under the notion that it was all make-believe, but now her heart was pounding hard and she scanned the room for exits to make an escape.

The woman let out an exasperated sigh. "They've told you nothing of us? Nothing of your responsibilities to us?"

"I don't even know who you are," Charlotte said. "And where's my mom? Do you have her?"

"It's worse than I thought," the woman said, turning to pace the room. She wore a thin gown of green that trailed the mossy floor behind her and revealed a flash of leg as she moved. Her feet were bare and her toes unpainted. Her golden hair was thick and wavy and moved like a cloak as she walked. She paced to a window and slouched against the colorful glass.

Charlotte's hands started to tremble. She held Mom's sandal and scarf close to her chest, clinging to the only things she could make sense of. "What are you?" she whispered.

"What am *I*?" The woman turned and flashed Charlotte a white smile. She held out her arms in a grand gesture. "I'm the reason the Great Tree stands. I'm the protector of your beloved Greenwood, and of Lyra." She shook her head and let out a small, sad laugh. "I'm a dryad, Charlotte. But what are you?"

What am I? Charlotte had no idea how to answer that. And what was a dryad?

"You don't even know," the dryad whispered, almost to herself. "She doesn't even know," she repeated to the oak men, who shook their heads and sighed. The dryad strode across the mossy floor and glowered down at Charlotte. She stood a head taller than Charlotte even without the added height of her antlers. "Have you ever heard of the Shrine Keepers?"

Charlotte didn't trust her voice, so she just shook her head.

"Of course not. They're only your ancestors, your own blood. Why would you know about them and their work?" The dryad pressed her fingertips to her brow and sighed. When she looked back up, her eyes were narrowed. "You hail from a long line of Shrine Keepers, Charlotte, humans tasked with caring for our shrines, places of immense power. You used to see us when you were a child, did you not?"

Charlotte swallowed a lump of fear and nodded. "I used to see things," she whispered.

"Not *things*," the dryad corrected her. "You saw the fae. And now you don't anymore. Why is that?"

"I don't know." Charlotte averted her eyes.

"Yes, you do. You deny our existence and our power, just like your grandmother and her mother before her."

"Grandma can see you?" Charlotte asked, perking up. She thought she was the only one.

"Not anymore, clearly." The dryad shook her head. "Once a Shrine Keeper stops believing, they lose the Sight forever. But not you." The dryad pointed one long, thin finger at Charlotte. "You still believe in us, you'd just prefer that we didn't exist. Is that right?" When Charlotte didn't answer, the dryad went on. "And your headaches? Those must be terrible."

"How do you know about those?" Charlotte asked. It felt like her skin was crawling with ants. How did the dryad know so much about her?

"The Sight is powerful," the dryad explained. "Denying it is more painful than using it."

"What do you want from me?" Charlotte whispered.

"I want you to do your job." The dryad reached out and took Charlotte's chin in her hand. "I want you to do what your grandmother failed to do."

Charlotte wrenched her face away and felt the dryad's nails scratch her skin. She fought the tears that threatened to stream down her face. She didn't know whether to be scared or angry. "What did Grandma fail to do?"

The dryad smiled. She gave the oak men a nod, and they scurried away into the maze of plants filling the room, then returned a moment later with what looked like a stone birdbath. It took all three of them to carry it, and they grunted under its weight as they placed it before the dryad. Another oak man poured water from a wooden pitcher into the bowl, and the dryad reached down to place a gentle pat upon his head.

"Thank you," she said, and her helpers smiled and blushed. They seemed to be enthralled with her. "Come," the dryad said, beckoning Charlotte closer. She reached up and snagged a pinch of moss from her antlers and sprinkled it into the bowl. Then she blew across the surface of the water and it trembled. As Charlotte watched, the surface shimmered and then showed her an image of the Greenwood. Or, more specifically, two men putting up a sign that read "Nolan Enterprises" in the Greenwood.

"These men intend my trees harm," the dryad said, her head and shoulders drooping. "For years they've been coming. Men of all kinds, trying to destroy what I've worked so hard to protect. But this time they'll succeed, because I don't have the power to stop them."

"Why not?" Charlotte asked.

The dryad smiled. She dipped a finger into the water and swirled it around. When the surface settled, a new image floated there. It was the ring of standing stones Charlotte had found in the woods. She still felt that they were familiar in some way, but she couldn't figure out why.

"This is one of many shrines of fae," the dryad explained. "The five standing stones represent the elements: Spirit, Water, Fire, Earth, and Air. And see these small stones within them?" She pointed one pale, round nail at a glowing orb in the belly of each stone. "Those are fairy stones. Each fairy stone acts as one of five hearts within the shrine. All five are needed to power the shrine and provide magic to the fae that live in the area. But these five fairy stones, small and beautiful as they are, have attracted the attention of humans and have been stolen from us." The image in the water shifted and the vibrant colors faded, as if the life had been sucked out of the forest. "Without the five fairy stones, the shrine cannot work in the way it's supposed to. Fairy magic in the Greenwood is running out, Charlotte." The dryad raised a hand and turned it palm-up. "In Lyra and the rest of the fairy realm, I am powerful." She waved her hand, and the plants filling the room started to grow out of control. They snaked across the walls and tangled into knots tight enough to block out the sun. "But in the Greenwood," she continued, "I am all but powerless." She dropped her hand, and the previously luscious plants wilted and turned brown, drooping off the walls. "The magic in the Greenwood isn't powerful enough to maintain me. This is why I can't stop the men that intend my forest harm." She sighed, and her long lashes brushed her pink cheeks as she dropped her gaze. "The human realm and fairy realm depend on one another, Charlotte. The connection between our realms has suffered in this last century, and the tether between Lyra and the Greenwood is about to snap."

"And what do I have to do with any of this?" Charlotte asked, stepping back from the bowl. "I didn't steal the fairy stones. I have nothing to do with that."

"You may not have stolen them, but you bear equal responsibility. You are the last remaining Shrine Keeper in your family line, and so the task falls to you to heal the damage that has been done and return what is rightfully ours."

"And if I don't?" Charlotte asked. She didn't want anything to do with this. She'd been avoiding contact with this world for eight years and had no desire to return to it. Children's stories gave everyone the idea that fairies were joyous creatures that liked to nap on flowers and bring spring to lands blanketed in winter, but not all fairy creatures were kind and gentle. Charlotte remembered the creature with glowing eyes and black horns crouched in the bushes and forced the memory away so violently that she felt her stomach turn. She wouldn't relive that—not now, not ever.

"If you don't," the dryad said, with sadness in her voice, "then your mother will never come home."

Charlotte's gaze locked on the dryad, and she narrowed her eyes. "What do you know about Mom?" she asked.

"I know that she has lovely golden hair," the dryad said casually, "and that she talks in her sleep, often of you."

"What did you do with her?" Charlotte asked, her voice an angry whisper.

"She's here," the dryad said calmly. "And here she will remain until you restore the shrine to its former glory." The dryad turned to look out a window, and Charlotte followed her gaze. "The new moon will rise tomorrow evening. I'll give you one moon cycle to do as I ask, or else you'll suffer the loss of another loved one."

"What?" Charlotte asked, her heart beating wildly beneath her ribs. "I don't understand."

"Retrieve the five fairy stones and I will release your mother. But fail to do so and I will imprison another of your loved ones, and so the cycle will repeat on every new moon until you have completed the task I've assigned you."

"Why can't you retrieve your own stones? Why can't they get them?" Charlotte pointed at the oak men, and the oldest one lifted his lip in a snarl.

"I forget how little you know," the dryad said in a small, tired voice. She took a few steps to her throne and collapsed down into it. "Our kind can't touch the stones. They're infused with magic that would kill any one of us in an instant. It keeps our power in balance, you see. No one fae can become stronger by acquiring the stones. This is why there are Shrine Keepers—you can handle the stones without being overcome by their power. Our realms are meant to work harmoniously together, though yours seems to have forgotten our existence entirely." She dropped her forehead into her palm and sighed.

Charlotte clenched her fist around Mom's scarf. She didn't know how much of this to believe. It all felt so foreign to her, so different from her mundane life, that she struggled to wrap her head around it. But if this was real, and if the dryad was telling the truth, then she had a decision to make. "I want to see my mom," Charlotte said, her voice small.

"By all means." The dryad sat forward on her throne. "I'd be happy to take you to her. Oh, but first . . ." She stood and waved Charlotte forward. "If ever you need to speak with me, you can access Lyra through the Greenwood portal. Come closer, Charlotte. I don't bite."

Charlotte stepped hesitantly forward and flinched when the dryad placed her cool fingers on either side of her temples. A song flowed into her mind, its melody soothing her strung-out nerves. She struggled to figure out what key it was in, which was usually an easy task for her. It sounded unlike anything she'd ever played before, and yet she felt as though she'd known the song her whole life. It left her feeling strangely at peace, and her heart calmed at the sound of it.

"That is my song," the dryad explained, removing her hands. "You need only play it amongst the stones to find yourself here. Now come, we'll visit your mother."

The dryad set off into the thick greenery, and Charlotte had to hurry after her. The dryad had long, lithe legs and moved swift and smooth over the moss and through the plants. They pushed through soft leaves and ducked under hanging ivy, and in moments Charlotte felt helplessly lost. It was a maze in here, almost as difficult to navigate as the Greenwood was.

The dryad walked silently over the moss, her lovely green gown trailing behind her. A bird fluttered down to perch on her antlers, and Charlotte was struck by what a strange and exotic place this was.

They continued through the plants, and when Charlotte was about to ask what was going on, the dryad pulled back a curtain of ivy and gestured for Charlotte to step through.

"What is this?" Charlotte asked.

"A safe place," the dryad said, offering Charlotte a smile. "I'll be here waiting when you are finished."

Charlotte had no other choice, so she ducked through the ivy, keeping a suspicious eye on the dryad until she was safely through. A glade of green waited on the other side. It was bathed in warm sunlight from the stained-glass windows and blanketed in moss. Butterflies floated on the balmy air and sprinkled silver powder on a woman sleeping amongst the flowers.

"Mom!" Charlotte called, rushing forward. She collapsed by her mom's side, hands trembling as she reached out to jostle her shoulder gently. "Mom?" she asked again, shaking her mom's shoulder a bit harder.

Mom shifted and smiled, but her eyes didn't open. Her blond hair was spread out around her like a halo, and her eyelids shimmered with the strange silver powder drifting down from above. Charlotte trailed a finger along Mom's neck, and it came away coated in the shimmery substance. She gave it a tentative sniff and yawned.

Sleeping powder? An hour ago she wouldn't have believed it, but now she wondered.

"I brought you something," Charlotte said softly, placing the red scarf under Mom's hand. Mom's fingers were still stained with paint and charcoal, and Charlotte smiled. It really was Mom, in the flesh, and she was okay. She was under a fairy spell and trapped in a world Charlotte hadn't even known existed, but she was alive.

"I'm so sorry this happened to you," Charlotte whispered, finally allowing herself to cry. Tears ran down her cheeks and dripped off her chin as she stroked a hand gently over Mom's golden hair. She took Mom's hand between her own and clung to it. "I'm going to make everything better. I'm going to bring all the stones back and then you can come home, okay?" She leaned forward and buried her face in Mom's neck, breathing in her comforting scent in the midst of this terrifying place. There she remained, crying and holding fast to her mom's hand, until the dryad poked her head through the ivy and beckoned to Charlotte with long fingers.

"Come," she whispered.

Reluctantly, Charlotte sat up and wiped her eyes. She remembered the sandal and gently slipped it onto Mom's one bare foot. Then she kissed Mom's silver cheek.

"I love you," she whispered, and then she stood and backed away before she could start crying again. Leaving Mom behind twisted Charlotte's insides and made her feel sick to her stomach, but she had no choice.

She ducked back through the curtain of ivy and found the dryad on the other side. Now there were birds of all colors resting upon the dryad's antlers, and they fluttered away when she turned her head.

"Why is she asleep?" Charlotte asked, wiping salty tears from her cheeks.

"It's most comfortable for her that way," the dryad explained. "She'll stay here with me, lost in sweet dreams, until you bring her home."

Charlotte nodded and averted her eyes. She felt like she might cry again, so she looked down at her muddy socks and crossed her arms.

"So you'll help us?" the dryad asked, with a hint of excitement in her voice.

"Yes," Charlotte whispered.

"You're doing the right thing," the dryad said, her voice gentle.

Charlotte nodded. Together they walked back through the maze of plants, and the dryad led Charlotte outside. An audience of oak men and women had gathered around the doors, and the dryad laughed when she saw them.

"Oh my," she said. "Have you all come to say hello to our Keeper?" There was a chorus of responses as the oak men looked back and forth between Charlotte and the dryad. They wore a mixture of expressions: excited, angry, frightened. Charlotte felt itchy under their scrutiny. She just wanted to go home.

The oak men called out to the dryad in fast, high-pitched voices that Charlotte couldn't quite make out. Finally, the dryad held up a hand to quiet them. "Charlotte is going to work hard to restore our shrine," she said, putting a hand on Charlotte's shoulder. "So please, do your best to support her in this endeavor."

The oak men exploded into sound again. Some of them applauded and others shook their tiny fists in the air. One small child stepped forward and handed Charlotte an indigo-petaled flower. Charlotte smiled at the child and then tucked the flower behind her ear. The dryad's guards came out from the Great Tree to hold back the hordes as Charlotte and the dryad passed through the village and across the creaky old bridge. They walked back down the path of glittering stone, and the sounds of the village faded away in the balmy breeze.

"Are there other Shrine Keepers?" Charlotte asked.

"Of course," the dryad said. "One family is assigned to each shrine, and the women of that family maintain it."

"Only the women?"

"Yes," the dryad said, a soft smile curling the corner of her pink lips. "Times have changed, Charlotte. Domestic magic used to be a woman's domain." When Charlotte didn't say anything, the dryad continued. "We've been waiting for you for a long time."

The dryad led her into the shadow of the trees, her gown whispering through the grass, and paused outside the circle of standing stones.

"Are there many of these?" Charlotte asked, breaking her silence.

"Yes," the dryad replied, "but not nearly as many as before. Your world has changed, Charlotte, and many sacred shrines have fallen into decay. If not for the Shrine Keepers, it would only be a matter of time before fae magic was entirely gone from your world."

Charlotte wondered if perhaps that wouldn't be such a bad thing, but she didn't mention this to the dryad.

"Step into the center of the stones," the dryad explained, "and I'll send you home."

Charlotte did as she was told. She walked across the forest floor and positioned herself in the center of the five standing stones. They towered over her head, terrifying in their magnificence. Her heart started to race.

"Goodbye, Charlotte," said the dryad, and she lifted a hand. The stones began to gently hum, and Charlotte felt herself start to shake. This was scarier than the roller coasters at the amusement park, and she hated roller coasters.

"Do you have a name?" she asked suddenly as the stones hummed to life around her.

The dryad smiled. "I do, and perhaps someday I'll share it with you."

Charlotte wanted to ask what she meant, but her vision started to swim and she had to kneel to keep from falling over.

The feeling of nausea passed as quickly as it had come, and when Charlotte looked back up, she felt a sprinkling of rain across her face.

She was home.

CHAPTER FIVE

Charlotte squinted up at the treetops and had to shield her eyes from the rain. The glimpses of sky between the fire-orange and red leaves were dark and stormy. She stood up slowly and wiped the mud from her hands.

I'm back home, she thought. The standing stones around her were in a state of decay again. They were worn and crumbling and covered in vines and weeds. The ground under her feet was rain-soaked and slippery, nothing like the warm soil in Lyra.

Lyra, she thought, running the name through her mind. *A world of fairies.* A powerful shiver raced across Charlotte's skin. *It was real*, she thought. *It was real.* Thunder rumbled overhead, and it startled her back to reality. It was wet and cold out here, and she had to get home.

Still wearing only socks, Charlotte started back the way she'd come. She pushed through the trees and crossed the abandoned hiking trail, her teeth chattering hard as the cold set in. Rain ran into her eyes and dripped off her chin, blinding her as she struggled back toward the house. She slipped and fell in the mud twice while descending the embankment behind the house, and by the time she climbed the porch stairs she was soaked through and coated in leaves and muck. Her trembling hands slipped on the door handle, and she had to try a few times before successfully opening it. The door swung open, and her dad and grandma stepped out of the kitchen to see who it was.

Both of their faces blanched, and Grandma's mouth fell open.

"What in the world," Dad said. "What are you doing?"

"I found Mom," Charlotte said, breathless from her long trek through the woods.

"Where?" Dad asked, his eyes going wide and hopeful.

"She's with the fairies. The dryad took her because of the missing stones and now I have to find them, but Mom's okay, she's just sleeping and—"

"Stop," Dad said, holding up a hand. The hope in his eyes had vanished.

"Dad, I'm serious, Mom is—"

"Charlotte, please don't." Dad ran a hand over his face and sighed. "I thought we were done with this. It's been so many years." He dropped his head, and his shoulders sagged.

"Listen to me! The fairies took Mom—I saw her!" Charlotte stomped her foot, frustrated tears springing to her eyes. "I saw her," she repeated, quieter this time, and then she started to cry.

Her parents had never reprimanded her for the stories she used to tell about the fairies in the woods, but she realized now that they had never believed her, either.

"Honey, I know this is stressful," Dad said as he wiped tears from Charlotte's cheeks, "but I need you to stay calm for me, okay?" He grabbed his keys off the hallway table and pulled on his rain jacket. "I'm going to drive back into town and look for her again. Maybe she's just waiting out the storm." He sounded hopeful and pitiful at the same time.

"She's not in town," Charlotte said through her tears. "She's with the dryad—I swear!"

"Call me if you hear from her," Dad said, looking at Grandma. Then, without replying to what Charlotte had said, he slipped past her and out the front door. He yanked up his hood while he hurried through the rain to his truck. It roared to life, and a moment later the tires were slinging mud as he threw it into gear and tore off down the driveway.

Charlotte stood in the doorway, staring after him long after his truck was out of sight.

"Come on, dear." Grandma pulled at Charlotte's soggy sweatshirt. She peeled it off and tossed it onto the front porch. "We'll get that cleaned up later," she said. "Now drop those muddy clothes at the door so you don't track it all over the house. I'm going to get a bath started for you."

She set off down the hall, and Charlotte called out to her. "Do you believe me?"

Grandma paused, took a slow breath, and smiled over her shoulder.

"Let's get you cleaned up, and then we can talk."

Grandma ran a hot bath with a few drops of lavender oil and then left Charlotte to soak. The hot water burned her frozen skin as she sank down into the deep tub, turning her arms and legs bright red. She dunked her head beneath the water and scrubbed at her scalp with her fingers. Her long, curly brown hair floated on the surface of the water around her, the individual strands twirling like skaters on a frozen pond.

She could partially understand why Dad didn't believe her, but she'd never lied to him before. Why couldn't he see that? The look in his eyes when he'd pushed past her had made her stomach sink like it was filled with stones.

Charlotte grabbed the bar of almond soap and started scrubbing the grime from her skin. She scrubbed her legs and her hands and her face, rubbing vigorously as if she could wash the entire day away.

After she'd finished, she stood to step out of the tub and spotted something floating on the surface of the soapy water. She scooped it up with one hand and let out a slow, relieved sigh.

It was a small flower with indigo-colored petals. She'd not imagined Lyra after all.

Charlotte stepped out of the tub and wrapped herself in a robe before heading into the kitchen. She found Grandma brewing tea at the stove and sat down on the couch in the living room to wait for her to finish. Out the front window, Charlotte watched the rain coming down in sheets and hoped Dad would drive carefully. She didn't need to lose two parents in one day.

A minute later Grandma came into the living room and set the two mugs down on the low table before sitting down beside Charlotte. "Much better," she said, patting Charlotte's hand. "Now, tell me everything that happened. Don't leave anything out."

So, between sips of chamomile tea, Charlotte did just that. She started with seeing the flash of color out the window, described the chase through the trees and stepping into the ring of standing stones, and tried her best to explain the magnificence of the Great Tree. Then she told Grandma all about the dryad.

"She told me I'm a Shrine Keeper," Charlotte said, "and that you and great-grandma were supposed to be Shrine Keepers, too."

"Shrine Keepers? I don't know anything about that," Grandma said, shaking her head. Her eyes grew cloudy as she settled back into the couch and sipped her tea. "I had imaginary friends when I was young, like most children do, but my mother was upset when I told her about them. I'd get punished if she saw me talking to them, and eventually I didn't want them around anymore. I'd throw water at them in the garden or run home when I saw them in the trees. After a while, I stopped seeing them altogether." She frowned, and her silver eyebrows knit together. "It's been a long time since I thought about any of this."

"So, you had the Sight?" Charlotte asked.

"I had a wild imagination," Grandma said, and it felt like a punch to the gut.

"I'm not a child, Grandma, and I don't have a *wild imagination*. You used to see fairies, and you never even told me about them." Charlotte's throat felt tight, and she struggled not to cry.

"They weren't real, dear." Grandma reached out to take Charlotte's hand, but Charlotte pulled away.

"You don't believe me?" If Grandma didn't believe her, then who else could she tell? Not Melanie, that was for sure. She hadn't even believed in Santa Claus as a kid—there was no way she'd believe in fairies.

"It's not that I don't believe you, dear. I believe that you saw these things, but I also know that the Greenwood can play tricks on the mind. Sometimes stress can blur the lines between fiction and reality."

"Didn't you wonder where I was?" Charlotte asked. They must have noticed how long she was gone.

"Hardly twenty minutes had passed," Grandma said. "I thought you were in the studio, trying to cope with all this."

Twenty minutes? Charlotte thought. No way she was gone for only twenty minutes. It must have been an hour, at least.

"Listen," Grandma said, interrupting her thoughts. "You go get some comfy clothes on and I'll start dinner. We'll feel better after we have something warm in our bellies."

"I'm not hungry." Charlotte didn't want to eat dinner—she wanted her family to believe her. "I'm going to my room." She slammed her mug down on the living room table and ignored the tea that sloshed over the rim. With that, she stood up and went to her room, slamming the door behind her.

Grandma came to get her a bit later for dinner, but Charlotte refused to eat. She couldn't stand that Grandma didn't believe her. Why would she lie about something like this? What could she honestly be trying to accomplish by coming up with such a ridiculous story? She paced back and forth from her bedroom door to the window, her stomach tied in angry knots.

She heard Dad get home later that evening. She cracked her door open and looked down the hall, and there she saw Dad crumpled against Grandma's chest, crying. Grandma looked up and gave Charlotte a small, sad smile.

Grandma had always been the rock. She bandaged bloody knees and mended broken hearts, and the only time Charlotte had ever heard her cry was when Grandpa died. Even then she'd mourned alone in her bedroom, the closed door muffling her sobs.

Charlotte cried herself to sleep that night. She cried for Mom, all alone in a foreign place. She cried for Dad, sleeping alone for the first time in over twenty years. And she cried for herself, the girl who could see fairies.

Her dreams were haunted by horns and glowing eyes that night. She dreamed of running through the Greenwood dressed in only socks and a nightgown, and no matter how fast she ran, the creature that pursued her was always right on her heels. His gray hands reached out, and only when his claws scraped her skin did she wake, panicked and soaked in sweat.

The creature hadn't haunted her dreams in years, but now she felt like a kid again, hiding under her covers and trying to push thoughts of him from her mind. She tried to pretend he didn't exist, and as soon as she did, a headache blossomed to life behind her eyes.

Charlotte had the urge to crawl into bed with Mom, but then she remembered that Mom wasn't here. There was no one here to gently massage her temples or sing her to sleep when the headaches got too bad, and the realization of it had Charlotte crying into her pillow for the second time that night. For the first time in her life, she felt completely alone.

CHAPTER SIX

The weekend passed by in a blur of officers, phone calls, and never-ending rain. When Charlotte wasn't answering questions about her mom's disappearance, she was in her bedroom with the door closed and her face in a computer screen, trying to figure out what a fairy stone was and how the heck to find one. She replayed the conversation with the dryad over and over in her mind, wondering if perhaps she'd missed some sort of clue as to where the fairy stones could be found.

Officer Beck came by the house again on Saturday, asking for more information about Mom and conducting another sweep of the house, this time with an entire team. She hinted at the possibility that Mom may have decided to up and leave, but Dad assured her that wasn't the case.

Search and Rescue volunteers flooded the neighborhood on Sunday and scoured the Greenwood for signs of Mom. They brought dogs and maps and bright orange vests, and a helicopter circled overhead.

Charlotte didn't involve herself in the search—she knew they wouldn't find anything.

Monday arrived, and with it a clear blue sky. The rain had finally let up, and Mapleton could start drying out.

Grandma already had coffee brewing on the stove by the time Charlotte made her way into the kitchen, so all she had to do was pour it into her favorite mug and add a dash of almond milk. But as she poured, she glanced up through the window over the sink and was startled so badly that she poured coffee all over herself.

"Shit," she mumbled, hurrying to wipe the coffee off before it could burn.

"What is it?" Grandma asked, coming to stand beside Charlotte at the sink. Her eyes were red and rimmed in dark circles.

"Fairies," Charlotte said, pointing out the window.

Two squirrels sat on the deck railing, and the fairies riding them wore tiny acorns on their heads. The fairies pointed and stared and spoke to one another in voices Charlotte couldn't hear, and then the squirrels dived off the porch and disappeared into the Greenwood, carrying the fairies with them.

Grandma frowned into her cup of coffee, but she didn't say a word. Dad walked into the kitchen a moment later, his curls standing up on one side and completely flat on the other.

"Get any sleep?" Grandma asked as Dad poured himself a cup of coffee.

"Not a wink." He kissed Grandma on the cheek and looked over at Charlotte. "Shouldn't you be getting ready for school?" he asked.

"Oh," Charlotte said, looking down at her pajamas. She'd assumed Dad would let her stay home, and she'd planned to surf the Internet all day trying to figure out where she could start her search for the fairy stones. Pre-Calc was low on her list of priorities right now.

"I know you're stressed," Dad said softly, "but you can't let your studies fail. I need you to keep it together, okay?" The smile he gave her looked worried, and Charlotte couldn't find it within herself to argue with him. He already had so much on his plate, and she didn't want to make it worse.

"Okay," she mumbled.

"I wish I could help you out there today," Grandma said, her lips pulling into a frown.

Charlotte had seen Grandma out the bedroom window on Sunday, wearing rain boots and carrying a yellow umbrella, and it had made her cry to see Grandma calling Mom's name in the rain.

"I know you do," Dad said, giving Grandma's hand a squeeze, "but I really need someone here in case Em comes home."

Grandma set her lips in a hard line and nodded. After that, Dad went back to his bedroom, probably to get ready for another long day of searching the Greenwood.

"I wouldn't mention fairies around your father." Grandma sighed as she sank down into a chair at the table.

"Can I mention them around you?" Charlotte asked, leaning back against the kitchen counter.

"Of course," Grandma said, offering Charlotte a smile that didn't quite reach her eyes.

Charlotte knew that she wasn't convinced—it was going to take time.

"You'd better get going," Grandma said, glancing at the cuckoo clock on the living room wall. "The bus will be here soon."

"Oh no," Charlotte said, realizing how late it was. Today was going to have to be a hoodie and hair-in-a-bun day, or else she'd never get to class on time.

After getting ready, she hurried down the porch steps and set off across the gravel drive. She had her rubber rain boots on and could hear the mud squelching under them as she walked. The sky was light blue and the air was crisp, and if she listened carefully she could hear birds and squirrels in the oak trees lining the long driveway.

Charlotte arrived at the bus stop just in time, and the bus driver tipped his fishing hat to her, just like he did every morning. She slipped into her favorite seat by the window and settled in for the drive to school.

Charlotte pulled a granola bar out of her pocket and was just about to take a bite when she spotted something out the bus window.

A deer stood watching her from the trees. His antlers were big and beautiful, and Charlotte thought instantly of the dryad. The buck's antlers weren't draped in moss and flowers, but they were lovely all the same.

He stared at her, and she stared back.

The bus window fogged up with Charlotte's breath, and when she wiped the condensation away, the buck was gone. It had vanished, as if into thin air.

✣

School sucked in general, but it was nearly unbearable when Melanie was absent. She didn't show up for orchestra and didn't text back when Charlotte asked where she was, which usually meant she was skipping. Not having Melanie around meant Charlotte had to eat lunch by herself, and there was no way she was going to eat in the cafeteria all alone, so when the lunch bell rang after orchestra class, she headed up to the library to sit and eat in peace.

The library was on the second floor and had a wall of windows that let the sun stream in. It was filled with yellow light and the air was balmy, so Charlotte shrugged out of her jacket as she looked around.

She scanned the tables and reading nooks and spotted only two other students. One girl sat at a table with biology books spread out around her, and there was another student sitting on a couch by a window, his hood pulled up and his face turned toward the glass. Neither one of them looked up when Charlotte walked in, so she felt good and alone, just the way she liked it.

Before sitting down, she took a stroll through the FOLKLORE & MYTHOLOGY section of the library. She'd never actually checked out a book from her school library, because everything she ever needed for research was available online, but today she found herself curious about what these dusty bookshelves had to offer. Perhaps she could find some information on fairy stones, or fairy portals, or something that would give her some idea about how to move forward. She found a book labeled *The Total Encyclopedia of Fairies*, and then another titled *All About Fairies, Nymphs, and Forest Spirits*, which was full of colorful illustrations. She grabbed the two books and picked her way through the rows of bookshelves to find her favorite reading nook.

She wasn't supposed to have any food or drink in the library, technically, but the old librarian preferred to sit behind her desk and read romance novels rather than bicker with teenagers, so Charlotte wasn't too worried about getting caught and scolded. She sat down on the floor with her back against the wall and spread the books out in the square of yellow sunlight filtering through the window. Then she pulled out the sack lunch Grandma had packed and started to read.

"Hey, no food in here," said a sharp voice overhead, and Charlotte was so startled that she dropped the carrot she'd been about to munch down on. She looked up, ready to be reprimanded, but was surprised to find not the bespectacled librarian, but a boy. He pushed back his hood, and the sunlight illuminated his eyes, turning them pale green. It was Tomas's older brother.

"You scared me," Charlotte said, picking her dirty carrot up off the floor. It had a long strand of hair stuck to it.

"Sorry," he said, running a hand through his messy brown hair with a smile. "You know you're not supposed to eat in here, though."

"Yeah, I know," Charlotte said, putting her carrots away. "But it beats eating in the cafeteria."

"Ain't that the truth." He laughed. "Anyway, I spotted you and wanted to give you that ten dollars I owe." He pulled out his wallet, which now had fresh bills tucked inside, and handed Charlotte a ten-dollar bill.

"Thanks," Charlotte said, reaching into her backpack to find her wallet. While she struggled, the boy cocked his head sideways to look at the books she was reading.

"Fairy folklore?" he asked.

"Uh, yeah," Charlotte mumbled, hoping he'd leave it alone.

"Sweet," he said, crouching down to spin *The Total Encyclopedia of Fairies* around. Charlotte noticed a smudge of charcoal across his knuckles and almost smiled. He leafed through a few of the pages and then stopped on a photo of a dwarf with a long beard and an assortment of gemstones adorning his fingers. "I love this stuff. I went to Ireland with my family last year, and I picked up a book of folktales while we were there. It just got me interested in all this." He reached down to turn a few pages again, and Charlotte admired the rings he wore on a few of his fingers. She was about to ask him if he'd bought his Celtic charm bracelet in Ireland as well, but then the bell for next period rang, signaling that she had ten minutes to get packed up and fight her way through the halls toward English class. Which reminded her, she still had a paper to write.

"Well, thanks for squaring up," she said, avoiding eye contact.

"No problem. I don't like owing anyone, you know?" He stood and then surprised Charlotte when he waited for her to pack up. Then he offered his hand and pulled her up.

"Thanks," she said, a little flustered to be standing so close to him now. He was cute, and she didn't have much experience with good-looking, messy-haired boys.

"I'm Art, by the way." He held out his right hand, and Charlotte gave it a shake.

"Charlotte."

"I know." He flashed her a smile. "My brother talks about you all the time. He likes you a lot."

Charlotte smiled. "Tomas is great," she said. "A little prone to distraction, but he's a good kid."

"Sure is," Art said, burying his hands in his pockets. "Anyway, class?"

"Oh, yeah." Her cheeks warmed, and she looked away.

Art walked with her through the library and out into the main hall, at which point they went opposite directions.

"By the way," Art called out as he walked backward down the hall, "you can borrow my books sometime if you want."

"I'd like that!" Charlotte had to holler back for her voice to carry over the sounds in the hallway.

Art gave her a sideways smile before disappearing into the sea of students.

❦

Charlotte was sitting at the bus stop after school when Melanie called.

"Hey," she said. "Where were you today?"

"Hello to you, too," Melanie said on the other end of the line.

"You sound annoyed." Charlotte picked at a loose thread on her hoodie.

"Yeah, I fought with my mom today."

"Oh. What about?"

Melanie launched into a tirade about how her mom was always pushing her too hard. She pushed Melanie to study more, practice her violin more often, strive to get into a better school.

"She's driving me crazy! We went to tour college campuses this weekend, and I swear she nagged at me the whole time. God, it's like she doesn't see how hard I'm trying already." Melanie sniffled into the phone.

"Hey, it's okay," Charlotte said, standing when she saw the bus in the distance. She quickly boarded and swiped her bus pass, then found a spot alone in the back. "Your mom just wants the best for you, that's all."

"No, she wants what she *thinks* is best. There's a difference."

"Have you told her that?"

"No," Melanie said, and then sighed. "I can't talk to my mom like you can talk to yours. Can your parents just adopt me already?"

Charlotte laughed, but her heart felt heavy. Melanie was right—she *could* talk to Mom about anything, and she never felt judged or embarrassed or misunderstood.

"Anyway," Melanie continued, "I should probably pull my violin out. Was Mr. Hamilton pissed that I wasn't in class?"

"Not really. The violas totally butchered that section in the Bach piece again, so he was focused on them all class."

"Phew," Melanie said, and then laughed. "Okay, I'll let you go. Say hi to everyone for me, okay? And ask your grandma when she'll be making that weird potato dish again. I've totally been craving it."

"I will," Charlotte said, smiling into the phone. "Love you, Mel."

"Love you too, Char."

The call disconnected, and Charlotte immediately started to cry. She buried her face in her hands and wiped her nose on the sleeves of her hoodie, trying not to let the other passengers hear her.

She probably should have told Melanie about Mom, but something held her back. She didn't want Melanie to ask all the questions that she'd no doubt ask, and she didn't want to sob into the phone like she knew she would have. Admitting that Mom was gone felt like it made everything real, and Charlotte wasn't ready for that yet. She needed to keep this to herself for a while longer.

This was on Charlotte's mind as she walked up the long gravel road from the bus stop. She stared at her boots as she walked, watching the mud squelch out from beneath the rubber soles. When she heard a strange sound, she looked up and stopped in her tracks.

There was a fairy creature on the porch. It had wrinkled skin and wore tattered clothing, and floppy ears poked out from beneath its cap. It smeared mud all over the front porch, grumbling to itself as it worked.

"Hey!" Charlotte yelled, getting up her courage as she stomped toward the porch. "What are you doing? You're making a big mess!"

The creature jumped, startled, and when it looked up at Charlotte, it seemed familiar for some reason. Her mind struggled to dredge up one of the old, buried memories from her childhood, and when it did, she remembered the creature. He'd been friendly when she was a child, and she used to watch him pick weeds in the garden and water the flowers from a small green watering can that he carried in a satchel on his back. But what had he become, all wrinkled and scowling and angry?

The creature narrowed his eyes and glared at her. "Lazy human," he muttered, reaching down into the mud to grab a sloppy handful. He packed it between his hands while he grumbled under his breath.

"You need to clean up this mess," Charlotte said, sounding like Grandma.

"Clean up mess," the creature mocked, and before Charlotte could say another word, he drew back his arm and pelted her with the mud ball.

"Hey!" she yelped, her mouth falling open in surprise. "Don't!"

But the creature didn't stop. He threw another mud ball, which hit Charlotte in the chest and splattered across her face.

"Knock it off!" she yelled. She ran around the back of the house, ducking as mud balls zoomed over her head, and hurriedly jammed the key into the back doorknob and wrestled herself into the house. She slammed and locked the door behind her, then looked up into Grandma's confused face.

"Hi, Gram," Charlotte said, wiping mud off her lips.

"Get those dirty clothes off," Grandma said, scowling at the mess on the floor, "and then we'll talk."

✖

Grandma was the queen of clean, and she had the kitchen floor wiped up and the dirty clothes in the laundry by the time Charlotte emerged from her bedroom. Charlotte placed the two fairy books she'd borrowed from the library on the kitchen counter while Grandma arranged crackers and hummus on a plate.

"Well then," Grandma said as she sat down, the chair squeaking under her weight. "Care to tell me what that was all about?"

"Okay." Charlotte took a deep breath. "I'll tell you, but you have to promise to be open-minded, okay?"

"Is this about your fairies?" Grandma asked, sounding hesitant.

"Yes, but just hear me out."

"Fine, fine," Grandma said, waving a cracker. "Go on."

Charlotte explained, to the best of her ability, exactly what the creature had looked like and what he'd done. Grandma's silver brows pinched together while she listened, but she didn't interrupt.

"He's the one that's been spreading mud all over the porch," Charlotte said, throwing up her hands. "Not the raccoons."

Grandma sat back in her chair and took a slow breath. She watched Charlotte through narrowed eyes, her lip moving as she chewed on it.

"Listen," Charlotte said, holding out her hands. "You don't have to believe me, but will you at least help me go through these books and try to figure out what that thing is?"

"That I can do." Grandma held out her hand.

Charlotte gave her one of the fairy books, and they started to read.

Charlotte flipped through the pages, looking for a picture of the creature, but she didn't have any luck. She found passages on mermaids, pixies, dwarves, and other fairies, but nothing that looked like the little creature that had tormented her outside.

Half an hour and a plate of crackers and hummus later, Grandma tapped the book she was reading and smiled. "Look here," she said. "Is this about right?" She handed over the book so Charlotte could see.

The illustration was almost spot-on, except for the ears. In the picture, the fairy had small, flat ears, but the creature outside had long, floppy ears.

"The brownie," Charlotte read out loud, "typically has a wrinkled, shaggy appearance. He stands at approximately two feet tall and appears naked or dressed in tattered brown clothes. The brownie may adopt and tend to a house, caring for animals and finishing work left undone in the evenings. However, if he feels they merit it, he may plague the residents for their laziness or idleness." Charlotte looked up at Grandma with wide eyes. "This has to be right," she said. "He even called me lazy!"

"Hmm," Grandma said, leaning forward to get a better look at the book.

"Didn't you say last summer that you'd go outside sometimes and your plants were already watered and weeded?" Charlotte asked. "Maybe that was the brownie!"

"Hmm," Grandma said again, starting to chew on her pinky nail. She always did that when she was thinking hard about something.

"There's more," Charlotte said. "Listen to this." She read on. "Brownies are known to have unpredictable behavior, and one would be wise so as not to offend. For all his work, the brownie asks only for a bowl of cream or milk and a biscuit spread with honey." Charlotte looked up. "Maybe that's it," she said. "Maybe he's upset that we haven't left anything out for him. Do you have a biscuit and honey?"

"I should," Grandma said. "And I bought a fresh carton of soy milk today. It's in the pantry."

"Let's try it," Charlotte said, and was happily surprised when Grandma shrugged and agreed to help.

Grandma opened a new roll of biscuit dough and baked it just for the occasion. Charlotte kept an eye on the porch, but she never saw the brownie again. Dad got home right as the oven timer dinged.

"How was your day?" Grandma asked.

"Long," Dad said, rolling out his neck. "Long and useless." He rubbed a hand over his face and rubbed his swollen eyes. "Any phone calls?" He sounded hopeful.

"No," Grandma said, her gaze falling.

Dad let out a tired sigh and walked down the hallway and closed the bedroom door behind him.

Charlotte wished she could get Dad to believe her. He was wasting his time with the cops and all the searches—they weren't going to find anything, and his energy would have been better spent helping her figure out where the fairy stones were.

"Here you go," Grandma said, licking a drip of honey from her finger as she handed the platter of biscuits over to Charlotte.

Charlotte balanced the platter on one hand and picked up the bowl of milk in the other. "Can you get the door for me?"

Grandma unlocked and opened the back door, and Charlotte stepped out into the autumn air. The biscuits steamed in the cold, and Charlotte peered into the dark, searching for movement or a pair of eyes staring back at her.

"Hurry up, you're letting the heat out," Grandma said from the door.

Charlotte put the plate and bowl down on the deck before scurrying back inside.

She stood at the door, staring out, waiting for the brownie to show up, but he never did. The biscuits were still steaming when Charlotte turned away and slid the curtains closed.

CHAPTER SEVEN

The alarm wailed on Charlotte's bedside table, and she smacked it with such force that it fell to the floor. She rolled over in bed and sat up, and it hit her: the brownie!

With newfound energy, Charlotte shoved her feet into her slippers and pulled on her robe, and then she rushed down the hall, through the kitchen, and out onto the back porch.

The sun was barely starting to come up, and a few rays of pale light illuminated the yard. The back garden sparkled with frozen dew, and Charlotte could see her breath as she pulled her robe tight and shuffled across the deck toward the plate and bowl. She smiled.

The bowl of milk was drained, and the plate of honeyed biscuits was licked clean, with not a drop of the sugary goodness to spare. And on the plate, as vibrant as its autumn surroundings, was a single red flower. Charlotte knelt to pick everything up, and on her way back into the house, she twirled the flower between her fingers and smiled.

"It worked," Charlotte said when she came back into the kitchen and found Grandma yawning over the sink. Grandma slid her bright blue glasses onto her nose and pursed her lips when she saw the flower.

"What's that?" she asked. She took the flower from Charlotte and examined it through squinted eyes. "This is a Shirley poppy."

Charlotte started rinsing the dishes in the sink. "And?"

"And they don't bloom until spring." Grandma looked up at Charlotte with a troubled expression. "Where did you get this?"

"It was on the plate outside." Charlotte dried off her hands and gave Grandma a kiss on the cheek. "I think the brownie left it for me."

✺

Despite success with the offering, two full days passed without any sign of the brownie, and Charlotte was getting worried. She blamed his absence on the ever-present SAR team and local volunteers, who still searched the woods despite not having found anything. Their presence made Charlotte antsy. She appreciated their dedication to finding Mom, but she wanted them gone. Fairies wouldn't be very likely to show themselves if people were constantly swarming around.

It was already the sixth of October, and nearly a week had passed since Charlotte spoke with the dryad. She'd looked up the moon cycle online and knew that the new moon would rise on the thirtieth, so she had just over three weeks to find all five stones. Unfortunately, the search wasn't off to a great start.

Charlotte was wondering whether she should put another offering out for the brownie when she walked out the front door on Thursday morning and gasped.

The brownie was on the porch, sweeping with a broom of twigs and dry grass, and he was humming to himself.

"Ah," he said when he saw Charlotte, and his wrinkled face turned up in a smile as he removed his hat in polite greeting.

"Uh, good morning," Charlotte said, glancing around. There were still SAR volunteers in

the area, their cars abandoned in the driveway. If other people saw her, would they think she was talking to herself?

"And good morning to you, Shrine Keeper." The brownie slapped his hat back onto his head. "Thank you for the gifts. They were much appreciated." He bowed his head to her, and his long ears flopped down.

"You're welcome. And, uh, thanks for the flower."

"That is quite all right." He put a wrinkled hand to his heart. "I know what you seek, and I can take you there."

Charlotte's heart tripped. "Wh-what do you mean?"

"The stones of fairy," he said. "I know where one is. Come, shall we go there now?"

The front door opened, and Dad stepped out onto the porch.

"Hi, honey," he mumbled, touching Charlotte's shoulder as he passed by. He bumped the brownie, who stumbled back and had to catch the porch railing to keep from falling. The brownie growled, but Dad didn't even glance his way. "I'm headed to the station—the incident commander needs to talk to me."

"About what?" Charlotte asked, tearing her eyes reluctantly away from the brownie.

"Calling off the search, probably." Dad sighed. "We haven't found any sign of her, Charlotte, and the SAR guys doubt she was ever in the woods to begin with." He pinched the bridge of his nose and took a slow, deep breath. "Come on, I can drop you off at school on my way."

"I don't feel very well today," Charlotte said, holding her stomach. "Can I stay home?"

Dad paused and gave her a look. "I don't think so," he said. "I told you that you can't start failing school. I need you to keep it together. For me, please?" He reached out and gave Charlotte's shoulder a squeeze and then headed across the driveway to warm up the truck.

Charlotte sighed. She pulled out her cell phone and pretended to take a call, then turned her back on Dad and looked down at the brownie.

"Why couldn't Dad see your broom?" she asked, speaking quietly so that Dad couldn't hear her.

The brownie grumbled and shook his head. "Humans don't see things they don't want to see. This broom has been touched by fairy." He held it up in his hand. "One must believe in magic to see the things that magic touches." He turned away from Charlotte and continued to sweep.

"Come on!" Dad called from the truck.

"Coming!" Charlotte called back. "I'll be back later today," she whispered to the brownie, but he ignored her. Reluctantly, she backed away from the house and went to climb into Dad's truck.

Charlotte thought about the brownie all through class and was so distracted in orchestra that Mr. Hamilton made her play through an entire section by herself, just to "get her head back in the game," as he put it.

"Are you okay?" he asked after class as the other students said goodbye and filtered out of the room. "You seem distracted lately."

"Just stressed," Charlotte said. It was only a matter of time before the authorities notified the school about Mom's disappearance, and Charlotte wasn't looking forward to it. She didn't want their pity.

"I'm sure you are. But don't forget about the little things. I know your audition piece for Bellini is your focus right now, but remember, we need you too. The orchestra looks to you for guidance, okay?"

"Okay," Charlotte said, giving him a nod. Mr. Hamilton had a point, but it was hard to focus on trivial things when so much hung in the balance. "I'll work on it."

"Thank you. Now get outta here. Lunch calls."

Melanie was waiting for Charlotte in the hall, and they went outside to eat their lunches in the sun. There were picnic tables on the patio outside the cafeteria, but those were always crowded on sunny days, so instead Charlotte and Melanie went around the side of the building to a secluded garden where the drama department always performed skits in the springtime. Today, the lone bench beneath the oak tree was empty, and Charlotte brushed orange and yellow leaves away before she sat down.

"What was up with you in class today?" Melanie asked, braiding her silky black hair away from her face. "I think that's the first time I've seen Hamilton call you out like that." Melanie finished the braid and pushed the shiny strand over her shoulder, then pulled out the bento her mom always packed for lunch.

Charlotte sighed and looked up at the leaves overhead. "I'm really stressed right now. I feel like everything is happening all at once."

"What, like, with Bellini? You still have almost a year to get prepared for your audition. Why are you freaking out?"

"It's not just that," Charlotte said, frustration creeping into her voice. "It's everything. School, music, my family."

"Whoa." Melanie held up a hand. "What's wrong with your family? I thought nothing ever went wrong in the Barclay house?"

Charlotte turned and met Melanie's gaze. She had deep brown eyes and a handful of freckles sprinkled across her nose. Now, as Charlotte stared into her eyes, she wondered how well they truly knew each other. Sure, they'd had countless sleepovers and could run through each other's houses blindfolded without so much as stubbing a toe, but what truths had they always hidden away? Charlotte had never once told Melanie about the fairies she could see, and Melanie never spoke about her father, even though Charlotte knew his excessive drinking caused major problems in the family. Charlotte would have loved to tell Melanie about the dryad, and the oak men, and the grumpy brownie, but something told her not to. She didn't want to hear Melanie's laugh at the ridiculousness of it all or her serious voice when she told Charlotte to stop playing around. So instead of telling the truth, Charlotte lifted her shoulder in a shrug. "My parents just work all the time. I feel like we don't get to spend time together anymore."

Melanie pointed her fork at Charlotte. "Enjoy it while you can. I wish I could get my mom to leave me alone."

"Oh, stop. You love your mom. You guys get along really well."

"Sure, until she starts nagging at me." Melanie shoved a forkful of rice into her mouth and rolled her eyes. "Anyway, let's talk about something else."

"Well, I met a guy," Charlotte said, and Melanie's dark brows shot up. She had a light dusting of glitter on her eyelids, and it sparkled in the warm afternoon sun.

"Oh my God," Melanie said around a mouthful of food. "Spill."

And just like that, Charlotte's worries started to melt away. Talking about boys was easy, and it was a welcome distraction from all the stress she'd been feeling lately. Melanie wanted to know everything about Art: what he looked like, how tall he was, what kind of shoes he wore. She pestered Charlotte with questions until the bell for next period rang, and then Charlotte headed into English class feeling better than she had all day.

After school Charlotte headed into town rather than to the bus stop. She had the fairy stones on her mind, and she wished she could have gone straight home to find the brownie, but she taught violin lessons on Tuesdays and Thursdays and it was too late to cancel now.

The bells over the door chimed as Charlotte stepped into Mélodie. Freddy was behind the register, rocking her purple hair in twin buns and humming along to a cello sonata playing over the store speakers. Charlotte had heard Freddy playing her cello in one of the practice rooms once, and she was *amazing*.

"Hey," Freddy said when Charlotte walked in. "How's it goin'?"

"Eh, could be better." Charlotte could have told her about Mom, but it didn't feel right. The news about Mom's disappearance hadn't come out to the public yet, and she wanted to keep it that way.

Freddy laughed. She lifted a hand to brush back a stray purple hair, and a ring flashed on her finger.

"Wow." Charlotte leaned in to take a closer look. "Where did you get that?" The stone on the ring was massive, and it looked so heavy that it was a miracle Freddy could move her finger.

Freddy held up the ring for Charlotte to see. The stone was metallic black and shot through with shimmery blue veins. "Aspen gave it to me for our anniversary. Isn't she the best?"

"Where'd she buy it?"

"She made it. Pretty cool, huh?"

"Huh," Charlotte mumbled.

Freddy looked up as the bell over the door chimed, announcing the arrival of Charlotte's first student. Charlotte turned and smiled at the family as they walked in. Only three lessons today, and then she'd get to go home and figure out what to do about the brownie.

Tomas was her final student of the day, and now her most highly anticipated. His mom dropped him off a bit early, and Charlotte could see him waiting patiently in the sheet music section through the tiny window in the practice room door. When it was time for his lesson, he came in carrying a note.

"My mom said to give this to you," he told Charlotte.

She took it and read it quickly. The note apologized for sending Art without proper payment last time, but promised he'd have the cash on hand today when he came to pick Tomas up. With a small smile, Charlotte folded up the note and stuck it in the back pocket of her jeans.

"Okay," she told Tomas. "Tune up that violin. Let's get started."

Right away, Charlotte noticed a difference in Tomas's playing. His bow still had the tendency to drift sideways across the strings, but he stood taller and played louder than he ever had before. Something was different about him, but she couldn't put a finger on what it was.

"What happened?" Charlotte asked when their lesson was over and Tomas was packing up his violin.

"What?" he asked quietly.

"You seem more comfortable playing in front of me now. And your posture was fantastic. What happened?"

"I don't know," Tomas said with a shrug and a small, embarrassed smile. "My brother has been helping me."

"Does he play?"

"No." Tomas shook his head and picked up his violin. Then he met Charlotte's eyes. "He just watches and listens to me play and tells me when I'm slouching."

Charlotte smiled. "Well, it seems to be helping. Keep up the good work." She opened the practice room door, and they stepped into the main lobby.

Tomas gave Charlotte a small smile just as Art showed up in the store, weaving through the displays of expensive instruments.

"Hey bud!" he said loudly, eliciting a dirty look from the young girl practicing the piano in the corner. "How'd it go today?"

"Great." Tomas gave Art a big smile.

"I hear you've been listening to him play," Charlotte said, leaning up against the door frame. "It's made a huge difference already. He's much more confident." She smiled down at Tomas.

"Ah, it's no big deal," Art said. "He plays and I listen. It's a good way for us to hang out."

Charlotte disagreed. It *was* a big deal. She'd tutored her fair share of students, and most of them would have benefited greatly from having someone listen to them. Her whole family used to sit down in the living room to hear her play, and knowing they cared made all the difference in the world.

"You finish those books yet?" Art asked, catching Charlotte off guard.

"Books?"

"The fairy books from the library."

"Oh, uh, not quite. I wish the library had more of them, though. I'll have to try the Mapleton Public Library next."

"Like I said, I've got a ton of books. You could borrow them, if you want." Art put one hand on Tomas's head and then pulled out his wallet. "I might have more than the school library and public library combined."

Charlotte laughed. "Sure, that would be great." She took the cash Art offered her and tucked it carefully in her pocket.

"Here, I'll give you my number, too. Just let me know when you want those books." He pulled a scrap of paper and a broken pencil from the pocket of his ripped black jeans and scribbled his number down.

"Perfect." Charlotte took the scrap of paper with a slightly shaky hand. She couldn't remember the last time a boy had given her his number, or had asked for hers. It was probably back in eighth grade when she went to the ice cream social with Melanie and a boy she liked had pulled her ponytail and made fun of her until she finally gave him her home number. He called, once, and Grandma had answered. He never called again after that.

Charlotte wasn't good with boys. She liked them just fine, but they never seemed to like her back. But here was a boy with floppy hair and a quick smile, and Charlotte had his number now. Her stomach fluttered with butterflies at the very thought of it. She would worry about what to actually do with his number later.

Art and Tomas waved goodbye when they left, and Charlotte had a giddy, excited feeling in her stomach while she packed up her violin and reset the room so it would be ready for the morning tutor.

"New friend of yours?" Freddy asked as Charlotte was leaving. She wiggled her eyebrows suggestively.

"Maybe," Charlotte said, unable to keep from smiling.

"You get it, girl."

Charlotte laughed and waved goodbye before stepping outside.

She felt strangely positive the whole way home. The air was fresh, the brownie was going to lead her to the first fairy stone, and she had Art's cell phone number in her pocket. Everything felt right.

That was, until she made it home and saw the news van parked on her front lawn.

CHAPTER EIGHT

The white van on the front lawn read *Pinewood County News* on the side. A man in a backward ball cap leaned out of the passenger seat and spotted Charlotte. He hollered something to someone she couldn't see, and a woman holding a microphone came around the van.

Oh no.

"Miss?" the woman said, hurrying over with the man, who now hoisted a large camera on his shoulder. "We're with PCN. Can we ask you a few questions about the disappearance of Emily Barclay?"

"Um," Charlotte mumbled.

"You must be Charlotte, Emily's daughter. Where do you think Emily is right now? Police investigators have found no evidence of foul play, and Search and Rescue volunteers told us they haven't found any sign of Emily in the Greenwood. Do you think your mother ran away? Was there anything wrong at home? Domestic disputes?"

Charlotte stepped back to get space from the microphone and glassy camera lens.

"No," she mumbled. "No, I don't think she ran away. Things at home are fine."

"No fights with her husband, William Barclay? Does he have a history of violence?"

"What? No, that's ridiculous."

"Where is she, then? If she didn't run away, what do you think happened to her?" The woman took a step forward and shoved the microphone under Charlotte's nose again. Before Charlotte could think of a response, Grandma came out on the front porch, wearing her toadstool apron and wielding a whisk.

"Leave her alone!" she shouted, her pink nails flashing as she shook the whisk over her head. The reporter stepped back and lowered the microphone. "Charlotte, come here, hurry up," Grandma called.

Charlotte couldn't get out of there fast enough. She ducked around the reporter, trying to avoid the camera, and ran up the porch steps and into Grandma's open arms.

"What are they doing here?" Charlotte asked as Grandma ushered her back into the house.

"They must have been tipped off about the missing person report," Grandma said as she slammed and locked the door.

"They think Dad did it," Charlotte said, a lump forming at the back of her throat. She took slow, deep breaths to calm her beating heart.

Just then Dad pulled up, and Charlotte ran to the window to watch. He left the engine running when he jumped out of the truck, face red and arms flailing. Charlotte couldn't make out what he was saying, but she could sense his anger in the way he stormed across the drive and pushed the camera out of his face. It didn't take long for the reporters to jump into their van and reverse down the drive.

Dad finally shut off his truck and started for the house. The front door opened and then slammed again.

"Assholes." He tossed his keys down on the table, and Charlotte jumped. "Investigators were trying to keep things quiet while they worked our case, but it's going to be everywhere now. And to make matters worse, the incident commander wants to pull SAR."

"What?" Grandma snapped. "Why?"

Dad slumped against the kitchen cabinets and sighed. When he looked up, there was hopelessness in his eyes. "Because they don't think Emily was ever in the woods. They think she left me, Mom."

✶

Charlotte closed herself in her bedroom early that night, wanting to do more research and be angry and sad and not have to speak to anyone. She wanted to talk to the brownie, but he was nowhere to be found. Charlotte opened her laptop and conducted a few web searches, but she kept finding more of the same—information about different fairy creatures, the holidays they celebrated, and stories about them. She shut her laptop and sighed. She worked on her Bellini audition piece for a while after that, but she kept hitting the notes too flat and finally got so frustrated that she knocked her sheet music to the floor and flopped down in bed with a disgruntled sigh.

"Is everything all right in there?" Grandma asked through the door.

"Fine," Charlotte grumbled.

There was a long silence, and then Grandma sighed. "We all miss her, Charlotte. It's okay to grieve."

"She's not *dead*, Grandma. I just wish someone would *listen to me*!" Charlotte yelled the last bit, and then she felt bad about it. After a while she heard Grandma's slippers slap against the hardwood floor, and then the bathroom door clicked shut. She threw an arm over her eyes and tried to get her mind in order.

She, more than anyone else, needed to focus on *not* grieving. Sitting around crying all the time wasn't going to bring Mom home. She needed to figure out a plan.

A small sound caught Charlotte's attention, and her jumbled thoughts cleared. She sat up in bed and heard the tap again, more like a distinct *clink*, and turned to her window. She jumped and let out a yip of surprise, and the fairy clinging to the outer windowsill got startled and fell off.

Charlotte crept across her room, heart beating fast, and peeked out the window.

The fairy was struggling to its feet, and once it got back up, it tipped its head back and looked at Charlotte with big, sad eyes. Its tiny cap had slipped off its little head and lay in the dirt at its feet. Charlotte couldn't help herself—she opened the window.

"Are you okay?" she asked quietly, hoping Dad wouldn't hear her. He'd be mad if he thought she was on about fairies again.

The small fairy, which looked like a hedgehog, picked up its cap and held it between trembling paws.

"Keeper," he said in a tiny, shaking voice, "I come seeking your help."

"Oh," Charlotte said, unused to hearing herself referred to in that way. "Hang on, just a sec." She went to her closet and pulled out an old wicker basket she'd gotten for Easter one year. Her parents never let her eat candy, so it had been full of ripe fruits and veggies instead, and she had loved it just the same. She grabbed an old hanger as well and hurried back to the window. "Here, crawl in and I'll lift you up." Charlotte leaned out into the chilly night air, her belly across the windowsill, and lowered the basket to the ground. The fairy sniffed it and crawled in. Charlotte hooked the handle with the coat hanger and carefully lifted the basket through the window.

"There, that's better," she said, setting the basket on the floor to close the window. "It's cold out there." She smiled, but the fairy just hunched low in the basket. "Are you all right? What's wrong?"

"I am fine, Keeper. It is my family that needs your help." The fairy removed his cap and wrung it between his paws. "Something happened at our home. I was on my way back when I saw them. The *humans*." He made it sound like a dirty word. His paws shook as he clutched his cap. "They put something in the log—a stick of fire. There was an explosion." He let out a sob and wiped his eyes on his cap. "My mate and children are still trapped inside. I was too weak to move the rubble, and they can't get out. Please, Keeper, please help them." The fairy crawled out of the basket and knelt at Charlotte's feet. "Please help us."

Charlotte looked out her bedroom window. The night was inky black, and wind rattled the dry leaves on the trees. The last thing she wanted to do was go into the forest she knew to be crawling with the fae. But the fairy still knelt crying at her feet, and she didn't know how to tell him no.

"I'm not sure," she said, pulling nervously on the hem of her T-shirt. "The other fairies can't help?" Charlotte knew she'd said the wrong thing when he burst into wild, uncontrollable sobs.

"Please," he begged. "The other fairies just l-laugh at us from the t-trees." He cried into his cap, soaking the material with his tears. "I have no one else. You're my only h-hope."

Charlotte bit down on her lip, completely torn. She hadn't been in the Greenwood after dark in years. But she'd have to face her fears eventually, and this fairy needed her help. So, despite the fear already clawing at her belly, she knelt and smiled into his brown eyes. "I'll help you," she said. "Just show me the way."

✷

And so Charlotte found herself, in a heavy coat and hiking boots, walking through the Greenwood late on Thursday night.

They headed up the embankment behind the house, and Charlotte clicked on the flashlight she'd brought along. She swept it back and forth in a slow arc, hoping not to come across any creature, fairy or otherwise, looking for a late-night snack. The fairy led her up the abandoned hiking trail, which Charlotte figured was probably not so abandoned after all. The forest service didn't maintain it anymore, but that didn't mean teenagers never came out here looking to cause trouble. The woods had a magic about them that could bring out the animal in people, and the night felt full of eerie possibility.

"We're almost there," the fairy said after they'd been crunching up the leaf-covered trail for five minutes or so.

Charlotte was relieved. She'd worried that his home may be further away than she'd anticipated, but five minutes was doable. She could help them out and then get the hell out of here.

"There!" he said, right at the same time Charlotte smelled the sting of sulfur. It reminded her of lighting candles with long matches and watching the fireworks show in town on the Fourth of July. She knew right away what the fairy meant when he said "stick of fire."

The fairy led her a short distance off the trail, and Charlotte had to push through low-hanging branches that draped damp leaves across her shoulders. Whoever had done this was long gone, and only the smell of sulfur and a blackened log remained. The fairy ran ahead and put his tiny paws on the splintered wood.

"The Keeper has come!" he shouted. "She's going to get you out!" He put his head beside the rubble and perked up after a moment. "They're alive," he told Charlotte, "but please hurry."

Charlotte pulled gloves out of her coat pocket and yanked them on before starting to move all the large, splintered pieces of wood. They were heavy, almost too big for her to lift, so it was no wonder the fairy hadn't been able to free his family. He hovered around her feet while she worked, scurrying this way and that, peering in through the dark spaces between the splintered pieces of wood. And finally, when Charlotte pushed away the last remaining fragment of log, he jumped into the hole she'd uncovered and disappeared.

The forest shifted around Charlotte, and she tried to ignore the darkening shadows that stretched and yawned from between the oak trees. It was funny how one little hedgehog fairy had made her feel so safe, and now without him she felt small and afraid.

The dirt around the hole shifted, and a tiny hedgehog appeared, coughing and sputtering. Charlotte knelt and held out a hand. "Are you okay?"

The tiny fairy squeaked and scurried away, darting into the underbrush nearby.

Another fairy climbed out of the dirt and debris. This one was smaller and rounder than the male, and it had lighter brown eyes. "You must be the Keeper," it said in a distinctively higher voice.

Charlotte nodded. "Yeah, but you can just call me Charlotte." She sat back on her heels and glanced in the direction the other fairy had run.

"Oh, that one's Butternut, my youngest. I apologize about that. It's just that we haven't had many, well, *pleasant* interactions with humans. Not in many years."

The male fairy crawled out of the dirt with one more in tow, this one just slightly larger than Butternut. It smiled up at Charlotte.

"Hello, Keeper. I'm Flora. Did you already meet my sister?"

"I tried to," Charlotte said, "but I think I scared her."

"I'll go get her." Flora ran off on all fours into the dark to find her sister.

"I apologize for failing to introduce myself earlier. I was out of sorts." The male removed his cap. "My name is Fiddleleaf, and this is my mate, Blue."

"Thank you so much for saving us," Blue said. "We heard our Keeper had returned, and I'm so glad to see now that it's true. We've needed you for so long." She stepped forward and offered her paws to Charlotte. Charlotte reached down, and Blue took hold of her fingers. "We will be grateful to you always, Keeper. Pixies never forget."

"None of the other fairies have told me their names," Charlotte said, remembering how the dryad had withheld her name when asked.

"Well, names have power," Blue explained, releasing her hold on Charlotte's fingers. "In our world, you must earn the privilege to know another's name, and you certainly earned ours tonight."

Charlotte couldn't deny the pride she felt at that. And at least she knew now why the dryad and the brownie had failed to introduce themselves.

"Where will you go now?" Charlotte asked. "Our world seems like a pretty dangerous place for you."

"Aye," said Fiddleleaf, "but the fairy realm isn't much better. At least there aren't any trolls around here."

"Trolls?" Charlotte asked. "That's a real thing?"

"Of course! Lyra has been rid of them for many years, the lady dryad saw to that, but venture too far into the mountains and you best beware."

Flora returned, carrying Butternut on her back, and she plopped her sister down in the dirt at Charlotte's feet. Butternut trembled, her round eyes wide and her paws shivering. She couldn't have been much larger than a mouse.

"It's okay," Charlotte said softly. "I won't hurt you."

"At least say hello," Flora said.

Butternut gulped. "H-Hello," she whispered.

Charlotte smiled. This felt like one small victory.

"Do you need us to walk you home?" Fiddleleaf asked, and Butternut ran to his side.

Charlotte shook her head. "No, I'll be okay. It's a short walk from here."

"Wait." Blue scurried through the dirt, digging through the underbrush until she found what she was looking for. It was a small seed, and she held it in her paws and whispered words over it that Charlotte couldn't understand.

"It's not much," Blue said, offering Charlotte the seed, "but it will keep you from losing your way. Without the stones, much of our magic is lost, but this is the least I could do."

Charlotte accepted the gift. "What do I do with it?" she asked.

"When you're ready to go, crush the seed beneath your boot, and it will show you the way."

"Thank you," Charlotte said, turning the seed between her fingers. "Will I see you again?"

"I truly hope so," Fiddleleaf answered. He hoisted Butternut onto his back and then dropped to all fours and waddled away.

"Goodbye, Keeper!" Flora called, waving before she followed her father. Blue was the last to go, and she gave Charlotte's fingers a squeeze.

"If you ever need anything, we would be honored to serve you."

"I appreciate that." Charlotte smiled down at Blue and then watched the family walk away until they were swallowed up by the darkness.

The wind rattled through the dry leaves overhead, and Charlotte pulled up her hood and hunkered down against the cold. She looked down at the seed in her palm, and then shrugged before placing it on a rock and crushing it under her boot. A tornado of leaves swirled to life around her, then fell to the forest floor, settling into a path that led back the way she had come.

"Cool," Charlotte whispered to herself, then clicked on her flashlight and followed the trail of leaves.

An old fear lurked in the back of her mind, but she disregarded it by focusing on the magic leaves, which continually swirled up and around her before settling like stepping stones to guide her through the forest.

She followed them all the way home, and soon the warm yellow lights on the front porch bled through the darkness. She navigated down the embankment slowly, being careful not to slip on the piles of damp leaves. When she stepped onto the back lawn, the magic leaves swirled into a vortex and scattered back into the trees, leaving her alone and awestruck. She slipped inside with a smile on her face.

Before she went to bed that night, there was one thing she had to do. She went into the kitchen to get milk and a biscuit and then went and sat on the back porch. The night air was still cold and the leaves in the trees were still rustling, but the Greenwood didn't look so eerie from here now. It looked like a place she'd just ventured into and returned from alive, and she felt empowered.

It didn't take long for the brownie to appear out of the shadows in the back garden, and he walked right up and plopped down beside Charlotte on the porch step. He looked at the biscuits, and the tip of his pink tongue poked out from the side of his mouth.

"I met a family of pixies tonight," Charlotte said. "I saved them."

"From what?" the brownie asked, his eyes on the biscuits.

"From people," Charlotte said, her smile faltering. "But anyway, I wanna go."

"Go where?" the brownie asked. He wasn't paying much attention to her.

"To get the stone. Can you take me?"

His floppy ears perked up, and his eyes grew wide. Then he smiled. "Yes, Keeper. I will take you."

"When? Tonight?"

"No, no, not tonight."

"Not tonight?" Charlotte asked. "Why?"

"The stone is not far from here, but it will be a long walk through the woods. Better to start a journey with the morning sun." He reached for a biscuit, and Charlotte pulled it away.

"Are you serious?" she asked.

The brownie growled deep in his throat and glared up at her.

"Okay, fine, tomorrow. You promise you'll take me?"

"I promise," he said, his eyes flicking between her and the biscuits.

With an exasperated sigh, Charlotte handed them over.

CHAPTER NINE

The incident commander working on Mom's case pulled SAR, so by Friday morning the patrols, volunteers, and law enforcement officers sweeping the Greenwood had dispersed. Dad didn't leave his room that morning, so it was easy for Charlotte to sneak into the woods without him knowing she was gone. She'd never skipped school before, especially not without telling her parents first, and slipping quietly through the oak trees now made her heart pound with anxious excitement.

The sun was just rising, and Charlotte shivered in the sharp October air. She was bundled up in multiple layers, thick socks, and carefully laced hiking boots. Her backpack was full of snacks that she'd hastily stolen from the cupboard before Grandma woke up, and a water bottle sloshed in the side pocket.

It wasn't hard to find the brownie. All Charlotte had to do was sit down on a rock, pull out the container of milk she'd brought along, and wait.

It took about thirty seconds, then a bush to her right wiggled and the brownie's head poked out. "Are they gone?" he asked.

"Is who gone?"

"The humans," the brownie said, stepping out of the bush and brushing himself off. "Humans are bothersome. Trampling everything and being loud." He made a disgruntled sound in the back of his throat.

"Well, I'm a human. Am I bothersome?"

The brownie shrugged. "Not quite," he said, his tone unconvincing. He

looked away and mumbled, "Especially now that you're doing your job."

Charlotte ignored his comment and handed him the container of milk. "Which way do we go?"

The brownie slurped the milk and pointed up the abandoned hiking trail. "It's that way."

"Okay," Charlotte said, standing up and slinging her backpack onto her shoulders. "Let's go find it."

The brownie led the way across the rocks and up the trail. He moved much faster than Charlotte and often vanished from sight when he'd duck around a tree or under a bush, but he would always reappear, waving his hat to catch her eye.

"Where are we going?" she asked once she had caught up with him.

"To the lake."

"The lake?" She hadn't hiked to the lake in years, not since she was a child. The family used to go swimming there when she was young and Grandpa was still alive. She could still picture him sitting in a lawn chair, his toes in the water, a beer in one hand. He passed away when she was young, but she still found herself missing him. And she knew Grandma missed him. She sometimes heard her talking to him while she was working in the kitchen. She'd chat about her day and about the family, and ask him what he thought about this or that. Charlotte wondered if Grandpa ever answered.

It was cold enough to need a jacket, but her body warmed up fast as she hiked. She unzipped the jacket a bit and enjoyed the cool air on her neck. The pale morning sun filtered through the leaves overhead, turning them brilliant shades of red and orange. The warmth and shadows played across her face, and she smiled. Mom would love this.

The trail, which they had been climbing for the better part of twenty minutes, leveled out and then made a smooth descent into the valley below. The Valley of Thorns, as the locals called it, was densely packed with bushes, trees, and foliage.

Charlotte picked her way down the trail and through the thorns carefully, thankful she was wearing thick-soled hiking boots. The brownie yelped when he got a thorn in one of his bare feet and then pulled it out with his teeth before continuing on his way.

"Come, Keeper," he said, waving her forward. "We are close."

The brownie slowed down, his feet whispering over the dry leaves as he led the way through the tangles of vines and sharp-toothed bushes. Charlotte struggled through the dense foliage for another ten yards, and then the way was clear. No more thorny bushes or creeping vines, just leaves and dry grass and a small, beautiful lake. It was fed by a river creeping down the mountainside, and the water was clean and clear.

"It is there," the brownie said, pointing toward the reflective surface of the lake.

"Where? In the lake?"

The brownie nodded. "Yes."

"How do you know?" Charlotte suddenly didn't know if she trusted the brownie. What if he was leading her into a trap? Dammit, she'd be screwed if something happened to her now. She pulled out her phone and checked her cell service. Only one bar.

"We can feel the stones," the brownie explained. "They have a heartbeat." He closed his eyes and tapped his fingertips against his chest. "Can you feel it?"

Charlotte tried, but all she could feel was the cool wind on her face and the sweat in her thick socks. "No. I can't feel anything."

The brownie shrugged. "In time, Keeper, the stones may speak to you."

Charlotte frowned at that. His words made her feel pitiful, like a fairy without wings or a bird who couldn't sing. It was a strange thing, to feel that being a human was somehow lesser than being something else.

"How do I get it?" Charlotte asked, approaching the edge of the lake. The surface was still and reflected her face back at her.

"I don't know," the brownie said. "I only said I could show you where it was."

Charlotte sighed, then used the toe of her waterproof boot to touch the edge of the water.

"Be careful," the brownie warned, but Charlotte ignored him.

She walked further up the shore, curious about how deep the lake was. She couldn't touch the bottom when she was a kid, and her parents always warned her not to swim out too far, but could she dive to the bottom and retrieve the stone now that she was bigger? And even if she could, how was she going to see through the dark water? She chewed on her lip, mulling over the possibilities.

She found a big stick half buried in the sandy bank and knocked it loose with the heel of her boot. She picked it up and brushed the wet sand off, then walked further along the bank, searching for a spot to test the water depth. The brownie trailed after her, muttering things under his breath.

"Beware the water," he said clearly when Charlotte found a good spot and stepped up to the edge of the lake.

"I'm not going to fall in." She poked the stick into the water, feeling around for the sandy bottom.

"I don't mean beware of falling in," the brownie said, standing a few feet back from the edge of the water. "You don't want to anger the spirits."

"The spirits?" Charlotte asked, whipping around to look at him. "You never mentioned any spirits before." The stick suddenly jerked, and Charlotte lost her balance. She fell, arms flailing as she hit the water. It swirled around her head and stole the air from her lungs, choking her with its icy claws. Charlotte fought her way back to the surface, coughing and sputtering as she tried to maneuver through the freezing water. Her clothes were heavy and tried to drag her down, but she clung to the muddy bank and kicked her legs hard, trying to propel herself out of the water and onto the bank.

"Hurry!" the brownie yelled, running back and forth in a panic. "Get out of the water!"

Charlotte gasped for air as she hauled herself up over the edge of the muddy bank, coating her clothes in filth. She was almost out of the water when something strong and sure wrapped around her ankle. It gave a mighty yank, and Charlotte slid through the mud, back toward the murky lake.

"Help me!" she yelled at the brownie. He just buried his face in his hat and sobbed. Charlotte kicked her legs hard and struggled against the force trying to pull her back in. She twisted her body around to get a look at what had a hold on her leg.

In the water below, narrowed eyes in a green face caught the yellow sunlight. Long black hair webbed through the water, and the scales on the creature's brow sparkled as it yanked again, pulling Charlotte further down the bank.

"Let. Me. Go!" Charlotte kicked and thrashed. Whatever that was, she refused to let it have her. She twisted and writhed, trying to free her ankle. The creature's grip faltered and then returned, but all it had a hold on now was her boot. Charlotte gave another mighty kick, and her boot slipped loose and came off, sinking down into the murky water with the scaled creature.

Suddenly free, Charlotte scrambled up the muddy bank and yanked her knees to her chest so the scaled hand couldn't grab her again. Sopping wet and covered in mud, she collapsed onto her side and began to cry.

She heard the brownie approaching and then felt his hand on her shoulder.

"There, there," he whispered. "It's okay."

Charlotte sat up, her hair dripping cold lake water into her eyes, and resisted the urge to shove the brownie away. "Why didn't you tell me about that, that, *thing?*"

"I tried to—"

"I could have *drowned,*" she snapped. "It almost got me . . ." She started to cry again, her chest heaving as she gulped in the fresh air. The brownie sat beside her and crossed his legs.

"She's a naiad," he said, folding his hands in his lap.

"A what?" Charlotte asked through her tears.

"A water spirit, just as the dryad is an oak spirit. She protects this lake and nourishes it with her magic. Or, she used to, at least." The brownie sighed. "There used to be three naiads living in this lake, all sisters. I saw one rescue a drowning child once—delivered it safely to the mother's arms."

"Wh-what happened to them?" she asked, her teeth chattering from the cold.

"The same thing that's been happening to all the fairies. Without the stones, our magic weakens. We are not immortal, Charlotte, and without magic we'll die, or else have to return to the fairy realm. That's why you're so important."

"Then why'd she try to drown me?" Charlotte gestured angrily toward the lake. The water shifted threateningly.

The brownie dropped his head and frowned. "The naiad is not as she used to be. Her sisters are long dead, and only malice keeps her alive now."

"The small one speaks as if he knows," said a cold voice.

Charlotte whipped around.

The naiad lurked near the bank, only her head above the water. Her dark lips glistened in the morning sun. "It is *your* fault my sisters are dead," she hissed. "Our magic weakens by the day, and yet you sit comfortably in your human home, unaware and uncaring."

"She's here now," the brownie said.

"Too late," the naiad said. "Now she must suffer as we have suffered in her absence." With that, she sank below the surface, her fin splashing water across the bank.

"I want to go," Charlotte said, struggling to her feet.

"But what about the stone?" the brownie asked.

"You think I can go back in there and get it now? She'll kill me!" She wrapped her arms around herself. The brownie seemed to shrink, his shoulders drooping. "We'll have to figure something else out," Charlotte said, wringing the water from her long, curly hair. "But right now, I want to go home." She started back the way they'd come, hobbling along with one boot and one soggy sock.

The brownie followed behind her, silent and moody. He vanished into the bushes halfway home, and Charlotte walked the rest of the way without him.

✖

Over dinner that night, Dad made it very clear that skipping school would not be tolerated.

"How could you do this?" he asked while Charlotte pushed the food. around on her plate with a fork. "I'm stressed as it is trying to find your mom, and now *this*? What were you thinking?"

"I'm sorry," Charlotte said, not meeting his eyes. "I didn't mean to worry you."

"You terrified me, Charlotte. How do you think it feels for a father to receive a call that his daughter never showed up to school?"

"Horrible," Charlotte answered quietly, and Dad let out a long sigh.

"Just don't do it again, okay?" He reached out and put a hand over hers. "We have to stick together. No more scaring me like that."

Dad had forgiven her by the time Grandma's oatmeal raisin cookies were ready. He tried to excuse himself to go back to his room, but Grandma stood in his way.

"We are spending some family time together," she said. "Put your butt on that sofa. And Charlotte, you pick a movie for us."

Charlotte pulled out the family's collection of DVDs and listened halfheartedly to the news channel Dad had put on. There was something on about a Mr. Arthur Nolan, who had won a state art competition, but hearing about it just made Charlotte think of Mom, so she tried to ignore it.

"How about this one?" Charlotte asked, holding up a DVD over her head. Dad let out a little gasp, and she turned to look at him.

"What is it?" she asked.

"Holy shit," he murmured.

Charlotte looked up at the screen, and she wasn't sure what she was seeing. Just a bunch of trees and a long gravel drive. Then it cut to a shot of a quaint home with a teal front door, and Charlotte realized what it was.

"We're in Mapleton, Colorado, at the home of William and Emily Barclay. William is a local restaurateur, and Emily is well-known in the Mapleton art scene. The Barclay residence is the last known location of Emily before her disappearance early Friday morning. Officers have swept the house and immediate surroundings, but no sign of Emily has been found."

The reporter went on to interview several SAR volunteers, and then there was a rough cut to the next scene. There were clips of Dad, his face blurred out, as he stormed across the driveway waving his arms and yelling. Then there was a clip of Charlotte running toward the house and the front door closing behind her.

"The family has declined to be formally interviewed at this time," the reporter said into the camera from the passenger seat of the van. "We will keep you updated with any additional information we receive. Stay safe, Mapleton, and think twice before leaving your doors unlocked tonight. Signing off from Pinewood County News."

Charlotte collapsed back against the couch. Dad didn't move, just sat there with his elbows on his knees, staring hard at the flickering images on the television screen.

"Everyone is gonna know now," Charlotte said. "The whole town." All the kids in her school would know, and oh God, Melanie was going to know. What was Melanie going to think? What were the kids in her classes going to say?

Dad turned off the TV, gently placed the remote on the coffee table, and then retreated to his bedroom without a word.

"I haven't put fresh linens on," Grandma said.

Dad opened the hall closet, pulled out fresh sheets, and then closed the bedroom door behind him. Grandma sighed, ran a hand over her gray hair, and gathered up the sheets she'd dropped on the floor.

"Now what?" Charlotte asked, twisting around to face her.

"Now nothing. We do the best we can, and we ignore what everyone else says." Grandma rearranged the load in her arms and gestured for Charlotte to follow her. "Come help me fold the laundry."

Charlotte sighed. She hated folding laundry. She got up and followed Grandma anyway, through the kitchen to the tiny room on the side of the house that used to be a walk-in pantry. Grandma stuffed the dirty linens into the washer and then pulled the fresh clothes from the dryer and dumped them on the table for Charlotte to start folding.

"I still can't figure out where that Shirley poppy came from," Grandma said as she folded one of Dad's shirts.

"I told you where it came from," Charlotte responded. "You just don't believe me."

They folded in thoughtful silence while the washer churned and sloshed beside them. After a while, Grandma put down the socks she was sorting and sighed. Without a word, she pulled Charlotte in for a hug.

Charlotte tucked her head against Grandma's neck and started to cry.

"I just miss her so much," Charlotte said between sobs. "It's all my fault."

"Shh, it's not your fault. Don't say such things." Grandma held her closer and stroked her hair. "We're going to get through this. One day at a time."

Charlotte pulled back, wiped her eyes, and nodded. "One day at a time."

CHAPTER TEN

"I'm going into town today," Grandma said over breakfast on Saturday morning. She'd roused Dad from sleep and dragged him to the kitchen table, where he now sat staring down at his oatmeal. "I need more herbs. I want to get some eucalyptus to hang in the shower."

Charlotte nodded, but her mind drifted. She thought about the horrible nightmares she'd had last night of gagging on murky water and seeing flashes of silver scales as she drowned. She hadn't slept well, to say the least.

"Charlotte, you can come with me."

"What?" Charlotte looked up from her maple and brown sugar oatmeal. She'd hoped to spend the day researching naiads, but she couldn't tell Grandma that with Dad sitting right beside her, so she just shrugged. Going into town wouldn't be too bad. It might be nice to get away from Dad's negative energy—it felt like a vortex of gloom was spinning around him, trying to suck the joy out of everything it touched.

An hour later, Charlotte was in the passenger seat of her grandma's pink VW Bug headed into Old Town Mapleton. Grandma drove with one foot on the brake and the other on the gas, so it was a rough ride. Charlotte had smacked her head on the window enough times to know to keep her face well away from the glass.

As they passed by Savior of the World church, Charlotte saw Melanie and her family standing on the steps out front. Melanie's parents were pillars of the church community and could usually be found there most nights of the week. Melanie attended church on Wednesdays and Sundays, and when they were younger Charlotte used to tag along. They liked to play in the pews and sing off-key during the hymns, and eventually Charlotte stopped getting invited. It had been years now since she'd stepped inside that church.

Melanie looked over as the Bug rolled by, and Charlotte raised a hand to wave, but Melanie just frowned and watched them drive by.

What was that about? Charlotte wondered. But then she remembered the news broadcast and thumped her head back against the headrest.

"What's the matter?" Grandma asked, looking over.

"Grandma, eyes on the road," Charlotte murmured. "It's just that I didn't tell Melanie about Mom, and I think she's upset now. She must have seen the news."

"Why didn't you tell her?"

"I don't know." Charlotte turned her head to look out the window. "I just wasn't ready to. It kind of feels like a bad dream still, and I felt like talking about it would make it . . . real." Charlotte reached out and touched the dry flowers hanging from the rearview mirror. Wherever Grandma went, flowers and herbs followed.

"She must be worried about you," Grandma said, taking a rough left turn in front of a truck. The driver just shook his head, which made Charlotte think he'd had this happen before. Grandma and this pink Bug had a bit of a reputation around town. People had mostly learned to stay out of the way.

"I hope she's not pissed off at me," Charlotte muttered.

"And if she is," Grandma said, "just apologize to her. And *mean* it."

Charlotte gave Grandma a little smile, then gripped the sides of her seat as the Bug cut to the right and came to a screeching halt in one of the few available spots left on Main Street.

Old Town Mapleton was the hub of activity in town. Main Street was lined on either side with shops owned by the locals, and on the weekends it was rare to find a good parking spot.

"You have to lift the handle and then push the lock down," Grandma told Charlotte for what she swore was the thousandth time. Some high school kids had stolen the Bug to take a joyride a few years back, and ever since then Grandma had been obsessive about making sure the doors were always locked.

It was a sunny, pleasant day, and Charlotte unzipped her jacket as they walked down Main Street. There were lots of families out this morning, shopping and sipping steaming coffee from paper cups.

Charlotte and Grandma walked through the Oval, which was paved with cobblestone and had old lampposts that were hung with lanterns every evening in the winter. It was one of those old, weird traditions that Charlotte adored. She also loved the fountain in the center of the Oval. It was a giant moose standing on a log, and during the warmer months, water would crash around the log, sending up a mist before settling in a pool below. Now, the pool was dry and the moose sparkled with a dusting of frost that would soon melt away in the afternoon sun.

Grandma walked faster as they entered an alley off the Oval, and Charlotte doubted anyone else in this town was as excited about herbs as Grandma was.

The shop was called Garden of Thyme, and the display windows in the front were full of beautiful green plants. A little bell chimed over the door when Charlotte and Grandma walked in, and the overwhelming smell of herbs and burning incense filled the air. Charlotte could pick out the smells of eucalyptus, sage, and rosemary, but the others were foreign to her.

Plants hung from the ceiling, grew from boots in the windowsills, and sprouted from adorable porcelain pots on every flat surface. Charlotte could feel their energy electrifying the air, and she breathed in their fresh scents with a smile. Plants gave off a vibrant energy and filled a space with light and life. Gemstones and minerals were the same, but their energy was often so strong that it gave Charlotte a headache. There was a rock shop only a few blocks from here, called Carnelia, that she refused to go into anymore because of the headaches the natural stones gave her. She'd told Melanie about it once, but Melanie had just laughed her off and called her crazy. She'd never brought it up again after that.

"Hello, hello!" called out a female voice from somewhere among the plants, and then a curvy woman with a mass of beautiful red curls popped out from a back corner full of green herbs. She wiped her hands on her soil-streaked smock and then tucked her hair behind her ears, which were adorned with silver earrings. She had a necklace with a pentacle hanging around her neck, and the silver flashed in the sunlight streaming through one of the windows. "Oh, Patty, it's you." The woman held out her arms, and Grandma walked into them. The two women shared a long hug and then turned to look at Charlotte.

"This is my granddaughter," Grandma said. "And Charlotte, this is my good friend, Loreena."

"So good to finally meet you." Loreena gave Charlotte's hand a strong shake. "Your grandma talks about you every time she comes in. I was wondering when she'd bring you along." Loreena put her hands on her hips and sighed. "I saw the news last night," she said, and the words had a tentative heaviness to them. "I am so sorry for what you must be going through. I'm here if you need anything. I make a mean potpie, all you've gotta do is say the word."

Grandma laughed. "We'll keep that in mind. For now, we just need some eucalyptus. You have any?"

"Absolutely," Loreena said, setting off through the plants.

Charlotte followed the two women through the store, reaching out to touch the pretty plants that caught her eye. The air was warm and humid, a welcome relief from the dry air outside.

Loreena helped Grandma pick out the best herbs she had in stock and then led the way to the register, which was hidden in the back behind a veil of broad-leafed plants.

Loreena blew a wisp of red hair out of her face as she punched numbers into the old register. She had shelves on the wall behind her, and they were lined with trinkets, minerals, and stones. And she also had . . . fairies?

Charlotte squinted her eyes to look closer.

There was no mistaking it. Three small fairies, their wings beating wildly, buzzed around a beautiful stone on one of the high shelves. They never touched it, only got close enough for a look and then flew away again. Their bodies looked human, except they had gangly limbs and pointed ears. They each had a different skin color, ranging from pale pink to deep forest-green. One fairy sat on the edge of the shelf, its little legs dangling down. When it saw Charlotte looking, it tipped its head at her, then said something to the other fairies in a tiny voice that sounded like bells ringing. There was a moment of stillness as Charlotte and the fairies stared at one another, and then the fairies erupted into movement.

They swarmed around the shelves and knocked the trinkets to the floor. A porcelain elephant crashed to the ground and shattered, making Charlotte, Grandma, and Loreena jump. The fairies knocked all the stones off the shelf except for the largest, the fist-sized black stone with veins of shimmering yellow in its surface.

"Not again," Loreena muttered to herself, dropping to the floor to gather up all the trinkets and stones that hadn't shattered. "I'm sorry about that. I'm going to grab the dustpan and be right back." Loreena's cheeks flushed red before she turned and disappeared into a back room.

The fairies landed on the shelf with the one remaining stone and called out to Charlotte in tiny, twinkling voices. They wailed and buzzed and raised such a ruckus that the shelf started to shake. "What's going on?" Grandma asked.

"Fairies," Charlotte whispered.

"Fairies?" Grandma asked, pulling back in surprise. The shelf rattled as the fairies screamed, and Grandma's eyes darted toward it. "Are you sure? What are they doing?"

"They're flying around that rock up there." Charlotte pointed to the one remaining stone.

And that's when she realized what the stone was. It had to be. It was the one object on the shelf that the fairies hadn't touched, and it had a sort of magical quality that drew her eyes to it again and again.

"I think that's one of the stones," Charlotte whispered.

"One of the ones you need?" Grandma asked, and Charlotte nodded.

Loreena came out of the back wielding a broom and dustpan. "I'm so sorry about that," she said, and the fairies screamed in their twinkling voices and swarmed around her head. Charlotte tried to keep a passive, uninterested look on her face.

"It's not a problem." Grandma placed the money she owed Loreena on the counter. "Is that stone up there for sale?" She pointed to what Charlotte assumed was a fairy stone.

"That old thing? No, no, just a decorative item."

"Oh, that's too bad. It sure is beautiful. Say, could you show me one more thing? Do you have any oils here? Pine, lavender, tea tree?"

"I sure do," said Loreena. She finished sweeping up and then put Grandma's money in the register. "Follow me, they're right over here." Loreena set off through the shop, and Grandma gave Charlotte a look over her shoulder.

They disappeared into the plants, leaving Charlotte alone. She stared at the stone, and her stomach pinched. What was she supposed to do, just take it? Was that Grandma's plan? And did that mean Grandma was starting to believe in the fairies after all? Charlotte knew she had to decide fast. She'd never stolen anything before, but she'd also never had to complete a fairy quest before.

"Shit," she mumbled, knowing that she had to do it. She stepped behind the register and reached up to grab the stone. The fairies attacked her hand, screeching with mouths wide open. One of them bit Charlotte's thumb, and she gasped in pain.

"Stop it!" she whispered fiercely. "I'm trying to help you!" She snatched the stone and dropped it into her purse.

The fairies swarmed her, screeching as they pulled her hair. The buzzing of their wings was loud in Charlotte's ears as she shielded her eyes from their sharp claws. Grandma and Loreena would be back any second—they couldn't see her like this.

Charlotte rushed for the door, stumbling as the fairies yanked her hair and screamed in her ears. They followed her out into the alleyway, refusing to give up.

"Stop it!" Charlotte yelled, swatting one fairy away before it could claw her face. A couple was walking by, and they gave her weird looks and went as far around her as they could. One fairy had a clump of Charlotte's hair in its mouth and was yanking on it like a dog. "I'm not stealing it," Charlotte whispered, glancing around for any other passersby. "I'm taking it back to the shrine, okay?"

All at once, the fairies settled. The forest-green fairy that had been pulling her hair sat down on her shoulder, and the other two landed on her purse. Just like that, their tantrum was over. Charlotte let out a heavy sigh and ran a hand over her tousled curls.

The bell over the door rang, and Grandma stepped out of the shop, Loreena behind her. They said their goodbyes, and then Loreena looked up and met Charlotte's gaze. Her red lips pursed. She crossed her arms and leaned against the doorway, and Charlotte could feel Loreena's eyes on her back as she walked away.

She knows. Charlotte glanced back one last time, but Loreena was gone.

"Did you get it?" Grandma asked as they walked back down the alley toward the Oval.

"Yeah," Charlotte said, feeling the weight of the stone in her purse. She looked down at her bag and sighed.

The fairies sat on the top of her purse, holding on to the strap and laughing in their high voices as the bag jostled.

"Grandma," Charlotte whispered, looking around to make sure no one could hear her. "The fairies followed me." She pointed down at her bag. "What should I do?"

"They probably want to stay with the stone," Grandma said simply, as if she'd studied fairy behavior in school. "Get that stone to where it needs to go and I bet they'll go with it."

"Wait," Charlotte said, stopping in her tracks. Grandma paused and looked back. "Do you *believe* me?"

Grandma was quiet for a moment, then she shrugged. "You've never been a liar, Charlotte, not even when you were little. Who am I to say what does and does not exist?" She smiled and reached out a hand, and with a sigh of relief Charlotte took it.

They stepped out of the alley and back into the Oval. There was a boy near the fountain setting up his supplies and examples of his caricature drawings, and Grandma headed straight for him.

Grandma had a thing for caricature art. She had a stack of drawings in her bedroom that Charlotte flipped through on occasion. Most of them were of Grandma and Grandpa, drawn at fairs and festivals they'd attended over the years. And that was why Charlotte smiled and nodded when Grandma asked if she wanted her picture drawn. It used to be something her grandparents did together, and now that Grandpa was gone, Charlotte felt she needed to take his place.

The artist looked up as they approached, and Charlotte's heart tripped.

"Charlotte!" Art said, his face breaking into a smile as he tipped back his hat. He wore black, thick-rimmed glasses that made his freckles stand out against his pale cheeks.

"Hey, Art," Charlotte said, feeling Grandma's curious eyes on her. "You draw?"

"I suppose so." He glanced down at all his pens and brushes and sticks of charcoal. Then he looked over at Grandma and smiled. "I'm Art," he said, holding out his hand.

"Patty Barclay," Grandma said, shaking his hand. "Well, Art, I'd like to have my picture drawn. Can you do that?" She sat down on the stool across from him without waiting for his response.

"I sure can," Art said, laughing. Then he smiled at Charlotte and gestured to the free stool beside Grandma.

Charlotte looked down at the fairies still sitting on her bag. She just hoped they would behave long enough for her to get this done and then get home.

She sat down, and Art had her twist her body a bit so that she and Grandma were closer together.

"Perfect," he said, pulling a stick of charcoal from a pouch. "Now just try to stay still." Art rolled up the sleeves of his plaid button-up, revealing the smooth, pale skin on his toned forearms. He started to sketch, and the sound of the charcoal scratching against the paper soothed Charlotte. She could picture Mom painting in her studio and remembered the sound of the bristles swishing across the canvas.

When Charlotte was a little girl, she would cuddle up on a chair in Mom's studio and close her eyes, and that sound would send her off to sleep. How she wished she could go home this evening and find Mom curled up in the corner chair in the living room, staring out the window with those dreamy eyes of hers while her tea went cold in the mug beside her. The thought of it nearly brought tears to Charlotte's eyes, and she had to distract herself by watching the water from the melting frost drip off the buildings behind Art's head.

"I meant what I said about those books," Art said, his eyes flicking between Charlotte's face and his canvas.

"Books?" Grandma asked, her tone curious.

"Yeah, I saw that Charlotte was interested in fairy lore, and I've got a bunch of books at home. Charlotte, could you look at me, please?"

Charlotte had been trying to keep her cheeks from going red by looking anywhere except at Art, but now she forced herself to stare at him. The late morning light hit his eyes just right and turned them a brilliant shade of green. Wisps of dark hair poked out from under his hat to touch the tips of his ears.

"I would like to borrow them," she said. "The only reason I haven't called is because I dropped my phone in the lake."

"The lake?" he said, glancing away from the canvas to quirk an eyebrow at Charlotte. She remembered that it was October and no regular person would be messing around at the lake.

"Uh, not the lake," she said, laughing awkwardly. "I meant the toilet. It just slid right off the sink and plop. It's sitting in a bowl of rice though, so hopefully it'll dry out." She averted her eyes and scratched nervously at her palm.

"Toilet bowl phone," Art said, laughing to himself. "Gross."

Charlotte didn't say anything else, just tried not to cringe at the awkwardness of it all. She let Art finish the piece in silence.

"Almost done," he said after a while. "Just putting some finishing touches on it."

"Could you add a few fairies?" Grandma asked, and Charlotte gave her a frustrated look. She wanted this to be over already.

"Uh, sure," Art said. "What kind of fairies?"

Instead of answering, Grandma looked over at Charlotte. "What kind of fairies?" she asked.

Before she could stop herself, Charlotte looked down at the fairies sitting on her bag. When she looked back up, Art was watching her curiously.

"Small," she said, "with big eyes and pointy teeth." Her hand still throbbed where the fairy had chomped down on it earlier.

"Wings?" Art asked as he started to sketch.

"Yeah. But they're thin, almost translucent. Kind of like dragonfly wings."

She probably shouldn't have been giving him all the details, but she was curious to see how Art's version of them turned out. He sketched for a while and then squinted at the canvas before pushing back his hat.

"Done." He pulled an adhesive spray out of his bag and coated the paper with it. "Here you go." He handed the caricature sketch to Grandma, and she laughed.

"This is wonderful," she said, throwing her head back to laugh again.

"Let me see." Charlotte took the picture and was pleasantly surprised. Art had done a wonderful job at capturing their likeness, and the three fairies he'd added were very close to the real thing. Their fingers didn't have little claws like the real fairies did, but otherwise they looked quite similar.

"What do you think?" Art asked. He leaned lazily forward with his elbows on his knees and his charcoal-covered hands clasped together.

"It's amazing," Charlotte said, and meant it. "I love it." She ran her thumb gently across Art's logo in the bottom right corner—his initials, A.N., in a funky script.

He gave her a small but genuine smile, and Charlotte's stomach filled with butterflies.

"What do I owe you?" Grandma asked, pulling a sequined wallet from her purse.

"Don't worry about it," Art said. "Just give me that call about the books and we'll be even." He gave Charlotte a sideways smile, and she couldn't help the grin that spread across her face.

She had to look away and pretend to be busy fussing with her purse to keep herself from breaking into nervous giggles.

Grandma gave Charlotte an obvious bump with her elbow, which was totally embarrassing, and they took the caricature and headed across the Oval toward the car.

"So, what's next?" Grandma asked.

Charlotte glanced down at the fairies and smiled. "Now I return that stone."

CHAPTER ELEVEN

"He's just a boy," Charlotte explained to Grandma on the way home. "He's the older brother of one of my students." The old Bug wheezed and clunked through an intersection as the fairies clung desperately to the straps of Charlotte's purse. She knew exactly how they felt, and gripped the handle on the door as Grandma took a hard turn onto the gravel road that led to their home in the woods.

"He seems like a sweet lad," Grandma said, and Charlotte suspected she'd been reading those Scottish romance novels again. "You should give him a call. What harm could it do?"

"I need to stay focused," Charlotte said, staring out the window as the oak trees flashed by. They were on fire with fall colors, but soon they'd be bare and the snow would fall. She hoped Mom would be home in time to see it. They always made a big deal of the first snow, brewing coffee and baking cookies and curling up by the front window to watch it fall. The thought of it made Charlotte frown. *I'm coming, Mom.*

Grandma pulled up in front of the house, and the Bug jolted to a stop. One of the fairies fell off Charlotte's purse, and she reached down just in time to catch it. It looked up at her with narrowed eyes, as if it wasn't sure whether to bite her or not. It was amiable, thankfully, and let Charlotte help it back onto the bag without sinking its teeth into her palm.

"I'm just saying," Grandma continued as she gathered up the purchases she'd made at Garden of Thyme, "you should give the boy a chance. People come into our lives for a reason, Charlotte. Don't be so quick to shut people out."

Charlotte climbed out of the car and headed toward the house. The stone was heavy in her bag, and the fairies had started to squabble with one another, vying for the best seat on the purse. She needed to find the brownie.

Charlotte spotted him through the kitchen window while making herself a sandwich. She hurriedly slapped the rest of the fixings together and slipped out the back door onto the porch.

The brownie was digging around in the flower beds, and his hands were covered in dirt.

"Hey," she said, and the brownie jumped straight up into the air.

"You scared me, Keeper." He wiped his dirty hands on his tattered tunic.

"What are you doing?" Charlotte asked, staring down into the dirt he'd been digging through.

"Replenishing the soil," the brownie explained. "The earth must be turned to fill it with life. Otherwise, the soil will not feed the plants in the spring." He wiped his brow and left a big streak of dirt across his forehead. "One of many reasons why your realm needs us," he grumbled.

"Oh," Charlotte said. She smiled down at him, and eventually he tipped his head to the side and narrowed his eyes at her.

After a moment his ears perked up. "What is that?" he asked. "Do you feel that?" He looked around curiously.

"I found one," Charlotte said, then took a bite of her sandwich, smiling smugly around the mustard.

"One what?"

"One of the stones." Charlotte wiped a dab of mustard from her lip and smiled. "Want to go with me to take it back to the shrine?"

"Keeper found a stone," the brownie whispered, his eyes lighting up. "Of course, I'll join you!" He stepped out of the flower bed and then paused. "But first, some milk if you please?"

Charlotte rolled her eyes in good nature. "Fine. I'll be right back."

She came back outside with a mug of soy milk, her purse, and the three fairies still in tow. When the brownie saw them, he turned up his nose and mumbled something under his breath.

"What is it?" Charlotte asked.

The brownie said something into his mug that she couldn't understand.

"What?"

"Pesky fairies," he repeated after he'd finished the milk and wiped his mouth. "Watch out. They bite."

Charlotte looked down at her thumb, which was still red and swollen. Too bad she'd had to learn that the hard way.

"I can feel the stone." The brownie reached a hand toward Charlotte's bag and closed his eyes. "Its magic is strong." He opened his eyes. "Come. We must hurry." He turned and ran toward the trees, and Charlotte would have to sprint after him to catch up.

She jumped off the porch and ran through the back garden, glancing over her shoulder once to make sure Dad wasn't watching out his bedroom window. Thankfully, his blinds and curtains were closed.

"Wait!" she called out as she struggled up the steep embankment behind the house. "You're going too fast!"

"Keeper is too slow!" the brownie called from up ahead.

"Why the rush?" Charlotte asked, walking the rest of the way up the embankment in an attempt to catch her breath.

"Fairy magic is dying," the brownie said. "The sooner that stone is returned to our shrine, the sooner our magic will return." He didn't explain himself any further, and Charlotte didn't have the excess air in her lungs to ask him to. She followed him across the old hiking trail and onto a smaller game trail, and as she walked through the leaves and trees, she glanced down every so often to make sure the fairies were still clinging to her bag. They may have been nasty little things, but she felt like it was her job to protect them, and whether they bit her or not, she was going to get them, and that stone, to the shrine.

Charlotte and the brownie picked their way through a particularly dense patch of trees. Charlotte had to carefully duck under a spider web glimmering with dew, and she even paused to admire the bulbous spider sitting in the middle of her creation.

"Come," the brownie said. "We are almost there."

The foliage in this part of the Greenwood was so thick it looked impossible to get through, but the brownie waved her forward and showed her the way. She'd come this way not too long ago, chasing Mom's red scarf through the trees, but she'd been in such a state of adrenaline that she couldn't remember it now. The only thing that looked familiar was the tangled trees up ahead, with a space between them just large enough for Charlotte to squeeze through.

She was careful to handle her purse gently as she shimmied through, and then she emerged on the other side with a breath of relief. The brownie had done it—he had led her back to the shrine.

Warm afternoon sun shone down on the five standing stones, casting long shadows on the forest floor. Despite their crumbling appearance, the standing stones stood tall and proud, reaching well over Charlotte's head. Grass and plants tangled around the base of each stone, while the circle of mushrooms that had transported Charlotte to Lyra looked gray and decayed.

"What will happen if I step into that?" Charlotte asked, pointing at the mushrooms.

"Nothing," the brownie replied. "It is wise to fear fairy rings, but the magic in this ring has already been spent. It is safe."

With a nod, Charlotte took another few steps and came to stand in the center of the five powerful stones. Their energy hummed deep and low, vibrating through her chest.

It was clear that these stones had been forgotten for many years, and yet something about them looked familiar. As she turned in a circle and swept her gaze over the area, she remembered a day long ago when she'd gone hiking with her grandfather.

"I think I know this place," she whispered. Hazy memories returned to her in bits and pieces. She could remember the picnic her grandfather had brought along and could still hear the way he snored when he fell asleep on the checkered picnic blanket in a patch of golden sunlight. She had grown bored and decided to go exploring on her own, and that was when she discovered this place and its tall standing stones.

"I'm not surprised," the brownie said. "These stones call out to you. It's only natural that they drew you here." He removed his cap and approached the stones slowly. For the first time since leaving Garden of Thyme, the fairies that clung to Charlotte's bag loosened their hold and spread their wings. They buzzed around one of the standing stones before settling down on the moss that covered its head. Then they looked back to Charlotte, their wings gently opening and closing as a chilly autumn breeze swept through the trees.

Charlotte opened her bag and removed the stone carefully. The veins of yellow glittered when she held it up to the light. The stone seemed to vibrate in Charlotte's hands, and she could almost feel it tugging at her, trying to return to where it belonged.

"Let it guide you," the brownie whispered, watching Charlotte with intense eyes.

The stone vibrated in her hands as she turned left and right, and its vibrations got stronger as she neared the fifth standing stone in the formation. The little notch in its belly was empty, and Charlotte took a slow breath before reaching out and sliding the smaller stone into the empty space.

The standing stone gave off a sudden pulse of energy, so powerful that one of the fairies tumbled off the top. Charlotte's curls lifted on a warm current of air and her fingers tingled. The brownie, who had dropped to his knees in the leaves, sniffled into his cap.

"Are you okay?" Charlotte asked. She knelt and placed a hand on his shoulder, and he smiled up at her.

"Just look around," he said, and then started to laugh.

Charlotte looked up and her breath caught. All around her, animals and fairy creatures emerged from the woods. A small herd of deer paused at the edge of the glade, their hooves stirring the leaves so they caught the air. Fairy creatures with wings and wide eyes peered out of the darkening forest shadows. A blue jay chirped from one of the low branches of a nearby tree, and on its back rode a fairy with streaming golden hair.

"What's going on?" Charlotte whispered, being careful not to make any sudden movements as she stood up.

"We feel the power of the stone," the brownie said, putting his hat back on his head. "They're coming to see who is responsible. And to thank you."

Tiny particles of what looked like dust materialized out of thin air and gathered around, landing on Charlotte's hands and arms, and she looked to the brownie for explanation.

"Air spirits," he said. "I haven't seen them here in years. There hadn't been enough air magic in this realm for them to appear." He held out a finger, and one of the air spirits landed gently on it. Charlotte laughed and the spirits lifted into the air, floating around her like the seeds of a dandelion before drifting off into the trees.

The assembled creatures and fairies started to leave, but a few stopped by to say hello. The blue jay flew over and landed on Charlotte's shoulder, and the fairy on its back tucked a flower behind Charlotte's ear before brushing a kiss across her cheek. The fairy was so small that it felt like the briefest tickle, and then the blue jay flew away, carrying the fairy with it.

Charlotte stood in the center of those standing stones until every fairy creature, except for the brownie, had retreated into the trees. A shaft of golden light filtered down through the trees to warm her face. She felt, for the first time, that she might be able to pull this off. She could bring Mom home.

⟡

That night before bed, Charlotte invited Grandma into her bedroom to tell her about the standing stones and remembering the shrine from her hike years ago with Grandpa.

"I wish he was here to see you now," Grandma said, patting Charlotte's hand. "He'd be so proud of what you're doing for this family." She stood and went to the bedroom window, tucking her robe more tightly around her. A frown came over her face as she stared out into the dark. "I'll be taking over your dad's place at the Blue Moose starting tomorrow. The sous chef and a few senior employees came by today and asked your dad to come back to work, but he refuses. So that leaves it to me." She rubbed her wrinkled hands together, and Charlotte frowned.

"I'm going to bring Mom home, and then everything can go back to normal," Charlotte said from where she sat cross-legged on the bed. "Dad can go back to work so you don't have to."

Grandma walked over to press a kiss to Charlotte's forehead. "And we'll all be thankful when you do."

Grandma went to bed after that, and Charlotte turned off her lights and slipped beneath her covers. She wondered if Grandma truly believed her now, or if she had just given up hope of Charlotte ever going back to normal. Either way, it felt good to be able to talk to someone about what she was experiencing with the fairies. She thought about texting Melanie but decided it would be better to talk to her in person on Monday. Text messages skewed everything.

Charlotte snuggled down into her blankets and buried her face in her pillow. No sooner had her eyes closed than she began to dream.

She stood in the Greenwood, her bare feet in the dry grass, while wind shook the trees around her. She couldn't feel the cold, but she knew from the color of the sky that it was going to snow soon. She tried to move but couldn't; all she could do was stare straight ahead.

Deep in the trees, a figure stood hunched and waiting. Its long arms hung down toward its knees, and its shoulders rose and fell with each breath it took.

"What are you?" she yelled at the dark figure, and it let out a guttural growl in response. It was the same creature she'd seen as a child, but she had no name for it. Its eyes started to glow, and when it opened its mouth, Charlotte gasped. Its throat was full of human body parts, all ripped apart and strewn together. She tried to turn and run, but no matter how fast her legs moved, she didn't make any progress. She could feel the creature gaining on her, and she let out a wild scream.

Charlotte woke up panting, her brow and neck damp with sweat. She pulled her knees up to her chest and squeezed her eyes shut, trying not to cry.

The more she allowed the fae back into her life, the more likely it was that she would come across the fairy from her nightmares, and she wasn't ready for that yet.

CHAPTER TWELVE

Charlotte spent the weekend thinking about her encounter with the naiad. She also kept replaying the nightmare she'd had, wondering what it meant, but no matter how much time she spent fretting about it, no answers were revealed to her. So, on Sunday, after she'd already finished her homework for Pre-Calc and got a start on her reading of Shakespeare, Charlotte sat down at her laptop and typed *Naiad* into her browser search. A definition popped up in a small white box, explaining that naiads were water nymphs of classical mythology that inhabited bodies of water such as lakes, rivers, and waterfalls. They were the female spirits of fresh water and were worshiped in archaic religious ceremonies and by cults.

She continued her reading and took notes on the info that might come in handy. She read that worshipers often wove garlands of flowers to present to the naiads, and Charlotte opened a new tab in her browser to learn more about it. Maybe it wouldn't be such a bad idea to take the naiad an offering. All she needed was for the water spirit to hear her out. If she understood what Charlotte was doing there, then maybe she'd help the cause, or at least stop interfering.

Charlotte continued her search until her eyes were dry and her head hurt from staring at the bright screen for so long. Then she flopped into bed and looked at the notes she'd collected. There were dark question marks scribbled across the page, an obvious indication that she still knew nothing.

With a sigh, Charlotte put the notebook on her bedside table and wondered, as she drifted off to sleep, if Shakespeare had ever actually met the king and queen of the fairies.

✖

Charlotte almost forgot that she'd been on the news Friday night, but the moment she walked into her first class on Monday, she was reminded.

"Charlotte, I was so sorry to hear about your mom," said a girl in Pre-Calc that Charlotte hadn't spoken to since elementary school. She put a hand on Charlotte's shoulder and frowned.

"Uh, thanks," Charlotte mumbled.

The rest of the day proceeded in a similar fashion. People stared as Charlotte passed them in the halls, and teachers pulled her aside to offer their condolences. Many eyes narrowed as she walked past, and Charlotte heard whispers of "the husband" and "murderer."

By the time Charlotte got to her orchestra class, which was third period, she'd had about all the hugs, stares, and shoulder squeezes that she could bear. But now she had to deal with what she'd been worrying about all morning: Melanie.

Melanie already had the music stand and chairs set up, and she stared straight ahead with her violin propped up on one knee. Charlotte got her instrument ready slowly, glancing over her shoulder every so often as the other students filtered into the classroom and started setting up their stands. Charlotte finished putting rosin on her bow just as Mr. Hamilton came out of his office waving his music folder.

"Come on, people! We're starting with the Bach piece." He made his way to his conductor's podium as Charlotte slipped into her seat beside Melanie.

"Hey," she whispered, "thanks for setting everything up."

"Yeah," was Melanie's only response. Her silky black hair hung like a curtain between them, shielding her face from Charlotte's view.

"What's wrong?" Charlotte whispered, but then Mr. Hamilton smacked the podium with his hand and pointed at Charlotte.

"D Major scale, with arpeggio," he said.

Charlotte sighed and then gripped her violin beneath her chin and played the scale and arpeggio.

"Next," Mr. Hamilton said, pointing at Melanie.

It took over twenty minutes to get through the orchestra, and half of the students didn't even know how to play an arpeggio. If Charlotte weren't so busy trying to bring her mom home, she may have offered to start holding early-morning sectionals for the second violins.

Mr. Hamilton was in a particularly picky mood that day and spent ten minutes making the cellos play the same seven measures over and over. Melanie didn't say a word, so eventually Charlotte stopped trying to get her attention. She assumed that Melanie had watched the news and was upset that she hadn't said anything about Mom sooner. The truth was, Charlotte didn't want to talk about Mom yet. She didn't know how to bring it up without telling Melanie about everything else, and there was no way Melanie would believe her. Not saying anything seemed like it would be the most painless route, but now Charlotte wasn't so sure.

"That's enough," Mr. Hamilton said right before the lunch bell rang. "Cellos, we're going to revisit that section tomorrow, so you'd better be practicing. And Charlotte, I'd like to speak with you in my office. That's all, classmates. Get outta here!"

The room erupted into movement as sheet music was shoved inside folders and plastic chairs were stacked up in the corner. Melanie took the folder of music and walked away, not giving Charlotte the chance to speak to her.

"Charlotte." Mr. Hamilton crooked a finger at her. "My office, let's go."

Charlotte stood up and followed him to his office, violin and bow still in hand.

"Shut the door," he said, so she did. "Would you like to sit?" He offered her a squeaky wooden chair that looked ready to topple.

"I'm okay, thanks."

"I heard about your mom," he said, leaning back in his office chair. Posters from his favorite '80s bands decorated the wall behind him. "How are you doing?"

Charlotte thought about lying to him, but it felt like too much work. She sighed. "It sucks," she said honestly, "but I'm getting through it." If she hadn't been aware of where Mom was this whole time, things would be very different. She felt like a fake for some reason, like she didn't have the right to be sad and depressed since she'd seen Mom and knew she was okay.

"How are the other students treating you?" Mr. Hamilton asked. His features had softened, and he gave her his full attention.

Charlotte sighed. "Most of them have just been telling me sorry all day." She looked down at her boots and rubbed her toe into a stain on the old carpet. "But some people are saying things about my Dad, which are total lies." Tears started to well up in her eyes, so she turned quickly away, willing herself to get it together. "It's just so stupid."

"Well, I'm here if you ever need to talk. I'm a good listener, you know." He smirked, and it made Charlotte laugh. She'd never met anyone else who had such a sensitivity to pitch as Mr. Hamilton did.

"Thanks," she said. "I'll remember that."

"Good. Now get to lunch, kid." Mr. Hamilton waved her away before turning back to his desk.

Charlotte pulled the office door open and headed back into the orchestra room. Most of the students were already gone, including Melanie.

She didn't wait for me, Charlotte thought, feeling her pulse race. She put her violin away as quickly as possible and stepped out into the music hall. She walked by the choir classroom and the piano room and emerged in the main hallway. The hall was crowded with students heading to the cafeteria or out the main doors into the parking lot, so it was a miracle that Charlotte spotted Melanie's head bobbing through the crowd. With angry determination, Charlotte pushed her way through the crowd, ignoring the startled or irritated glances from her peers.

"Melanie!" she yelled, and was surprised that Melanie stopped and turned around. "What's your problem?" she asked when she caught up.

"Excuse me?" Melanie asked in the sassy, sarcastic voice she used whenever she got upset.

"You ignored me all day, and then you just leave without waiting for me?" Charlotte's voice was raised, and a circle of onlookers started to form around her.

"Oh, I'm sorry, did I hurt your feelings?" Melanie quirked a sharp black eyebrow. "How do you think I felt having to find out through the news that your mom is missing? We're supposed to tell each other everything, and you just happen to forget that detail?"

"Are you serious?" Charlotte snapped.

"Of course I am!" Melanie said, raising her voice. "I love your mom, too, and I deserved to know about this. I can't believe you would keep this from me." She shook her head as her eyes started to get glassy.

"Mel," Charlotte said, softer this time. Her anger was cooling, and the tears in Melanie's eyes hurt.

"I just can't," Melanie said, waving Charlotte away. "I can't do this right now." She turned and pushed through the gathered onlookers.

Charlotte's eyes teared up, and as she turned away, she caught a glimpse of Art in the crowd. Before he could see her cry, she hurried up the main staircase to the second floor where the library was.

Charlotte sniffled as she rushed into the library, and the old librarian peeked over the top of her romance novel. She weaved through the rows of bookshelves and found her favorite sunny spot beneath the window, then tossed her backpack on the floor and sat down.

Melanie's voice echoed in her mind. Was it wrong not to have told Mel about Mom? She hadn't thought of how Mom's disappearance would affect anyone else. Maybe that was selfish of her—she didn't know.

She wiped the tears from her eyes and pulled out her phone, still surprised that Grandma's phone-in-rice method had worked. Her phone had dried out completely after its little dunk in the lake and was working just fine. Well, it smelled a little bit like lake water, but that could be remedied with a rag and some rubbing alcohol. No problem.

She scrolled through her contacts until she found Melanie's name, but when it came to typing out a message, she didn't know what to say. So instead, she decided to text Art. She'd entered his number into her phone days ago but hadn't decided when an appropriate time would be to text him. She still didn't know if it was a good idea to get involved; she had so much on her plate already. But what harm could come from one text message? Besides, those books he offered to lend her might come in handy.

She opened a new text and typed: *Fighting with friends sucks . . . sorry you had to see that.* She thought about adding an emoji, but none of the programmed smiley faces properly communicated how she felt. So, with a deep breath, she closed her eyes and hit Send.

She didn't know what to expect. Flirty text messages weren't her thing, mostly because she didn't text very often and didn't have anyone to flirt with. She'd heard from Melanie that you had to wait a certain amount of time before texting back to make yourself seem more mysterious or desirable or something, so she didn't expect to hear from Art right away. But then her phone buzzed and his name appeared on the screen.

Happens to the best of us. I happen to be available, if you need a friend in the meantime.

Charlotte sniffled one last time and then smiled. She thought about taking her time texting back, like Melanie would tell her to do, but decided against it. Melanie and her boyfriends were always breaking up, so maybe her method wasn't such a good idea. Besides, she'd have to be back in class soon, so this would be her only chance to talk to him. She went through a few different options and then settled on sending him: *I'd like that. What should we do first, friend?*

She felt a little nervous sending it but hoped the question would prompt him to respond again. And she was right. Her phone buzzed, and she smiled before even reading what he said.

We could hang out on Sunday. Are you free?

"Oh my gosh," she whispered to herself, her heart beating fast. She'd expected small talk, maybe a phone conversation, but not to hang out with him so soon.

She ate half her lunch while thinking about how to reply, and only when lunch break was almost over did she finally work up the nerve to text him back.

"You can do this," she whispered to herself while typing a message in return. *I am – how about 12?* She bounced her knee anxiously, watching as one minute, and then two, ticked by. When her phone buzzed, she nearly squealed.

Meet you at the moose in the Oval. She'd barely read the message before another one came in. *Looking forward to it.*

✺

When Charlotte got home from school, she threw herself into more naiad research. She could have practiced her violin or done homework, but that all seemed to be less important to her these days.

That evening when Grandma got home, Charlotte could barely wait to tell her what she'd discovered. Dad didn't eat that night, so Charlotte whispered to Grandma over the dinner table while they ate. She told her about the research she'd been doing and her discovery that naiads used to be worshiped by pagans.

"So, what are you saying?" Grandma asked, a bit droopy after her long day at the restaurant. Her gray hair was frazzled, and there were bags under her eyes. "You want to worship her?"

"Not exactly. But maybe there's some sort of blessing or ritual I could perform, you know, something to show her that I respect her and mean no harm. Maybe then she'd let me close enough to get the stone." Despite her rough day, Charlotte was brimming with excitement. She'd been worrying about the stone since Friday, and now she'd found a possible solution to the problem. It was worth a shot.

"I don't know anything about rituals or blessings," Grandma said, sitting back from the table. She crossed her arms and sighed, chewing her lip in thought. After a moment she smiled. "I know who you can talk to. Remember Loreena?"

Charlotte nodded, but a ball of dread started to grow in her stomach. She'd hoped never to return to the scene of her crime.

"Well," Grandma continued, "she's a practicing witch, so if anyone in Mapleton knows about rituals, it'd be her. You should take some time to stop by and talk to her." Her cell phone buzzed from somewhere in her bedroom, and she got up to answer it, leaving Charlotte alone at the table.

Loreena may be a great place to start, but Charlotte didn't know how to face her. Did she know about the fairy stone and what Charlotte had done? She sat back in her chair irritably and turned to stare out the kitchen window. The oak trees shifted in the darkening night, and Charlotte wondered if Mom was alone right now. She sighed.

If facing Loreena meant getting a step closer to rescuing Mom and moving on with her life, she'd do it.

CHAPTER THIRTEEN

On Tuesday afternoon before she had to be at Mélodie to teach lessons, Charlotte walked down the alley that branched off from the Oval. She'd been dreading this walk all day, afraid of what Loreena might do or say, but now she felt a sense of calm as she opened the door to Garden of Thyme and the bells chimed overhead.

"Back here!" called Loreena.

Charlotte couldn't see her through all the plants and foliage, and she had to push large-leafed fronds out of her way as she headed toward the back of the shop.

A woman stood across the register from Loreena, her dark curls pulled up in a bun. She laughed at something Loreena said and then turned away, purchases in hand, and stopped when she saw Charlotte.

"Oh, hello." Her voice was warm and familiar. She smiled. "I'm not used to seeing you outside of Mélodie."

It was Claire Nolan, Tomas's mom. Charlotte didn't know much about her, but she liked Mrs. Nolan nonetheless. She was easy to talk to, didn't loiter after lessons, and paid on time. She was the perfect client.

"I'm about to head over there," Charlotte said, lifting her violin case for Mrs. Nolan to see. "Will Art be picking Tomas up tonight?"

"No, his dad will be picking him up. Have you ever met my husband?"

Charlotte shook her head.

"Well, you'll know him when you see him. Tall, dark hair, probably talking on his cell phone." She sighed and brushed a strand of hair out of her face. A ring flashed on her finger, and Charlotte recognized it as the same pentacle that Loreena wore on a chain around her neck. "Anyway, I'll be going. See you later, Loreena. Bye, Charlotte." She waved and disappeared into the greenery, and a moment later the bells chimed over the door as she left.

Now they were alone. Charlotte turned to face Loreena, who stood with her hands on either side of the register, her eyebrows raised and a quirk in her lip.

"I was wondering when you'd return," she said.

"You knew I'd come back?"

"I had a feeling." Loreena cast a glance toward her shelves, now missing the yellow-veined fairy stone. "And now here you are."

Charlotte cast her gaze to the floor and took a steadying breath. A small sliver of light filtered in past the plants desperately reaching for it and illuminated a single leaf on the tile beside her boot. She knelt and picked it up, running her thumb across its smooth texture as a means of comforting herself.

"I asked my grandma for advice, and she said I should come to you."

"About what?" Loreena crossed her arms and tipped her head to one side, her stare curious and intense.

How to say this? Charlotte wondered, rubbing her thumb in small circles across the silky leaf. What if her grandma was wrong about Loreena? The pentacle likely proved otherwise, but it would be embarrassing to ask someone about witchcraft only to find out she'd been completely wrong. She took a breath.

"Do you know anything about rituals?"

Loreena let out a long sigh. "Do you like tea?" she asked, and Charlotte smiled. "Do you have time for a cup?"

Charlotte checked the time on her phone. She still had half an hour before she needed to be at Mélodie, so she nodded.

"Let's sit down."

Loreena led her into the room behind the register, holding aside the beaded curtain so Charlotte could step through. It opened into a quaint room lit by sunlight coming in through a small window in the back door. Loreena gestured for Charlotte to sit down at a yellow table with daisies painted on it.

"Lavender chamomile okay?" Loreena asked, already mixing leaves while the electric tea kettle heated up.

"That would be great."

Charlotte looked around the room while Loreena prepared the tea. Plants hung from the ceiling with vines that crisscrossed the length of the room, almost completely camouflaging the overhead tiles. A stick of half-burned incense sat on a side table near the door, still smelling of musky sage.

Loreena handed Charlotte a cup of steaming tea and sat across from her at the table. "So," she said between sips, "what is it that you want to know about rituals?"

Charlotte was ill-prepared. She didn't know how much to tell Loreena about the fairies, or if she should say anything at all.

"Well," Charlotte said, staring down into her tea, "do you believe in spirits and stuff?"

"Sure do," Loreena said, stirring her tea. "What kind of spirits are we talking about here?"

"Um, water spirits. Like, the ones that live in lakes and stuff."

"Okay," Loreena said slowly, prompting Charlotte to look up. "So, what are you asking for, exactly?"

"I want to perform a ritual, or a blessing, or something, at the lake in the Valley of Thorns."

Saying it out loud sounded ridiculous, but Loreena didn't laugh. Rather, she sat and quietly sipped her lavender tea, her auburn brows drawn down over her eyes.

"What makes you so sure there's a spirit in this lake?" she asked as casually as one may inquire about your weekend or wonder about the weather.

"Well, she tried to drown me." Charlotte said simply.

Loreena put down her tea, and her lips puckered into a surprised O. "When did this happen?" Loreena asked.

"Um, last Friday," Charlotte said, tracing one of the painted daisies across the tabletop with her finger.

"Dear," Loreena said, sounding very much like Grandma, "it's the middle of October. This is no time for swimming."

"I know, I know. It was an accident." Charlotte waved a hand, trying to deter Loreena from asking any more questions. "Would you be able to help me?"

Loreena tapped a finger against her chin. "You want to perform a ritual to, what, placate the spirit?"

"I guess so. I read online that people used to honor the spirits all the time, and I thought it might help."

Loreena nodded. "I'll have to get the coven together for this one." She took another sip of her tea and looked up at the vines.

"Wait," Charlotte said, "you believe me?"

"Of course." Loreena laughed. "I felt it the day you walked into my shop. There's an energy to you, Charlotte, a power that not many people have."

"Do you have it, too?"

"Oh, no." Loreena waved a hand. "I wasn't born into a family of witches. I learned and practiced on my own for years before joining a coven. I practice herbal magic, mostly. But you're not a witch, are you?"

Charlotte shook her head.

"Will you tell me what you are, then?" Loreena asked, leaning over the table. Charlotte shook her head again, and Loreena laughed. "Ah, well. I do love a good mystery. I'll get in contact with the other ladies. It's a full moon this weekend—the perfect time for a ritual. Does Sunday work?"

"Uh, yeah, that's fine." Charlotte remembered that Sunday was the day she'd agreed to hang out with Art and backtracked. "Wait, does Sunday night work?"

"Absolutely," Loreena said. "I prefer to work under the moon." She winked and then stood when the bells up front chimed. "Meet me here around six thirty, and you can help me close up shop before the others arrive. Deal?"

"Deal," Charlotte said, and then gathered up her belongings and moved toward the exit.

"And, Charlotte," Loreena said behind her.

"Hmm?" Charlotte turned.

Loreena stood with her arms crossed and her red lips turned up in a smile. "Thank you for ridding me of that stone. It was gifted to me many years ago. I knew there was something different about it, and that's why I could never get rid of it. I'm glad it's back where it belongs."

Charlotte gave Loreena a small smile. "You're welcome," she said softly.

"Hello?" called a customer from somewhere in all the plants, and Charlotte laughed.

"See you Sunday," she told Loreena, and then she headed out of the shop.

The bells chimed overhead as she pushed through the door, and then she paused in the alley to collect her thoughts. *It worked*, she thought, a smile turning the corners of her lips. She couldn't believe her good fortune, or Loreena's good graces.

She had to teach her first violin lesson in half an hour, so Charlotte hurried back down the alley into the Oval. It was crowded, as usual, with people shopping, families dining, and children chasing each other across the cobblestone in clouds of laughter. The moose fountain was turned off, and some older children crawled through its legs and onto its back even though the sign clearly said not to. She wondered where their parents were.

"Charlotte!" called a familiar female voice. She turned around and saw Freddy coming toward her through the crowd, lilac hair bouncing around her shoulders. She dragged her girlfriend, Aspen, through the Oval behind her. "Hey! Aren't you supposed to be at the store?"

"I'm headed there now." Charlotte gestured to her violin.

"Ah. Hey, have you met my girlfriend?" Freddy asked, pulling Aspen up beside her.

"Not officially. I'm Charlotte." She held out her hand, and Aspen gave it a firm shake.

"Aspen. Nice to meet you."

Aspen had light brown hair that fell silky straight around her face. Her nose ring flashed in the afternoon sun as she turned to put an arm over Freddy's shoulders.

"Did you see what she made me?" Freddy asked, sticking her hand out for Charlotte to see her ring.

"Yeah," Charlotte said, her attention drifting. She needed to get to the music store before her student arrived. But then the ring, still as flashy as Charlotte remembered, caught her eye for a different reason. It looked exactly like the stone she'd taken from Garden of Thyme, except it had veins of shimmery blue instead of yellow. "You made this, right?" she asked, and Aspen nodded. "It's gorgeous. Do you mind if I take a picture of it?" She wanted to be able to show the brownie later and get confirmation that it was a fairy stone.

Freddy beamed, but Aspen quirked a brow curiously.

"Of course not!" Freddy squealed happily. "Flash away." She smiled and brushed kisses along Aspen's cheek while Charlotte took out her phone and snapped a few pictures.

"Thanks. It really is gorgeous." Charlotte put her phone away and took a step back. "I've really got to go, but it was nice meeting you, Aspen."

"You, too." Aspen gave Charlotte a small, polite smile.

"See you on Thursday!" Freddy called, and then Charlotte lost sight of her when a group of ladies from the senior center scuffled by with their glorious hats and wisps of curly silver hair.

❧

Tomas had made considerable progress with a piece they'd been working on, and Charlotte was pleased to hear that Art had still been listening to him practice. It made a stark difference, and Tomas seemed to notice it as well. He even pointed out measures in the piece that were tripping him up so that Charlotte could go over them with him.

His dad was perfectly on time and, as Mrs. Nolan had predicted, he was on his cell phone when Charlotte and Tomas stepped out of the practice room. They waited a moment before he spotted them, and then he clapped a hand over the speaker on his phone and walked across the store to greet them.

"Hey, bud," he said to Tomas. And then, "You must be Charlotte. Gerald Nolan." He held out a hand and gave Charlotte's a firm shake.

Charlotte saw some of Art in him, with the same dark hair and green eyes, but he smelled like cologne and didn't have holes in his jeans. He pulled a crisp bill out of his wallet and thanked Charlotte before leading Tomas from the store.

"Bye," Tomas mouthed as his dad led him away, and Charlotte lifted a hand to wave.

❧

"Look at this," Charlotte said to the brownie later that evening, holding out her phone for him to see.

"Too bright," he said, shielding his eyes from the backlight on her phone. She dimmed the screen and offered it to him again. He held it awkwardly, like a child holding a baby for the first time, and squinted at the screen. After a moment his eyes widened. "Where did you find this?"

"It belongs to a girl I know."

"It belongs to the fae," the brownie corrected, and Charlotte sighed.

"I know, I know. But she *thinks* it's hers. And I don't know what we're going to do about it."

"We take it back," the brownie said simply, but it wasn't that simple.

"This was a gift. It would break her heart if we stole it."

The brownie grumbled under his breath and shoved the phone back into Charlotte's hands. "It was easy enough to steal from us. But we cannot steal back?"

"We know better." Charlotte slipped her phone into her coat pocket and shivered. She could see her breath, and the evening sky was streaked with thin gray clouds. "Any other ideas?"

"Hmm." The brownie took off his cap and scratched his head. "The dwarves used to make jewelry, but their forges are quiet now. Not enough magic."

"Dwarves?" Charlotte asked. "You know a *dwarf?*"

"I do."

"Then can you ask him about making a replica? It's worth a shot, right?"

"Very well," the brownie said. "I'll speak to him." He slapped his cap back on and crossed his arms moodily as Charlotte yawned. "Why so tired?" he asked.

"I've been having bad dreams lately."

"It may be the Sight," the brownie said casually. "Depending on the Keeper and their connection to the natural world, the Sight can exhibit strange powers. Your dreams may have something to do with it."

"What, like my dreams can tell the future or something?"

"Perhaps. Or maybe they tell the past, or the present, or nothing at all."

At that moment a group of three child-sized fairies came traipsing into the backyard. They had pastel skin, and their eyes were big and beautiful. They laughed joyfully as they dived into the old vegetable garden and started slinging dirt at one another.

The brownie shot up angrily, muttering something about hobgoblins under his breath as he struggled down the porch stairs and ran off into the garden to scare the troublemakers away. Charlotte was cold anyway, so she yelled "Goodnight!" and then went inside to warm up.

Before she went to bed, she pulled up a new tab on her Internet browser and typed in *What do dreams mean?* Thousands of pages showed up in the browser search, and Charlotte let out a slow breath as she started clicking through them. Each link she clicked on led her to another one, and soon she was taking notes and watching videos and ignoring the hour growing later and later. She found an especially interesting site called Stones and Psychics and read that amethyst was one of the most powerful stones known to boost dreamwork and psychic abilities.

She wrote *amethyst* in capital letters and circled it.

CHAPTER FOURTEEN

Charlotte stood in the late afternoon sun staring into Carnelia's window display. The minerals in the window gleamed in the sun, sending prisms of rainbow light dancing across the delicate pillows they nestled on.

As soon as Charlotte stepped through the door she felt a wave of nausea roll over her. Her head felt full, and her ears buzzed as if she'd been listening to loud music with her earbuds for too long. She reached out to steady herself on a nearby wall and took a few sips of lukewarm water from her water bottle.

"Are you okay?" someone asked, and Charlotte looked over her shoulder. Aspen stared back at her, eyes narrowed and lips pinched in concern. When she recognized Charlotte, she smiled. "Oh, hey."

"Hi," Charlotte said, straightening up. "Yeah, I'm fine. Just felt a little nauseous when I stepped through the door."

"Ah," Aspen said, crossing her arms and smiling. "It's the stones. You must be hypersensitive to them. Some people are. I used to get headaches a lot when I started working here, but they're not so bad now." She tucked a strand of brown hair behind her ear. "Is there anything I can help you find?"

"Yes, actually. I'm looking for amethyst."

"This way." Aspen led Charlotte through the shop, which had skylights overhead and was filled with warm yellow light. They walked through rows and rows of gemstones, all varying sizes and colors. Charlotte wanted to reach out and trail her fingers across all the gorgeous crystals, but Aspen was walking fast, and she had to keep up. "Here they are," Aspen said, stopping at a display covered in purple crystals. "Do you want it for something in particular?"

Charlotte hesitated. She tried to recall what she'd read about amethyst last night. "I've been having weird dreams," she said, "and I read that amethyst might help me make more sense of them."

"For sure," Aspen said, surprising her. "It's great for dreamwork, tarot readings, divination, all that third-eye stuff. If you want to do dreamwork, I'd recommend getting a small piece so that you can put it under your pillow."

"How do I choose one? There are so many." The entire display was covered with them. There were crystals the size of Charlotte's fist and collections of smaller crystals in tiny wicker baskets.

"Touch them, look at them, feel their energy. The right crystal will choose you. You'll know when it does." Another customer entered the store, and Aspen smiled politely at Charlotte before departing to go greet the new shopper.

On her own, Charlotte reached out and started sifting through the baskets of small amethyst stones. Some were tumbled and round on the edges, while others were roughly cut and dug into her palm if she held them too tight. She picked up all the stones that caught her eye and finally found the one that called to her. It was a beautiful dark purple with swirls of lilac, and it felt snug in Charlotte's palm. It was tumbled into an oblong shape that was smooth and cool against her skin, and she knew it was hers the moment she held it in her hand.

Aspen had just finished with the other customer when Charlotte stepped up to the register.

"Find one you like?" she asked.

"Absolutely." Charlotte held up the stone for Aspen to see. "It chose me, just like you said it would."

Aspen punched numbers into the old register, and Charlotte recognized the ring she had on her finger. It was the same five-sided star that Mrs. Nolan had been wearing when Charlotte saw her at Garden of Thyme. Aspen caught her staring, and Charlotte brushed it off with a laugh.

"I was just thinking about that ring you made for Freddy. Did you buy the stone here?"

"Nope. I found it when I was hiking in the Greenwood a few years ago. It felt magical, so I kept it. And then what do you know, I met Freddy a few days after that and now we've been together for a year. Crazy how things work out, huh?"

"Yeah, crazy," Charlotte mumbled. This confirmed her suspicions—the stone on the ring had to be a fairy stone.

"Do you need a small bag for that?"

"No, I'll carry it. Thanks for your help."

"Sure. Hope it helps you figure out your dreams."

Charlotte pushed out the door, stone in hand, and the vibrations in her head calmed down the further away she got from Carnelia. It was a gorgeous fall day, cool and sunny, and she decided to snag a free spot on a nearby bench and bask in the warmth rather than go home and close herself away in her bedroom. Dad had been in horrible spirits lately and barely left the house. He called the police station so frequently that they'd sent investigators and volunteers out a few more times to sweep the house and surrounding property, but nothing was ever found. Now Dad just prowled from the bathroom to the kitchen in an old robe and ripped sweatpants and never brushed his hair, which had become a nest of dark curls. Charlotte had Dad's same curls, the unmanageable kind that always looked like bedhead. Today she wore her hair in a single long braid down her back, which she pulled over her shoulder before she sat down and leaned back on the bench.

The amethyst glimmered in the sunlight as Charlotte tilted it this way and that on the palm of her hand. She wondered how much difference such a small stone could make in her life. She would put it under her pillow when she went to bed and see if it helped make sense of her dreams.

A shadow fell across Charlotte's lap and she looked up. Then her heart dropped into her stomach and her pulse started to race.

"Hey," Art said, smiling down at her. His dark hair was tousled, and he had a baggy sweater on. "Cool stone. What is it?"

"Amethyst," Charlotte said, holding it out for him to see. "I just bought it."

"It's beautiful. My mom is really into stones. She has a collection of them. You should put it on a windowsill tonight or smudge it with sage. That's what my mom does whenever she gets a new stone. It cleanses the energy or something."

"I'll do that, thanks." Charlotte smiled up at him, and he smiled back. His pale cheeks were scattered with freckles, and his green eyes crinkled adorably in the corners when he smiled. Charlotte got nervous and broke eye contact first. "What are you up to?"

"I'm headed to the art supply shop to pick up some more charcoal pencils."

"They're out of stock," Charlotte said with absolute certainty. Then she took a moment to assess how exactly she knew that.

Art tilted his head curiously. "Really? Were you already there today?"

"No," Charlotte said softly. "I don't know where that came from, actually." She tried to laugh it off. "Just a prediction, I guess."

"Well then, now you'll just have to come with me. I'll bet you five bucks you're wrong."

"Deal," Charlotte said, less because she believed in her strange prediction and more because she didn't want to turn down the chance to spend a bit more time with him. She didn't even know if she had five bucks cash on her.

She gathered up her things and accompanied Art across the Oval and through Old Town. She'd visited the art supply shop with her mom hundreds of times, and walking through its doors today made her heart ache. The air smelled of new paper and rubber erasers, and it was the smell of long days spent browsing the shelves with Mom. The grief and longing squeezed at her chest and robbed the air from her lungs. She had to turn away and pretend to be interested in a display of chalk pastels until she could catch her breath and quickly wipe the tears from her eyes.

"Over here," Art said, waving to her from the next aisle. She joined him, and together they made the short trip down the aisle to the charcoal pencil section. And, lo and behold, the display case was empty and had a small sign that read: OUT OF STOCK. NEW SHIPMENT ON MONDAY. WE APOLOGIZE FOR THE INCONVENIENCE.

"No way." Art turned to Charlotte with a look of disbelief. His mouth parted just enough to show a hint of white teeth, and his eyes narrowed suspiciously. "Seriously, how did you know they were out? You really weren't already here today?"

"I really wasn't. I told you, it was just a guess."

"It didn't sound like a guess," Art said as he pulled out his wallet and handed over a five-dollar bill. "It sounded like you were pretty sure of yourself." He lifted one dark brow and gave Charlotte a small smile. "Well, guess this was a wasted trip. Are you headed home now?"

Charlotte nodded, although she would have much preferred to walk around Old Town some more and enjoy the day with Art.

"I can walk you home," he offered.

Oh my God, Charlotte thought. *Is this boy even real?*

"I'd like that," she said, tucking her hair behind her ear. Rebellious strands of hair were always escaping from her braid and getting snagged on things. "It's a long walk, though. I live up Old Hickory Road."

"Good, because it's a beautiful day for a walk." He held the door open for Charlotte on the way out of the shop, and then they walked side by side through the Oval and past the bus stop where Charlotte usually waited for a ride home. As they walked out of Old Town and into the Greenwood, she watched the trees carefully. She was used to riding her bike down this path, but it was nice to have Art with her. She was still nervous of the trees and the fairies that lived in them, and Art felt like a shield, like nothing bad could ever get past the bubble of happiness and calm he radiated. Even now he was talking and laughing, going on about how fun it was to paint trees in the fall.

"My mom loves to paint these trees." Charlotte smiled up at them as she walked through a shaft of golden light.

Art got strangely quiet, and when she turned to look at him, he was staring down at his feet. "I saw the news," he said quietly, and Charlotte's stomach pinched.

She wasn't sure she could handle any more fake sincerity. But when he looked over at her with sad eyes and a deep frown, Charlotte knew he wasn't about to fake it.

"Do you have any idea where she is?"

I know exactly where she is, Charlotte thought, but instead she shook her head. "Search and Rescue came out and swept the Greenwood, but they didn't find any sign of her. Some people think she just left us."

"Do you think that?"

"No way," Charlotte snapped. "She's going to come home. I know it."

A smile spread slowly over Art's face, brightening his eyes. "You are so positive," he said, laughing. "I love that."

Charlotte's cheeks warmed. He *loved* something about her. No boy had ever loved anything about her before.

"It doesn't do any good to think negative thoughts," she said.

"Yeah," Art agreed, "it's better not to put those out in the universe. Stuff like that will come back to you."

They crossed the intersection and headed up the winding gravel road toward Charlotte's house. Other families lived along Old Hickory Road, but the houses were hidden back in the trees and each had its own private drive, which made the road feel abandoned.

Charlotte's house was at the top of the hill, and despite walking home from the bus stop every day, she felt winded.

"Come on, Mountain Lady," Art said, hurrying on ahead of her. "You've gotta keep up!" He took off running up the gravel road, and Charlotte groaned before struggling after him, her lungs burning with the effort.

She found Art lounging on the front porch steps, his elbows on his knees as he drank in big breaths of the fresh mountain air.

"I love it up here," he said. "You're so lucky you get to live here."

Charlotte put her hands on her head, trying to catch her breath. "Yeah," she said between gasps. "It's pretty awesome. Where do you live?"

"In town," Art said. "Not too far from Old Town, actually."

"Seriously?" Charlotte said. "That's such a long way back! Do you want me to ask Dad to give you a ride home?"

"Nah, I like being out in the trees. Makes me feel alive. Besides, now I get to ride this all the way down." He stood up and pulled a small skateboard out of his bulky backpack. But before taking off, he paused. "Hey, are we still on for Sunday?"

"Absolutely," Charlotte said, thinking that he was probably going to crash on the way down the hill. She hadn't ever ridden a skateboard, but she was pretty sure they didn't do well over gravel.

"Great. Okay. I'll see you then. Don't forget!"

"I won't," Charlotte said. She hoped he would hug her goodbye, but instead he just bumped her playfully with his elbow when he walked by.

"I'm looking forward to it," he said.

"Me, too." She held her breath as he stepped onto his board and started a bumpy descent down Old Hickory Road.

Charlotte made it all the way to the front door before she wondered how Art knew which house was hers.

✖

That evening, Charlotte took her freshly cleansed amethyst (Grandma had some sage sticks she hadn't burned yet) and opened the door to Mom's studio. She stepped inside and closed the door as quietly as she could. She didn't want Dad knowing she was in here. He'd been so depressed and angry lately, and Charlotte felt like he was claiming Mom all for himself. Even though he hadn't said it outright, she had a feeling he'd be upset if he found her in here.

She felt her way carefully through the dark to turn on the desk lamp. The lightbulb buzzed and cast a dim light at first, but after it warmed up, it filled the room with a comfortable glow. Charlotte sat down in Mom's work chair and sighed as she leaned back. More than anywhere else in the house, this was where she felt Mom the most. The door and window had been kept closed since the day she disappeared, so there was still the lingering scent of her essential oil perfume on the air. Someone, probably Grandma, had put Mom's paints away, so the work desk was clean and organized, a rare sight in this studio.

Charlotte opened one of the deep desk drawers and pulled out a file folder overflowing with old paintings and sketches. She smiled as she opened it and started flipping through the artwork. A bunch of Mom's work-in-progress sketches were in the folder, as well as some paintings she remembered doing as a child. There was one of a toad waiting out a rainstorm beneath a cluster of lilac flowers, which she had painted late one spring while Mom crouched beside her holding a bright yellow umbrella. Then there was the one of the doe and her fawn grazing beneath the oak trees in the backyard. Charlotte could still remember how frustrated she'd been while trying to get the proportions of the doe's legs right. She would either sketch them too long or too short and would have to erase it all and start over again. Mom tried to teach her a method of measurement using her pencil at an arm's distance, but she still couldn't get it right. In this final version, the doe's legs were a tad too long and the fawn's were a bit short. Despite the frustration it had caused her, Charlotte smiled at it now.

She continued flipping through the old paintings and drawings until she came to one that caught her eye. It was a sketch of Charlotte playing in the garden as a child, at maybe eight or nine years old. She was wearing a big floppy hat and had mud up to her elbows as she worked tirelessly on building mud homes for the toads that frequented the garden. Charlotte could still remember that summer and how she'd spent every morning after breakfast working on the toad village. She'd been devastated when they all got washed away in a week of rainstorms toward the end of the summer and hadn't ever built one again.

But this sketch, done in charcoal pencil, wasn't one of Mom's. Charlotte had spent enough years watching Mom make art to know at first glance when a piece of art was hers. This one wasn't. The lines were too careful, too dark. Mom sketched quickly and lightly, only glancing down at her paper every so often. Charlotte was always shocked by how well her mom could capture a subject's likeness while hardly ever taking her eyes off it to look down at what she was doing.

This drawing wasn't like that at all. Every line and shadow looked carefully placed and meticulously shaded. It had more roundness than Mom's work did, which was mostly angles and sharp lines until she went back in with pastels or paint to bring it to life.

There was a signature in the bottom corner, a logo of sorts, but it was too smudged to read.

Putting the mystery away for now, Charlotte slipped all the artwork back into the file folder and closed the desk drawer. She stood up from Mom's chair, pulled the chain on the desk lamp, and found herself in complete darkness. A sliver of moonlight leaked in through the space between the curtains, and Charlotte walked over and peeked outside.

The side yard was bathed in a pale silver glow that made the shadows between the trees look like impenetrable pits of darkness. Charlotte thought briefly about what kind of fairy beasts may be lurking in those trees, and as she did so, she reached into her pocket to touch the amethyst. As soon as her fingers brushed its smooth, cool surface she was launched into a jostling daydream.

She saw Mom sitting at her desk, her blond hair pulled back in a ponytail at the nape of her neck while the autumn sun leaked golden light across her newest painting. Then she heard music, and it was startling in its beauty and perfection. Charlotte recognized it instantly as the song she heard while walking home through the Greenwood at the end of September.

Mom lifted her brush, tucked a stray hair behind her ear, and cocked her head to the side to listen. The light coming through the window made her eyes shine, and Charlotte felt a pang of loss and grief at the sight of her.

Mom stood up, slipped her feet into her sandals, and went to the window. The music grew louder, and Charlotte watched as the fairy magic did its work. Mom climbed out the window and hurried across the side yard in nothing but her sandals and her house robe, and didn't notice when her red scarf slipped off and fell to the grass at her feet. And then she was gone, swallowed up by the trees behind the house, on her way to the fairy shrine that would whisk her off to Lyra.

When Charlotte came to from the vision, she reached out to steady herself against the wall. Her stomach rolled and the room swayed around her, and it took a minute or so before she regained her balance.

She'd just witnessed Mom's last few moments in this room, and the amethyst had somehow triggered it. She took her hand out of her pocket and slid down the wall to sit on the floor.

Mom had already been gone that day she'd arrived home from teaching lessons and found the door to her studio closed. If only Charlotte had knocked, or reached out and tried the handle, then maybe this could have been avoided. Maybe there would still have been time to save her before the dryad had stolen her away.

With a fresh wave of guilt, Charlotte dropped her head into her hands and cried quiet tears. She felt like so much of this was her fault. If only she'd done this or that, if only she'd been more aware or had worked harder, maybe none of this would have happened.

When Charlotte felt the grief about to drag her under, she pulled in a sharp breath and sat up straight. *No*, she thought. *Do not give in to this. Pull it together.* She scrubbed her hands across her face, wiping away the tears, and then stood up.

Before Grandma could get home and find her in there, Charlotte went back to her room, leaving Mom's studio the same way she'd found it. She dressed for bed and carefully pulled the amethyst out of her pocket, thankful that it didn't send her spiraling into a new vision. She fell asleep with it under her pillow that night and dreamed of being someplace cold, wet, and dark. And amidst it all was a kiss. A warm, lingering kiss that left her yearning when she woke the next morning. She pulled the amethyst out from her pillow and quickly made a note of her dream in the journal beside her bed. What did the dream mean? What did the *kiss* mean?

Despite everything going on, Charlotte thought of Art.

CHAPTER FIFTEEN

The week dragged by, and all Charlotte could think about was the upcoming weekend. By the time Saturday arrived, she had already picked an outfit to wear on Sunday to hang out with Art and had watched how-to videos online for styling curly hair. She felt prepared, and now all that was left to do was wait.

She finished up her homework on Saturday and spent the rest of the day practicing her audition piece for Bellini, which had been neglected in light of the circumstances. She'd played through it hundreds of times by now, and sometimes listening to herself sounded like listening to a word said over and over. After a while, it loses its meaning, and that was how her piece sounded as she played through it again that afternoon.

Frustrated, Charlotte collapsed into her desk chair and sighed. She'd recorded herself playing on her cell phone a few times, but she wanted someone else's opinion. Grandma was at the Blue Moose working the full day shift, which meant Dad was the only one home. She sat in her room and waited until she heard his door creak open and his feet slap down the hallway toward the kitchen. She jumped out of her chair and pulled the bedroom door open.

"Hey, Dad?"

"Hmm?" He turned to face her, and she tried not to frown. His facial hair was long and unkempt, and his eyes had dark circles under them. Dad had always been the one who had it together. He got up early, ate healthy, and exercised on the weekends. He owned a restaurant, loved his wife, and laughed often. But now he was just a shell of a person, moping around and living in a dark room. Charlotte didn't know who this person was.

"I've been practicing my piece all day, but I don't know if it sounds right. Would you listen and let me know what you think?"

Typically, Dad was always happy to sit down and listen to whatever she was working on, but today he sighed and averted his eyes. "Maybe later," he said. "I'm not feeling very well right now."

"Oh." Charlotte sagged against her doorframe.

"I'm sure it sounds great." A hint of a smile tugged at his lips, but it didn't make it all the way to his eyes.

"Thanks, Dad," she said quietly. Then she closed the door, turned the radio on loud, and crumpled onto her bed to cry. She buried her face in her comforter as sobs shook her shoulders and jostled her bed springs. She'd never felt so unimportant and cast aside by her own dad. He'd always been the first one to stand up in the audience and cheer at the end of her orchestra performances, but now he couldn't even rouse enough energy to sit on the couch and listen to her play. The realization hit her like a punch in the stomach. She knew Dad was sick and that he was spiraling into something deep and dark, but the only way to help him was to bring Mom back. And even though Charlotte was doing the best she could, it didn't seem like enough.

✱

Sunday rolled around and Charlotte was eating breakfast with Grandma when she heard her text alert go off. Grandma didn't budge, just kept reading her book about kitchen herbs, so Charlotte quickly slid out of her chair and slipped into her bedroom to check it. She tried not to get her hopes up, but really, who else would be texting her on a Sunday? It was Art.

Good morning! Still on for 12?

Charlotte grinned and checked the time. It was nine o'clock and she hadn't showered or even brushed her hair, so she was going to need some time to get ready.

That's perfect. Still meeting at the moose?

He texted back within the minute. *Yes, ma'am. I'll be the goofy one in glasses.*

Charlotte giggled to herself, thinking that Art looked anything but goofy.

Looking forward to it :)

She did a little dance and went back out to the kitchen to finish breakfast with Grandma.

"Who was that?" she asked without looking up from her book.

"Art," Charlotte said casually.

"Art?" Grandma put down her book and pushed her bright blue glasses onto her head. "Is that the boy who drew our picture?"

"Yup." Charlotte chased a plump grape around her plate with a fork, trying not to make eye contact. If she looked Grandma in the eye, she was going to blush and then Grandma would know just how much she liked this boy.

"What did he want?" Grandma leaned across the table, her eyes shining.

Charlotte thought about whether or not to tell her, and then decided to just go for it, since she really didn't have anyone else to talk to. Mom was trapped in Lyra, Dad was equally as unreachable, and Melanie still hadn't spoken a word to her since their fight.

"We're going to hang out. Probably walk around Old Town. Maybe get lunch at the Moose." She smiled. "I think I really like him." She bit down on her bottom lip to keep her grin from stretching any further.

"Have you told Melanie about him?" Grandma asked, and the grin fell away.

"No."

"Why not? You girls have been friends forever."

"We fought about Mom." Charlotte sat back in the chair and pulled her sleeves down over her hands. Ever since she was a kid, having her hands tucked safely away in her sleeves made her feel safe and protected. Dad used to get upset that she would stretch her sleeves out, but Mom would just laugh and tell him to leave it alone.

"You girls will work it out," Grandma said, sliding her glasses back onto her nose. "And you should probably take a shower and get ready, hmm? You look like a ragamuffin." She winked.

"Hey!" Charlotte said. "So rude." But she laughed as she stood up and collected the breakfast plates to wash. Grandma laughed quietly behind her, and when Charlotte caught a reflection of herself in the window over the sink, she realized Grandma was right. Something needed to be done about the rat's nest atop her head before she took a single step out of this house.

The bathroom, although tiny, was one of Charlotte's favorite rooms in the house. She'd spent many hours in here with her violin because the acoustics were so good. She used to have trouble holding her bow arm correctly, so she played in front of the mirror until she made sure she got it right. That was years ago, but she still liked to come in here every so often to hear the songs she played echo back at her. She never had a plan when she held her musical bathroom concerts, but that was what she enjoyed most about it. She felt closest to her music when she didn't have any sheet music in front of her.

Charlotte closed the door behind her and stared at herself in the oval mirror over the sink. Her skin was pale from spending most of the summer indoors, and it made her brown curls look almost black. They kinked and curled and spiraled all over the place, and Charlotte was glad to see that her hair now reached halfway down her back. She'd received a bad haircut at the beginning of sophomore year, which Melanie had assured her would look cute, and it had taken this long to grow it back out.

Charlotte undressed and stepped into the clawfoot tub. A bundle of eucalyptus hung from the shower head, and it gave off a pleasant smell as the hot water created a humid mist.

Is this a date? she wondered while rinsing conditioner from her hair. *No, we're just hanging out. If it was a date I'd know it.*

After showering, Charlotte slipped into her comfy robe and used Mom's hairdryer and a diffuser to carefully dry her curls. She wished Mom was here to do her makeup and ease the nervous knots she had in her stomach.

Back in her bedroom, she braided the top half of her hair like she'd seen in the video online and dressed in the outfit she'd picked out the previous day. She turned this way and that, wondering whether she should add earrings, or change her shoes, or paint her nails to match her coral top. In the end she left her outfit just the way it was: a cute sweatshirt, skinny jeans, and her favorite pair of fringe boots.

Around eleven thirty she got a text from Art and clicked on it with a trembling finger.

Heading out now! Meet you there.

Me too, she texted back, struggling to hit the correct letters on the screen because her hands were shaking so bad. *See you soon.*

She slid her phone into her small backpack and went out into the kitchen to fill up her water bottle.

"You look cute," Grandma said. "Do you need a ride? I'm about to head to the Moose."

"No, I'm gonna take my bike. Thanks, though." She headed toward the front door.

"Put on some chapstick!" Grandma called back, and Charlotte laughed as she left the house.

Put on chapstick? Does she think I'm going to kiss him? Oh my gosh, am *I going to kiss him?* Butterflies fluttered around in Charlotte's stomach as she went around the side of the house and pulled her old bike out of the shed. She closed and locked the shed behind her, took a deep breath, and swung her leg over her bike and pushed off. The crisp autumn air played in her hair as she descended the long and winding gravel drive. It was a gorgeous morning, and the leaves on the trees glowed when the sunlight filtered through them just right. The road was scattered with dry leaves that crackled as the bike tires rolled over them. It wouldn't be long now before all the leaves fell and snow blanketed the forest.

She got to the Oval at 11:55 and found a spot to lock up her bike. She considered herself early, but Art had beaten her there. She spotted him before he saw her, and she paused for a moment to take him in. He stood staring up at the moose fountain, his head tipped back and his hands in his pockets. He wore a knitted black cap and thick-rimmed black glasses, and Charlotte half expected him to pull out a cigarette and a guitar and start singing the blues. But instead he turned and spotted her, and his lips lifted into a small smile.

"Hey," Charlotte said breathlessly as she walked up. The bike ride through the woods didn't have her out of breath so much as her nerves and the sight of him did.

"Hi," Art said, his white teeth showing when he smiled. "Do you think this statue is actual size?"

"Um, what?"

"The moose." He turned to look up at it again. "Do you think a moose could actually be this big?"

Charlotte stood beside him and looked up at the gleaming statue. "I think so. My dad went snowmobiling with his friends a few years ago and they saw one. He said it was so tall they could have driven right under it."

"Seriously?" Art shook his head and laughed. "That's crazy. I don't think I'd ever want to come across one of these in the woods."

"Me neither," Charlotte said, but she was thinking that there were much worse things in the woods to be worried about. There was a pause during which they both stared up at the statue and said nothing. Charlotte started to worry. Was the entire day going to be like this? Was she too boring for him? What if they had a horrible time and never spoke again after this? That had happened last year with the boy Melanie went to homecoming with. After that night he just ignored her in the halls. Melanie said it was because she refused to make out with him in the car afterward, and Charlotte hoped Art wasn't one of those boys. She reached up and nervously twirled a long strand of hair around her finger.

"Hey, would you mind going to the art supply store with me?" Art asked. "I was so distracted last time I was there," he said, giving her a look, "that I forgot to get everything else I needed."

Charlotte smiled. "Sure."

Art kept his hands in his pockets as they walked, and Charlotte held on to the straps of her backpack. There were already morning crowds in Old Town, and Charlotte smiled at the families sitting on the patio at the old breakfast cafe. She used to eat breakfast there with her family every Sunday, but then Dad got too busy with the Blue Moose and they stopped going. The Moose opened at twelve o'clock, so it would start getting busy soon. Charlotte hoped Art would want to eat lunch there, because she was really craving an avocado black bean burger. They were the *best*.

Art held the door open for her as they stepped into the art supply store. "I need more textured paper and kneaded erasers. Think those are in stock today?"

Charlotte stroked her chin and stared off into the distance. "The voices tell me yes," she said, and they both laughed. She still wasn't sure exactly what was going on with her dreams and that crazy vision she'd had, but the amethyst certainly had something to do with it. She'd left it on her bedside table that morning. Today, of all days, she didn't want any added weirdness.

Art led her through the crowded store, and Charlotte's cheeks grew warm when he glanced back over his shoulder at her and smiled.

"These are the ones I use for my charcoal sketches," Art explained, holding up a gray kneaded eraser. He picked up a few of them and then waved Charlotte after him. She was pleased to follow along, comforted by his presence and the bustle of the store around her.

Art picked out a new pad of textured paper and then paid for his wares. After they left the shop, Art stretched his arms overhead and yawned. "How about lunch? I think my blood sugar is low."

"I know just the place," Charlotte said, smiling. "I can get us in for free."

"Free food? I'm game. Lead the way."

They walked across the Oval, being careful not to run into any of the children playing tag around the fountain, and then Charlotte led the way to the Blue Moose. It had a prime location in the Oval, just off Main Street in a corner unit that had a gorgeous patio seating area wrapping around the outside of the building. A few families were already seated on the patio for lunch, and Charlotte checked to make sure her favorite table in the corner was still available.

Inside, the hostess greeted Charlotte with a hug and handed her two menus.

"I'm going to take Table 18 on the patio. Does that work?"

"Sure. I'll let Patty know you're here." The hostess turned away to mark something down on the seating chart, and Charlotte led Art outside.

"This is my favorite table," she explained. "In the summer, all the plants in these potters grow so tall that it's like a secret garden back here."

Art laughed as he took off his backpack and slid into his chair. "So, does your family own this place?"

"Yeah, my dad does. But he's not doing too well right now, so my grandma is managing everything."

"And how are you doing?" he asked. He folded his arms on the table and leaned forward a bit, the afternoon sunlight shining off his glasses.

"Better than my dad," she said honestly. "He's pretty much lost all hope I think, but I'm just trying to stay positive. I have a feeling everything will work out in the end."

"Kind of like your 'feeling' that the store was out of charcoal pencils?"

"Exactly." Charlotte gave him a sly smile. A moment later Grandma walked around the corner, wearing an apron with chili peppers all over it. "Hi, Gram," Charlotte said. "You remember Art?"

"Of course." Grandma pushed her glasses up on top of her head and smiled. "The *artist*!" she said with a funny accent.

Art laughed. "That's me."

"What can I get you kids?"

Charlotte wasted no time. "Avocado black bean burger, no cheese, onion rings. Uh, please." She gave Grandma an innocent smile.

"And for you?" Grandma asked Art. "Any allergies I should know about?"

"Nope. I'll just have what Charlotte is getting, please."

"Okey doke. Two black bean burgers and some o-rings."

"Oh, and two chocolate shakes, please," Charlotte added. "With almond milk."

"You got it," Grandma said, then squeezed Charlotte's shoulder before walking off.

"Your grandma is the coolest," Art said, sitting back in his chair. "My grandparents live in Virginia, so I barely know them."

"Yeah, I'm pretty lucky. I grew up with my grandparents living in the same house, so I've always been really close to them. Grandpa died a few years ago, so it's just Grandma now, but we have a good time."

"She seems like a lot of fun."

"Yeah, she is." Charlotte smiled and looked down at the table. A few moments of silence passed, and Charlotte listened to the family a few tables down. The daughter kept trying to pour apple juice on her plate, and her mom and dad were laughing and filming her on their phones. They sounded so lighthearted and happy, and Charlotte hoped that she'd be able to enjoy a meal like that with her parents again sometime soon.

"Oh, hey, I brought you those books to borrow." Art opened his backpack and pulled out a stack of books. He handed them to Charlotte and their fingertips brushed. Her stomach somersaulted.

"Shit," Art said, digging through his backpack. "I forgot one."

"Oh, it's not a big deal," Charlotte said, transferring all the books into her backpack.

"No, really, it's a good one. Do you wanna swing by my house after this and pick it up?"

Her stomach flip-flopped again. "Sure, if you think it's that important."

"Definitely. It's one of my favorites." He smiled at her, and she almost combusted right there.

The waitress walked up a moment later to deliver their burgers and shakes, and that was that. She was going to Art's house.

✖

Art lived in a simple two-story in one of the older districts in Mapleton. Charlotte had always loved this side of town because she thought it had so much character. The streets were wide and had tall trees that created a canopy over the road during the summer. Now they were bright with fall colors, and walking under them made Charlotte feel like she was passing through a portal into another world.

All the houses on this street were painted in pastel colors and had a quaint, cozy appearance that Charlotte loved in old homes. Pumpkins, bats, and scarecrows decorated the yards and front porches of most of the houses, reminding Charlotte that Halloween was near. It was already October 16th, meaning Charlotte only had two weeks left to complete the dryad's task. The thought of it made her slightly nauseous.

A breeze rustled the old oaks and sent a few dry leaves swirling down from overhead and skittering along the sidewalk as Art led the way up the stairs to his front door. He stepped through first and held it open wide so Charlotte could enter.

"Mom, I'm home!" he called. "Charlotte is with me!" He closed the door just as his mom walked into the front hall. She wore yoga pants and had her hair pulled up in a bun.

"Hey, Charlotte. Good to see you."

"You, too," Charlotte said. "Is Tomas here?"

"No, he's at a birthday party, which means I'm in zen mode." Mrs. Nolan touched her thumb and forefinger together, and Charlotte laughed.

"Okay then, we'll be going now." Art placed his hand on Charlotte's back and guided her toward the staircase.

Despite how gentle his touch was, she could feel heat radiating through her clothes and onto her skin. Her cheeks warmed when she wondered how it would feel if he slid his hand under the fabric to touch the small of her back.

"Mine's on the left," he said, removing his hand to point down the hall.

Charlotte froze as soon as she stepped through the door. Art had to wiggle his way in behind her while she stared at the pictures and paintings on the walls. Watercolor, charcoal, acrylic, pencil, pastel—almost every inch of wall and ceiling space was covered up with his artwork.

"I know it looks kind of ridiculous," he said, tossing his backpack on the bed before he went to his bookcase, "but I like being able to see them all. It's like a constant reminder of who I am."

"It's beautiful," Charlotte said, drifting toward a wall plastered with watercolor paintings. They looked strangely familiar, but it took her a moment to figure out why. "These look kind of like my mom's." She leaned closer. The same gradation of light, the same wash of colors. When Art didn't say anything, she turned to face him. He found what he was looking for on the bookshelf and then stood and sighed.

"You don't remember, do you?"

"Remember what?"

"The student your mom used to tutor. Must have been about . . . nine years ago. Maybe ten."

As soon as he said it, Charlotte remembered. She used to get so jealous of the boy that would come to the house, art bag in hand, because he got to draw and paint pictures with Mom all day while she was banished to the garden out back.

"Oh my gosh," she said. "That was you?"

"Yup. She really influenced my style."

"Why didn't you tell me?" Charlotte asked, turning back to the paintings.

"I thought you knew."

She shook her head. "I guess that explains why you knew the way to my house the other day."

"Yeah, that would be why." He laughed, but it faded quickly. "I was really upset when I heard about what happened. It's crazy. Stuff like this isn't supposed to happen in Mapleton, and especially not to people like your mom."

Charlotte kept her eyes on his wall of paintings and fought back the sudden tears that tried to fall. The mattress springs squeaked as Art sat down, and Charlotte wiped her eyes before she turned around.

Art smiled and offered Charlotte the book. "Here you go. If I gave you too many, then read this one at least. It's the best, I think."

She took it and read the title. *Beasts of Faerie* by Alexander C. Coyne. She added it to her backpack, which was already heavy with books, and then turned back to Art. "Thanks, I really appreciate you letting me borrow them."

"No problem. It's fun to have someone that I can talk to about these things."

He was still sitting on his bed, and as silence settled between them, the room felt like it started to shrink. All Charlotte could focus on was his bed, and his green eyes, and the small step it would take to close the distance between them. She wondered if he felt it, too. His lips slightly parted and his eyes narrowed in focus. But before anything could happen, the door downstairs slammed and they both jumped.

"Dad must be home," Art said, wiping his hands across his jeans.

Charlotte stepped toward the door. "I should be going. I'd like to get started on these books."

They walked down the hall and descended the stairs, and Charlotte came face-to-face with Art's dad at the door. She remembered him from their brief meeting at Mélodie, but today he wore a jacket and carried a hardhat under one arm. The logo on his jacket read Nolan Enterprises, and suddenly the pieces came together.

Nolan Enterprises was responsible for the new building site in the Greenwood. Tomas's last name was Nolan. Art's last name was Nolan.

Charlotte felt sick to her stomach. How could she have been so clueless? This man was partly responsible for Mom getting kidnapped. If not for him, maybe none of this would have happened. Her head spun.

He said something to her, but she brushed past him without offering any sort of greeting. And even though she heard Art calling her name, she slammed the front door as she left and didn't look back.

CHAPTER SIXTEEN

Charlotte was still upset that night on her way to Garden of Thyme. She thought back to that day on the bus when she saw the sign out the window. Nolan Enterprises, it was so clear. How was it that she didn't put two and two together and figure it out? And how was it that she felt like Art was somehow to blame? He didn't know the truth behind the Greenwood and Mom's disappearance, so how could he be held accountable? Charlotte knew she shouldn't be upset with Art, but she couldn't help it. He'd called her cell phone a few hours ago, but she'd silenced it without answering.

She stepped through the door into Garden of Thyme right as the last customer was leaving.

"Loreena?" she called out tentatively.

"I'm back here!" Loreena called, and one hand shot up out of some foliage.

Charlotte wove her way through the store and ducked under low-hanging vines before she found Loreena in the back with a hose. It was a good thing the floors were concrete, because the plants were dripping water everywhere.

"Hey, how can I help?"

"You can water all the plants in this corner for me," Loreena said. She handed over the hose and wiped her hands on her smock. "Water it until the soil is dark and then let it soak in. If water drips out of the bottom, then you know you've watered it enough. I'm going to close up the register so that we can head out of here on time." Without further instruction, Loreena ducked under the vines and was gone.

Charlotte knew a thing or two about plants from spending so many summers working in the garden, but she didn't want to be responsible for the plants that were the backbone of Loreena's business.

She was so timid and careful about not over-watering that it took her twenty minutes just to finish up that one corner. Loreena laughed when she came back to check on her.

"What's taking so long?" she asked, hands on her hips.

"I didn't want to drown them," Charlotte said, turning off the hose.

"And I appreciate that, but it's almost time to go. The other ladies will be here soon, and I need help loading some stuff in the car. Could you give me a hand?"

Charlotte followed Loreena through the store, keeping close by so as not to lose her in the maze of plants. Her stomach twisted when she stepped into the back room and saw the basket of artifacts sitting on the table.

"Do we need all of this for the ritual?" she asked. "Because I don't know what to do with any of this."

"Don't worry about it," Loreena said, coming around the table to give Charlotte's shoulder a squeeze. "I'm going to walk you through it. There's nothing to be worried about."

The bell over the door chimed, accompanied by a babble of female voices.

"We're back here!" Loreena yelled.

Charlotte took a steadying breath. The women poured into the tiny back room, and Charlotte was surprised to see not just one familiar face, but three. And they seemed equally as surprised to see her.

"Hey," Aspen said, her surprise giving way to a friendly smile.

Mrs. Nolan's surprise was harder to shake. She looked at Charlotte with her lips puckered and her eyes narrowed. Despite the pentacle ring she wore, Charlotte never would have guessed she was in the coven, not with her fancy blowouts and manicured nails. But that just went to prove that she couldn't, and shouldn't, judge people based on their appearance alone.

The third woman, Melba, was one of Grandma's old friends, and she was also someone the school brought in every year to speak at an assembly during Culture Week. She was from Nigeria and had gorgeous dark skin and long hair that she wore up in elaborate braids. Tonight, she wore a loose-fitting black shawl over her shoulders and had bracelets of silver and gold on each wrist.

"Ladies," Loreena said, "if you don't already know, this is Charlotte. Charlotte, this is Aspen, Claire, and Melba."

"Oh, Charlotte," Melba said, coming forward to wrap her in a hug. Her arms were strong, and she smelled like jasmine. "I was so sorry to hear about your mother, and your grandmother has been so busy I've hardly been able to speak a word to her on the phone."

Charlotte stepped back from the hug. "Yeah, Dad's not doing well, so Grandma is running the Blue Moose for him right now."

"You have such a beautiful family," Melba said. "Things are going to work out. Just stay the path." She gave Charlotte a reassuring smile.

"Okay, enough chat." Loreena clapped her hands. "Let's get the SUV loaded up and get this show on the road."

✖

Mrs. Nolan climbed into the passenger seat while Charlotte, Aspen, and Melba piled into the back. It would be a short drive to the trailhead, but it was enough time for the witches to ask Charlotte why she wanted to hold this blessing in the first place. Charlotte felt awkward trying to explain it, mostly because it sounded ridiculous to say out loud, and she was thankful when Loreena explained it for her.

"There's an angry water spirit in the lake in the Valley of Thorns. She might be dangerous to swimmers come summer, and Charlotte thinks holding a water blessing might help."

"How do you know?" Aspen asked, turning to look at Charlotte curiously. "Did you see her?"

"Well, no," Charlotte said, looking down at her feet.

"Then how do you know there's a spirit in the lake?"

"She tried to drown me," Charlotte said quietly.

"You're sure it wasn't lake plants or something? I've heard of people getting tangled up in lake plants and drowning."

"I'm sure," Charlotte snapped, the words coming out harsher than she'd intended.

Aspen shrugged and turned to stare out the window.

The city center and all its lights faded into the distance as Loreena drove out of town and into the Greenwood. She followed the familiar road toward Charlotte's home, but at the intersection she took a left instead of going straight, and from there she found a trailhead and pulled off the road.

It was unsurprising that the parking lot was empty—not many people wanted to go hiking in the woods after dark, especially with winter so near. The trees, however, cackled with life. Charlotte heard fairies as soon as she got out of the car. She listened to their snickers and chatter while the other women pulled the bags out of the back of the Suburban.

"It's a bit of a hike, so I hope you all have good shoes on," Loreena said as she led the way toward the trail. "Here, Charlotte, you can borrow my extra headlamp." She tossed Charlotte a headlamp and then clicked hers on.

Charlotte fell into line behind her, careful to make sure she wasn't at the back. She adjusted the headlamp strap around her curls and then pulled up her hood against the cold, dry air.

Gravel crunched under their boots as they walked, but the rattle of dry leaves and the shrieks of fairy creatures overhead nearly drowned out the sound. Charlotte kept peeking up into the trees, and every time she did, the fairies would tilt their heads and stare back at her with big, bulbous eyes. One of them dropped down suddenly, like a spider on a web, and Charlotte jumped. Aspen put a hand on her shoulder.

"You okay? The woods can be a bit eerie at night, huh?"

"Yeah, spooky," Charlotte said, careful to walk around the creature with the gaping mouth as it hung upside down from a rope of leaves.

She kept expecting the fairies to get aggressive. She thought they would scream and snap their jaws and throw rocks and fly down from the trees to pull Aspen's hair, but they did nothing of the sort. They stayed up in the trees, for the most part, and watched curiously as the witches passed by. Charlotte didn't understand at first, but it eventually occurred to her that these witches, contrary to popular belief, were connected to the natural world in ways many people weren't. After seeing the pentagram Loreena wore on her jewelry, Charlotte had done some research on it. She'd always thought it was some sort of dark symbol, but it represented something much different. The five points of the star represented spirit, water, fire, earth, and air. Witches could, supposedly, tap into the natural world and the magic inherent in all things, which may have been why the fairies stayed at a respectful distance.

Charlotte felt like the hike would never end. Her nerves were on edge the entire time they walked through the trees, and she kept jumping and frightening the other ladies whenever a squirrel would run by or a bird would swoop overhead.

Charlotte knew where they were going, so it was easy to point out the abandoned hiking trail that had been sectioned off by the forest service. They had to step over a fallen tree and shimmy around a "No Hiking in Unauthorized Areas" sign, and then they started up the long, rocky trail that would lead to the Valley of Thorns.

Charlotte mostly kept her head down, focusing on the way her breath sounded rather than on the fairies rattling the naked branches overhead. All she had to do was keep putting one foot in front of the other. Take just one more step, climb one more hill, and eventually she'd be there and they could get this over with. Inside the pockets of her jacket, her hands shook.

She followed close behind Loreena as they descended into the valley and pushed through the thick brush toward the lake. Charlotte's heart pounded as soon as she saw the water sparkling dimly beneath the gray moonlight. The evening breeze sent ripples across the water, and Charlotte watched for the naiad to surface and reach out a slimy hand.

"Okay, ladies, you know what to do," Loreena said. "Charlotte, you want to learn a thing or two?"

"Sure," Charlotte said, trying to keep her teeth from chattering. Whether she shook from the cold or her nerves, she wasn't sure.

Loreena unzipped the bag she'd brought along and pulled out a silver cup.

"This is a chalice," Loreena explained. "It represents water and the feminine energies of the universe. Quite fitting for this situation, I'd say." She handed the chalice to Aspen and then pulled out four colored candles. "Candles can have many different meanings, but tonight we'll be using them to call on the powers of the elements." She handed the four waxy candles to Melba. Finally, she pulled a silver blade with an ornate black handle from the bag. "And this is an athame," Loreena said, holding it up so that the moonlight reflected off the double-edged blade. "I'll use it to direct energy during the ritual." She zipped the bag back up, and Mrs. Nolan moved it out of the way.

"Here you go," Aspen said, handing Charlotte the blue candle. "You'll stand over here."

"Wait, I'm part of this?" Charlotte asked. She'd hoped to stand by and watch and be ready to run at any moment.

"Of course," Aspen said, as if it was that obvious. "This is your ritual. It won't work if you don't take part in it, too."

Aspen handed out the other candles and took her place across from Charlotte. Melba and Mrs. Nolan took their spots on either side of

Charlotte, and together they made up a witchy circle. Meanwhile, Loreena strapped the athame to her hip and then walked toward the lake, the chalice held high. Charlotte wanted to call out and warn her not to get too close to the water, but fear and insecurity kept her quiet. She watched as Loreena knelt and filled the chalice with lake water, and thankfully the naiad didn't surface.

"You can't leave the circle once the ritual has started," Aspen whispered, "so if you have to pee, I recommend you do it now."

Charlotte shook her head. Go pee in those woods? Yeah right.

Loreena stepped into the center of the circle and held up the athame. All the women fell silent. She chanted words under her breath while she traced an invisible line around the circle with the tip of the blade. Then she slipped it into a sheath at her hip and raised the chalice of water. Again, she whispered something under her breath and then dipped her thumb in the water and pressed her finger to her forehead. She passed the chalice around, and each woman did the same. Charlotte tried to look like she knew what she was doing, but her hands shook as she held the chalice and a splash of water spilled out.

"Sorry," Charlotte whispered, handing the chalice back to Loreena. Loreena only smiled before setting the chalice down.

"The circle is drawn," she announced, holding out her arms. "Nothing may enter or leave this sacred space until the ritual is complete." She caught Charlotte's eye and smiled, but it did nothing to calm the beating in Charlotte's chest.

"Lift the pillars," Loreena said, and Charlotte followed suit when the three other witches lifted their candles. Mrs. Nolan held up a green candle, Aspen held up a yellow candle, Melba's was orange, and Charlotte's was blue. It was heavy and waxy in her hands and smelled of tea tree oil.

Loreena pulled a box of matches from a deep pocket in her black robe and struck one. It burned bright against the dark shadows from the trees and threw dancing yellow light across her face. Match in hand, she approached Aspen first.

"Guardians of Air in the East," Loreena called out in a level voice. She lifted her athame and pointed it east. "I call upon you to watch over our rites this night. We ask that you guard and protect us. Let all who stand within this circle under your guidance do so in perfect love and perfect trust."

Aspen repeated the phrase, and afterward Loreena lit the yellow candle. Charlotte watched carefully, trying to memorize the lines before Loreena arrived at her.

Loreena moved to Melba. "Guardians of Fire in the South, I call upon you to watch over our rites this night. We ask that you guard and protect us. Let all who stand within this circle under your guidance do so in perfect love and perfect trust." Loreena lit the orange candle after Melba had repeated the phrase, and then she turned and smiled at Charlotte.

Charlotte's heart pounded as Loreena stood over her, the flame from the match flickering in the cool breeze. Loreena pointed her athame to the west and then began to speak, slowly. "Guardians of Water in the West, I call upon you to watch over our rites this night." Charlotte repeated the phrase madly in her head but kept jumbling the words. "We ask that you guard and protect us. Let all who stand within this circle under your guidance do so in perfect love and perfect trust."

Charlotte cleared her throat. "Guardians of Water in the West," she began, her voice small and unsure, but the ladies nodded at her with encouraging smiles. "We ask that you guard and protect us. I call upon you to watch over our rites tonight—"

"This night," Loreena whispered.

"This night," Charlotte corrected herself. "Let all who stand within this circle under your guidance do so in love and—"

"Perfect love and perfect trust," Loreena whispered.

"Can I start over?" Charlotte asked, and Loreena nodded.

"Say it clearly and loudly," she instructed. "You want the Guardians to hear you."

Charlotte took a deep breath and started again. "Guardians of Water in the West," she said more loudly. "We ask that you guard and protect us. I call upon you to watch over our rites this night. Let all who stand within this circle under your guidance do so in perfect love and perfect trust."

Loreena smiled and lifted the match, bringing it forward to light the wick on Charlotte's blue candle.

"Well done," she whispered, and then moved on to Mrs. Nolan.

"Guardians of Earth in the North, I call upon you to watch over our rites this night. We ask that you guard and protect us. Let all who stand within this circle under your guidance do so in perfect love and perfect trust." Mrs. Nolan repeated the phrase, and Loreena lit the green candle.

With all four candles lit, Loreena sheathed the athame and lifted the chalice of lake water. She held it up like an offering to the sky and began to chant.

"Blessing this Water, Renewing our Earth; We are Her Children, bringing Rebirth. We are the Flow, and We are the Ebb; We are the Weavers, healing the Web."

She repeated it, and the other witches closed their eyes and joined her. Their voices waltzed, spinning together like white magic under the pale moon. A shiver raced across Charlotte's skin as she drew in a breath.

"Blessing this Water," she whispered, "Renewing our Earth." Then she had to listen to the next line and try again. She had to do this multiple times, but finally she said it all together. "Blessing this Water, Renewing our Earth; We are Her Children, bringing Rebirth. We are the Flow, and We are the Ebb; We are the Weavers, healing the Web."

As soon as she completed the chant, a strong wind whipped up from the direction of the lake and extinguished all four flames, drowning Charlotte and the witches in darkness.

The other women breathed hard in the darkness, and wind whispered through the trees. Charlotte thought she felt a spider on her cheek, but when she reached up to brush it away, it was only a tendril of hair. Her hands trembled in the cold, and her breath hitched when something moved in the lake, splashing water onto the shore.

Her eyes adjusted slowly, and when she could finally see again, she looked up at the lake and her heart dropped into the pit of her stomach.

Emerging from the murky lake water was a woman whose wet skin glistened under the moonlight. Her long black hair clung to her naked body and was tangled with lake plants. She walked slowly, deliberately, as though she were unsteady and uncertain on her feet. With each step she took, Charlotte's heart beat harder and faster.

She longed to run, but she couldn't move. She was frozen in place and felt helpless as warm, salty tears began to stream down her face.

The naiad walked toward the circle. As she drew nearer, Melba shivered.

"It's here," Melba whispered.

Charlotte longed to call out, to point and scream until the others

saw the naiad with her sickly green skin and black eyes, but she could barely breathe, let alone speak. And still the naiad drew closer.

She dripped water as she walked, leaving a trail of wet scum behind her. Her long arms dangled limp at her sides, and her mouth hung slightly open.

When the naiad reached the circle, she paused and snaked out a hand. As soon as she touched the invisible line Loreena had drawn, she yanked her hand back and let out a hiss that raised goose bumps on Charlotte's arms and made her flinch.

"Hey, are you okay?" Aspen asked.

"Focus!" Melba hissed. "Something is trying to get in!" Melba's silver and gold bangles shone in the moonlight as she lifted the orange candle over her head and began to chant.

"Shrine Keeper," the naiad hissed, reaching out as if to touch Charlotte. She paused and pulled back at the last moment before the power of Loreena's circle could touch her. Her lips pulled into a grimace. "Traitor," she whispered. Water drained from the naiad's mouth, and it took all Charlotte's strength just to remain standing. The other witches were all chanting now, their eyes closed and candles raised.

"I didn't know," Charlotte whispered, tears still coursing down her cheeks, "but I'm going to fix it. I'm going to restore the shrine."

"Is that so?" the naiad asked, taunting Charlotte as she shifted closer and then stepped away, always hesitating before she could touch the circle of protection.

"Let me help you," Charlotte whispered, starting to tremble.

"*Let* you? Where were the Keepers when the human stole the stone in the first place? Where were you when the lake filled with trash and human scum? Where were you when my sisters became nothing but a memory?"

"I didn't know," Charlotte repeated, refusing to look the naiad in her cold, black eyes. "But I'm here now. Let me help you." She held up the blue candle, and the naiad paused to consider this.

"How?" the naiad asked. "How can you undo the wrong that has been done?"

"I'll do anything. Just tell me how to help you, and I will. I'll clean up all the litter."

The naiad snorted and water sprayed out of her nose. "You think that is enough? Hardly."

"I'll do anything," Charlotte whispered again.

"We will see. Your words mean little. Only your actions can speak now."

The naiad pulled away. "You will return."

Charlotte nodded. She would have agreed to nearly anything at this point, just to get the naiad to go away. She smelled of fish and filth, and Charlotte tried not to gag on the smell.

"Very well." The naiad opened her mouth and lake water poured out of it, splashing into the dirt and soaking Charlotte's boots. The naiad continued to spew water as she melted into the puddle in the dirt, until all that was left of her was a stringy lake plant curling through the mud.

Once the naiad had gone, Charlotte sucked in a breath, as if she'd been drowning and had just broken the surface. Aspen and Melba tried to rush forward, but Loreena waved them off.

"Charlotte?" she asked quietly as Charlotte bent over with her hands on her knees. "Are you okay?"

Charlotte continued to suck in deep gulps of air, but it was just making her lightheaded. She straightened up and put one hand on her heart to feel how fast it was beating. "I'm okay," she said finally. "Holy shit."

"What happened?" Aspen asked.

"Don't ask her to explain," Melba said quietly. "You aren't obligated to tell," she told Charlotte.

"I'm ready to go," Charlotte said, wiping the tears from her cheeks, and Loreena nodded.

They finished up the ritual, and Loreena ceremoniously cut the circle of protection so that the witches were free to move.

"Here, drink this," Melba said, removing a thermos from her bag. "It's herbal tea. Tastes bad but will replenish your energy." She handed the thermos to Charlotte.

The tea inside smelled like dirt, but Charlotte gulped some down anyway. Then she passed it around so everyone could have some of the smelly concoction.

Aspen hung by Charlotte's side the entire walk back, slowing to hike over tricky sections of the trail together or to offer her hand when the walking got rough.

"That was amazing," Aspen whispered while they walked. "It's like I could feel the energy getting sucked out of me."

"You enjoyed that?" Charlotte asked.

"Absolutely. I've been practicing witchcraft for years, but I've never felt anything like *that* before." Aspen's smile glowed in the dim light.

When they got back to the car, Loreena offered Charlotte a blanket and she cuddled up in it on the ride home. No one spoke much on the drive back, and Charlotte realized that Mrs. Nolan had barely spoken a word to her all night. Her eyes had been attentive and watchful at the ritual, but now she stared out the passenger side window, her lips pulled into a frown. Charlotte caught her eyes in the rearview mirror, but then Mrs. Nolan looked quickly away.

She helped the ladies unload the Suburban when they got back to Garden of Thyme and then thanked them all for coming. Aspen gave Charlotte a hug before she left, and Melba told Charlotte to take care of herself and that grandmother of hers. Mrs. Nolan hovered and hesitated, and it was only when the others had left that she spoke up.

"I'm glad you're okay," she said, and Charlotte smiled. "I, uh, just wanted to express how important it is that this stays between us." She looked into Charlotte's eyes with grim determination. "My husband and the boys don't know about the coven. They have no idea I'm a witch." She crossed her arms, and Charlotte understood now why she'd been quiet all night.

"I won't tell them," Charlotte said. "It's your secret to share, not mine."

"I appreciate it. I think Arthur would be fine with it, but my husband would need time to warm up to the idea."

Arthur, Charlotte thought, and the name sounded familiar. It took a moment to place it, but then everything clicked together. Art was Arthur, the boy who'd been on the news for the art competition the night the story on her mom aired. Of course he was the only Arthur in Mapleton that was participating in art competitions. She felt ridiculous realizing it only now.

"I won't tell him, so you have nothing to worry about."

"Thank you," Mrs. Nolan said, and her eyes softened. "And I'm so sorry about your mom. Truly." She gave Charlotte a reassuring squeeze before calling out a goodbye to Loreena and walking outside to find her car.

After the other women left, Loreena offered to drive Charlotte home. Charlotte accepted gratefully.

The ride home was quiet, thoughtful. Finally, Loreena spoke up.

"You did well tonight," she said. "Do you think it helped?"

"Yeah, I think so." She heard the naiad's watery voice in her mind and goose bumps rose along her skin. "It's not over, though. There's still more work to be done."

"Anything else I can help you with?"

Charlotte shook her head. "This next part I can handle on my own. Thank you for everything, though."

Loreena gave Charlotte's hand a soft squeeze. "I'm here for you," she said, "whenever you need it."

Charlotte smiled and then turned away, finding her eyes overflowing with tears.

Mom, I miss you.

�

After dinner, Charlotte headed to her room. She picked up her cell phone off her desk and plopped down onto her bed. Then, before she could talk herself out of it, she called Art. He picked up after the second ring.

"Hey." His voice was warm.

"Hi."

"I was hoping you'd call me back." There was a rustle of fabric and then the squeak of old bed springs.

Charlotte pictured him lying there, staring up at the ceiling with her voice in his ear. She played with a loose thread on her comforter and wondered what he was wearing.

"What happened?"

She cleared her throat. "Um, it was your dad."

"What about him?"

"I didn't realize until today that he's the one that's going to rip up the Greenwood . . ."

"Oh, that." Art sighed. "Yeah, that sucks."

"Wait, what? You're not mad?"

"No. I mean, I was earlier, but I get it. A lot of people are mad. Last weekend some lady yelled at Dad for like fifteen minutes at the grocery store when she found out who he was. I don't think anyone really likes what he's doing."

"What about you?"

Art shuffled around and then sighed into the phone. "I don't really like it, but I don't have a choice. I've talked to Dad about it, but he just calls me his crazy environmentalist, so I stopped." He laughed, and the sound was breathy in Charlotte's ear.

Right then, Charlotte wanted to tell him her secret. She wanted to tell him about Mom and the fairies and the dryad. But what if she told Art and he laughed at her? Or what if he got angry and thought she was a creep? She couldn't risk it, especially when their friendship was still in such an early phase.

Through the phone she heard a muffled knock and then Tomas's voice asking Art to listen to a new song he was working on. She heard Art agree and smiled.

"Hey, I've gotta go. Tomas wants me to come listen to something he's working on."

"Remind him to keep his bow straight," Charlotte said. "Oh, and congrats for winning that art show. You deserved it."

"I will," Art said. "And I appreciate that." She could hear the smile in his voice. "I'll talk to you soon."

"Sounds good," Charlotte said, already looking forward to hearing his voice again. "Bye."

After they hung up, she tossed her cell phone onto her desk and flopped down on her pillow. A strand of hair brushed her face and it smelled like the lake.

Tomorrow, she thought as she got up and headed into the bathroom for a shower. *Tomorrow, I'll show the naiad that she can trust me.*

CHAPTER SEVENTEEN

Mondays sucked in general, but this Monday started off even worse than usual. Charlotte's curls were frizzy, there was a quiz in Pre-Calc that she wasn't prepared for, and on her way to orchestra she saw Melanie and Marco making out in the music hallway.

Melanie's back was up against the lockers, and she had her arms wrapped around Marco's neck. She was smiling with all her teeth showing, which was something she only did when she was ridiculously happy. Charlotte knew that smile well.

She was happy for Melanie, *really*. What hurt was realizing that something this monumental in Melanie's life had occurred and she didn't find it necessary to call and tell Charlotte about it.

With a jolt, Charlotte realized that this was probably how Melanie felt the whole time. It made her feel insignificant, small, and unimportant. But this wasn't how she had meant for Mel to feel at all. Charlotte had simply been protecting herself by not telling her about Mom, and in the end, she'd hurt someone she cared about.

Charlotte glanced back over her shoulder and caught Melanie's eye. Melanie's smile faded as they watched each other, but then Marco leaned in to kiss her cheek and she laughed, her attention stolen away. Charlotte slipped into the music room without another look.

All class period Charlotte wanted to turn to Melanie and wrap her in a hug, but she held herself back. She was nervous that Melanie would pull away or yell at her, and she couldn't stand that rejection right now. So, instead, she sat quietly staring off into space, hoping Mr. Hamilton wouldn't call her out on it.

After class, Charlotte packed up her violin slowly to allow Melanie time to leave. Part of her hoped that Melanie would be standing in the hall when she left, leaning up against the old lockers, waiting for her like she'd done so many times before, but when Charlotte made her way into the music hall, Melanie was nowhere to be found.

Charlotte headed up to the second floor using one of the side staircases and then squirmed her way through the flow of students heading down to the cafeteria. The librarian was busy showing a boy how to use the scanner and didn't even look up when Charlotte passed by. Her eyes instantly slid toward the seating area by the windows where she'd first spotted Art, but he wasn't there. Her heart sank. She'd been hoping to see him.

Alone, Charlotte wandered through the rows of bookshelves and then plopped down in her favorite spot beneath the window. She'd brought one of Art's books with her and opened it up while she ate. It was *Beasts of Faerie* by Alexander C. Coyne. Holding the book made her feel closer to Art in a way. He'd probably never lent these books to anyone before, and knowing she had the opportunity to see this side of him made her giddy with happiness.

The book gave Charlotte the creeps. It may have been entertaining to someone else, but Charlotte knew that the world of faerie existed, and these beasts may very well have inhabited it. There were goblins that washed their caps in the blood of humans they killed, and carnivorous horses that would drown and devour anyone who tried to ride them. Charlotte shook her head as she turned the page.

And then she froze. Her breath caught and her stomach clenched. Blood rushed through her ears as she stared down at the dark, inky illustration on the page.

It was an illustration of a fairy with the head of a goat and the body of a man. Just seeing the illustration on the page made Charlotte's hands clammy with sweat.

According to the author, the phooka was a shape-shifting goblin. Its horns were tall and sharp, and the hair covering its body was thin and dark. It had the arms and hands of a human, but with fingernails like talons. The eyes were what caused a shiver to travel up Charlotte's back. She could still remember the way the phooka had tipped its head and lurked over Dad's shoulder. Its eyes, luminescent in the dark, were burned into her memory.

The school bell rang so suddenly that Charlotte jumped, knocking the book to the floor. Her heart pounded, and she leaned up against the wall and took a few breaths to slow it down. She packed up her lunch and the *Beasts of Faerie* book and headed out into the hallway with only one thing on her mind.

The phooka.

With lunch over, students flooded the hallways. In a daze, Charlotte headed down the main staircase and got caught up in the clog of people trying to funnel through the hall. Still running the phooka over and over in her mind, she failed to step out of the way when a boy carrying a slushie stepped into her path. She smacked into him, and the bright blue slushie spilled down the front of her sweater. The boy gasped and then spewed forth a slew of apologies, and behind him his friends just laughed. People passing by stopped to shake their heads or roll their eyes, and in the sea of faces, Charlotte spotted familiar green eyes. She caught Art's gaze for the briefest moment before she turned and shoved her way through her staring peers and rushed out the front door.

I can't go to class like this, she thought, feeling pitiful as blue slush ran down the front of her sweater and splattered on the concrete. She smelled like artificial syrup and food coloring.

"Charlotte!"

She turned. "Art," she said, trying to cover the stain on her sweater as he made his way toward her through the sea of students. "Hi."

"Hey," he said, running a hand through his dark curls. "Geez, I hope that doesn't stain."

"It's okay. I'll soak it when I get home."

"You're skipping class?" He quirked a brow.

Charlotte shrugged.

"You want some company?"

Butterflies filled Charlotte's stomach. "You'd skip with me?"

"I'm a senior, and I'm going to community college next year." He shrugged. "I'm not too concerned about missing Econ. That class sucks."

"Oh, well, okay." Charlotte smiled and ran a hand over her frizzy curls. Dammit, if only they'd cooperated today. "I was just going to head home, but we can do something else if you want?"

"Nah, no way. I'm just tagging along. Do what you've gotta do." He put his hands in his pockets and smiled.

They walked to the bus stop together, and Art pulled out his skateboard to show Charlotte a few tricks he'd been working on.

"I've been working on my kickflip." He tossed his backpack down and rolled up his sleeves, revealing angry red scabs that snaked down the length of his forearms.

"Oh my God," she said, pointing them out. "What happened?"

Art gave Charlotte a sheepish smile. "Let's just say that gravel and skateboards don't mix." He coasted by her on the board, and her hair ruffled in a mint-scented breeze.

"Even I could have told you that," she said playfully.

"Oh yeah?" He stepped off his board and smirked. "If you're such a pro, show me what you've got." He pushed the board toward her and she stopped it with the toe of her boot.

"I don't demonstrate my skills in public. Don't want to make anyone feel inferior."

"I already know I'm inferior," Art said with a mischievous twinkle in his eye. Then he held out a hand. "Come on, I'll help you."

Charlotte looked down at the scuffed board, then at his outstretched hand. With a breath, she put one foot on the board. "Don't let me fall," she said, and Art shook his head.

"Never."

She took the hand he offered, which was warm and strong around hers, and then stepped onto the skateboard.

It immediately shot out from under her, and Art jumped forward to catch her under the arms.

"Shit," she mumbled, trying to regain her footing.

"Told you," Art said, and then smiled as the bus pulled up behind them.

Charlotte shook her head as he grabbed his backpack and fetched the rogue board.

"I knew that was a bad idea," she said as she boarded the bus. She swiped her bus pass and found a seat. Art didn't have a pass, so instead he had to pay a few dollars, and then he took a seat next to her. The bench seats were so small that they had to squish together, their legs pressed up against each other, and Charlotte tried not to let Art see her smile.

"Oh my gosh," she exclaimed, and Art's brows shot up.

"Uh, you forgot you actually had an exam in English?"

"Psh, no. I started reading those books you gave me. I'm working on *Beasts of Faerie* right now, and . . ." She trailed off, realizing she'd been about to tell him about seeing a phooka on Halloween eight years ago. Talking with him was just so comfortable—it made her almost forget the secrets she had to keep.

"Freaky, right?" He laughed and she was off the hook. "That's my favorite book, which is why I dragged you all the way to my house to get it yesterday."

There was a moment of silence as Charlotte remembered being in Art's room. She could picture the way he sat on the bed and the space just big enough for her beside him. She wanted to know if he'd done it on purpose, but of course she didn't get the chance to find out.

"Sorry it got a bit weird there at the end," Art said, readjusting himself on the squeaky seat.

"You don't have to apologize. I'm the one that was acting weird. I hope your dad doesn't think I'm horrible now."

"Of course not. I doubt he even realized it."

Something about the way Art said it made Charlotte turn to look at him. "What do you mean?"

Art shrugged. "Eh, just that if it's not a call on his work phone or an email from some business guy, then it usually doesn't rank too high on his list of priorities." He tried to stretch out his legs, but they were too long and his knees pressed on the seat in front on him. "I don't really get along with him, if you couldn't tell."

"Why not?"

"We're just different." He didn't explain any further, and Charlotte didn't push him.

The bus dropped them off at the bottom of Old Hickory Road, and Charlotte thanked the bus driver as she stepped off. She and Art talked the rest of the way home, and in the back of her mind she wondered what was going to happen when they got there. She'd never had a boy over before, or not a boy alone, at least. She could vaguely remember birthday parties as a child that kids from her homeroom class would come to, but those stopped once she hit the seventh grade, and after that, birthdays consisted of family dinners (with Melanie of course) and trips to the Colorado Symphony Orchestra in downtown Denver. But as far as cute teenage boys with green eyes and a passion for fairy tales went, the Barclay residence hadn't seen one of those in all Charlotte's years.

Her dad's truck was, unsurprisingly, in the driveway when they got there.

"My dad's here," she said.

"Awesome," Art replied. "He was always cool to me."

Charlotte stepped in front of him as they climbed the few stairs to the porch. "He's having a hard time," she warned, "so he's probably not the way you remember him."

Art smiled. "It's fine. You don't have to worry about me judging, or whatever."

Charlotte couldn't help but smile as she turned the key in the lock and opened the front door.

The first thing she did was kick off her boots in the hallway and rush into the living room to open all the blinds. Grandma had been so busy lately that she'd abandoned her morning routine. She used to open all the blinds, light up a cone of incense, and start the coffee, but now she barely had time to eat a quick breakfast and take all her vitamins before she had to rush outside and head to work. Things were falling to pieces, and Charlotte felt some responsibility for it. Nothing could go back to normal until she brought Mom home.

When Charlotte turned around, she spotted her dad standing in the kitchen. He had the medicine cabinet open and was staring at the old bottles of painkillers the family had collected over the years.

"Dad?" she called, and he jumped as if he hadn't realized someone was there.

"Hey, honey." He closed the cabinet and turned to face her.

"I brought a friend home today. This is Art." She gestured to Art standing in the hallway and watched confusion, and then slow recognition, spread over Dad's face.

"Arthur?" he asked hesitantly, and when Art nodded, he held out his arms for a hug. "Come here, kid! It's been too long!"

Charlotte wouldn't have wanted to hug her dad, seeing as he was in a bathrobe and looked like he hadn't showered in a few days, but Art stepped forward and embraced him without so much as a wrinkled nose.

"It's good to be back," Art said, and Charlotte wished she remembered as much about him as Dad did.

Dad held Art at arm's length and shook his head. "God, Emily would have loved this." He started to get choked up and cleared his throat. "Anyway, it's good to see you."

"You too." Art stood there smiling as Dad retreated to his bedroom. As soon as the door clicked shut, he dropped his head and rubbed at the back of his neck. "Geez," he mumbled, then took a shaky breath. "This sucks."

Even though it wasn't very eloquent, it was one of the most heartfelt sentiments Charlotte had heard so far.

"That's her studio, right?" Art asked, pointing at the closed door with the afternoon sunlight seeping through the cracks.

Charlotte nodded.

"Is it okay if I look inside? I understand if you don't want me to, but—"

"Go ahead," Charlotte said, cutting him off. "I'm gonna get changed real quick and then I'll meet you in there." She opened the door for him, and he stepped over the threshold slowly, as if stepping into another world. The sunlight cast him into a yellow haze and made his skin glow.

Right then, he was the most beautiful boy she'd ever seen. He moved like a worshiper through a sacred space, treading softly and breathing so gently that the air in the room barely shifted. She watched him trail his fingers across the back of Mom's chair and then lean over the desk to look at the work she'd been poring over just before her departure.

Tears sprung to Charlotte's eyes, and she hurried to her room next door before Art could see her. She closed the door quietly and pulled off her stained sweater. She wiped away the tears that had yet to spill and took a deep breath.

There was a knock on the window, and Charlotte was startled to find the brownie's ears and big eyes peering over the windowsill. She quickly pulled on a hoodie and then slid the glass open.

"What are you doing?" she whispered, trying not to let Art hear her.

"I was about to ask you the same question," he said in a grumpy tone. "You've told me nothing of the ritual for the naiad. It's all anyone can talk about." He jabbed a thumb over his shoulder toward the forest, and a few small fairies fluttered into the trees. "Well?"

"I can't talk now, I'm busy."

"The stones are more important than the pretty boy next door," the brownie said, his eyes narrowing.

"Oh my God," Charlotte whispered irritably. "I told her I'd come and clean up the lake. It's a start, at least."

"Then what are you waiting for? You're the Shrine Keeper—you're supposed to take care of us."

"I am," Charlotte snapped. The brownie's ears drooped, and she immediately regretted her harsh tone. "Okay, okay," she said, more gently this time. "I'll do it as soon as I can. I promise."

"Don't make promises lightly," the brownie mumbled, and then he turned away from the house and walked across the yard toward the back garden.

Charlotte sighed and closed the window quietly. Then she finger-combed her curls before tying them back in one long, thick braid. She put a fresh coat of chapstick on her cracked lips and assessed her appearance in the mirror before going to find Art.

He was standing at the window when she walked in, hands in his pockets and head tipped slightly to one side.

"What do you see?" she asked, crossing Mom's studio to stand beside him in the warm patch of afternoon sunlight. Outside, the trees were yellow and red and the grass had started to fade from green to brown. The brownie was nowhere to be seen.

"I used to watch you play out this window," he said, glancing at Charlotte from the corner of his eye. "You'd wear this floppy hat and carry around a handful of flowers and talk as if all the plants were listening."

"They *were* listening," she said softly.

Art smiled. "I wanted so badly to go out and play, but my mom would never let me stay late after my tutoring sessions. And besides," he said, turning toward her, "I don't think you even knew I existed."

"Of course I knew," she said bashfully. "But you were always stealing Mom's attention. I just wasn't interested in floppy-haired boys back then."

"And now?" he asked.

It felt like all the air had been sucked out of the room. Art stood so close that she could see each individual freckle sprinkled across his nose. When he breathed out, she breathed in, and that shared air was the closest she'd ever come to a kiss. And then, in a fraction of a moment, it was broken.

Art laughed and stepped away from the window. Charlotte's heart pounded as she stood frozen in place.

"Sorry," he said, running a hand through his dark hair. "Stupid question." He cleared his throat. "So, what now? What does Charlotte do on the days she plays hooky?"

Charlotte was still so shaken that she said the first thing that came to her mind. "Want to go to the lake?"

"The lake?" he asked, eyebrows inching closer together.

"Uh, yeah, the one in the Greenwood. I volunteered to clean it up, and I still haven't done it yet." Even as she spoke the words, she wondered why she was lying to him. She shouldn't have even mentioned the lake, because now he was smiling and nodding like volunteer service was his favorite thing to do.

"That would be awesome. It's been years since I went to the lake."

"Okay, great." She gave him what she hoped was a convincing smile.

✲

That was how Charlotte ended up in the woods, carrying trash bags and work gloves, with Art by her side. He was way more excited about the possibility of cleaning up trash than she was, but for good reason: he knew nothing of the fairies or the creature in the lake.

She'd brought her backpack along and had filled it with a few water bottles, snacks, and some of the fairy books Art had lent her.

They didn't talk much as they hiked, but Charlotte felt comfortable in the silence. Leaves crunched under her boots, and the smell of fall in the air made her want to go back home and curl up in a blanket after lighting pumpkin-scented candles. She loved the cool weather and musky smell of leaves but knew that it wouldn't be long before the snow started to fall and the Greenwood would be nothing but a soggy brown mess. She had to enjoy this beauty while it lasted.

"Wow," Art said as they pushed through the snarled tangle of bushes that encircled the lake. "I don't remember this at all." He looked down at all the thorns in the dirt and grimaced. "And to think I used to run barefoot through here. Kids are crazy."

"Yeah, my dad used to mountain bike through here a lot, but eventually he stopped because the thorns put holes in his tires. Whoa!" Charlotte's boots slipped on the dry grass, and Art held out an arm to steady her. She took it, and they laughed as they jogged the rest of the way down to the lake.

"I seriously don't remember the lake like this," Art said when Charlotte released his arm. He took a few steps closer to the water, and she almost called out a warning. "It's such a mess now. Look at that." He pointed at a tangle of twigs and leaves and pop cans floating on the surface of the lake. "It's disgusting."

There was trash everywhere, and it was way worse than Charlotte remembered from the day she came here with the brownie. There were cigarette butts in the dirt, plastic bags in the bushes, and random decaying articles of clothing strewn about the shore.

"I'll work near the water," Charlotte said as she pulled on the work gloves she'd borrowed from Grandma's flowerbox. "Do you want to start over in the bushes?"

"Sure," Art said, and Charlotte breathed a sigh of relief. If he stayed away from the water's edge, he should be okay. Unless the naiad decided to step out of the lake in her gloriously wet, naked form. Then neither of them would be safe.

Charlotte opened her trash bag and started cleaning up the cigarettes and odd pieces of trash that had become lodged in the soft, wet dirt along the lakeside. She kept a close eye on the water, so she knew exactly the moment when the naiad surfaced. She heard the soft shush of water as it parted, and then looked up into the black eyes hovering just above the surface. Despite her pounding heart and the instincts that told her to run, Charlotte forced herself to stay put and to nod, just slightly, to acknowledge the naiad's presence. The water nymph didn't move or say a word. She remained watchful, and her eyes followed Charlotte wherever she went.

"Hey, look what I found!" Art yelled, and water splashed when the naiad whipped around to see where the voice had come from.

Art stood half-hidden in the thick brush and held a sign over his head. It had a picture of a swimming stick figure crossed through with a big red slash. The words read NO SWIMMING. Both Charlotte and the naiad watched as he moved the sign to a better location and pounded it into the soft dirt using a rock. Then he gave Charlotte a thumbs-up and turned back to what he'd been doing.

"He's helping," Charlotte whispered when she felt the naiad's gaze on her. "We're not all bad, you know." At that she heard popping bubbles, as if the naiad had snorted or laughed underwater.

Charlotte returned to her work, picking up an abandoned flip-flop and shoving it into the trash bag. She continued to clean, and after a while she noticed that the naiad had stopped staring at her and was watching Art instead. When the naiad noticed Charlotte watching, she rose out of the water just enough to reveal her head and gave Charlotte a wet smile.

"That's a pretty boy," she said in a slippery voice. "I wonder what he feels like."

Charlotte swallowed and her stomach twisted into knots. She glanced over at Art just in time to see him pull off his dark hoodie. His T-shirt rose up slightly, and she caught a glimpse of his stomach before he yanked the fabric back down and returned to his work.

"Have you touched him?" the naiad asked, wading slowly closer to where Charlotte worked along the shore.

"Oh my God," Charlotte whispered. "No, I have *not*."

The naiad laughed. "But you want to," she said, and when Charlotte looked up, they made eye contact. "Yes," she hissed. "I can always tell, and you want that boy."

Charlotte's cheeks warmed at the thought of Art's exposed skin. She turned away, and the naiad laughed again.

"Don't be so shy," the naiad said. "Life is nothing without love." She sighed, and in another moment she'd sunk below the surface of the water and disappeared.

Charlotte glanced over her shoulder and watched Art work. He pushed through the bushes with vigor, his lips slightly parted and his brows drawn together in focus. In comparison, Charlotte was moving at a snail's pace, and she put it into her head to work as hard as he was. There were still pop cans and plastic bottles sticking out of the sand along the shore, and she got to work picking them all up.

The sun inched its way across the sky as she filled up her trash bag, and the air was getting considerably cooler by the time Art came to find her on the far end of the lake. He had his sweatshirt back on and his brow was damp.

"Done," he said, holding up his full trash bag. "I can't believe how much crap people leave around here."

"Tell me about it," Charlotte agreed. "I had to pick up a pair of underwear with a stick."

Art dissolved into laughter, and over his shoulder Charlotte spotted the last bit of trash. It was the tangle of bottles and lake plants floating on the surface of the water.

"Let me get this last little bit," she told Art, "and then we can go." She walked to the water's edge to assess how best to retrieve the floating trash. It was just far enough away that she couldn't reach out and grab it, so she went and found a long stick to help. But unfortunately, no matter how hard she tried, the trash floated right out of her reach. A few times she bumped it and it seemed as if it would float right into her outstretched hand, but then it would drift just far enough away to be out of her reach again. After a while, Art came over to try to help, and together they used sticks to try to prod the trash to the water's edge. Charlotte was frustrated and about to give up when a dark shadow rose up from under the water.

"Hang on," she told Art, stepping back. He lowered his stick and looked at her.

The naiad surfaced slowly, and she cupped the trash in her green palms and pushed it just hard enough to send it right into the soft bank. Charlotte knelt and picked it up, her eyes locked on the naiad.

"You've done well, Keeper." The naiad's black eyes flicked toward Art. "Perhaps it is as you say." She lifted a glistening eyebrow. "I have one final task for you. Return here without the boy and prove yourself loyal to the fae. Only then will I give you what you seek." With that, she sank below the surface without so much as a splash, and Charlotte shoved the nasty, slimy soda bottles into her trash bag.

"How did you do that?" Art asked.

"Do what?"

"Get the bottles!" He pointed at the lake. "They were literally floating in the opposite direction and then suddenly they floated right to your feet."

Charlotte laughed. "I'm just lucky, I guess. The universe works in mysterious ways."

Art gave her a look, and she knew he didn't believe her, but he didn't question her any further. Instead he looked at the sky and sighed. "Sun's going down, and those clouds look like they might dump on us. Think we should start heading back?"

"Absolutely." She hefted her bag up over her shoulder and followed Art away from the lake and back up the slight rise to the trail.

Art hiked fast, and when he glanced back and saw Charlotte struggling, he stopped and gave her a guilty smile.

"Sorry, I just don't want to get caught in that storm." He glanced toward the darkening sky, and the gray light caught his eyes, making them shine.

"What's so bad about a little bit of rain?" she challenged, and his eyes met hers as he smiled.

"Nothing, unless you're like me and are so sweet you're made of sugar. I'll melt right down and you'll have to carry me home in one of those nasty plastic bottles."

"What if I didn't get all of you scooped up?" Charlotte teased as they hiked. "And then when you solidified you were missing an eye or something?"

"That'd be pretty sweet, actually. I think I would have liked to be a pirate in another life. Argh!" He jumped up on a nearby boulder and grabbed a stick to brandish at Charlotte like a sword. "You, lady, must walk the plank!"

"I think not," Charlotte said, playing along. "I'm the captain of this ship, sailor." She said it in a pirate's accent and squinted one eye as though she had a patch.

They both burst into laughter, and Art jumped down from the boulder. He bumped into Charlotte as they walked, and she bumped him back.

Charlotte stepped down and felt a distinct pop, as if she'd stepped on a water balloon. Art must have felt it, too, because he paused and looked down. Charlotte lifted her foot and saw a tendril of green smoke drift upwards and blow away in the wind.

"What the hell?" she whispered.

"Um, do you know where we are?" Art asked.

Of course she did—she'd walked this hiking trail hundreds of times when she was a kid. But despite that, when she looked around she found herself unsure of where they were. She turned back the way they'd come. Just a minute ago she'd known exactly where she was heading, but now nothing looked familiar. It was as if she'd been spun too many times in Mom's office chair and couldn't get her bearings.

"I could have sworn this was the right way," Art said, looking around with wide eyes, "but I don't recognize anything now."

"Me, neither," Charlotte whispered. She thought of the pop and the smoke and wondered if that had something to do with it.

The trees rustled and sent red and orange leaves falling around Charlotte's head. She brushed the leaves out of her hair and looked up.

Two fairy creatures sat on a low branch, swinging their legs and laughing. They had gray-blue skin and bulging eyes, and rows of sharp teeth flashed when they opened their mouths to sneer.

"What are you looking at?" Art asked, peering up into the tree. The creatures rattled the branch again, and more colorful leaves swirled down. "What was that?" Art whispered, but Charlotte just shook her head.

"Pixie-led, pixie-led," the fairies howled. "Now you'll never find your bed!" They screamed and laughed and shook the branch until twigs fell off and all the leaves were gone.

"Pixie-led, pixie-led," Charlotte repeated quietly. "Now you'll never find your bed."

"Huh?" Art asked.

"Pixie-led. We've been pixie-led. Do you know what that means?"

"No. What are you talking about?"

Charlotte knelt and took off her backpack. She pulled out the books she'd brought along and handed one to Art. "Let's look through these. Try to find a definition for pixie-led."

Art took the book but shook his head. "Not until you tell me what's going on."

"Help me first," Charlotte said, "and then I'll answer your questions. Please?"

Art didn't look particularly pleased, but he opened the book she'd handed him and started to read.

"Check the glossary, too," Charlotte said as she skimmed the book in her hands. She heard Art flip to the back of the book and start turning pages.

"Got it," he said. "Page 320." He flipped back through the book, found the page, and started to read. "A traveler will become pixie-led if they step on a stray sod, which is a clump of grass that has been enchanted by the pixies. The traveler will become disoriented and will never find their way home." He glanced up at Charlotte with a look of confusion. "The simplest way to break the spell is to turn your jacket inside out."

The pixies in the tree started to howl in displeasure, and Charlotte grimaced. Art put a finger in his ear, and Charlotte wondered if perhaps he had some very low-level awareness of the fairies after all. Maybe everyone did, but they just ignored it or attributed it to something else.

"Let's do it," Charlotte said, trying to ignore the pixies having their tantrum.

"You think we've been pixie-led?"

"What's the harm in trying? I thought you loved all this old fairy lore?"

She started to unzip her jacket as Art sighed. Eventually he put down the book and yanked off his sweatshirt. They both turned their clothing inside out and then put it back on.

At first nothing happened. Charlotte still didn't know where she was, and the pixies continued to shriek in the trees. But then, after a few moments had passed, the forest seemed to change right before her eyes. It was like watching a dense fog lift to reveal a place you'd known your entire life. Soon she recognized the boulder Art had jumped up on, and then she recognized the tree nearby with the hole in its bark where an owl had lived when she was young. The relief was immediate, and she looked over at Art with a grin.

He looked starstruck. "What the hell was that?" he asked.

She had to tell him. All this time, ever since their first conversation about fairies, she'd wanted to tell him the truth. She'd never had solid reason to before, but now it couldn't be avoided. He'd been pixie-led right alongside her, and now it was time to tell him the truth. But before she could figure out the best way to start, thunder rumbled overhead and the wind started to blow. The pixies jumped from the low branch and spread their dragonfly-thin wings, soaring away through the trees.

"We should find shelter and wait this storm out," Art said, his eyes on the sky. As if he'd summoned the rain himself, fat droplets started to fall. "Hurry! Follow me!"

Charlotte stuffed the books into her backpack, grabbed the bag full of trash, and hurried after Art as the rain pattered down across her hair and shoulders. The rain turned the dirt a dark, muddy brown, and the wind blew more leaves from the trees. As Charlotte followed Art through the rain, she couldn't help but smile. She felt alive, more alive than she'd felt in so long. The rain was wet on her shoulders and the thunder vibrated in her chest.

"In here!" Art called, and he led her up a slippery slope and under a rocky overhang that kept them sheltered from the rain.

They dropped their trash bags outside because there was only enough room for the two of them to huddle beneath the rock. Their shoulders pressed together as they struggled to get further back and out of the rain, and finally Charlotte relaxed and leaned back against the mossy rocks.

Despite it all, she smiled. There was so much to grieve for, but she just wanted to soak in the feeling of being here, pressed up against Art's damp sweatshirt, while the rain poured down around them. She took a deep breath and smelled the wet leaves and the dirt and moss all around her, and for the first time in a long time she felt connected to the forest in a way she hadn't since she was a little girl. She used to love hiding out in the trees and building forts to play in with her fairy friends. It pained her to know how far separated she had become from it all.

"Okay," Art said, wiping rain from his eyes. "I'm ready." He turned his head and gave her a reassuring smile.

"I've never told anyone this. Well, besides my grandma, but she doesn't know everything either." Charlotte took a slow breath. She wanted to make what she had to say sound cool and mysterious, but unfortunately all that came out was, "I can see fairies."

She expected Art to laugh or call her a liar, but he didn't. He narrowed his eyes, dark brows drawing together. "Fairies? Like, the ones on TV?"

"No." Charlotte pointed to her backpack. "Like the ones in the books you gave me. *Real* ones."

Art smiled. "Are you joking around? Trying to tease me?"

Charlotte shook her head.

His smile faded. He turned to stare out into the rain. "Okay. How long have you been able to see them?"

"Ever since I can remember." Charlotte pulled her legs up to her chest and rested her chin on her knees. "It's called the Sight."

"I've read about it. It runs in families, right?"

Charlotte nodded. "Yeah. My grandma had it, but her mom kind of repressed it, and after a while she stopped believing and it just went away."

"But you never stopped believing?" he asked.

"I tried," she admitted, "and for a long time I didn't see them. But I still knew they were there."

"So, what changed? Why are you seeing them now?"

This was it, the big question. It was the reason for everything that had happened the past two weeks.

"Because they took my mom," she said quietly, and watched confusion cross Art's face.

He opened his mouth as if to ask a question, but no words came out. He just kept shaking his head, like this was too much to get his mind around. Finally, he uttered one word.

"Why?"

She told him about the stolen fairy stones and how fairy magic was dying. He listened intently while she told him about the oak men and the dryad with her antlers. She told him about the naiad, and the pixies, and the brownie that looked after her family's home. And, finally, she told him that his father's company planning to start construction in the Greenwood was the final straw.

"You're being serious right now?" Art asked, and it was just a whisper.

"Yes," Charlotte said softly. "I wouldn't lie about this. I didn't know who else to tell . . ." She let out a long, slow sigh, then glanced over at him from the corner of her eyes. "Do you believe me?"

Art was quiet for a long time—for such a long time that Charlotte felt icy fear start to constrict around her throat. *He doesn't believe me. He thinks I'm crazy, too.*

"I am so, so sorry," he said finally. "I want to help make it right."

Charlotte didn't know what to say. She was shocked into silence as he moved closer and wrapped his arms around her. Suddenly she was pressed up against his chest, buried in his sweatshirt that smelled like rain and leaves, and she liked it there. She hugged him back, slowly wrapping her arms around him and gripping his sweatshirt in her fingers.

And there they sat as the rain poured down, turning the brown earth black and bringing the smells of the forest to life. Charlotte watched the Greenwood over Art's shoulder, and when the rain had become no more than a drizzle, she shifted and pulled back.

"It stopped," she said quietly, almost afraid to ruin the perfect moment with words.

Art cleared his throat and smiled. "Great. Let's head back then. I'm still soaked."

He offered her a hand and helped her out of their mossy sanctuary. They walked side by side, and on the way home he asked her more questions about the fairies. She told him about the hedgehog family, and the tiny fairies that rode birds and squirrels, and more about the brownie and his tendencies to be a grump.

"Wait a minute," he said, stopping suddenly. "So that day your grandma had me draw fairies into the caricature with you, were they actually there?"

"Yup," Charlotte said, feeling like a weight had been lifted from her shoulders. It felt so nice to talk to someone about all this. Grandma wasn't home very often anymore, and when she was home she was tired, so speaking to her had become more and more difficult.

"So, what were we actually doing at the lake? Was that really some volunteer project?"

"Definitely not," Charlotte laughed.

By the time they slipped down the muddy embankment and walked across the yard to Charlotte's front door, she had told him nearly everything she knew about the fairies. The only thing she didn't share was the frightening experience she'd had with a phooka all those years ago.

"I have to return all the stones by October 30th," she explained as they took the porch stairs to the front door, "or else the dryad will kidnap someone else that I love." She ran a hand through her hair. "I just don't know where the rest of the stones are, and I'm kind of freaking out, and—"

"I'm going to help you," Art said, reaching out to touch Charlotte's sleeve. "With whatever you need, seriously. You don't have to do this alone anymore. And no way we're going to let that dryad-lady take anyone else. I'm just a phone call away, okay?" He smiled at her and his eyes crinkled in the corners.

"Okay," she said, "I'll call you."

"Good," he said, backing down the stairs slowly. "Sooner rather than later, okay?"

"Definitely," Charlotte agreed, and then she waved goodbye and went in the house. As soon as her boots were off, she ran to the living room window to watch Art walk back down the gravel road, throw the trash bags in the big dumpster at the end of the drive, and then get swallowed up by the old oak trees as he headed home.

CHAPTER EIGHTEEN

By late Tuesday morning the clouds had become fat and gray, likely the sign of an oncoming storm.

Charlotte was excited to get a text message from Mrs. Nolan stating that Tomas wasn't feeling well and they'd have to cancel his lesson that day. Now she'd be able to get to the lake before the sun went down.

Charlotte had been antsy and impatient on the bus ride home, but seeing the brownie digging around in the flowerbeds out front lifted her spirits.

"Hey!" she called to him, and he jumped in surprise.

"Perhaps you could announce yourself next time, Keeper," he grumbled.

"Sorry, but listen. I talked to the naiad. I did what she wanted, and she said I just have to come back to the lake and do one other thing for her and then she'll let me have the stone. Will you go with me?"

At her request, the brownie's eyes lit up. He wiped his hands, still dirty from the flowerbeds, on his tunic and nodded. "I will accompany you."

"Thank you! I'm going to go inside and get changed, and then I'll be right back." She ran up the porch stairs and into the house. In her bedroom, she changed into warm hiking clothes, thick socks, and a stocking cap. Grandma had knitted it for her years ago and it was still her favorite cold-weather accessory.

Dad's bedroom door was still closed when she stepped out of her room to leave, and she wondered if he'd left his room at all that day. A familiar pang of guilt rose up in her, but she pushed it down and replaced it with determination. *I have to focus on Mom.* She closed the front door behind her and set off into the trees with the brownie in tow.

Charlotte hiked quickly, wanting to get to the lake and back home before the sun went down. It was already chilly out, and she had no desire to be caught in the woods with the fae after dark. The brownie kept pace with her, and unlike the last time they'd hiked together, he remained by her side rather than rushing ahead. Despite being the short, frumpy-looking creature that he was, he moved quite smoothly through the trees and thick underbrush. Charlotte admired him for it and mused that beauty could truly be found in the most unlikely places.

"You're different," he said to her as they neared the Valley of Thorns.

"How so?"

"You're more . . ." He paused and searched for the word. "Alive."

"What do you mean? I've always been alive."

"Yes. But now the magic is inside you." He touched his chest and gave her the briefest of smiles.

The naiad was waiting when Charlotte arrived. She swam in lazy circles, just her head and shoulders above the water, dark eyes watchful.

"You've returned," she said as Charlotte stepped toward the lake and let the water just barely touch the toes of her old hiking boots.

"Of course," Charlotte said. "You didn't think I would?"

"I don't know what to think of you. Humans can seldom be trusted."

"You can trust me," Charlotte said, and the naiad quirked a brow. "I'll prove it to you. Just tell me what I have to do next."

Without answering, the naiad dived under the water and disappeared into the murk. Charlotte looked at the brownie for an explanation, but he only shrugged.

"Hello?" Charlotte called. "Hello?"

The naiad returned, her slick black head sliding through the surface of the water. "Patience, Keeper."

"Sorry," Charlotte mumbled.

The naiad held up a pearly white shell. She peeled it open to reveal a collection of shimmering scales. "These are all I have left of my sisters," she said, her lips pulling into a frown. "But they don't belong here. They belong in the realm of fae, where we came from."

Charlotte squatted down at the edge of the lake. "Why haven't you taken them back?"

"I can't. I don't have enough magic to open the portal, nor can I hold my glamour long enough to walk to the shrine." She sighed. "That's why I need you to return them for me."

Charlotte drew back. "You want me to take them to Lyra?"

The naiad nodded. "Please, Keeper. My sisters deserve more than this. They deserve to go *home*." She extended her arms, offering the shell and its contents to Charlotte.

Charlotte reached out, slowly, and took the shell from the naiad. It was slick and cold in her hands, and the scales inside shimmered in the pale afternoon light.

"Where are they supposed to go?" she asked.

"Once in Lyra, follow the river north and you'll find a deep pool fed by a waterfall. That's where my sisters and I were born, and it's where they should return."

The brownie bumped Charlotte's elbow and gave her an encouraging nod.

"I've only been to Lyra once before," Charlotte said. "I don't even have my violin. I can't open the portal."

"We'll help you," said a tiny voice, and Charlotte turned.

It was the family of hedgehog pixies: Fiddleleaf, Blue, Flora, and Butternut. They waddled toward the lake, their paws leaving prints in the damp sand.

"We were out and about and heard your voice, Keeper. It's so nice to see you again." Blue reached out and placed one small paw on Charlotte's thigh. Flora, still smaller than her parents, struggled up onto Charlotte's leg and peered into the shell.

"Pretty," she said, which made the naiad smile.

"You need to get into Lyra?" Fiddleleaf asked, and Charlotte nodded. "We can help you with that. Together we have enough magic to get you there." He took Blue's paw and kissed it.

"Well then," the naiad said, "I suppose it's up to you, Keeper." She leveled a stare on Charlotte and waited.

"Okay," Charlotte said, letting out a long breath. "Let's go."

✻

The family of pixies led the way while Charlotte and the brownie followed close behind. Flora circled around to walk beside the brownie, but he shooed her off with his hat, grumbling to himself.

"It seems you're making friends in these woods," Blue told Charlotte while they walked.

"I hope so," Charlotte replied.

"The naiad must trust you, or else she'd never give you something so precious."

Charlotte reached into the pocket of her hoodie to touch the shell. She nodded to Blue, then fell into her own thoughts as they hiked the rest of the way to the shrine.

"Ah, here we are," Fiddleleaf said when they arrived.

Butternut had clung to his back the entire way, but now he pulled her off and set her down in the grass. She cowered back against one of the standing stones, her tiny body shivering, and Charlotte gave her a soft smile. The pixie twitched her whiskers and huddled further into the grass.

"You don't need music to open the portal?" Charlotte asked, turning her attention to Fiddleleaf.

"Oh, no." Fiddleleaf chuckled. "Each fairy has its own store of magic, and we use that to open the portal. The naiad must be running very low on magic if she is unable to open it herself."

"Poor dear," Blue said, shaking her head. "I don't think she's gone back home since her sisters died."

"Why not?" Charlotte asked.

Blue shrugged and flicked her tiny ears.

"Gather around!" Fiddleleaf called. "You too, Butternut. Come now." The four pixies joined hands, and then they started to spin. They spun round and round, the four of them twirling so fast that it made Charlotte dizzy to watch. She looked away, only to see the brownie cross his arms and glower at the pixies.

"What's wrong?" she whispered.

"I could have opened the portal for you," he grumbled, looking away.

Charlotte smiled.

"Hurry, now!" Blue called, and Charlotte turned.

The four pixies stood waiting for her in a circle of toadstools and flowers. It looked like the fairy ring she'd stepped into the day her mom went missing.

"Are you coming with us?" Charlotte asked, and Blue shook her head.

"No, not today. We're going foraging for tubers." She smiled. "Will you be able to get home all right?"

"Yeah, I'll have the brownie with me." Charlotte glanced over her shoulder at him, and he perked up.

"Good. The magic won't last long, so you'd best get a move on."

Charlotte double-checked that she had the shell in her pocket, and then she took a deep breath and stepped into the fairy ring.

Stepping into Lyra felt like walking into summer. The cold, sharp October air gave way to warmth and the scent of flowers. Wind blew through the trees overhead, making the leaves rustle.

The brownie appeared at Charlotte's side, still wearing a frown.

"Do you know where the pool is?" Charlotte asked him, and he nodded.

"It's this way," he said, and then led the way into Lyra.

Charlotte took off her hat and peeled out of her winter jacket. She still had her hoodie on, with the shell tucked safely inside the pocket. They pushed through the trees, stepping out of the forest and onto the glimmering, silver-stoned path. The brownie continued ahead while Charlotte looked toward the Great Tree in the distance, wondering how Mom was.

"Come on, Keeper," the brownie called, waving her down the path.

Charlotte caught up with him, and they headed toward the oak man village. In the distance, smoke curled from chimneys and oak men crisscrossed the cobblestone streets. Charlotte and the brownie turned to the north and followed the grassy bank along the river.

"Have you been there before?" Charlotte asked. "To where the naiads live?"

"Yes," the brownie replied, the tips of his ears going red.

"What?" Charlotte asked, but the brownie just waved her off.

He led her through the soft green grass, and Charlotte reached out to snag a flower and tuck it behind her ear.

They followed the river as it twisted through the grassy meadow. The sun was warm overhead, and Charlotte tipped her head back to enjoy the heat.

"It's there." The brownie pointed ahead.

They'd come to a point where the river widened into a pool. Water tumbled over a slick rockface, sending up a fine mist that cast rainbows in the afternoon light. Rocks jutted out of the pool, providing spots for the naiads to warm themselves in the sun.

Charlotte hesitated. The naiads had already seen her and watched with curious, narrowed eyes. Their hair hung long and cascaded across their wet shoulders, revealing their slick, naked chests. Charlotte gave the brownie a knowing look. His ears were red again.

"Come closer," one of the naiads called out, waving slender fingers in the air.

Charlotte took a deep breath before approaching. The brownie stepped into place behind her, hiding himself from the water nymphs.

"A human," one of the naiads said, and the scales along her neck shimmered when she tipped her head.

"Not just any human," said the other. She pushed a braided lock of crimson hair off her shoulder and leaned forward. "I know who you are. Everyone has been talking, saying our Keeper has finally returned." Her gaze shifted. "Ah, and you've brought a friend."

Charlotte glanced down, and the brownie ducked behind her again. She set her shoulders and looked the crimson-haired naiad in the eyes. "I was asked to return these to you." She pulled the pearly shell from her pocket and opened it, revealing the sparkling scales inside.

Both naiads promptly dived off the rock and swam to the bank. They propped themselves up on the edge of the pool, and the green-haired naiad held out a lithe, dark arm.

"Let me see," she said, her fingers grasping at midair.

Charlotte stepped back, and the naiad hissed.

"Hush," the other said. "Keeper, tell us, where did you get those?"

"From my world," Charlotte said. "There's a naiad in the lake near where I live, and she wanted me to return these. They belonged to her sisters."

"Of course," the naiad said, and tears welled up in her pale eyes. "Our sisters. You've finally brought them home." She held out her wet hands, and Charlotte gave her the shell, careful not to get too close.

The two naiads bent their heads together, crimson-red against dark green, and wept over their sisters' scales. They lowered the shell into the cerulean pool, and Charlotte leaned forward to get a closer look.

Water rushed into the shell and the scales began to sparkle. They glowed so bright that she had to squint against the light. The scales transformed into two fish, one white and one blue. The fish had long, draping tails and nearly translucent bodies, and they swam around the two naiads, making the sisters laugh and cry as they held tight to one another. The two fish made final circles and then dissolved into the water, leaving only the empty shell in their wake.

"Thank you," said the naiad with red hair. "We never thought they'd return to us. Now their souls are free to swim all the seas."

Charlotte knelt and ran her fingers through the warm grass. "Can I ask you a question?" she asked.

The sisters looked at one another, and then the dark-skinned naiad nodded.

"If you're both still here, then why did your sisters leave? I mean, if the human realm is so dangerous, then why go there?"

The naiad sighed. "I asked them that many times before they left. They wanted something new, something more. We were all born of this river, and we've lived our entire lives here." She turned and gestured to the sparkling pool, surrounded by tall grass that shifted in the warm breeze. "It wasn't enough for them."

"We begged them not to go," explained the other naiad. "We offered to swim downstream and find a new pool to live in, but it was no use. Once they'd decided they were going, we had no power to change their minds."

"Did you ever see them again?" Charlotte asked.

"No," the sisters said together.

"I'm sorry," Charlotte said softly.

"There's no need to be," said the yellow-skinned naiad. She pushed her crimson braid back and smiled. "You're here now."

"And you have our blessing," the other naiad said. "Take this back to our sister. She'll know what it means." She waved a hand over the pearly shell and it transformed into a single pebble. Charlotte reached out and took it.

"And this, too." The naiad pulled out a few strands of her red hair, tied them in a knot, and then wrapped them up in a purple plant she fetched from the surface of the water.

"What's this for?" Charlotte asked, taking the strange bundle from the naiad.

"It contains some of my magic. I imagine she could use some of that right about now."

"Will you run out now?" Charlotte asked, still confused about how their magic worked.

"Of course not." The sisters laughed. "Just as plants gather energy from the sun, we gather magic by being here in Lyra. Don't you know anything, little Keeper?" The sisters twittered again, and this time Charlotte rolled her eyes and stood up.

"I'll take it to her," she said.

"Come back soon," the green-haired naiad said. Then the sisters sank beneath the water, leaving Charlotte and the brownie alone on the bank.

"I'd say that went well," the brownie said, finally stepping out from behind Charlotte's back.

"I know now why you've visited here before," Charlotte said, and the brownie turned away with a huff and a blush.

They walked back the way they'd come, and Charlotte made circles with her thumb across the smooth blue pebble the naiad had given her. It had swirls of white that glittered in the sun, and she slipped it into her pocket for safe keeping.

"Look there," the brownie said, pointing.

The dryad stood on the bridge up ahead, her antlers towering gloriously above her. She was looking right at them.

"I'll be at the shrine when you're ready to leave," the brownie said, and then he dived into the tall grass and vanished.

The dryad still stood waiting, and she smiled when Charlotte approached.

"Keeper," she said warmly. "It's a pleasure to see you again. What brings you back to us?"

"I had to give something to the naiads," Charlotte said, standing uncomfortably at the end of the bridge. There was a long pause.

"And now you'd like to see your mother?"

"Yes." Charlotte held her breath for the dryad's response.

"Come on, then." The dryad waved Charlotte forward, and together they walked across the bridge into the village.

As they walked, the oak men paused to give the dryad fresh flowers and loaves of bread. She thanked each individually, and both the men and women blushed at her praise.

"They really like you," Charlotte observed, and the dryad laughed.

"Kindness is the surest way to someone's heart."

They passed three young girls braiding each other's hair, and one of them paused to smile at Charlotte and hand her a delicate pink poppy.

"For you, Keeper," she said, and the other girls giggled and hid their faces.

"Th-thank you," Charlotte stammered. She twirled the poppy between her fingers and smiled.

"You remind me of someone I used to know," the dryad said once they'd passed the girls.

"How?"

"She loved flowers, too. Always had one tucked behind her ear or braided into her hair." The dryad sniffed the bundle of flowers one of the oak men had given her and smiled, almost sadly.

"Who was she?" Charlotte asked.

"We called her Faer—a traveler. She wanted to see everything, learn everything, touch everything." The dryad laughed and discreetly dabbed at her left eye. "She used to love my antlers and would string them with the most beautiful garlands of flowers." She sighed. "I wish we could meet again."

"What happened to her?" Charlotte asked, curiosity getting the better of her.

"She grew old," the dryad explained. "And, like your kind do, she died much too soon."

My kind? A slew of questions formed on the tip of Charlotte's tongue, but they'd arrived at the Great Tree and the dryad became distracted talking and laughing with the guards at the grand doors. Charlotte stood back as the doors opened to admit them, and then she followed the dryad inside.

"I'm glad you've come back," the dryad said as they walked. "I hoped I hadn't scared you away." She glanced back at Charlotte, and her eyes were soft and glassy.

"I wasn't scared," Charlotte said, but it didn't sound convincing, and the dryad smiled knowingly.

"Your mother is here," she said, after having led Charlotte through the dense greenery growing inside the Great Tree. "I'm not able to stay. Will you be able to find your way home?"

Charlotte nodded. "I have the brownie with me. He can take me back."

The dryad reached out and put a soft hand on Charlotte's shoulder. "I hope to see you again." She pulled back the curtain of vines for Charlotte to step through.

The vines fell closed behind Charlotte, and she let out a soft sigh.

Mom was there, still asleep on the bed of moss. Tiny fairies fluttered around her, twisting her golden hair into braids as she slept. When they saw Charlotte, they fluttered away with laughter ringing out behind them.

Charlotte approached carefully and sank to her knees on the soft, warm grass.

"Hi, Mom."

CHAPTER NINETEEN

When Charlotte arrived back at the shrine, she found the brownie asleep in a patch of flowers beneath one of the standing stones. She tickled his nose with a long frond of golden grass, and he awoke with a sneeze.

"You should know better than to wake a sleeper," he said, and then stretched his arms and yawned. While he got to his feet, Charlotte reached into her pocket to touch the smooth pebble.

"Now, I've not done this in a while," the brownie said, looking up at the standing stones with a wrinkled brow.

"What?" Charlotte asked, alarmed. "Can you send us back?"

"Of course, of course. Don't get your knickers in a twist." The brownie gathered up a handful of dirt and rubbed it between his palms. He mumbled something over the dirt and then tossed it in the air. Charlotte shielded her eyes as dirt sprinkled down around them and landed in her hair.

Nothing happened.

"Well?" she asked.

The brownie didn't reply. He picked up another handful of dirt and repeated the process. Still nothing. Finally, he picked up a handful of dirt and threw it directly at the nearest standing stone.

The stone gave off a pulse of energy that knocked Charlotte and the brownie to the ground. The world spun around her, and by the time she finally got back to her feet, she was standing in the Greenwood.

"Smooth," she said, brushing dirt out of her hair.

"Like I said—it's been a while."

Charlotte pulled her jacket on, already chilly in the mountain air, and they headed back toward the Valley of Thorns.

Despite the time she'd spent in Lyra, there was still light in the gray sky as Charlotte descended the slippery slope toward the naiad's lake.

The naiad surfaced and swam in impatient circles. "Well?" she asked, the corners of her eyes pinched in worry. "Did you return them?"

Charlotte pulled the pebble out of her pocket and tossed it to the naiad, who snatched it out of midair. She ran a finger across the stone and sighed.

"Thank you, Keeper. You've set my heart at ease."

"What does that pebble mean?" Charlotte asked.

The naiad held it up, and the light reflected off the wet surface of the pebble. "I've always collected pretty stones, ever since I was young. It's my sisters' way of saying thank you, I suppose." She smiled.

"Your other sister gave me this, too," Charlotte said, pulling the still-damp clump of hair and plants from her pocket. She handed it over to the naiad and their fingertips brushed. Charlotte wiped the lake water on her jeans while the naiad untied the bundle.

"She gave me her magic," the naiad whispered, and a gentle smile lifted the corners of her lips. She carefully took each strand of her sister's long, crimson hair and tied it into her own. When she was done, a tiny glimmer of magic sparkled around her and she let out a sigh. "That feels better." She stretched her arms overhead, as if awaking from a long sleep. Then she looked at Charlotte. "Now, have you ever been kissed?"

Heat rose to Charlotte's face and she looked away.

The naiad laughed. "Very well. Remove your clothes and come closer."

"Oh my God," Charlotte snapped. "What is wrong with you?"

"She's a nymph," the brownie muttered. "What did you expect?"

A wall of water suddenly cascaded down on him, leaving his hat drooping off and his tunic sopping wet.

"Ahh, feels good to have magic again," the naiad said.

The brownie grumbled something in response that sounded very much like "fish face," but the naiad ignored it. Instead, she focused her gaze on Charlotte.

"Are you going to join me, or not?" She arched one dark, slick brow.

"It's cold out," Charlotte argued.

"All the better reason to stop wasting time. The temperature will drop when the sun goes down."

Charlotte looked at the brownie for support, but he was busy mumbling to himself and wringing lake water out of his hat. She drew in a deep breath and unzipped her jacket with resolve. "Okay. But first tell me why."

"I can't touch the stone. You should know that." The naiad gave Charlotte an amused look. "How else do you think it's to return to the surface, except by human hands?"

Once this fact sank in, another question surfaced. "I can't hold my breath for very long, so how——"

"You worry too much," the naiad said, cutting her off. "You need only to trust."

"You tried to drown me once," Charlotte said, removing her winter jacket. A cold breeze whistled through the oak trees and seeped into her hoodie, chilling her skin. She shivered.

"Yes," the naiad said, with not a hint of regret. "And you abandoned me once, yet here I am, ready to assist you. Remind me, Keeper, who is the least trustworthy amongst us?"

"I didn't know," Charlotte grumbled, but the naiad didn't respond. Charlotte pulled off her articles of clothing, one by one, until she stood at the edge of the lake in nothing but her bra and underwear. The sand was frigid beneath her toes, and the air raised goose bumps along her skin. She took a step into the water and held back a cry when the cold sucked at her toes. It was so much worse than she imagined it would be, so much colder than anything she could remember.

"The slower you go, the more painful it will be," said the brownie from the shore.

Charlotte wanted to flip him off, but she doubted he would even know what the middle finger meant. She gulped in a breath, counted down from five, and then took three big steps into the water.

"Shit!" she cried, the muscles in her legs tensing up in the cold.

"Swim to me," the naiad said. "Don't focus on the cold. Look at me." She lifted a dripping hand from the water and beckoned Charlotte forward.

Charlotte still didn't know if she could trust the naiad, and yet she had no choice. She pushed onward, gritting her teeth and cursing under her breath as the water swelled up and around her thighs, her hips, her belly button, her chest. And when her toes could barely brush the sandy, rocky bottom, there the naiad was.

Her eyes were so much blacker up close, but in them Charlotte saw glimmers of blue and green, so subtle she never would have guessed they were there. And the naiad's skin was green, but it looked soft and smooth, not sickly like Charlotte first thought.

"Almost there," the naiad whispered. "Are you ready to see my world?"

"Yes," Charlotte whispered through chattering teeth. And she didn't have the strength to pull away when the naiad took her face and pressed their lips together. The naiad's lips were surprisingly warm and soft, and as they moved against hers, Charlotte felt a new kind of breath filling her lungs. As she gave in to the kiss, the naiad pulled her swiftly beneath the surface.

Down and down they plunged, their lips still locked in a kiss. Frigid water washed over Charlotte, but the magic breath filling her lungs made her chest tingle with warmth.

The naiad released her, and when Charlotte opened her eyes, she was far beneath the surface of the lake and hovering in inky darkness. The late afternoon sunlight glowed on the surface of the water overhead, but down below the world was dark and cold.

It would have been pitch-black if not for the naiad, who glowed with her own radiant light.

She had a tail like a mermaid, but it was long and twisting and glistening with shimmering scales that gave off a gentle blue-green glow. Her black hair fanned out around her like a cape, and her fingers were webbed with thin skin that she used to propel herself through the water.

She held out one webbed hand to Charlotte. Charlotte looked down into the dark water beneath her pale, kicking feet and felt the familiar icy fear claw its way around her lungs. But despite it all, she accepted the naiad's outstretched hand, and together they swam deeper into the lake.

All the way down, Charlotte looked about her. The glow from the naiad's scales illuminated the lake as they swam, revealing years of human pollution. Shoes, ripped and disintegrating bits of clothing, fishing line tangled up in creeping lake plants. Charlotte even spotted her own hiking boot, half buried in mud.

It was only when they reached the bottom that Charlotte looked up and realized that she hadn't taken a breath since descending from the surface. It must have been the magic from the naiad's kiss, still warm in her chest, that kept her from gasping for air. And it was because of the naiad's magic, and her generosity, that Charlotte was now at the bottom of the lake, looking at a dimly glowing stone with veins of shimmering green. It lay buried beneath thick mud and sand and stringy green plants.

The naiad swam closer, her glimmering tail working the water in graceful arcs, to watch as Charlotte began the slow process of digging the stone out from the bottom of the lake. Her movements were slow as she pushed through the water and struggled against the muck and the plants and the pressure from the water overhead. Finally, after her fingers were aching with the effort and her feet were halfway buried in mud, the stone came free of its burial place, and Charlotte held it up over her head for the naiad to see.

Her sharp-toothed smile was bright and genuine. She clapped her webbed hands together, though Charlotte couldn't hear the sound. What she could hear was the naiad's happy laughter as she twirled through the murky water. Charlotte wanted to smile and laugh, too, but feared that opening her mouth would let the lake water rush inside.

With the stone clutched in one hand, Charlotte pushed off hard from the bottom of the lake and swam toward the surface. It was a slow, painful process, especially after seeing the way the naiad glided through the water like a figure skater over ice. She paused on her way up to fetch her poor, forgotten boot, and then put it under her arm. She kicked her legs and pulled herself through the water with cold, clumsy fingers. Her ears popped once, painfully. Then, when she least expected it, the naiad swam up, wrapped her webbed fingers around Charlotte's waist, and propelled her through the water. Her head broke the surface and she sucked in a deep, dry breath. As soon as the air hit her lungs, she felt the naiad's magic ebb away. The heat in her chest was replaced by a dry, aching cold, and her teeth began to chatter.

"Hurry," the naiad said as she helped Charlotte to the shallower waters. "Get dressed quickly before the cold sets in."

"It . . . already . . . has," Charlotte said between bursts of teeth-chattering. Her muscles ached with the cold as she pulled herself out of the water and walked, body shivering, up the shore to where she'd abandoned her clothes.

The brownie watched her with wide, fascinated eyes, but she knew his interest lay in the glowing fairy stone clutched in her hand. It felt warm against her skin, and she held it close as the wind picked up.

Getting dressed was a mess. Charlotte's wet feet were covered in sand, which she got all over her jeans as she pulled them on. The brownie offered her his hat to dry off, but unfortunately it was still damp and thus not helpful in the least. She turned her back on both of the fairy creatures and peeled off her sopping wet bra before putting her shirt, hoodie, and jacket back on. The clothing eased some of her shivering, but she was chilled to the bone.

She sat down to brush the sand off her feet before pulling on her warm socks and shoes. Then she twisted the water out of her hair, put it up in a high bun, and pulled on her knit cap.

Meanwhile, the naiad waded just offshore, watching Charlotte with those dark eyes flecked with colors of the sea. She swam closer when Charlotte stood and walked to the edge of the water.

"You've done us a great service," the naiad said.

"Thank you," Charlotte said, "for everything."

"Those that are deserving of help can always find it here." She smiled and lifted one dark brow. "As long as they don't bring any human filth with them. I still have my work cut out for me getting this lake cleaned up."

Charlotte laughed. "I'll come back and help you again. I just have to get these sorted out first." She lifted the stone for the naiad to see.

"Of course. You'd best hurry and get that to the shrine. We're all depending on you."

"Come, Keeper," the brownie said, tugging gently on Charlotte's jacket. "We must go before the sun sets. These woods are different after dark."

Charlotte nodded, and then she waved goodbye to the naiad and watched her sink gracefully below the water.

The brownie led the way through the trees, moving much quicker than Charlotte could. The icy cold clung to her muscles, making it difficult to keep up with the brownie's pace. She moved noisily through the trees, frightening a herd of deer that had gathered for the evening in a thicket and startling birds from the trees. She felt tired and sluggish, but kept pressing onward, relying on the glowing fairy stone to keep her warm.

She followed the brownie down the long, abandoned hiking trail and wished the naiad could have just transported her back to the shrine with fairy magic. She'd never walked this trail so many times in the same day.

The walk was long and painful on Charlotte's frozen feet, so she felt especially grateful to squeeze through the twisted trees and emerge at the shrine.

As with the last time she was here, she held out the stone and closed her eyes, feeling its vibrations from the tips of her fingers all the way up into her elbows. It wanted to return home, and it guided Charlotte forward, its vibrations increasing in intensity. The stone, which was inky black and glowing with flecks of luminous green, pulled her toward the southwest standing stone. As soon as Charlotte slipped the small stone into the niche in the larger stone's belly, the ground shifted under her feet, knocking her down.

Not again, she thought. She was going to be bruised and battered by the time this day was over.

"What was that about?" Charlotte asked, looking to the brownie for some sort of explanation.

"The dwarves," he said, tapping one foot on the ground. "They use earth and fire magic primarily."

Charlotte remembered the brownie's mention of dwarves, but still she shook her head. "Next you'll tell me dragons are real, too."

"They are," he said matter-of-factly. "You won't find any here, though. The human realm is too dangerous for them now, so they stay in the realm of faerie."

Charlotte wanted to laugh, but the brownie's serious expression kept her mouth closed. Just then, a fairy fluttered down from the trees and hovered in front of Charlotte. Charlotte held out her hand, and the fairy landed on it so gently that her feet felt like a flower petal. She pointed toward the ground, and after a moment of miscommunication, Charlotte finally understood and knelt. The fairy fluttered down into the grass, which was over her head, and stomped down some blades before kneeling and pressing her palms to the earth. Charlotte copied her, unsure of what she was feeling for until she felt the vibrations beneath her fingers. They were deep and slow, and they echoed in her chest like a far-off drum. She looked over to the fairy, and the tiny creature gathered up her locks of golden hair and dangled them under her chin like a beard. *Like a dwarf*, Charlotte thought, and broke into a smile. The fairy clapped and smiled back, and then spread her wings and fluttered off, her laughter ringing behind her like bells.

"That was awesome," Charlotte said, sitting back on her heels as she watched the fairy fly off into the yellow trees.

"It's progress," said the brownie, nodding his head slowly.

Charlotte laughed as she got back to her feet. "Let's go home," she said, and the brownie beamed.

✼

Charlotte soaked in the tub for an hour that night. It took nearly that long just to chase the cold from her bones. She'd added lavender essential oil to the bathwater, and now it smelled luxurious as she poured water over her head.

Her phone vibrated with a text message, and Charlotte dried off one hand before reaching out of the tub to grab it off the sink. She smiled as soon as she saw who the text was from.

Hey Charlotte! Art's use of punctuation always made him seem cheery. *I'm taking Tomas to the museum tomorrow. (If he's feeling better.) Thought you might want to join us?*

Charlotte dried off her other hand and typed out a quick response.

I'd love to! Haven't been there in years.

Art responded within sixty seconds. *Great! Let's meet up tomorrow after class. Can't wait.*

Charlotte let out a little squeal and kicked her legs in excitement, accidentally spilling bathwater onto the wood floor.

"Shit," she mumbled. "Dad's not gonna like that."

CHAPTER TWENTY

The next day, Charlotte walked out the front doors of Mapleton High School and found Art waiting for her at the bottom of the stairs. He was wearing a black jacket with a forest-green scarf bundled around his neck, and his cheeks were red from the cold.

Charlotte leaned against the railing at the top of the stairs and smiled down at him. She followed the lines of color in his eyes and found a scattering of freckles across his nose that were so faint she'd never noticed them before. He must have been doing the same thing, because his gaze roamed her face, making her cheeks warm.

"Thanks for waiting," Charlotte said.

Art smiled and gestured gallantly. "After you, m'lady."

Charlotte rolled her eyes, but she couldn't stop the smile stretching across her face.

They had to fight through the clusters of students pouring out from the school and spilling over onto the parking lot and sidewalks. Art led the way, more prone to cut in front of people and barrel his way through the crowds than Charlotte was, and he made quick work of it.

"I'm so ready to be out of here," he said to her as they walked side by side down Main Street toward the elementary school.

"You're a senior, right?" Charlotte asked, pulling up her hood against a blast of frigid wind.

"Yeah. Only two months and one more semester, and then I'm free of this place." Art hunched down against the cold.

"Ugh, I'm jealous," Charlotte said. "I wish I was graduating this year."

"You're so close," he said, giving her a friendly nudge. "Don't give up just yet. Senior year is the best, by far."

"And where does junior year rank?"

"Second worst," he said, smiling. "Freshman year is definitely the worst, but junior year sucks because of ACTs and SATs, and because you're in this weird limbo where you're almost done but you still have another year to go."

"Wow," Charlotte said. "You really just did a horrible job of consoling me."

"You're right. I kind of suck."

They both laughed as they continued down Main Street. Mapleton Elementary School was only a few blocks down from the high school, which made it easy for the older kids to swing by and pick up their siblings after class.

Charlotte and Art joined the crowd of parents standing outside the school, and a few minutes later the bell rang. All the classroom doors swung open and students rushed outside, their backpacks bouncing as they ran across the dry grass to show their parents what they'd made or worked on that day.

Tomas didn't run—he walked. He carried his violin at his side, his backpack heavy and drooping down as he made his way across the grass to join Charlotte and Art on the sidewalk.

"Hey, bud," Art said, taking Tomas's backpack and swinging it up onto his shoulder.

"Hey, Tomas." Charlotte gave him a small smile.

"Hi," he said, averting his eyes to look at his shoes.

"Are you feeling better?" she asked.

"Yeah, my stomachache is gone. I think Mom's stew was bad."

Art cracked up laughing and threw an arm around Tomas's shoulders.

The three of them headed back down Main Street, their shoes crunching across the dry leaves on the sidewalk.

The Mapleton Museum of History was at the end of Main Street and around the corner. It was an old house that had been built in the early 1900s and renovated to suit the city's need of a historical center.

The house had recently been repainted and looked creamy white in the pale afternoon sun. Charlotte had flashbacks as she walked up the sidewalk and climbed the stairs to the large wraparound porch. She remembered visiting this place as a child and thinking it was fascinating. She didn't have many friends in elementary school, so she usually ended up wandering through the rooms and exhibits by herself or at the back of the group, pausing to look at war memorabilia or the dead, stuffed animals. Their glass eyes were so flat and emotionless, and even at that age she knew that what she was seeing made her sad. She wasn't looking forward to seeing those animals today.

The door creaked as Art pulled it open, and Charlotte thanked him when he held it for her. Inside, the museum smelled of stale air and rugs that needed replacing. However, the chandelier overhead glowed with warm light, and it was a pleasant escape from the biting air outside. There was an older woman sitting at a desk in the front room, who Charlotte recognized and waved to. Melba lifted her arm and waved back, her white teeth flashing when she smiled. She was on the phone and talking rapidly, so Charlotte left her be.

She unzipped her heavy jacket and looked around while Tomas rifled through his backpack. He found the folder he was looking for, fished a pencil out from the front pocket on his bag, and was ready to go.

"Okay," Art said, standing over his brother's shoulder to look down at the stapled packet of papers. "What are we looking for today?"

"It's a scavenger hunt," Tomas explained. "I have to find all these things and then write down their exhibit number." He started to read off the lengthy list of items as Charlotte turned away to look at the old photos on the walls. They were black and white, and from the looks of it they were photographs of the family who built and lived in this house back in the early 1900s. The woman wore a stiff dress buttoned up to her neck and had her dark hair twisted up on the top of her head. Her look was focused and stern, and Charlotte knew from research she'd done for a project that most people in old photos looked this way because they had to sit still for so long to have their picture taken.

"Hey, Char, you ready to go?" Art asked from behind her.

"Yeah," Charlotte said, keeping her face down as she turned away from the photos so he wouldn't see the smile his nickname gave her.

They started out in the Hallway of Time, the long hallway on the main floor that was filled with pictures chronicling the creation and evolution of Mapleton over the last hundred years. Charlotte had always enjoyed this hallway because it had an old photo of her great-great-grandparents, who had built the family home in the Greenwood all those years ago. Charlotte found the photo and smiled at it. Great-Great-Grandpa squinted at the camera, his arms crossed and his head tilted to one side. He had one boot propped up on a tree stump and wore an old-style hat with a feather tucked into its brim. Great-Great-Grandma stood beside him, a child perched on her hip. Her hair was loose around her shoulders, and she had a flower tucked behind one ear. Behind them, the family cottage sat in the shadows of the old oak trees.

"Here it is," Tomas said, pointing at an old photo of a train. He wrote down the exhibit number and then proceeded down the hallway with Art and Charlotte in tow. Charlotte reached out and snagged a bit of Art's sleeve.

"What is it?" he asked.

Charlotte glanced around, making sure none of the other museum visitors were listening before she leaned in and spoke. "I went back to the lake yesterday, and I got the stone."

"No way!" Art said, loud enough to cause the family looking at a display nearby to turn around. Charlotte put a finger over her lips to shush him. "Sorry," he whispered. "What happened?"

She told him about the naiad while they followed Tomas from exhibit to exhibit, and her cheeks got hot when she told him about the kiss. She didn't tell him it had been her first kiss, because she probably would have melted into a puddle right there out of sheer embarrassment. He seemed to go a little red himself when she told him about it.

"So, you kissed a mermaid, she gave you the power to breathe underwater, and then you swam all the way to the bottom of the lake to retrieve a magical long-lost stone? All on a Tuesday afternoon?"

"Yes, sir," Charlotte said playfully.

Art shook his head and smiled. "You are literally the most amazing person I have ever met." His cheeks went red again, and he reached up to run a hand through his dark hair.

Behind him, Charlotte spotted a pair of beady eyes watching her from a dark doorway. The creature was hard to see in the shadows, but it looked like an older, more wrinkled version of the brownie. She smiled at the creature, and then it vanished into one of the off-limits areas of the house.

Charlotte and Art followed Tomas up the stairs into the Rocks and Minerals exhibit on the second floor, and Tomas stopped to address them for the first time since they'd started their conversation.

"Are you two in love?" he asked matter-of-factly, with his packet of papers open in front of him and his pencil poised and ready to write. He looked like he was about to take notes on their current relationship status.

Charlotte looked to Art for an answer, unsure of what to say.

"Well, define love," Art said, and when he turned around, something over his shoulder caught Charlotte's eye.

It was a stone about the size of a baseball, and if its shimmery black surface didn't give it away, then the veins of deep burgundy shot through it certainly did.

"Oh, my, God," Charlotte whispered, grabbing Art's arm.

"What is it?" he asked, turning to look around the exhibit.

"That," she said, pointing at the stone. "That's one of them."

It was in an exhibit with a weird wax statue of a miner and a sad stuffed mule pulling a minecart full of rocks. The fairy stone was on top of the pile and glittered softly under the yellow exhibit lighting.

"No way," Art said. "Are you sure?"

"Positive. It looks just like all the other ones."

"All the other what?" Tomas asked.

"Oh, uh, all the other rocks in my collection," Charlotte said.

"You collect rocks?" Tomas asked, quirking a dark brow. "I thought only hoarders did that."

"How do you know what a hoarder is?" Art asked.

"I saw it on TV." Tomas shrugged and then wandered away to look at a different display.

"What are you going to do?" Art asked, turning his attention back to Charlotte. "You have to take it, right?"

"Shh," Charlotte said, glancing around to make sure no one else was in the exhibit. "Don't let anyone hear you." There wasn't anyone else in the exhibit to hear them, which wasn't a surprise since it was literally just full of rocks, but she was shaken nonetheless.

"You can't just leave it here," Art said, checking over his shoulder to make sure no one came in. "You said you need them to get your mom back, right?"

"Yeah," Charlotte said quietly. She felt suspicious standing there staring at it, so she turned around casually to look at a display of minerals that had been discovered in the nearby area. As she turned, she glanced up at the ceilings. There was one camera in the corner, an old hulk of a thing, but it was pointed at the other end of the room. Charlotte followed the camera's gaze and found a display of diamonds and chunks of gold behind a glass display case.

"This is your only chance," Art whispered. "I'm going to go stand in the doorway, and if anyone is coming, I'll say something really loud."

"I don't know if I can do this," Charlotte whispered back, curling her fingers nervously into fists as she stared at the stone on the pile of other rocks.

Art put a hand on her shoulder. "You can do this. The railing is low, so just hop over it, grab the stone, and get out. You've got your backpack, so just slip it in there and then we'll leave."

"I wish you would do it," she grumbled.

Art laughed. "This is your fairy quest, not mine." He gave her shoulders a squeeze and pushed her gently toward the display. "Hurry," he whispered, "before someone comes in." Art walked off to stand in the doorway.

Charlotte looked back at the display and glared at the glassy eyes on the wax miner. "I can do this," she whispered, not sure if she was saying it to herself or to him. She double-checked to make sure Tomas was distracted writing in his packet and then, before she could overthink it, stepped over the low railing and into the exhibit.

The lights were warm on her back and made her feel like she was in the spotlight on a stage. She knew the feeling well from playing solos during the orchestra performances at school, but those performances always made her feel proud. At the moment, she just felt shameful.

The display had looked so small, but now it felt like it was a mile long. She crept across the display, and the closer she got to the stone, the more sure she was that it belonged to the fairies. The red veins glowed under the exhibit lights, and she could feel its buzzing energy as she got closer. She walked very carefully around the stuffed mule and thought how cruel it was that they were forced to work such laborious jobs. Even long dead, the mule looked miserable.

"Pretty cold outside today, huh?" Charlotte heard Art say, loudly. Way more loudly than any casual conversation called for.

Charlotte ducked quickly behind the minecart and folded herself into the square shadow it cast. She dropped down low to peek under the wheels and saw Tomas staring in her direction.

Art was still talking in the hallway, and a few seconds later Melba stepped into the doorway. Charlotte pulled her legs tight into her chest and held her breath. How would she explain what she was doing if Melba found her?

"Where's Charlotte?" she heard Melba ask Art, and he laughed easily.

"She went into one of the other exhibits," he said. "The mule really freaked her out. She doesn't eat animals, you know, so it really bothered her seeing it in here."

Despite the situation, Charlotte smiled. She didn't think Art would have remembered that.

"Oh, I didn't know," Melba said.

Charlotte heard her moving around in the doorway but didn't bend down to peek again for fear of being spotted. Now all she could hope for was that Tomas would stay quiet and not give her away.

"Are you working on something for school, young man?" Melba asked.

"Yes," Tomas said in a small voice.

"Do you need help finding anything?"

"No," Tomas said. "I'm finished."

"Ah, what a smart boy." Melba laughed. "I'll be around if you need me."

"Thanks," Art said, cheerful as ever, and then the exhibit was quiet.

Charlotte peeked under the minecart and saw that the room was empty again. With a breath of relief, she reached up to grab the fairy stone. Her fingers brushed its warm surface, and as soon as she picked it up, a jolt of energy shot through her arm. Startled, she let out a squeak and dropped the stone. It clattered across the display, scattering rocks as it went, and then finally landed heavily on the wood floor and rolled toward the doorway.

Charlotte stood up, meaning to retrieve the stone before anyone saw her, but then Melba appeared in the doorway. She bent down to pick up the stone and then looked up at Charlotte. Her eyebrows drew down over her dark eyes.

"Ms. Barclay," she said slowly, "*what* do you think you're doing?"

Charlotte had never been so humiliated. She was promptly escorted into the front office, where Melba closed the door behind them.

"Care to explain yourself?" Melba asked, her gold bangles jingling when she crossed her arms.

Charlotte didn't know what to say. She glanced at the fairy stone sitting on Melba's desk, opened her mouth to explain what had happened, and then stood there without saying a word. The thought of explaining everything made Charlotte feel tired—there was no easy way to tell Melba what was going on.

Melba walked around her desk and sat down. She propped her elbows up on the desk and shook her head. "I know you're going through a lot right now, but that doesn't give you the right to damage historical artifacts." She gestured to the stone. "I've never known you to be so reckless."

The office door creaked open, and Charlotte turned around. The creature she'd seen earlier, indeed an old brownie, shuffled into the room. Melba stood up to close the door, mumbling about door hinges, and then took a seat behind her desk again.

"Do you know what the purpose of a museum is?" Melba asked. "It's to preserve history. How can we preserve history if visitors climb into the displays or steal our artifacts?"

Melba continued with her lecture, but Charlotte was distracted by the brownie. He made his way slowly across the room, then used a stack of books and a filing cabinet to crawl up onto Melba's desk. He was careful to avoid the fairy stone, but knocked a stack of papers to the floor. While Melba bent over to pick them up, he leveled his gaze on Charlotte.

"You must be the young Keeper I've heard about," he said in a sandy voice, and then had a fit of coughing before he could continue. "It pleases me that you are here. What you did was very brave. Our curator does not . take grievances lightly." He smiled at Melba as she finished gathering up the papers and sat back in her chair.

"What do you have to say for yourself?" Melba asked. She leveled her dark eyes on Charlotte.

"I'm sorry," Charlotte said quietly.

"I will help you," the old brownie said, at the same time Melba said something about talking to Grandma. He plucked a leaf from a nearby plant, crushed it in his palm, and whispered, "Bit by bit, shall you forget." Then he blew the dry leaf particles into Melba's face.

Melba coughed, wiping at her eyes. "Allergies," she said between fits of sneezing. She reached for a tissue to dab at her nose, but then her hand dropped and her head fell back against her office chair.

"She's only asleep," the brownie said in a voice more tired than before. He slouched toward the desk and fell to his knees. "Hurry, take the stone before she wakes. She won't remember you were here."

"Are you okay?" Charlotte asked, reaching out a hand.

"I've used the last of my magic," the brownie said, coughing. He waved at the stone. "Take it. Go."

Charlotte grabbed the stone and dropped it into a small pouch on her backpack. Then she held the backpack opened wide to the brownie. "Come on," she said. "I'm not leaving you here."

The brownie smiled up at her from where he lay crumpled on the desk.

"You remind me of her," he said. "Same eyes." He coughed again, and his frail shoulders shook.

"Who?" Charlotte asked, leaning close to hear the brownie's fading words.

"Faer," he said. A smile pulled at the corner of his lips, and Charlotte reached out to trail a gentle hand over the wisps of hair on his balding head.

"Tell me about her," Charlotte whispered.

He blinked his eyes open and they glistened. "Oh, Keeper, there's so much to say. She was always so kind to me—so gentle. She wouldn't have harmed a fly, that one." He started to laugh, and the sound was breathy and tired. "She brought me biscuits once, and they were just *horrible*. Tasted like biting into a sack of flour." His laughter turned into tears that streaked down his old cheeks. "But she did try. She tried so hard."

"She sounds wonderful," Charlotte said, still trailing her fingertips over his forehead. "What's your name?" she asked softly.

The brownie blinked up at her with a smile in his eyes. "Barrow," he whispered. "My name is Barrow." Then, with a sigh, Barrow closed his eyes as his body turned to dust.

Melba's office window was cracked, and the particles of what used to be the old brownie swirled into the air and drifted out on the cold October breeze. Not a speck of him remained—it was as if he had never been.

Charlotte stared at the window long after the brownie was gone. Her hands trembled. *He sacrificed himself . . . for me.* All this time, all these years, she'd avoided these magical beings, only to realize that she'd done herself, and them, a great disservice. Had she never abandoned them, maybe they wouldn't be running out of magic. Had she never abandoned them, maybe Mom never would have been taken. Had she not abandoned them, maybe this all could have been avoided. Maybe Barrow would still be alive.

Melba stirred in her office chair, already starting to wake up. Charlotte stood and wiped the tears from her cheeks.

"Thank you, Barrow," she whispered, and then slipped from the office before Melba could wake.

Art and Tomas were waiting in the Hallway of Time. They rushed over as Charlotte eased the office door closed behind her.

"What happened?" Art asked.

"Are you in trouble?" Tomas asked.

"Did you get the stone?" Art asked.

Charlotte held up a hand to stop their questions. "I got it, I'm not in trouble, and we need to go. Come on." She reached for the handle on the front door but had to step back when it swung open.

Melanie and Marco stepped inside, and Charlotte's stomach hit the floor. The two of them were laughing and their cheeks were red from the cold.

Melanie's face froze when she met Charlotte's eyes. "Oh, hi," she said, stopping dead in the doorway.

Marco had to shimmy in behind her just to get the door closed.

"Hey," Charlotte responded, feeling Marco's and Art's eyes on her. She stared at Melanie and Melanie stared back. A few quiet moments ticked by before Marco held out his hand.

"Hey," he said. "I'm Marco."

"Charlotte," she said, shaking his hand. "Nice to meet you."

"I've heard a lot about you," he said, his face breaking into a big smile. "I kept asking Melanie when she would finally introduce us." He jostled Melanie with his elbow, and she looked mortified, her head down and her arms crossed. But Charlotte was glad to hear it.

"I've heard a lot about you, too," Charlotte said, and meant it. "Oh, this is Art. And his little brother, Tomas." Charlotte gestured to them, and Art shook Marco's and Melanie's hands. Tomas just looked bored.

Melanie met Charlotte's eyes with a curious look. Charlotte gave her a little smile, and Melanie's pink lips returned the gesture.

And just like that, the tension between them seemed to loosen its grip. Suddenly they were just two teenage girls standing in the company of two cute boys, and they were blushing and smiling like they hadn't been at odds with each other for the last few weeks. And it felt *good*.

"Oh," Art said, his gaze flicking toward Melba's office door. "Hey, it was nice meeting you guys, but we've gotta go. Come on, Char, we don't want to be late."

At Art's use of the nickname, Melanie lifted her brows. Before Melba could open the office door and ask what had happened, Charlotte lifted a hand in farewell and followed Art out into the cold.

"Bye," she said. And to Melanie, "It was nice to see you."

"You, too," Melanie said. "See you in class tomorrow." And then the door shut between them and Art hurried Charlotte down the stairs and away from the Mapleton Museum of History.

Once they were far enough away to know that Melba wasn't following them, Art stopped short and turned to Charlotte. "What happened?"

"Melba was lecturing me," she said, "and then an old fairy came in and helped me."

"There was a fairy in there?" Art's eyebrows shot up.

"Yeah." Charlotte scuffed her toe into the sidewalk, fighting the tears that threatened to spill as she pictured the way Barrow's body had turned to dust.

"So, what now? You return the stone?"

"Yeah." Charlotte looked up at the sky. "I'd like to return it today, but it's getting a bit late. I probably wouldn't make it before the sun went down."

"I could drive you," Art offered. The breeze ruffled his dark hair, and Charlotte couldn't resist when he gave her that smile.

"Okay," she said, nodding. "Let's go."

They dropped Tomas off at Art's house, despite his protests. He wanted to come with them, but Charlotte knew how finicky the fairies could be and advised Art against it.

Art didn't have his own car, but his mom was home and she agreed to let Art borrow hers. Mrs. Nolan had a nice SUV, and Charlotte felt giddy climbing into the passenger seat. She'd never driven anywhere with a boy before. The only times she'd ever gone out with boys was in a friend group and her dad always dropped her off, but this was different.

After buckling her seatbelt, she glanced over at Art and watched him adjust the seat to his height. He had long legs and had to scoot the seat way back from the steering wheel.

"Okay," he said once he'd adjusted the mirrors. "You ready?"

Charlotte gave him a nod, and he smiled.

"Here we go!"

Despite the chill in the air, Charlotte rolled down her window to smell the fresh fall leaves and watch Mapleton flash by. Old Town was decorated for Halloween, with pumpkins on every corner and fake cobwebs clinging to the bushes. Charlotte loved how festive her town was, even if she didn't participate in the celebrations.

The drive to the Greenwood was brief, and the sun was still in the sky when Art parked the car and they both climbed out. There were two other cars in the lot, but Charlotte wasn't worried about bumping into their drivers. The fairy shrine was well off the beaten path, and most hikers didn't wander too far off the marked trails, especially at this time of day. The sun would set soon, and no one wanted to be lost in the Greenwood overnight.

With Art's comforting presence at her side, Charlotte led the way without hesitation. She was finding that the closer she got to the fairy world, the more the Greenwood seemed to be revealing itself to her. She had traversed these trails hundreds of times as a child, all the way up until the evening she saw the phooka. Now her memory was resurfacing, and paths she thought she had forgotten opened up before her like an outstretched hand.

"This way," she said, directing Art down a narrow path away from the main trail. The shadows were darkening and the wind was cold, but the trembling Charlotte felt in her fingertips was from something else entirely. She could feel Art right behind her, his footsteps matching hers, and she listened as he breathed in and out. She thought about his lips and smiled to herself when she remembered that she'd officially had her first kiss. It still counted even if it wasn't with a human, right? It had been warm and wet and terrifying, but she'd done it, and now she wanted to do it again, preferably with a human boy.

"Are you sure you know where you're going?" Art teased as Charlotte led him deeper into the Greenwood and further from the popular hiking trails.

"Don't you trust me?" Charlotte asked over her shoulder, using a more playful tone than she usually did with him. He gave her a crooked smile.

Charlotte turned back around and lurched to a halt. She held out an arm to stop Art and felt his chest brush her arm when he bumped into her.

"What is it?" he asked.

"Shh," she said, and then pointed. "Look."

Just up ahead and to their left was an open area where a few old trees had fallen, leaving a grassy spot where a herd of deer had gathered. They nibbled on the grass and flicked their tall, furry ears, ever aware of their surroundings. One deer in particular looked a bit different than the rest. It didn't have its head down eating and seemed uninterested in the grass. Instead, it stared through the trees at Charlotte and Art, its dark, intelligent eyes looking back and forth between the two of them.

"I think I've seen that one before," Charlotte said. Its antlers were impressively tall, and it looked like the deer she'd seen on a few other occasions, including the day she saw the workers putting the Nolan Enterprises sign up in the Greenwood.

"It's gorgeous," Art whispered. "It's watching us."

It was. Its gaze remained fixed on the two of them, ever curious and watchful.

"Come on," Charlotte whispered, taking a step back. "Let's go this other way so we don't disturb the herd." She turned away to take a different path through the trees, but even as she walked away she could feel the deer's gaze on her back. She felt goose bumps prickle across her skin and tried to shake off the feeling of being watched.

"That was awesome," Art said when he caught up to her and the path widened enough for them to walk side by side. Their arms bumped as they walked, and Charlotte spread her fingers open, just in case. "I've never seen a deer act like that before. It just stared at us."

"Maybe it was actually a fairy," she teased.

"But I can't see fairies."

"Maybe it was wearing a glamour," Charlotte countered. "I read about them in one of your books. It's like a second skin fairies wear so they can interact with the human world."

"I know what a glamour is," he said, giving her a playful shove. "I lent you those books, remember?"

She turned to look at him and then gasped when she saw three fairies lurking in the tree over his head. They had heads like turnips and sharp-toothed smiles, their fingers ending in claws that allowed them to cling to the branches. They each held a small rock, and before Charlotte could tell Art to duck, the fairies pulled their arms back and fired. The three pebbles pelted Art in the back of the head in rapid succession.

"Ow!" He whipped around to see what had hit him. The fairies hissed and rattled the tree limbs, their teeth gnashing and claws swiping at the air.

"Leave him alone," Charlotte snapped, flapping her hands at the troublemakers.

They hissed at her, too, before spreading their wings and flitting away into the orange and yellow leaves.

"What the hell was that?" Art asked, still rubbing at the back of his head.

"Fairies," she said, "but they're gone now."

"Really?" Art sounded excited. "What did they look like?"

"Um, kind of like the fairies you sketched into my caricature that day. Except meaner. With funny looking heads."

"Sweet," he said, sounding genuinely pleased. "But why are they throwing things at me?"

Charlotte shrugged. "They don't know they can trust you yet. They used to act like that toward me, too, pulling my hair and stuff."

Art smiled to himself in a silly sort of way, prompting Charlotte to ask, "What are you smiling at?"

"You said 'yet,'" he explained, "which means you think they *will* eventually trust me. Does that mean you're going to bring me along on these adventures more often?"

Now it was Charlotte's turn to give him a silly smile. "We'll see how you do on this one first. We're almost there."

Art was quiet after that. He fell a step behind her as she led the way through the trees. The hike had taken longer since they had to backtrack around the herd of deer, and the sun was sinking toward the horizon, casting slanting sunlight and shadows through the trees.

Charlotte felt a sense of relief when she found the twisted trees, knowing that she'd found her way. She squished herself through the narrow space between the two trees and waited for Art to shimmy through behind her. On the other side of the tangled trees were the five standing stones rising toward the darkening sky. The standing stones cast long shadows across the ground, but the sunlight fell through the trees in just such a way as to light up the grass all around them like blades of gold. Colorful leaves crunched underfoot as Charlotte moved, and overhead they spun lazily down from the trees to settle upon the ground.

"Oh my God," Art breathed, his pale, freckled face gone slack as he looked up at the shrine. "I can't believe I'm seeing this."

"It gets better," Charlotte said, removing the fairy stone from her backpack.

As she held it up for Art to see, the air seemed to shift and suddenly fairies were creeping out of the shadows and popping their heads out from holes in the trees to see what was going on. They all looked at Art with narrowed, cautious eyes, but Charlotte smiled to assure them that everything was all right. As with the other two, she let the stone guide her. Its energy tugged at her hands and led her forward, and she placed it into the belly of the corresponding standing stone. As soon as it had settled snugly into the niche, a gust of air rushed around the stones, so hot that Charlotte held up a hand to shield her face. It felt similar to the way the potbelly stove spit heat into her face whenever she tried to use it.

"Did you feel that?" she asked Art.

"Yeah—what was that? I thought my eyebrows might melt off."

"*That* was the fire stone. See that one over there?" She pointed to the stone with veins of yellow. "That's the air stone, and that one in the middle is the earth stone."

"I can't believe this is happening," he said quietly, and then sat down in the grass in the center of the five stones.

Charlotte sat down beside him, close enough that their thighs brushed.

"What can you see right now? Are there fairies around us?"

There sure were. Those that had been hesitant and hiding in the shadows before came out as soon as the fire stone was in place. They swirled over the standing stones and chased each other through the deep grass and dry leaves. Two squirrels with fairy riders raced by.

"See those squirrels?" Charlotte asked, and Art nodded. "There are fairies on their backs. They're playing some sort of game." She looked around for more whimsy to describe to him. "And see that boulder over there?" She pointed to the edge of the forest where a few boulders sat in the shadows. "There's a tiny man sitting on it, and he's playing a song on a little wooden instrument."

The music the small fairy man played had the other fairies dancing and twirling through the leaves and the sky. Charlotte laughed as she watched them, but she couldn't shake the sadness it gave her to know that Art couldn't see this world. He sat beside her happily, though, with a small smile and his head tipped back so that his curly hair shifted off his forehead when the wind blew.

Unexpectedly, a small fairy with bright red hair and eyes the color of dandelions alighted on Art's shoulder. She had wings like a butterfly, and she opened and closed them slowly as the sun danced across their vivid colors.

"Sit very still," Charlotte whispered. "One just landed on your shoulder."

Art did as he was told, and Charlotte held in a squeal of joy when the fairy leaned in and kissed him on the cheek. Then the fairy laughed and lifted into the air, her bright hair trailing behind her.

Art brushed his fingers across his cheek. "I think I felt something," he said, his eyes wide and glittering. "What was that?"

"A fairy kiss," Charlotte said through a big smile. "I think she likes you."

"Oh, you think so?" Art asked. He shifted closer and Charlotte's heart jumped.

She stared at him and he stared back. His eyes swept over her face, and she held her breath when his gaze settled on her lips. Art leaned closer and put a hand down in the grass to steady himself. Charlotte did the same, and then without a clue about what she was doing, she leaned in and bumped her lips against his.

"Oof," he said, pulling back suddenly, and the fairies overhead dissolved into laughter.

"Oh my gosh," Charlotte whispered, horrified that she'd just messed up the kiss she'd been thinking about for weeks.

Art laughed, and then he leaned in again. This time Charlotte sat very still, and when he brushed his lips against hers, it was soft and slow and perfect. His hand came up to trail a touch across her cheek and she leaned in to him for more. He parted her lips with his and their kiss deepened. Fairies twittered in the trees overhead, but she didn't care. She grabbed the end of his scarf and used it to pull him closer. She let his lips guide hers, and when his tongue touched her bottom lip she let out a small sigh.

Leaves of red and gold swirled down around them, and Art pulled back to look up.

"It's the fairies," Charlotte whispered. They were on the branches overhead, plucking the leaves off and scattering them like rice at a wedding.

She looked back to Art and found him smiling with rosy cheeks, and they beamed at each other before starting to laugh. Art stood and offered Charlotte his hand. Charlotte took it and he pulled her up.

"Thank you for bringing me along," he said. "This is probably the most magical place I've ever seen."

"Maybe you could come back with me some time," she said, testing the waters. Hopefully he wasn't still thinking about her muddled first attempt at a kiss. "The fairies are warming up to you."

"I'd like that." He offered her his hand. "Want a ride home?"

"Absolutely," she said, even though her house was only a short hike away. There was no way she was going to waste this opportunity to spend more time with him. She took the hand he offered, and her insides tumbled with joy as he laced his fingers through hers.

Art held Charlotte's hand all the way to the car and on the ride home. His hand was big and warm around hers, and the skin on his palm was soft. She wished it would last longer, but her family's home was only a short drive from the Greenwood trail system, so too soon it was all over. She wondered what to do as he pulled into her gravel drive and put the car in park. Was she supposed to hug him? Kiss him? Get out and wave goodbye?

In the end, he simply lifted her hand and kissed it gently.

"Today was awesome," he said. "Thanks for letting me tag along."

"I was glad to have the company. The fairies can be a little intimidating sometimes."

Speaking of fairies, one was sitting on the porch, and he jumped up and waved his hat when Charlotte saw him. "Oh," she said. "I have a visitor."

"A fairy?" Art asked.

"Of sorts. He's a brownie." She grabbed her backpack and opened the car door. "Thanks again for the ride. So, I'll see you later?"

"Absolutely. Maybe we can hang out this weekend or something."

Charlotte smiled. "I'd like that." She climbed out of the SUV and closed the door, then waved as Art reversed down the gravel drive and headed back into town. Then she turned her attention to the brownie.

"Where have you been?" the brownie asked. "I've been waiting for you all day."

"I," Charlotte said smugly, "found another stone today. The fire stone." She tossed her backpack down and took a seat on the porch steps beside the brownie.

His eyes went wide. "Interesting," he mumbled to himself. He jumped off the porch and began to pace, one hand stroking his chin thoughtfully. "That leaves the stones of water and spirit."

"I know where the water stone is," Charlotte said, and the brownie perked up his big ears. "Remember? That girl that I know wears it as a ring."

"Just take it," the brownie said, as if it were that simple.

"I can't just *steal* it," Charlotte argued, although she'd stolen two of the stones already.

"It's not stealing if you're returning it to its rightful place." The brownie sighed. "Humans are despicable."

Charlotte couldn't disagree, so she just dropped her head and kicked at the loose gravel underfoot. Then the brownie startled her when he snapped his fingers.

"Today you returned the fire stone, yes?" he asked, and Charlotte nodded. "With both the earth and fire stones returned, the dwarven forges should be operating at full power again."

"Did you ever ask that dwarf friend of yours about forging a new ring?" Charlotte asked, thinking back on their conversation. It felt like forever ago.

"I did, but he couldn't help us without more magic. Now that you've returned the fire stone, things may be different. I'll speak with him tonight. If he agrees, you'll need to meet him."

"You know where to find me," Charlotte said, gesturing at the house.

The brownie gave her a slight nod and ran off into the night, leaving her sitting on the porch in the dark.

When she was sure he was gone, she leaned back and looked up. The sun had gone down and only a few streaks of pale light lingered in the sky. She smiled to herself and laughed quietly, still in awe over this day. A fairy stone, a boy, and a kiss that still made her skin tingle to think of it—she must have been doing something right.

CHAPTER TWENTY-ONE

Charlotte was so lost in her thoughts walking home from school and violin lessons early Thursday evening that she didn't even see the brownie waiting for her on the porch. She was thinking about the way Art had been waiting for her out in front of the high school when she arrived that morning, and how he'd walked her to her first class and told her about the movie Tomas made him watch the night before. And then in orchestra, Melanie had actually said hello and complimented Charlotte's navy sweater (which Grandma had recently picked up at a thrift store in town). They weren't back to eating lunch together, but it was a step in the right direction.

"Keeper!" the brownie yelled in exasperation as Charlotte stepped up on the porch.

She jumped, startled by his presence, and almost dropped her violin case. "Geez," she said. "What is it?"

"My acquaintance has agreed to meet you, but we must go *now*."

"Your acquaintance?"

"The *dwarf*, Keeper," the brownie said with a hint of annoyance. "He has agreed to meet you, but we must go now if we aren't to be late."

"Oh, okay, hang on, let me just put this away. Do you want a snack?"

"Hurry!" the brownie snapped, which made Charlotte scuttle inside without another word.

She dropped off her violin and changed into her hiking shoes and big jacket, and then on her way out she saw that her dad's bedroom door was cracked and he seemed to be organizing things. He was walking around the room, going through the closet, and throwing things on the bed and floor. She wanted to go ask how he was doing, but the brownie was waiting for her and didn't seem all too patient.

As expected, the brownie was tapping his foot irritably when Charlotte got back outside.

"Come," he said, waving her forward before jumping off the bottom step and running into the trees that bordered the long gravel driveway.

"Slow down!" Charlotte called after him, glancing over her shoulder to make sure Dad wasn't watching through the front window.

Her violin lessons had taken a few hours after school, so the sun was already sinking as she crunched through the leaves and tried to keep up with the brownie. The light was darkening as the sun slipped toward the horizon. The shadows stretched long across the forest floor, and Charlotte felt the familiar prickling of fear in her belly as fairies and forest creatures moved in her peripheral vision.

"Hey," she called ahead to the brownie, who kept ducking out of sight only to appear moments later out of a bush or from around the trunk of a tree. "I can't keep up with you!"

"It's almost time!" the brownie called back, looking up through the trees toward the sun. "Hurry! We're nearly there!"

Charlotte wanted to complain, but instead she bit back her angry words and put her energy into moving quickly and not tripping on any of the roots or boulders littering the path. They were far enough into the Greenwood now that Charlotte couldn't see any hiking trails or signs of human life. The Greenwood was a lovely place to get outdoors and go camping, but as soon as you stepped off the marked trails, it became a maze of trees and bushes and rocks that all looked the same to the unfamiliar eye. There were still old photos of missing people posted at the trailhead, and Charlotte felt sick when she thought of how terrified they must have been to realize they'd gotten turned around and were lost in the trees. Some of the bodies of missing hikers had never been recovered, and a small part of Charlotte wondered if the fae had something to do with it. She'd spent more time reading through Art's books, and they all warned of the inherent danger of fairies. They could be conniving and clever, and supposedly, back when the veil between the realms was more permeable, people used to get kidnapped by fairies all the time. Charlotte knew, all too well, how possible that was and wondered if perhaps those missing hikers hadn't been so lost after all.

"We're here," the brownie said as they came across a rock garden.

The rocks were gray and black and made traversing the area difficult, so Charlotte had to slow down and hold on to the bigger rocks to keep from twisting an ankle.

They descended a sloping hill and stopped at the bottom, where Charlotte took a seat on a flat rock to catch her breath.

"Where is he?" she asked, looking around for a small man in a pointy hat carrying a pickaxe over one shoulder. She'd never seen a real dwarf before, so the only ideas she had to go off were those from movies she'd seen as a child.

"We made it just in time," the brownie said, squatting on a rock beside her. "He'll be here soon."

They sat there and watched the sun go down over the forest. The air was cold and Charlotte could see her breath, but she was comfortably warm inside her jacket and enjoyed the crisp breeze on her face.

"I met another brownie," Charlotte said quietly. She'd been unsure of how to bring it up, but it felt like the right time.

"Oh?"

"He helped me get the fire stone. His name was Barrow."

"Was?"

Charlotte scuffed her boot in the dirt. "He ran out of magic after helping me . . ."

"Ah." The brownie was quiet for a long time, and then he smiled. "Barrow was a good fellow. I'm sorry to hear he's gone."

"What happens when fairies die?" Charlotte asked, glancing timidly at the brownie.

"We return to nature, in one way or another. We may become a flower, or a blade of grass, or a puff of smoke."

"Barrow turned to dust," Charlotte explained, and the brownie nodded his head knowingly. "Do fairies live forever in Lyra?"

The brownie laughed. "We live long lives, Keeper, but we don't live forever."

Charlotte traced a line in the dirt with the toe of her boot. "What about humans in Lyra?"

"What about them?" the brownie asked, narrowing his eyes at the sinking sun.

"How long do they live in Lyra?"

"The same length of time as they would here, of course." He crossed his arms and sighed, and Charlotte went back to tracing lines in the dirt.

Only a few rays of sunlight still slanted across the forest floor when a brown toad hopped up on a rock across from where Charlotte sat. It croaked loudly, making her jump.

The brownie stood up and looked at the sky. "Not much longer now."

Charlotte watched the toad, and it seemed to stare right back with its bulging eyes. The rock it sat on was half-illuminated by the sun, and Charlotte watched the line of sunlight move as darkness fell over the Greenwood. She didn't know what they were waiting for until the sun fully set and the toad, despite how entirely unmagical it had appeared, began to twist and transform. Charlotte stood up, surprised and disgusted, but despite how grotesque it was, she couldn't look away. After a matter of seconds, a small humanoid creature stood where the toad had been. The dwarf opened his mouth to speak but only a croak came out. He cleared his throat, thumped once on his chest, and tried again.

"Evening," he said in a slow, deep voice. He nodded his bald head to Charlotte and then to the brownie. He did indeed have a beard, and it was decorated with beads made of glass and stone. He wore a green tunic and trousers belted at the waist. Standing on the rock, he came up to Charlotte's height, so he couldn't have been more than a few feet tall.

"You must be the Keeper," he said, and bowed low. "Our forges haven't produced anything more than dust and ash in many years, and thanks to you the fires are roaring once again." He let out a deep laugh, and his belly jiggled.

"I'm, uh, glad to hear it," Charlotte said. Nothing should have surprised her at this point, but there was still so much about the fairy world that she didn't know. What else lurked underground, or in the sky, or in the seas that she knew nothing about?

"I'm told that you have a request of me." The dwarf hooked his thumbs through the waistband of his trousers. "What is it that you need?"

"Yes, I do," Charlotte said, searching in her pocket for her cell phone. She pulled it out and found the photo she'd taken of Freddy's ring. "Do you think you can make a replica of this?" She held it out to the dwarf and he, like the brownie, shielded his eyes from the bright screen. Charlotte dimmed it and tried again.

"Aye, that's quite a stone," the dwarf said.

"I'd say," mumbled the brownie.

"And you want me to replicate this?"

"Yes, please. Do you think it's possible?"

The dwarf looked at the photo again and nodded his head. "Aye. With the forges up and running again, crafting a replica of that ring shouldn't prove too difficult."

"Oh, thank goodness," Charlotte said, letting out a sigh. That was such a weight off her shoulders.

"And what do you propose in exchange?" the dwarf asked, crossing his arms.

"In exchange? Like a trade?" Charlotte asked.

"Aye, like a trade."

"Um, I don't know." Charlotte glanced at the brownie for support, but he just shrugged. "What would you like?"

"Something equal in value," said the dwarf. He pointed at the studs she wore in her ears. "Let me see those."

Charlotte didn't like his pushiness, but the earrings didn't mean much to her so she took them off and handed them over. It took him only a moment to realize that they were fake diamonds.

"Lousy," he said, turning up his nose before he tossed them over. One fell in the dirt, and Charlotte felt a surge of irritation as she knelt to pick it up.

"Then what do you want?" she asked, putting her earrings back in.

"Something shiny, like those, but with real diamonds. My daughter's one-hundredth birthday is coming up, and she'd like those very much."

Charlotte wasn't sure what to be more surprised by: the fact that the dwarf wanted her to bring him *real* diamonds, or that dwarves lived to be over one hundred years old.

"I don't have any diamonds," she said. Frivolities like expensive jewelry were low on Charlotte's priority list. She'd much rather have a car or money to go to Bellini—if she even got in. She'd been so distracted by all this fairy stuff and Art stuff lately that she hadn't been practicing her violin nearly as often as she needed to be. Even that afternoon in orchestra she'd been so distracted thinking about her kiss with Art and wanting to tell her mom about it that she'd completely missed a measure and had thrown off the entire first violin section, eliciting a harsh look from Mr. Hamilton.

"Well," the dwarf said, shrugging his shoulders slowly as if he really didn't care. "If that be the case, then I won't be able to assist you after all."

Charlotte looked at the brownie, who looked as upset as she felt.

"What is the meaning of this?" he asked. "This is the Keeper you speak to, and we all must do our part to assist in her quest."

"Don't be so quick to forgive," the dwarf said in a low, threatening voice. "You seem to forget that her family betrayed us and allowed the shrine to fall into ruin. My trust won't be so easily gained."

"Okay, okay." Charlotte held out a hand for the two fairies to stop arguing. "I'll do it," she said, unconvinced even as the words came out of her mouth. "But I'll need some time."

"I'll give you twenty-four hours. I'll be here at dusk tomorrow. Bring the diamonds, or our deal is off." With that, the dwarf turned around to face the rock behind him. He held out one hand, whispered a few words in a language Charlotte couldn't understand, and then was illuminated by white light as it burst forth from fissures in the rock face. The light moved in a sweeping arc, carving a glowing doorway into the stone surface. The dwarf turned and nodded to Charlotte before he pushed the door open and stepped through. As soon as he was on the other side, the doorway sealed itself and the rock was as it had been before—solid and gray and entirely unmagical.

The brownie clambered up onto the rock so that he was at Charlotte's eye level and put his hands on his hips.

"Well?" he snapped. "How do you plan to acquire *diamonds* in the next twenty-four hours?"

Charlotte hated herself for thinking it, but there was only one place where she could get diamonds on such short notice.

Mom's jewelry box.

CHAPTER TWENTY-TWO

On the walk home, the brownie let Charlotte know just how displeased he was. He complained about dwarves and their selfish nature, and repeatedly muttered that the dwarf owed him double the favors now than he had before. Charlotte hardly listened. She was too caught up in her own thoughts.

As they approached the house, the brownie left her in silence and slumped away into the dying flower bushes as Charlotte took the stairs to the front door. Grandma wouldn't be home until late, which meant the house was dark and there wasn't any food boiling on the stove to fill the house with warm, delicious smells. Charlotte had half a mind to start eating at the Blue Moose in the evenings just to avoid having to fix another sad spaghetti dish or settle for a bowl of cereal. Tonight, though, she wanted to spend time in the kitchen and living room so that she could hear what Dad was up to. She didn't think he'd let her take the jewelry, especially with Mom being gone, so she needed to find a way to sneak in, grab the diamonds, and get out before Dad realized what she was doing. Just the thought of it made her stomach turn. Once Mom was home safe, Charlotte would come clean about everything she'd done and seek forgiveness for hurting anyone along the way. But tonight, she needed to be strong and get this done, or else she'd lose her only chance at securing the dwarf's help.

Charlotte was stirring pasta on the stove when Dad passed by carrying two full trash bags. She watched as he carried them outside to the truck and threw them in the back.

"Hey, Dad," she said when he came back inside, rubbing his arms to warm them up from the cold.

"Hey, kid. How was your day?" He looked up at her with dark bags under his eyes and a weariness that deepened his wrinkles and pulled his lips into a frown. These past few weeks had aged him.

Charlotte wanted so badly to sit him down and tell him everything she knew. She'd tell him about the dryad and her magical antlers. She'd tell him about the helpful, grumpy brownie and about the hundred-year-old dwarves that lived in a world far beneath their feet. But he wouldn't believe her. She'd already tried.

"It was good," she said. "I've been messing up in orchestra lately, though. I'm not practicing enough."

"We're all distracted," he said, his eyes glazing over.

He wandered back toward his room, and Charlotte held back the sudden urge to cry. She'd never seen Dad so beaten and battered, and felt partially responsible for all that he was going through. But *dammit*, if only he'd listen to her.

She was sitting on the couch watching a nature documentary and eating her pasta when Dad grabbed a towel out of the hall closet and headed into the bathroom. Her heart slammed up against her ribcage when she realized this was her chance. It might be her *only* chance. Once Dad was back in his bedroom, he'd likely be there all night.

She put her bowl down on the coffee table and listened. It took a few minutes, but then the pipes groaned and the shower came on in the bathroom.

Charlotte stood up.

Oh my God, she thought, *I can't do this*. But then she thought of her mom in the dryad's mossy prison and heard the dwarf saying this was her only chance, and that alone propelled her feet forward, her socks swishing quietly over the hardwood floor. She paused outside the bathroom, her heart beating as she listened to her dad adjusting the faucets on the old tub. Her parents' room was straight ahead, the light spilling through the doorway, warm and yellow.

She took a step forward, careful not to step on the old floorboard that always squeaked under her feet. She didn't hear any sign that Dad had heard her, so she took another step, and then another, until she hesitated in the doorway.

She used to come in here all the time when she was a child. She'd spend snow days in bed with Mom, reading stories and staring out their window into the back garden as it got buried under snow. As she got older she started entering their bedroom less frequently, more and more aware of how private and sacred a space it was.

But when she stepped over the threshold this time, it felt like she was committing a crime. The room she'd always known and had felt so comfortable in as a child felt like it was closing in on her. The swirls in the natural timber walls seemed to be staring at her, judging what she was about to do.

She spotted Mom's jewelry box on the dresser, right where she thought it would be. Charlotte crept toward the dresser slowly, listening for any sign that her dad might be coming in. All she could hear was the rushing of water through the old pipes and the groan of the timber beams as the wind blew outside.

The dresser was still littered with Mom's things: bottles of essential oils that she used as perfume and wore in crystal vials around her neck, a wooden comb with strands of blond hair still tangled in its teeth, a piece of paper she'd doodled a sketch on all those weeks ago. Despite all the cleaning and organizing Dad seemed to have done over the last few days, none of Mom's belongings had been touched. They all remained exactly as they had been the day she'd vanished, waiting patiently for her to return.

Charlotte pressed her tongue against the roof of her mouth in an attempt not to cry. She missed the smell of patchouli that wafted by whenever Mom passed through a room. She missed the humming that meant Mom was in a cheerful mood. And more than anything, she missed the life that Mom brought to the house. Without her, this cottage felt less like a home and more like a pile of wood.

Charlotte opened the lid of the wooden jewelry box carefully. The lid was inlaid with heavy, polished stones, and Charlotte settled it down slowly. A collection of glittering jewels winked up at her. There were rings, necklaces, earrings, bracelets, brooches, and more. She'd never seen her mom wear half the things in the box, but they'd been kept clean and pristine nevertheless.

Charlotte rifled through the pieces of jewelry, trying to figure out which piece would be best to give to the dwarf. There was a bracelet that looked promising, and Charlotte was holding it up in the light when the bathroom door creaked open and Dad's bare feet slapped down the hall. She froze.

And then he was standing there in the doorway, still unwashed and in his bathrobe, staring at her.

"Oh, hi," she said, trying not to let her voice quake. "I thought you were in the shower."

"I forgot my phone," he said, picking it up off the dresser. "I want to have it in case Officer Beck calls." He slipped it into the deep pocket on his bathrobe and crossed his arms. "What are you doing in here?"

Charlotte hadn't taken the time to come up with a story, because she hadn't planned on getting caught. But as she stood there holding the diamond bracelet, a lie came easily to her lips.

"A boy asked me out on a date, and Mom always told me I could wear some of her jewelry the first time I went out. I thought it would upset you, so I was trying to take it without you knowing." She hung her head in genuine shame. "I'm sorry."

Dad didn't say anything at first, and when she glanced up at him, she was relieved to see that the confusion and distress on his face had been replaced by a sad, knowing smile.

"I see," he said, walking over to join her at the jewelry box. "May I?"

Charlotte handed the bracelet over and watched as her dad held it tenderly between his fingers. He turned it this way and that, watching the light sparkle off the diamonds.

"Did you get this for her?" she asked.

"I did." He smiled to himself. "I gave this to her for our second wedding anniversary. She was so excited that she put it on right then, but for the rest of the night it was getting snagged in her hair and her clothes, and it even got stuck on my jacket at one point." He laughed. "She hasn't worn it but a few times since. I never bought her another bracelet after that." He handed it back to Charlotte. "Feel free to wear it, but be careful, because the clasp snags on everything."

Charlotte held it to her chest and gave him a small, sad smile. "Thanks, Dad." She gave him a hug and he hugged her back. "I'll take care of it."

"I know you will," he said, and the trust in his eyes stung. Charlotte reminded herself that she wasn't taking the diamonds to be cruel—she needed them to bring Mom home, and she'd give all the jewels away if that was what it took.

"Who's the boy?" Dad asked, and Charlotte was surprised he was interested at all. He'd been so detached lately that she'd started to believe he didn't care about anything she did.

"Um, it's Art, actually."

Dad smiled and shook his head as if it were no surprise. "I thought something was going on when I saw him here with you. He was always a good kid. I think your mom would be happy to hear that." Just as his eyes started to tear up, his cell phone went off and he dived into his pocket to grab it. He frowned when he read the caller ID.

"Your grandma," he whispered, and then walked away to talk.

Charlotte closed the jewelry box and sent a whispered thanks out to Mom before going back to her room for the night. All she had to do now was get the diamond bracelet to the dwarf and she'd be one step closer to bringing Mom home.

CHAPTER TWENTY-THREE

Pre-Calc was especially painful on Friday morning. All Charlotte could think about was Mom's diamond bracelet in the top drawer of her dresser at home, and the fact that it was already October 21st, meaning the new moon was drawing near. She still hadn't figured out where the fifth stone was, and now she had less than two weeks to return all five fairy stones to the shrine. The nerves had Charlotte's leg bouncing uncontrollably under her desk.

The teacher droned on about rational functions, and Charlotte was so bored and antsy that she'd taken to staring out the window and counting the cars that drove by. She'd brought her amethyst along today, hoping it would give her some sort of vision about the fifth fairy stone, but so far it had done nothing but weigh her pocket down. Now she took it out and pressed it into the palm of her hand. She continued to stare out the window, and a truck that looked like Dad's had just passed by when Charlotte felt a tingling sensation at the base of her neck.

She knew this feeling—it had happened when she stepped into Mom's studio and saw the day of her kidnapping. This one came on slowly, seeping into the edges of Charlotte's vision like ink through water. It was hazy and confusing, and the images that floated before her eyes kept shifting as if they were unsure of themselves. She saw Dad sitting in his truck outside the house, and all she could hear was him sobbing. The vision swam, distorting the images and the whiteboard at the front of the classroom, but it was clear enough for Charlotte to see the whiskey and a bottle of pills on the dashboard. Dad's hands shook as he reached for the whiskey, and then the vision cleared.

As soon as she realized what was going on, Charlotte jumped up from her seat and almost knocked her desk over in the process. Twenty-nine pairs of eyes turned to see what was going on, but Charlotte bolted from the room before Ms. Mullins could ask what the matter was. She ran down the hall, dodging students and ignoring the shouts of teachers telling her to slow down. The brick walls, covered in colorful posters advertising clubs and activities, flashed by in splashes of yellow and blue. Charlotte was so focused on getting home that she didn't even think to slow down before she took a corner too fast.

As soon as she bolted around the corner, she came face-to-face with Melanie, colliding so hard that Melanie dropped her books and stumbled back to brace herself against a wall.

"Oh my God, Charlotte," Melanie snapped, bending down to pick up her books. She flicked her straight hair over her shoulder irritably. Then she saw Charlotte's face and her expression changed. "Are you okay? What's going on?"

"It's my dad," Charlotte said, on the verge of tears. "I need to get home. I don't have time." She tried to hurry past, but Melanie reached out and grabbed her arm.

"Stop, slow down. I have a car. Can we take that?"

A few minutes later Charlotte climbed into the front seat of Melanie's white sedan. She'd ridden in this passenger seat a hundred times, but it felt foreign to her now. The dip in the seat below her was too large, too deep. She realized that this was Marco's seat now, and that he may have officially taken her place. But none of that mattered now. She leaned forward and then back, as if moving her body could somehow urge the car forward.

The vision she'd seen of her mom's kidnapping had been a vision of the past, and she hoped and prayed to whatever being could hear her that this wasn't the case with the vision of her dad. Charlotte couldn't imagine losing him, especially not when she was so close to bringing Mom home.

Melanie told her to put on her seatbelt, but she didn't want it to get in the way when she had to get out of the car. She kept one hand on the door handle and the other on the dashboard, as if bracing herself for an impact.

"Charlotte, God, sit back. You're freaking me out."

"Can't you go any faster?" Charlotte anxiously rapped her fingers across the dash.

"No. There's something called a *speed limit*."

Charlotte looked away and gritted her teeth. *I'm coming, Dad.*

Main Street had never felt so long, and by the time the car crunched up the gravel drive to the house, Charlotte already had the door halfway open and was ready to jump out.

Melanie slowed down as the house came into view, and Charlotte rocketed out of the passenger door. She sped across the driveway and ripped the truck door open.

Dad was sitting in the driver seat, *alive*, and had the bottle of whiskey in one hand and a handful of pills in the other. Charlotte snatched the bottle out of his trembling hand and threw it to the ground, ignoring the crash as it shattered and scattered shards of glass across the gravel. Dad made no effort to stop her when she took the pills and poured them back into the bottle. They were strong pain pills Grandma had used years ago after a severe back injury, and Charlotte remembered seeing Dad staring into the medicine cabinet only a few days ago. Was that when he got the idea to do this to himself? Had he been planning it all along?

"Charlotte? Is everything okay?" Melanie crept toward the truck, keeping her distance.

"Go get my grandma," Charlotte said over her shoulder, not taking her eyes off Dad. She heard Melanie's shoes crunching toward the house, and then the front door opened and closed.

"What the hell?" Charlotte whispered. "What were you thinking?" She took Dad by the front of his jean jacket and gave him a hard shake.

He burst into tears and dropped his head into his hands. All he could mumble was, "I'm sorry. I'm sorry."

Grandma sped out of the house a moment later, her long hair in braids and house slippers on her feet. "William!"

Charlotte stepped aside and sagged back against the truck. Her heart was beating so hard and fast that she thought she might pass out. She put a hand to her chest and took a slow, deep breath.

Melanie walked down the front porch steps and hesitated, hanging back from the chaos. Her pink lips were pinched together in a tight line, and there were worried creases on her forehead. Charlotte pushed off the truck and walked toward her.

"Is he okay?" Melanie whispered, shifting from foot to foot as she watched Dad and Grandma over Charlotte's shoulder.

"I don't know," Charlotte said, on the verge of tears. She ran a trembling hand through her hair. "Thank you for everything. I don't know what would have happened if I had got here any later." Just the thought of what could have happened caused Charlotte to burst into tears.

"Hey, hey, it's okay," Melanie whispered, pulling Charlotte in for a hug.

Charlotte wrapped her arms around Melanie and held on for dear life. She cried big, wet tears into Melanie's hair and soaked the shoulder of her jacket, but Melanie kept rubbing her back and whispering quiet words of comfort. Charlotte's whole body shook, but Melanie held on tight, a lighthouse in a storm.

How many times had they stood like this, holding on to one another just to keep from drowning? It was usually Melanie that needed consoling, either after a breakup or a fight with her mom, but today she was the rock, holding Charlotte steady so she didn't float away.

After a few minutes, Charlotte had cried herself out, and she wiped her nose on the sleeve of her jacket before pulling back and giving Melanie a thankful smile.

"I'm going to go back and get your backpack and stuff," Melanie said, reaching out to tuck a strand of Charlotte's hair behind her ear. "What class were you in?"

"Pre-Calc with Mullins."

"Okay. I'll bring it by at the end of the day, and I'll tell Mr. Hamilton you'll be out today."

"Thanks, Mel," Charlotte said softly.

"Charlotte, I need you!" Grandma yelled, and Charlotte turned around.

Grandma was in the process of getting Dad out of the truck, and it wasn't going well.

"I've gotta go," Charlotte told Melanie. "Thank you for everything." She reached out and gave Melanie's hand a squeeze before hurrying across the driveway to help Grandma.

She grabbed Dad and pulled his arm across her shoulders. He sagged heavily against her, and his breath stank of whiskey. She shouldered as much of his weight as she could, trying to take the load off Grandma.

"I'm sorry, I'm sorry," he whispered again and again.

"Then get your feet under you and *walk*," Charlotte snapped.

Surprisingly, Dad gathered himself up enough to get into the house and collapse onto the couch.

"Sit with him," Grandma said, then hurried into the kitchen to start water in a kettle on the stove.

Charlotte sat down in the plush chair across the living room and stared at Dad through narrowed eyes. Dad sat slumped over on the couch, his head hanging low while he sniffled and cried quietly to himself. Charlotte wanted to go over there and shake him until he snapped out of it, but she forced herself to remain right where she was, halfway across the room.

The tea kettle whistled, and Grandma brought the steaming mugs of tea into the living room on a tray. She set it down on the coffee table and then sat down beside Dad and offered him the cup. He shook his head at first, but she was persistent, and eventually he accepted the mug and took a small sip. Charlotte refused the cup Grandma offered her. She could smell the herbal mixture and knew it was Grandma's special concoction for sleep: a mix of hops, chamomile, and lavender. But Charlotte had no intention of sleeping.

"Explain yourself," she snapped.

Dad lifted his head and looked at her with red-rimmed eyes.

"Go ahead. Tell me why you thought leaving Grandma and me behind like that would have been a good idea."

"I'm sorry," he said, and Charlotte threw her hands up in the air.

"Yeah, I get that part. But *why?*"

"Emily," he said, and just saying her name brought him to tears. "She's everything to me." He cried harder.

"Then listen to me!" Charlotte yelled. She slapped a hand down on the coffee table so hard that the mugs of tea almost spilled. Grandma gave her a warning look, but Charlotte ignored it. "I told you she was alive, but you refused to listen to me. I've been working all this time to bring her back and you've been of no help. And now you do this? What the hell, Dad!" Charlotte stood up and stormed across the room to stare out the front window.

It was still early, and the sunlight glittered on the stones in the driveway and the fall breeze made the oak trees sway. Charlotte's anger vibrated through her chest, and she knew who she needed to talk to next: the dryad. This was all *her* fault.

"I don't understand," Dad said, tears still thick in his throat.

"Yeah, because you refuse to open up your mind to other possibilities."

"I don't know what you're talking about."

"Then *listen*," Charlotte said, turning away from the window. "Mom is *alive*. I've seen her. I tried to tell you that before but you wouldn't freaking listen to me."

"It's just not possible," Dad said, shaking his head.

"I'll prove it to you." Charlotte crossed her arms defiantly.

Dad looked up at her, and some of the despair in his eyes had been replaced by something curious, perhaps even hopeful.

Before Dad could say anything else, Charlotte stormed into her bedroom and grabbed her old violin case out of the closet. She hadn't used the beat-up violin since she got her new one, but her nice violin was still in Ms. Mullins's classroom, so this one would have to do.

"I'm going to prove it to you," she said as she paused in the living room on her way out the door, "and then you'll wish you'd listened to me from the start." With that, she stormed out the front door and slammed it behind her.

CHAPTER TWENTY-FOUR

Charlotte stormed out of the house and across the gravel drive without stopping to grab a jacket. She was so angry that sweat dampened the fabric beneath her arms. The handle on her violin case squeaked as she scrambled up the embankment behind the house and pushed through the old oak trees standing in her way. She mumbled under her breath as she hiked toward the shrine, her insides a scrambled mess of chaos. She didn't know how to feel about any of this. All she could do was put one foot in front of the other in the hopes of putting this behind her.

Fairies and birds sang and chirped in the golden treetops as Charlotte shimmied through the two tangled trees and emerged among the gray standing stones. Early afternoon sunlight filtered down through the treetops and made the fallen leaves surrounding the shrine look like fire underfoot. Charlotte set down her violin case and opened the buckles that squeaked with age. And then there it was, the violin she had learned how to play "Twinkle, Twinkle, Little Star" and "Mary Had a Little Lamb" on. It was a bit small for her now, but it brought back pleasant memories. She ran a hand over the strings and plucked them one by one, grimacing at the dissonance. She pulled out the violin and began to tune it as slowly and gently as she could, careful not to break the old strings.

She got the violin as in-tune as possible, and then she pulled out her discolored bow and tightened it up. There wasn't any rosin in the case, so when she stood up and pulled the bow across the strings, it squealed in protest.

"Work with me here," she whispered, and then took a deep breath. She could smell the dampness of the leaves underfoot and the thick, fertile soil that sprouted with mushrooms, flowers, and other plants.

As Charlotte raised the bow again, she realized that she couldn't remember the dryad's song. Her stomach twisted into nervous knots as her pulse quickened. What if she couldn't play the song? What if it didn't come to her?

"Relax," she whispered to herself, taking another slow, deep breath. Fairy magic worked its wonders in mysterious ways. She could still remember the way the music had flowed through her mind when the dryad had placed smooth, cool fingers on her temples. But the harder Charlotte tried to remember it, the further from her grasp the song seemed to slip. So instead of focusing too hard, she relaxed her shoulders, let the morning light fall on her eyes, and started to play.

It wasn't pretty, and the violin squeaked more than it sang, but she didn't care. She played the song that only she could—the song of the Greenwood. She played her violin for the hedgehog pixies that lived in the log, and for the squirrels and their riders that sped through the treetops. She turned in circles to watch the standing stones spin by, and in time she found herself smiling. How long had it been since she'd allowed herself the pleasure of playing simply for the joy of it? Nowadays she only played for two reasons—the school orchestra, and the audition piece for Bellini, which she hadn't looked at in over a week. But this was the way her music was meant to be played, out in the trees with nature pulsing around her and filling her soul with its own song.

She barely realized when her fingers started moving to another rhythm, playing a song that sounded familiar but that she hardly knew. She played the song of the dryad, and as she did, the treetops filled with fairy creatures who swirled through the sky and sang in voices too high-pitched for Charlotte to hear. And as she played the final few notes and drew her bow across the strings with a flourish, the Greenwood seemed to shimmer and then melt away, revealing a world much more magical in its place.

The five standing stones stood statuesque in the dappled sunlight, surrounding her where she stood in calf-deep grass that shifted in a soft breeze. The air was warm, almost balmy, and smelled of honeysuckle.

Charlotte knelt and hid her violin and bow in the deep grass at the base of one standing stone, and then she wiped the nervous sweat from her hands and took a deep breath.

Something rustled the bushes behind her, and she turned just in time to see three fairy children come barreling out of the foliage. They parted around her, laughing and pushing each other as they ran, and one stopped and looked back. He had skin like lapis that shimmered in the dim forest light and eyes as big as a doe's. His ears were long and delicately curved, and Charlotte wondered what kind of fairy he was.

"You're a human," he said, and she detected curiosity in his voice. "What are you doing here?"

"I've come to see the dryad," Charlotte explained. "Do you know where I can find her?"

"Sure," he said, flashing white teeth with two large, sharp canines. "Come on." Then he took off running, bounding through the trees like a deer.

"Slow down!" Charlotte called as she hurried after him, clumsy in the underbrush. What was it with fairies and always running off?

The fairy boy's dark skin allowed him to slip away into the shadows, but then he would appear a moment later, leaping and laughing and waving her onward. She felt a wave of relief when the forest came to an end and opened onto the field of tall, swaying grass and the Great Tree in the distance. The fairy boy stood waiting for her there, and seeing him in the sunlight caused her to pause, simply to admire him.

His skin was not one color, but many. It was primarily dark blue, but shimmered with undertones of green and brown and silver. He was like the ocean, or the night sky, beautiful and magical and terrifying all at once.

"Are you a Keeper?" he asked as they walked down the shimmering stone path.

Charlotte could see the village in the distance and smelled freshly baked bread in the air.

"Yeah. How did you know?"

"Only the Keepers know the way into our realm now," the boy explained, reaching out to snag a golden blade of grass. He twirled it between his fingers and it blossomed with flowers. "My dad used to know a Keeper. Mom doesn't like when he talks about it, but he tells me stories about her sometimes."

"Why doesn't your Mom like it?"

"Because he loved her, I think." The boy shrugged.

"Loved the Keeper?" Charlotte asked in surprise.

"Yeah, that's what I just said." The boy rolled his eyes. "Humans aren't too smart, huh?"

Charlotte turned to glare at him, and over his shoulder she saw a pair of great antlers rise out of the tall grass, and below those antlers was the dryad. She carried a bundle of flowers in her arms and wore a silk robe the color of sunlight.

"That's enough," she said to the boy, and he spun to face her. She shook her head at him. "Charlotte is our guest here, and you'll speak only kind words to her. Understood?"

"Understood," he said, then gave Charlotte a sly smile and winked over his shoulder before taking off across the field, shimmering blue under the sunlight as he went to greet his friends.

"A well-meaning child," the dryad said, running one hand over the tall stalks of grass. "But stubborn and spoiled. Most elves are. Especially the royal ones." She looked up at Charlotte, and the smile fell from her face. "What's wrong?"

"My dad could have died today." Charlotte let the anger from before bubble back up in her chest. "Because of you," she said, jabbing a finger toward the dryad, "I could have lost both my parents."

"What are you talking about?" the dryad asked, her brown eyes wide.

"He was going to . . . to . . ." Charlotte trailed off, unable to bring herself to say it.

The dryad gave Charlotte a soft smile. "My dear, nothing was going to happen to your father. It wasn't meant to be."

"What the hell is that supposed to mean? If I hadn't gotten there in time, he—"

"But you did get there in time," the dryad said. "Just as you were always meant to. Come, sit." The dryad waved her hand, and tree roots sprouted from the ground. They parted the dark soil and pulled the grass from the earth, tangling and entwining as they went. They creaked and groaned as the roots laced together and then stilled, providing a bench perfect for two to sit. The dryad took a seat, flowers in her lap, and patted the spot beside her.

Charlotte sat hesitantly and crossed her arms over her chest.

"Time, fate, destiny," the dryad said, "they're all concepts that humans struggle to understand." She picked up a sky-blue flower and smiled. "This flower, in all its lives and all its time, was always meant to be yours. It would never happen any other way."

Charlotte took the flower and twirled it between her fingers. As she watched the blue petals spin, her vision swam with tears.

"I thought I'd lost him," she said, and started to cry. She dropped her head into her hands, and a moment later the dryad wrapped a warm, strong arm around her shoulders. The dryad smelled of flowers and sunlight, and Charlotte allowed herself to be consoled as she cried.

"All is well," the dryad whispered. "Your father isn't going anywhere anytime soon." She lifted Charlotte's chin delicately and brushed the tears from her cheeks. "Would you like to visit your mother? Would that make you feel better?"

Charlotte nodded.

The dryad led the way to the Great Tree, her dress of shimmering yellows and golds catching the sun as she walked. Her antlers gleamed, all smooth and polished to a shine. Charlotte wanted to hate her, but she found it difficult to do. She'd always thought hate was simple, but it wasn't. She hated the dryad for kidnapping Mom, threatening her loved ones, and causing grief for her family. However, she enjoyed the dryad for her soft words, gentle magic, and way with the natural world. If she'd met the dryad under different circumstances, would they have been friends?

"You said that elf was a royal?" Charlotte asked, running her hands over the tall stalks of grass as they swished around her.

"Indeed." The dryad glanced over at her, a small smile tugging on her lips. "Sometimes I forget how little you know." She let out a small, breathy laugh. "Well, each species of fairy has a ruling family. The elves, dwarves, goblins, nymphs."

"Are you a royal?"

"Oh, goodness, no!" The dryad laughed, and it was a beautiful sound. "I'm one of many sisters, and I'm no more special than the rest." She gave Charlotte a small smile but didn't explain any further.

As they walked through the village, oak men came forward to offer Charlotte loaves of bread, dolls made of straw, and garlands of flowers. Charlotte knelt to accept one such gift, and the old oak woman placed a crown of flowers on Charlotte's head.

"Thank you," Charlotte whispered, and the woman smiled.

"Thank *you*, Keeper. For all you've done."

The dryad smiled at Charlotte and placed a hand on her back, guiding her forward through the crowd.

Four oak men stood outside the Great Tree, and they removed their hats and bowed to the dryad as she approached.

"Lovely day, my lady," said one, his cheeks turning pink.

"May I carry those for you?" asked another, offering to take the dryad's flowers.

"Thank you," the dryad said, kneeling to kiss the oak man atop his head, "but all I need is to step inside."

"Of course, my lady!" The oak man slapped his hat back on his round head. "Come, men!"

The four oak men lined up, two per door, and with grunts and a mighty pull, they yanked the heavy golden doors wide open, revealing the way into the Great Tree.

"Your strength never ceases to amaze me," the dryad said in her honey-sweet voice, and the oak men all but melted into puddles at her feet.

Charlotte stepped into the open, airy chamber and looked around while the dryad went about putting the bouquet of freshly plucked flowers into a vase of water. Despite being here before, the Great Tree still amazed her. The floor was covered in dirt and soft green moss, and everywhere she looked there were plants and flowers and creeping vines. It reminded her of the butterfly pavilion that she took a field trip to as a child.

"Your mother is through there." The dryad pointed toward a small path through the foliage. "You remember the way?"

"Kind of," Charlotte said, remembering how lost she'd felt the last time she was here.

The dryad lifted a hand and whistled. A small blue bird flitted out of the plants and alighted on the dryad's finger, chirping in her ear and fluttering its dainty wings. The dryad whispered something to the bird and then kissed its feathery head.

"He'll lead the way," the dryad said.

The bird let out a series of chirps and flew toward the trees. Charlotte followed it into the thick plants, leaving the dryad behind to tend to her flowers.

The plants grew tall, and they reached out to touch Charlotte's hair and trail their silky leaves across her skin. She pushed them gently aside as she went, listening for the bird as it sang through the leaves. She lost sight of the bird after a while, and it was only thanks to the bird's song that she found him again.

He nestled among a thick blanket of vines, his blue-feathered chest puffed out as he sang. Charlotte recognized this place, and she knew that just behind these vines was the glade where Mom slept.

"Thank you," Charlotte whispered to the blue bird, and then she pushed through the vines and stepped into the glade.

She found Mom asleep on a blanket of moss and flowers. Her skin was still soft and pink, and her lips were turned into a smile as she slept. Charlotte knelt by her side, careful not to let the butterflies overhead sprinkle their sleeping dust on her as well.

"Hi, Mom," she whispered, reaching out to trail her fingertips across Mom's cheek.

Mom shifted, nestling her head into the pillow of moss, but she remained fast asleep, lids closed over blue eyes. Charlotte wondered what she was dreaming about as she slept. Mom used to have crazy dreams, and Charlotte always looked forward to hearing about them over the breakfast table in the mornings. It was one of many things that she had taken for granted but now missed terribly.

"I miss you so much," Charlotte said, starting to cry. At first only a few tears ran down her cheeks, but then it was like the floodgates opened and she was sobbing. She collapsed forward and wrapped her arms around Mom, squeezing her tight and wishing she could hug back.

"You're not going to believe what Dad did," Charlotte said, finally able to stop crying and wipe her eyes. She told Mom about what had happened, breaking into a few more bouts of tears as she went. "And that's why I'm here," Charlotte explained, wondering if Mom could hear her. "I have to prove you're still here. I just—I don't know how. What should I do?"

She reached down and picked up Mom's hand, entwining their fingers together. Mom's wedding ring sparkled in the yellow sunlight streaming down from above, and Charlotte got an idea.

Of course, she thought, very carefully working the wedding ring off Mom's finger. Mom never went anywhere without it. She painted in it, showered with it on, slept with it, and would probably be buried with it. Dad knew this, of course, and had on multiple occasions asked Mom to take it off so that he could take it to the jewelers and have it cleaned. Mom always refused, opting instead to go with Dad to the jewelers so that she could watch them clean it.

"I swear I'll give it back," Charlotte said as the ring fell into her hand. "I'm going to show it to Dad so that he knows I'm telling the truth. He'll take care of it, I promise."

Charlotte looked down at the wedding ring and smiled. It had a band made of gold and a small diamond that sparkled in the sunlight. It was small and simple, just like Mom liked it.

"I'm going to get you out of here soon," she said, burying the ring in a deep pocket. She gave Mom a big hug and tried not to cry again. She needed to pull herself together and get back to Dad.

With great hesitation, Charlotte finally stood and backed away from Mom. Some sleeping dust had fallen in her curls, and she shook it out carefully. The butterflies overhead fluttered in dizzying circles, their wings a rainbow of colors as they floated on the balmy air. If Mom had to be in a deep sleep anywhere in the world, this was probably the most comfortable place to be. She was safe here, and Charlotte tried to remember that as she pushed through the vines and followed the blue bird back the way she'd come.

The dryad was nowhere to be found when Charlotte got back, but she didn't waste any time looking for her. With the wedding ring in her pocket and a renewed determination to bring Mom home, Charlotte set out from the Great Tree. No one stopped her on the way back to the standing stones, and this time when she picked up her violin to play the dryad's song, the notes came to her without pause.

The autumn sun was still high in the sky as Charlotte made her way home from the shrine. She'd been surprised to find how slowly the day was moving, but then she remembered that time flowed differently in the fairy realm than it did here.

Dad was pacing by the front window when Charlotte got home. He greeted her at the door and crushed her in a hug as soon as she walked in.

"I was so worried," he said into her hair. "You should have taken your phone."

Even if she had taken her cell, the service would have been out of range. She'd yet to see a cell tower in Lyra.

"I can prove it," Charlotte said, her lips pulling back into a smile.

Dad stepped back, holding Charlotte at arm's length. "What?"

Charlotte reached into her pocket and pulled out Mom's wedding ring. It shone dimly in the hallway lighting, not nearly as vibrant as it had been in the golden light of the glade. Charlotte placed the ring in Dad's outstretched, trembling hand. He cupped the ring in his palm like it was a baby bird, as if he had to be careful not to hold it too tight. He lifted it to his face and pressed it against his lips, and then he started to cry.

"Oh, and this," Charlotte added, taking the crown of flowers from her head. Dad took the flowers and ran his thumb across the petals.

"Come, sit," Grandma said, ushering them both out of the entryway and into the living room. "We have a lot to talk about."

Dad wanted to know everything, and he held the ring tightly while Charlotte explained as best she could. It took hours to talk through it all. She told him about the other realm and her duty to the shrine. She told him about the dryad and the Great Tree. And then she told him about Mom.

She told him about the glade full of sunlight and the smile on Mom's face as she slept. She told him about the butterflies and the sparkling silver powder and the birds that sang sweet lullabies.

"I just," Dad said, shaking his head, "I just don't know how to believe these things you're saying."

"Don't think about it too hard," Grandma said, after having been quiet for most of the conversation. She sat across the room in her plush rocking chair, one hand on her chin as she listened to Charlotte speak. "Just let it be, and know that Emily is safe and Charlotte is going to bring her home."

"Is there anything I can do?" Dad asked. "H-How can I help?"

"By going back to work," Charlotte said simply. "You have to get back to your life. I can't be worried about you every single day, and Grandma can't keep up this workload. You've got to start doing your part around here."

Dad frowned, and she wondered if she'd been too hard on him, but then he let out a long breath and sat up straighter.

"Okay," he said in a stronger and surer voice than he'd used in weeks. "If you say your mom is still out there, and that you can bring her back, then I'm going to do whatever you tell me to. Whatever I can do to help."

Charlotte let out a sigh of relief just as there was a knock at the door. She stood to go answer it.

"Hey," Melanie said when Charlotte opened the door. It was already getting dark and bugs buzzed around the porch light over Melanie's head. "I brought your stuff. I hope I got it all." She handed Charlotte her violin case and her backpack, heavy and weighed down with books. "And your jacket," she said, slinging the puffy winter jacket over Charlotte's head.

They both laughed, and Charlotte took it off and hung it in the hall closet.

"Thanks for all of this," she said, "and thanks for bringing me home today."

"You're welcome." Melanie stuffed her hands in her coat pockets. She looked down at her boots. "How's your dad?"

Charlotte glanced over her shoulder, but from where she stood, she couldn't see into the living room. "I don't know," she whispered. "Better, I think. We're going to keep a close eye on him."

Melanie nodded. There was a long silence, and then she looked up at Charlotte with a nervous smile. "You're still my best friend, you know."

"Marco hasn't taken my place yet?" Charlotte asked playfully.

Melanie shook her head. "Not so long as Art hasn't taken mine."

"Never." Charlotte gave Melanie a hug.

Melanie hugged her back, and after a minute she sighed and pulled away.

"I'm so sorry about your mom," she said, her eyes getting glassy. "I just—I couldn't believe it when I saw it on the news. And then I picked up the phone to call you, but I thought you must be mad at me or something, because why else wouldn't you tell me?" Melanie started to cry, and Charlotte reached out to pull her in for another hug.

"No, it was nothing like that," she said softly, holding Melanie tight. "I wasn't ready to talk about it, that was all. And I want to tell you about it, I do, but I don't think I can yet. I'm sorry."

"It's okay." Melanie pulled away, wiping her eyes. "I get it. Take your time. But I'm here if you need me, okay?"

"Thank you," Charlotte said. A bug buzzed toward the porch light and flew too close to Melanie's face in the process.

"Gross," Melanie said, trying to wave the bug away.

"You've gotta conquer that fear," Charlotte said, leaning on the door frame with a smile.

Melanie shook her head. "Nope. Creepy crawlies just don't work with me." A moth flew too close, and Melanie let out a squeal and jumped off the porch. "I'm getting out of here," she said. "See you at school?"

"Absolutely," Charlotte said. "I'll see you then." She waved until Melanie got back in her car and drove off.

"Who was that?" Dad asked from the living room after Charlotte locked the door and carried her stuff down the hall.

"Melanie. She brought my stuff from school." She lugged her backpack and violin case into her bedroom and put them on the floor. There was a tap on her window, and when she looked up she saw the brownie's big, round eyes peering through the glass. She went to the window and opened it.

"Keeper," he said, "we must go. The dwarf will not wait long."

"Shit," Charlotte mumbled. She'd nearly forgotten after all the craziness of the day. "Hang on." She went to her desk and picked up Mom's diamond bracelet. It was a dainty, beautiful little thing, lined with small diamonds that winked in the yellow light. She hoped the dwarf would like it.

"Here." Charlotte leaned out the window, handing it down to the brownie. He looked up at her in confusion. "My dad had a rough day," she explained. "I need to be here for him right now." She nodded to the bracelet in the brownie's hand. "Can I depend on you to get that to the dwarf?"

The brownie puffed up with pride. "Of course, Keeper. You can trust me."

"You're the best," she said softly, and could have sworn the brownie blushed.

Without another word he turned and ran off into the woods, and she took a deep breath of the outside air before closing the window and returning to her family in the living room.

"So, about the dryad," Dad said when she sat down. It was going to be a long night.

CHAPTER TWENTY-FIVE

The weekend that followed was the best Charlotte had had with her family since Mom's kidnapping. Dad ate breakfast with them, and on Sunday he went into the Blue Moose to meet with the employees and his sous chef. Charlotte had felt like she was drowning for so long, but the rocks that had been pinning her down were lifting, one by one, and she felt the surface drawing near. Now all she had to do was get the stone from Freddy, somehow discover the location of the last stone, and then Mom would be able to come home and she could put all of this behind her. The only problem was that the brownie hadn't come around since Friday night, and Charlotte tried to keep herself from suspecting the worst.

On Monday morning she was overjoyed to see Dad fill his travel mug with coffee in the kitchen. He'd gone to the barber on Sunday, and his curls were finally under control again. He wore a nice button-up and had a belt on for the first time in weeks.

"Looking good," she told him from the breakfast table, and he smiled at her around his mug. Only when he set it down did she see the chain hanging from his neck and the wedding ring dangling from the end of it. "Here," she told him, and then stood and tucked the ring into the collar of his shirt. She gave him a pat on the chest, and then Dad wrapped her in a hug.

"Thank you so much," he whispered into her ear.

Behind them, Grandma shuffled into the kitchen, wearing a robe and slippers.

"Ah, the sweet joy of retirement," she said, stretching her arms overhead. "It's about time you got back to work."

Dad nodded. "I'm trying to get back to my routine."

"It'll take time. Don't push yourself too hard. And you're going to that appointment after work today, right?" Grandma wanted Dad to go talk to a therapist, and she'd even called and made him an appointment.

"Yes," Dad said with utmost seriousness.

Grandma gave him a kiss on the cheek and walked him to the door. Charlotte watched from the front window as he walked across the gravel drive and climbed into his truck.

"Do you really think it's going to be okay?" she asked Grandma when she came back into the living room.

"All we can do is wait, and hope. But yes, I think we're all going to be just fine."

❧

Charlotte found the brownie on the front porch steps when she got home from school. He jumped up and ran toward her when she got near.

"Keeper, it's been done," he said, hardly able to hold still.

"What has?"

"The dwarf accepted your offering, and he has finished the ring. We're to meet him at dusk."

"Oh my God," Charlotte whispered, almost to herself. She looked up at the blue-gray autumn sky and started to laugh.

"Keeper?" The brownie sounded worried. "Are you all right?"

"Yes," she said between giggles. "It just feels good to have everything coming together." Charlotte squatted down and wrapped the brownie in a hug. He was soft and warm and smelled of dirt, and the scent brought back memories of her childhood.

"Keeper?" the brownie asked, going rigid in her arms. "What are you doing?"

She released him with a laugh. "Thank you for all your help. I couldn't have done any of this without you." She gave him a soft smile and watched his cheeks turn red. "Come on, I'll get you some biscuits and milk while we wait for the sun to go down."

Dad wasn't home and Grandma's pink Bug wasn't in the driveway, so the house was empty when Charlotte unlocked the door and invited the brownie

223

inside. She poured him a glass of milk and heated up some day-old biscuits in the toaster oven.

"Careful, they're hot," she said, handing the plate down to him.

He took it carefully, his ears perking up when he saw the flaky golden biscuits. Charlotte grabbed herself a few of the oatmeal raisin cookies Grandma had made over the weekend and then joined the brownie on the couch.

They sat there for a few hours together, flipping through the channels and trying not to get crumbs in the couch. The brownie was quiet at first, timid even, but it didn't take long for him to settle in. Eventually he was going through the kitchen cabinets and making messes as he pulled boxes of crackers and bags of chips off the shelves.

"Hey, I think it's time to go," Charlotte told him, and he stopped what he was doing in the kitchen. She had never been so thankful for dusk.

Charlotte grabbed a flashlight from the drawer in the kitchen and then zipped up her jacket and followed the brownie outside. He grumbled about how slow she was, but he stayed right next to her for the entirety of the walk through the darkening trees. They took the same path through the Greenwood that they'd walked the first time Charlotte met the dwarf, so when they came across the rock garden and scrambled around and over the assortment of gray-black boulders, Charlotte knew they had arrived.

The dwarf arrived a few minutes later, but not as a toad this time. A stone began glowing with a bright yellow light, as if it were being carved from the opposite side. The shape of a door appeared, and then it swung open and the dwarf stepped out. His beard was braided with beads, and his cheeks were rosy with color.

"My daughter's birthday just passed," he explained. "She loved the diamonds, Keeper. I'm the best father in the world now, I suppose." He laughed, and it was a robust sound.

"You're welcome," she said, exchanging a small smile with the brownie. "I'm glad she liked them."

"Yes, and you're going to like this." The dwarf reached into a small brown pouch at his hip and pulled out an exact replica of Freddy's ring. It had the same beautiful stone, dark and shot through with veins of shimmering blue, and the same exotic band with engravings and flourishes. He held it up for Charlotte to see but pulled it away when she got too close. "Heed my warning," he said slowly. "Dwarven magic comes at a price. It will resize itself to the first finger it adorns, and then must be worn by no other, lest it squeeze their finger right off." He made a popping sound with his lips, and the brownie jumped.

"I won't put it on." Charlotte reached for the ring again, and this time the dwarf let her take it.

She held it up to what very dim light was left in the sky and marveled at the beauty of it. Even in this low light it glistened, and Charlotte could tell that the dwarf had taken no shortcuts in its creation.

"This is gorgeous," she told him. "It's absolutely perfect. Thank you so much."

"It was my pleasure, Keeper. Without you, our forges would still be covered in dirt and ash, destined to rot into the earth for all eternity."

"So, does this mean you're not mad at me anymore?" Charlotte asked, quirking an eyebrow.

The dwarf sighed. "You have done great deeds for us, but that doesn't wash away the past. There is still much healing left to do."

The doorway the dwarf had carved into the stone was still open, and two voices rang out from the darkness inside. Before he could turn to close it, two small dwarves burst forth from the opening, running and tumbling over each other. "Grandpapa!" they yelled, jumping on him.

"Oh, you two," he said in a tone that reminded Charlotte of her grandpa. "You know you're not supposed to be up here." He picked up the dwarf children and placed one on each shoulder. They were a girl and a boy, and both had beautiful red hair and dark eyes.

"Is that her?" the girl asked, pointing a small finger at Charlotte.

"Yes, that's her," the dwarf said. "Our Shrine Keeper, returned."

The little girl blushed and buried her face in her grandpa's beard.

"Well then, I'd best get these two back to their mother. But thank you, Keeper, for all you've done. We won't forget this."

Charlotte smiled and waved goodbye to the little dwarves as their grandfather carried them back through the stone doorway. The girl lifted her small hand to wave back, and then the door swung closed behind them, resealing itself so that Charlotte couldn't even tell it had been there.

"Well," the brownie said, "what now?"

Charlotte dropped the ring into her pocket, careful not to let her finger slip into the band. "Now we make the switch."

"How?" the brownie asked.

Charlotte thought for a moment, and then she smiled. "I think I know exactly the person who can help us."

CHAPTER TWENTY-SIX

Charlotte's stomach was in nervous knots the entire next day at school as she wondered if her plan would work. Freddy never took her ring off at the store, so she knew there wouldn't be any opportunities to trade out the rings secretly. She was going to need to enlist the help of someone a bit closer to Freddy.

After school Charlotte packed up her backpack as fast as she could and took the back stairs to the side door to avoid the traffic jam of students that would be trying to squish themselves out the main doors.

The day was warm and the sky was blue, and Charlotte tipped her head up to the sun as she walked down Main Street toward the Oval.

The main square bustled with people, which was no surprise. The only time it was quiet in Old Town was the early morning before all the storefronts opened. It was always eerie to walk through the Oval when everything was closed and the store windows were dark.

Mom had painted a picture for one of the shops in town, and she had spent a week going into town in the early hours of the morning so she could paint without any distractions or people getting in the way. Charlotte tagged along on a few of those mornings, a thermos of hot chocolate in hand, and enjoyed the stillness of the place that was so rarely still. It felt like those days were so far away now.

Charlotte dodged young children and slow-moving grandparents as she hurried toward Carnelia. The door was propped open, and Charlotte could feel the buzzing energy of the stones and crystals before she even stepped inside.

A woman with pale hair and bright eyes greeted her at the door. "Welcome to Carnelia! Is there anything I can help you find?" Her voice was bright, and she wore a pendant of lapis lazuli around her neck.

"Yeah, I'm looking for Aspen. Is she in today?"

"Totally. I'll go get her for you. One sec." The woman whirled around, and the air filled with the smell of lavender.

It didn't take long for the shopkeeper to fetch Aspen, and Charlotte took a deep breath to calm her nerves.

"Hey," Aspen said, putting her hands on her hips. "What's up?"

"Can we talk? Outside? It's really important."

"Uh, all right." Aspen turned and shouted over her shoulder that she'd be back and then let Charlotte lead the way outside.

"Thanks for seeing me," Charlotte said once they were away from the doorway. She could think more clearly out here, away from all the stone energy.

"No problem, what's up?" Aspen cocked her head, and her nose ring flashed in the sunlight.

"Do you want to sit down?" Charlotte asked, motioning to the bench nearby.

But Aspen just shook her head. "No. I have to get back to work soon. What's this about?"

Charlotte took another deep breath and tried to steady her beating heart. "Okay, um, it's about Freddy's ring."

Aspen narrowed her eyes. "What about it?"

"You picked it up for a reason, right?" Charlotte asked. "It felt different from the other stones. It has a different energy around it. I know you can feel it."

Aspen quirked an eyebrow. "Yeah, so?"

"So, you know it's not an ordinary stone."

Aspen's eyes flicked away and followed a group of teenagers as they walked by, talking and laughing and snapping photos on their phones. She scratched at her arm and chewed her lip.

"Where are you going with this? What do you want with the stone?"

"It doesn't belong here," Charlotte said softly. "It doesn't belong to *us*, and I need to return it. And listen, I know this might sound crazy, but you were there that night at the lake, and I know you felt something. You know that we're not the only ones here, and that stone belongs to *them*."

Aspen didn't ask who "them" was. "No," Aspen said, shaking her head. "Freddy loves that ring."

"It's not safe for her to have it," Charlotte said. If the fairies found it, they would torment Freddy just like they did Loreena. She would never be safe with them lurking about. "And I don't want to take it. I want to replace it."

"It's irreplaceable," Aspen said, crossing her arms.

"Are you sure?" Charlotte reached into the tiny pocket on her backpack and pulled out the dwarven ring.

Aspen's eyes went wide when she saw it. "How did you do that? I made that ring myself. It's the only one of its kind." She reached out to grab it, but Charlotte pulled away.

"Listen to me," she said, leaning forward so that Aspen would pay attention. She lowered her voice so that the family passing by couldn't hear her. "The ring you made for Freddy is incredibly special, but she won't be safe as long as she wears it. That thing you felt at the ritual, it's involved with the stone. I need to return it to the place where it came from, or else something terrible will happen to my family. Again."

Aspen's face softened.

"Please trust me with this. Switch out the rings, and Freddy will never know." She held up the ring again for Aspen to see. The stone glittered softly in the afternoon light and the band shone brilliantly.

"It looks too big for her," Aspen said.

"It will resize itself to the first finger that wears it."

Aspen narrowed her eyes. "What magic is this?" she whispered.

"The old kind," Charlotte said softly. "Now will you help me? And if not for me, then for Freddy?"

Aspen stared long and hard at the ring in Charlotte's hand. The silence crawled by, making Charlotte's stomach go sour. She held her breath and waited.

"Okay," Aspen said, and Charlotte let out the breath in a sigh of relief. "But only because I want Freddy to be safe, and because I was there with you that night and I felt the presence around our circle. I know you've seen the other side."

"You have no idea how much this means to me," Charlotte said, "and to them."

Aspen reached for the ring in Charlotte's outstretched hand and picked it up carefully.

"Remember not to put it on. Freddy should be the only one to wear it."

"I'll trade them out tonight." Aspen slipped the ring into the pocket of her jeans. "Come back here at the same time tomorrow and I'll give you the original."

"Thank you so much." Charlotte threw her arms around Aspen in a hug.

"You're welcome," Aspen said, hugging her back. "But I've gotta get back to work, so . . ."

"Oh no," Charlotte said, reaching for her phone. Her first violin lesson was supposed to start in a few minutes. "I've got to go, but thank you so much! I'll come back tomorrow!"

Aspen shook her head and smiled, and then waved goodbye as Charlotte turned to head for Mélodie.

Charlotte hurried to Carnelia as soon as she got out of school the next day, but Aspen had customers, so she had to wait outside.

She paced back and forth in front of the shop, counting her steps and then turning and counting them again. She probably would have carved a rut into the cobblestones outside had Aspen not come out and stopped the incessant pacing.

"What are you doing?" she snapped. "You're probably scaring my customers away. Here." She reached into her pocket and pulled out a ring— *the* ring.

Charlotte could feel its trembling energy as soon as it touched the palm of her hand.

"You got it," she whispered, realizing that she hadn't known until this very moment if Aspen would follow through with it or not.

"Of course I did. Freddy takes it off every night when she showers, so I just switched them out."

"And? Did she notice a difference?"

"She mentioned this morning that her ring fits better. She seems pleased with it." Aspen gave Charlotte a small smile.

"Oh my God, Aspen. Seriously, thank you so much. This is amazing."

"I did my part," Aspen said, "now go do yours. Don't let that stone go to waste. It's special."

"It sure is," Charlotte said. "I'll take it back to where it belongs." She put the ring in her pocket just as two older women entered Carnelia.

"Gotta go," Aspen said. "I'll see you around, okay?" And with that she turned, her long skirt swishing around her, and disappeared into the rock shop.

Charlotte wasted no time. She hurried back through the Oval and up Main Street. It was almost three thirty, and it wouldn't be long before the sun started to set. She took a minute to text Art once she'd arrived at the bus stop.

Got the stone, she typed. It wasn't five minutes later that he responded.

YES!!!!! :D

She smiled and slipped the phone into her pocket. She waited anxiously at the bus stop, pacing back and forth rather than sitting on the bench. It took ten minutes for the bus to show up, and as soon as the door folded open, Charlotte sped up the stairs and threw herself into a seat as fast as possible.

The bus pulled away from the curb, hissing as the driver merged back onto Main Street.

Charlotte sat with the ring in her lap, turning it over and over in her hands as the bus wheezed out of Old Town and into the mountains. The ring was rather heavy, and Charlotte wondered how Freddy had ever gotten used to carrying it around on her finger all day. The black stone glittered in the yellow afternoon light streaming through the dirty bus window, and Charlotte smiled as she ran her thumb across the veins of blue. Carefully, she wiggled the stone and pried the metal back that held it in place. The stone fell into her hand, and she wrapped her fingers around it protectively.

Charlotte climbed off the bus at the bottom of Old Hickory Road, and she thanked the bus driver before beginning the long, uphill trek toward home. Gravel crunched under her boots as she walked, and a chilly breeze whistled through the trees overhead.

Rather than stopping at the house, Charlotte headed straight up the embankment that would lead her to the old fairy shrine. The quiet hike through the Greenwood gave her time to contemplate what she was going to do about the fifth stone. She did have that amethyst crystal at home, and maybe a vision was exactly what she needed. Maybe it could lead her to the stone somehow.

Charlotte was startled out of her thoughts when a flurry of feathered creatures flew out of the treetops to circle around her. She thought they were birds, but then she saw their arms and wide round eyes and knew they were some kind of fairy. They fluttered down and landed softly on her shoulders to hitch a ride through the Greenwood.

"Well hello," Charlotte said, reaching up to scratch one under the chin.

It had bright green feathers and a long, cat-like tail. She smiled when it started to purr. The other fairy whined in her ear, jealous probably, until she reached up and gave it a chin scratch, too. After that they were content to ride along in silence while Charlotte walked.

It had been less than a month since all this began, and yet she felt as if she had never given the Sight up. She had gone without it for all those years, scared of what she would see, when in reality the fairy world was full of beauty and gentleness just waiting to be discovered. There was the dark, of course, and malevolence that she had yet to discover, but for now this was enough, and she regretted ever turning a blind eye on such magic.

She followed the single-track trail through the trees, zipping up her jacket when it got cold in the shade. It didn't take long to find the pair of twisted trees, and the fairies on Charlotte's shoulders rearranged themselves on her back as she squished through the narrow opening between the two oaks.

Fairies were already waiting for her when she emerged on the other side. The two from her back flew off to sit in a nearby tree and watch.

"Hello, friends," Charlotte whispered to the eyes that stared out at her from the limbs and leaves. "I brought you something." She reached into her pocket, and the fairies in the trees stirred. When she held up the stone for them to see, they began to yip and howl and sing in celebration.

"Now where do you go?" Charlotte asked the stone, and held it out toward the five standing stones. It vibrated with warm energy in her hand, and she let the stone lead her like a metal detector, its vibrations becoming more powerful as she neared the place where it belonged. She placed it into the niche of the northeastern standing stone, and as soon as she did, a light drizzle began to fall. It was warm, like a summer rain, and misted over her face and hair, washing old dirt stains from the standing stones and leaving them a clean, fresh gray. "The water stone," Charlotte whispered to herself, holding out her hands to catch the rain as it fell.

Fairies flew down from the trees and scampered out from the grass to celebrate in the light rain. They hopped from stone to stone and spun each other in merry dances, and this time when they flew down to pull on Charlotte's hair, it was only to twist it into tiny, lovely braids that they tied off with grass and flowers.

❧

It was dark by the time Charlotte got home, still damp from her rainy celebration in the trees. Dad was on the phone with someone from work, and she could hear Grandma singing from the shower, so rather than chat, Charlotte went straight to her room and got changed into something warm and dry. She hoped the brownie would come to her window to tell her that he'd discovered the location of the final stone, but she had no such luck. Her window remained dark, quiet, and empty all the way up until she turned off her light and crawled into bed.

She stared at the amethyst on her bedside table as she lay awake, and decided to slip it under her pillow in the hopes that it would give her some clue as to where the fifth stone was. It took a bit of maneuvering to get comfortable, but once she settled into a good spot, Charlotte closed her eyes and started repeating the same sentence over and over.

"Show me the stone, show me the stone, show me the stone." And it was with those words on her lips that she fell asleep and started to dream.

The forest surrounded her. It was dark, and the sky was yellow-orange. Jack-o'-lanterns flickered in the corner of her vision, casting dancing shadows on the trees. Children ran through the forest, wearing white sheets with holes for eyes. Charlotte tried to get their attention, tried to tell them to get out of the forest, but they didn't hear her. One ran right past Charlotte, and she took off after it, chasing the child through the shadows. It darted behind a massive oak, and as Charlotte peeked around the tree trunk, she came face-to-face with glowing eyes in a goat's face. She pulled back as the creature lifted its head and opened its gaping mouth. Smoke billowed from its nostrils and fire burned in its eyes, and Charlotte screamed.

She woke herself up whimpering in bed, her forehead and pillowcase drenched in sweat. Charlotte sat up and put a hand to her chest, feeling her heart beating wildly beneath her ribs. Her lungs heaved for fresh air, but all she could remember was the smell of the forest and the leaves and the scent of smoke when the creature rose up before her. No, not just a creature. She knew its name now, thanks to Art's fairy book—the phooka.

She shivered at the thought of it and then turned and knocked the amethyst crystal out from under her pillow. She reached into her bedside table and pulled out the notebook she'd been recording her dreams in, then jotted down everything she could remember: Night, fire, pumpkins, children, ghosts, the phooka. She closed the journal and stuck it back in the drawer before flipping her pillow over to the dry side and flopping back down. She didn't know exactly what the dream meant, but deep down, in a place where she tried to hide her darkest thoughts, she knew it was a premonition. And she knew, despite all she'd done to avoid it, that she would meet the phooka again.

CHAPTER TWENTY-SEVEN

Days passed by in a blur. When Charlotte wasn't at home or teaching violin lessons, she was in her bedroom surrounded by candles, trying to meditate over her amethyst crystal. She didn't know what she was doing, but videos online had given her enough guidance to at least get started. She even called Freddy one night to talk to Aspen and had asked crystal and divination questions for an hour before Aspen finally had to go.

Charlotte would light her candles, clear her mind, and focus on one question: *Where is the stone?* At first nothing happened, and Charlotte got so fed up with the voodoo-weirdness of it all that she nearly tossed her amethyst in the trash. But then, when she least expected it to, the divination worked.

She was on her back on the floor, the amethyst crystal balancing on her forehead, when it happened. The thoughts that came to her moved slowly, spreading out like ink through water. She closed her eyes and let out a long breath as the vision came over her. It felt like being on the verge of sleep: awake but barely, with only a hazy idea of what was going on around her.

She saw pumpkins, so many pumpkins. Some had faces and stared at her with firelight in their eyes. Others were still on the vine, their skin pale and not yet ripe for the picking. No matter which way she turned, pumpkins followed, their eerie carved faces laughing at her shortcomings.

After the pumpkin vision passed, Charlotte rolled over and scribbled everything down in her journal. She let out a long sigh that ruffled the curls falling in her face.

It was the end of October, so Mapleton was in the middle of pumpkin season. Pumpkins lined the streets in Old Town, stared out from shop windows, and overflowed from big bins outside the supermarkets. She used to love going to the farm on the edge of town to pick a pumpkin and then go home and carve it for Halloween, but it had been years since she'd visited the patch. Was that what her vision meant? That she should go pick a pumpkin? It seemed unlikely.

"Pumpkins," she whispered. "Stupid pumpkins."

❧

By the time Sunday rolled around, Charlotte was frustrated and just about ready to fling her amethyst through the open bedroom window. She sat on her bed with her laptop open, frowning at the moon cycle on the screen. According to the search engine, the new moon would rise that night, meaning she'd run out of time.

A crisp autumn breeze blew through the window, shuffling the pages of the open book on Charlotte's desk. It was Art's book, and she pulled her phone out of her pocket when she thought of him.

Hey, she typed. *Trying to figure out where the final stone is, but I'm stuck. Wanna help?* She hit send and tossed the phone down on the bedspread, trying not to overthink it.

Art replied quickly. *Sure. Your house?*

Charlotte smiled. Dad was at work and Grandma was watching a show in the living room, so she headed out to ask if it would be okay to have him over.

"Grandma?" she asked, leaning over the back of the couch.

"Yeah?" Grandma sipped her tea and kept her eyes glued to the screen.

"Is it okay if Art comes over to hang out?"

"Sure, sure," Grandma said, waving a hand casually. "Just clean up the kitchen first."

Charlotte texted Art back to let him know he could come over and then tried to ignore the butterflies in her stomach while she hurriedly washed the dishes and wiped down the countertops. When she was done, she went into her bedroom to put away the clean clothes that were folded on the end of her bed and pick up the dirty clothes she'd left on the floor the night before. When all was tidy, she headed into the bathroom to finger-comb her hair and wash her face. She hadn't really been expecting him to say yes, and now she found herself nervously pacing the floor in her room, trying to spot anything out of place that she needed to clean up before he arrived. She nearly had a heart attack when there was a knock on the front door.

"He's here," Grandma called.

Charlotte took a deep breath before she walked down the hallway and pulled the door open.

Art stood there in an oversized sweater, black jeans, and frayed black tennis shoes that looked ready to fall apart.

"Hey," he said, flashing Charlotte a smile.

"Hi." She smiled and looked down at her feet, realizing that she'd forgotten to change out of her fluffy duck socks.

Art looked down at the same time and laughed. "Where'd you get those?"

"Grandma gave them to me for Christmas last year," Charlotte said, opening the door wide for Art to step through.

"Your grandma is awesome," he said.

"Damn right," Grandma called from the living room, making them laugh.

"We're going to my room," Charlotte told Grandma, and then walked Art down the hallway and into her bedroom. She pushed the door halfway closed, feeling too awkward to shut it all the way.

Art looked so dark in contrast to everything else in her room. She had white curtains and a pastel bedspread, and everything he wore was dark blue and green and black. His curls looked slightly damp, as if he'd taken a shower right before leaving the house, and they twirled around his ears and eyes, tempting Charlotte to reach out and touch them.

"You've been reading my books," he said, running a finger over the fluttering pages of the book that sat open on her desk.

"Yeah," she said, relieved to have something to talk about. "I've been trying to figure out where the fifth stone is, and I hoped to find some sort of clue in the books, but I'm not having any luck."

"You have no idea where it is?" he asked, glancing up at her with concerned eyes. They were green and lined with long, dark lashes, and they almost made Charlotte forget what she was about to say.

"Um, unfortunately not. The other four just kind of presented themselves to me. And I've been meditating and—"

"You meditate?" Art asked, his brows shooting up.

"Uh, yeah. I'm new to it."

"My mom meditates, too, but it's hard for me. My mind is always moving a million miles an hour." He smiled and leafed through a few pages of the book. "I can help you go through these," he said, putting his hand on the stack of fairy books at the edge of the desk. "I know it's a lot to read on your own. Just tell me what you're looking for, and I'll try to help."

That was how they ended up cross-legged on the floor with books spread out all around them. They checked the glossary and index of each book for any mention of *stone* or *shrine*, because Charlotte had no idea what else to look for. They talked while they read, and every so often Art would show Charlotte a picture he liked or wanted to do a charcoal study of when he got the books back. When he turned a book around and held up a photo of the phooka, Charlotte froze.

"Are you okay?" he asked.

She thought about lying and telling him she was just fine, but she was tired of keeping this secret to herself.

"I've seen that before," she said quietly, as if speaking the words would summon the creature into her bedroom.

"No way," Art said, flipping the book back around to look at the picture. It was the same photo Charlotte came across in her own reading, of a shaggy black goat with the body of a man and twisted horns with gleaming points. Its eyes were what struck her, glowing out from the page as if the phooka could see into her soul.

"The phooka," Art read aloud, "is a mischievous goblin known to take on different forms. It may bestow blessings or ill will, and has been known to harm or mislead weary travelers." He cleared his throat and closed the book. "When did you see it?"

"On Halloween eight years ago." She flipped the pages of the book in her lap but didn't pay attention to the words on the page. "I was trick-or-treating when I saw it."

"Oh my God," Art breathed. "What did it do?"

She shrugged. "It seemed curious, but it didn't try to hurt me. It was *huge*, though. Towered over my dad when it stood up." Goose bumps rose up along her arms as she thought of that night, and of the creature in the underbrush with strings of what looked like flesh dribbling from its jaws.

"That would have scared me shitless," he said, shaking his head, and something about the unwavering truth in his voice made Charlotte laugh. He looked up at her and smiled. "What?"

"It scared me shitless, too," she said. "I've been terrified of that thing for *eight* years!" It seemed ridiculous at the moment, and Charlotte laughed harder at herself.

The laughter was contagious, and soon Art was holding his stomach and had tears running from the corners of his eyes from laughing so hard. By the time they both stopped, they had collapsed back against the bed and had lost all focus on their reading project.

"You're the best," Charlotte whispered, and in reply Art slid his hand across the floor and pressed his fingertips against hers. Charlotte's stomach went warm.

"Knock, knock," Grandma said at the door before pushing it open. "Want anything from the store? I have to go pick up some things for dinner."

Art shook his head. "No, but thank you."

"Can you pick up some more green tea?" Charlotte asked. "I think we're almost out."

Grandma held up a scrap of paper. "It's already on my list." She slipped it into her pocket and pointed at Charlotte and Art. "You two be good. I'll be back soon." And then she winked. She actually *winked.* Charlotte thought she may shrivel up from the embarrassment of it as Grandma pulled the door closed.

"I wish my grandma was like that," Art mused. "She mostly just tells me to cut my hair and tuck in my shirt."

Charlotte smiled to herself and then glanced up at Art from the corner of her eye. "I think your hair looks nice," she said quietly, and it came out in a more sultry voice than she'd anticipated.

Art must have noticed, because the smile that spread across his face was slow and smooth. "I like yours, too," he said, and then Charlotte held her breath as he reached up and caught one of her curls between his fingers. He twirled it around and around, and with each twirl he leaned a bit closer. When his face was only a few inches from hers, Art reached his hand around to cup the back of Charlotte's neck and pull her in for a kiss.

Her back went stiff, and nervous thoughts about being a bad kisser and doing it wrong flooded her mind. But then Art scooted closer and his warmth surrounded her, and she let herself melt into his kiss, all worries forgotten. She reached up with one hand to play with his curls.

"Come here," he whispered, leaning back against the bed and tugging her closer.

She climbed on top of him, unsure and awkward, but when he placed his hands on her hips, his fingertips playing around the hem of her shirt, she relaxed into his touch. For a moment she admired him, his hair curling around his ears and his green eyes bright and alive. Then she lowered her face to his and, in a moment of bravery, caught his bottom lip between her teeth and tugged.

Art let out a low sigh, and his fingertips curled into the skin of her low back. His breathing quickened as he reached up to pull her closer, his other hand still lingering on her skin. She kissed him harder, allowing herself to succumb to the brush of his tongue against her lips and the warmth of his breath across her face. Her heart raced, beating hard against her ribs as her breath grew quick and shallow. Art's hand trailed up and down her back, his nails lightly scratching each time she deepened their kiss.

She didn't know how long they'd been kissing by the time she had to pull away and catch her breath. She smiled down at him, her hair falling like a veil between the outside world and their private sanctuary, and knew when he smiled at her that she was as good as gone. She'd never been in love before but imagined this was how it started.

Art reached up and brushed his thumb gently across her eyebrows, her cheeks, her lips, and then pulled her in for one final kiss, his lips barely brushing hers in the sweetest of sensations. "You are so beautiful," he said as Charlotte pulled back and stood up.

"Thank you," she said shyly, pushing a strand of hair behind her ear as he grinned up at her from his spot on the floor.

His phone went off then, and he pulled it out of his pocket. "It's my mom," he said, silencing it with his thumb. "She needs me to babysit Tomas today. But I'm glad that I got to see you for a while, at least."

"Me too." Charlotte offered him a hand and pulled him to his feet. "And thanks for helping me out. I know we didn't get very far, but I appreciate it."

"You are very welcome, Charlotte Barclay."

His use of her full name gave her butterflies, and they still weren't gone by the time she'd walked him down the hallway to the front door. She let him pull her in for one last kiss on the porch.

"Be careful tonight," she told him as he pulled away.

"What do you mean?" he asked.

"It's the new moon. Remember what the dryad said?"

He gave Charlotte a wicked smile. "I thought you said she would take a *loved* one if you didn't bring the stones back on time?"

The realization of this made Charlotte's cheeks heat up, and they were still warm as Art laughed and bounded down the porch steps to the car in the driveway.

"I'll be safe and sound," he said as he opened the door, "and I'll see you tomorrow." He gave her one more smile before sliding into the driver's seat and starting the engine.

Charlotte lingered in the doorway as he turned the car around, and then watched until the taillights disappeared into the trees.

She received a text message from him about half an hour later, letting her know he was home and looking forward to seeing her at school the next day. Charlotte smiled to herself, but despite everything, a nervousness had taken hold in her belly and was refusing to ease up. Even when Dad and Grandma arrived home and were ready to relax for the rest of the evening, Charlotte continued to feel unsettled. She tried not to let her family see her worry, because she didn't want them concerning themselves over something that may not even happen. The dryad had been in such good spirits the last time Charlotte had seen her, and perhaps she would be merciful. But even so, Charlotte made sure to double-check that all the doors and windows were locked before she went to bed, and then she stayed up until the clock struck twelve and signaled the start of a new day.

Charlotte slipped out of bed and crept down the hall to Dad's room. She could hear him snoring inside and let out a sigh of relief. Then she tiptoed to the other side of the house to Grandma's room. She twisted the doorknob slowly, and when the door was open just a crack, she peered inside. Grandma was in bed, her silver hair in a long braid on the pillow next to her, sleeping soundly.

With a small smile, Charlotte pulled the door closed and headed back to her room. She sent Melanie a text message, wanting to confirm that she wasn't locked away in Lyra somewhere, and was unsurprised when she texted back—she'd always been a night owl.

You dressing up tomorrow? Charlotte asked.

Of course – it's Halloween! But I bet you won't, lame-o ;)

Charlotte sighed and turned off her phone before settling back into the pillows.

"One more stone," she whispered to herself, "and this will all be over."

CHAPTER TWENTY-EIGHT

Charlotte woke in the morning with a stretch and a smile. The new moon had passed, her family was safe, and by the smell in the air, Grandma was making pancakes. Charlotte jumped out of bed, got dressed, and headed into the kitchen.

"Happy Halloween!" Grandma said, and Charlotte laughed when she saw her. Grandma wore a pumpkin sweater, a long black skirt, and a pointed hat. She even had ghost earrings dangling from her lobes.

"You look great," Charlotte said, sliding into her spot at the table.

"You're not dressing up this year?" Grandma asked casually, as if she didn't ask every year and get the same answer every year.

Charlotte opened her mouth to say no, but then she paused. "Hang on." She went into her room to rifle through her closet. "Bingo," she said when she found the old, sparkly fairy wings she'd worn for a silly play in middle school. She pulled the straps on over her arms and checked herself out in the mirror. The wings glittered and made Charlotte feel like a fairy princess.

Grandma clapped when Charlotte walked back into the kitchen.

"Happy now?" Charlotte asked, and Grandma nodded.

"Very. Now sit down. Pancakes are ready."

Half an hour later Charlotte had finished eating and was out the door, headed for school. She felt a bit silly in her wings until she made it into town, where people of all ages were walking around in costumes and Halloween sweaters. There was always a costume contest at school on

Halloween, so Charlotte wasn't surprised to see her classmates done up in extravagant makeup and costumes. Her wings paled in comparison, which was perfectly fine. She could blend in and still have fun at the same time.

Charlotte headed straight for the stairs where Art had waited for her last week, but he wasn't there when she arrived. She pulled out her phone and texted Art to let him know she was there, and then she waited until the first bell rang. She'd be late to math class if she waited any longer, so she headed inside and hoped to see him at lunch.

As it turned out, he wasn't at lunch either. Charlotte ate with Melanie and Marco on the patio outside the cafeteria, and she kept looking around but didn't see him anywhere.

"He must not be here today," Melanie said. "Maybe he's sick?" She had fluffy cat ears on and whiskers painted on her face.

"Maybe," Charlotte said, picking at her sandwich with disinterest. She wanted Melanie to be right, but something about it felt wrong. If Art was sick, wouldn't he have texted her to let her know? It was already the afternoon, so he wouldn't still be sleeping in, would he? She tried to ignore the bad feeling in her stomach. *He's fine.*

The last few classes of the day dragged on forever. Charlotte stared at the clock, rapping her nails across the desk and shaking her foot anxiously. *Could it be?* she wondered, but kept pushing that possibility away. She didn't usually look at her phone while in class, but today she kept it hidden inside her binder so she could peek at the screen without the teacher seeing. But each time she looked, the screen came up blank. By the end of the day, Art still hadn't texted her back.

Charlotte bolted out of the classroom when the final bell rang and pulled out her phone before she even got outside. She found Art's name in her contact book and hit the call button.

The phone rang, and it rang, and it rang. Finally, the voicemail picked up and Art's voice came on the line.

"Hey, you've reached Art. Leave a message."

Charlotte hung up.

"Hey!" Melanie yelled, coming up behind Charlotte and tugging on one of her fairy wings. "Want to go get coffee?" she asked, her brown eyes shining and her cheeks rosy from the cold.

"I'd love to," Charlotte said, and meant it, "but there's something I have to do first. I'll text you, okay?"

"Okay." Melanie pulled Charlotte in for a hug. "I'm glad we're back together again."

"Me, too," Charlotte said, and then watched Melanie run across the parking lot to her car. After she disappeared into the crowd, Charlotte turned away and headed quickly down Main Street. She knew where Art's neighborhood was, but only had a vague recollection of which house was his.

Charlotte walked under the same trees that she and Art had walked under only weeks before, but now most of the leaves were on the ground and the branches overhead looked naked and gray. A chilling breeze blew the leaves across the sidewalk, and the eerie sound caused goose bumps to rise on Charlotte's arms. Everywhere she looked there were kids in costumes and pumpkins with frightening faces watching her from front porches. She shivered in her sweater and wrapped her arms around herself as she walked.

She'd been worried at first that she wouldn't be able to find Art's house, but it ended up being easier than she thought it would be. Up ahead, at the end of the street, was a police car sitting outside a lovely two-story home— Art's home. Seeing the empty cop car brought back Charlotte's memories of the day the officer came to her house to ask questions about Mom. Her stomach twisted at the thought.

Charlotte walked closer to the house, checking the windows for anyone who might be watching outside. She could see into the front window, and Mrs. Nolan sat in the living room with the same yellow-haired officer that had come to the house to investigate Mom's disappearance.

Charlotte didn't need any more proof.

She turned and ran back the way she'd come.

✳

Charlotte was an anxious mess on the bus. She wished the driver would go faster, but he was being especially cautious today, probably because of all the crazy kids running around wearing sheets over their heads. Charlotte's leg bounced, and she tapped her fingernails against her chin, her other hand curled into a fist in her lap.

Charlotte wasted no time once she stepped off the bus. She hoisted her violin case high and ran the whole way up the long gravel road to the house. She yanked off her backpack and slung it onto the front porch, not even taking the time to step inside before she ran into the trees. She struggled up the embankment behind the house, breathing hard as she slipped in the leaves and soft dirt. Her heart pounded as she sprinted down the old game trail, her sparkly fairy wings glittering in the gray light. She saw the tangled trees up ahead and slowed down to squish her way through the narrow space between the two trunks.

The fairy shrine stood tall and stoic in the pale light. The sky overhead was streaked with clouds that looked like they could dump snow at any moment. A few feathered fairies sat along the tops of the standing stones, their wings flapping slowly behind them as they watched Charlotte with wide, curious eyes.

She knelt in the center of the stones and pulled out her violin. The polished wood shone as she lifted the violin and slipped it into the space between her shoulder and her chin. She turned to face the light, and as she did, the glitter on her fairy wings sent diamonds of fractured sunlight dancing across the trees and forest floor. She tightened up her bow, drew it across the strings, and began to play. Rosin lifted from her bow each time it sawed across the strings, and this time her fingers played the dryad's song as if she'd known the notes her whole life.

Charlotte closed her eyes, letting the music swell around her until all she heard was the sound of the bow across the strings and the beating of her heart, rushing, rushing, rushing. Her chest rose and fell as she breathed in the smell of the forest and the chill in the air, and her body began to tingle as the human realm fell away around her, piece by piece, as if being washed away in a summer rain. She didn't even need to open her eyes to know she no longer stood in the Greenwood. The smell in the air was more pungent, more exotic. The air across her skin was warm and damp.

Charlotte opened her eyes. She hid her violin away in the deep grass at the base of the nearest standing stone, and then she ran.

The vines and plants underfoot seemed to make way for Charlotte as she pushed through the forest and out into the open air. The tall grass shone like waves of gold under the sun, but Charlotte didn't pause to run her hands through it like she'd done before. Today she was anything but tantalized.

She sprinted down the long path, across the creaking wood bridge, and through the village.

The same guards stood outside the dryad's tree when Charlotte arrived. They didn't blush or take their hats off for her like they did for the dryad.

"What are you doing here, Keeper?" the older one asked. He eyed her fairy wings curiously.

"Please let me in," Charlotte said, gasping for breath. "It's important."

The four guards glanced at each other and then, without saying a word, they pushed open the doors and granted Charlotte access to the Great Tree.

Charlotte stormed inside as the doors closed behind her. She expected to find the dryad waiting for her, but the throne of branches and leaves was empty. She looked around the room and was startled, and somehow saddened, to see that the flowers the dryad had picked when she was last here had died and withered in their vase. The sight of them gave Charlotte a sick feeling in her stomach.

"Hello?" Charlotte called out, but no one called back. Birds didn't sing or flutter among the foliage, and the silence was unnerving. She'd come here to give the dryad a piece of her mind, but her anger had quickly given way to worry. She had to find Art and make sure he was okay.

Without really knowing where she was going, Charlotte set off into the jungle-like foliage, pushing leaves and flowers out of her face as she hurried along.

"Mom!" she called out, without expecting a response. "Art!" She let her instincts guide her as she half-jogged through the greenery. She somehow found where she was going, and she felt a prick of pride at being able to find her way around. She quickly pulled back the veil of vines and stepped through.

The glade on the other side was the exact same as the last time she'd been there, except for one addition.

Now Art lay asleep on the bed of moss, his green eyes closed and a sprinkling of sleeping dust glittering on his dark hair and cheekbones. Mom was asleep beside him, her pink lips smiling and her golden hair spilling out onto the moss around her. It looked longer than Charlotte remembered.

Charlotte knelt to wrap her arms around Mom's shoulders. She buried her face in Mom's hair, which smelled of flowers and sunshine. This time she didn't cry—she couldn't afford to waste any time.

She went to Art next. He looked so peaceful in sleep, and Charlotte couldn't help but reach out and trail her fingertips across his cheek.

"I'm so sorry," she whispered. "I never should have involved you in any of this." She bent forward and placed a gentle kiss on his cheek, and in response he stirred in his sleep. Charlotte sat back, hoping his eyes would flutter open, but he just yawned and turned over, lost in dreams.

A glimmer caught Charlotte's eye, and when she looked closer, she saw that it was the silver charm on Art's bracelet catching the light. She reached out and slipped it off his wrist, closing the bracelet into her fist as she stood.

Perhaps it was unkind of her to take something so dear to him, but she wanted some part of him to hold onto, if only to remind herself that something precious depended on her. And now she needed to get back and find that last fairy stone, or else Mom and Art were never going to come home.

Charlotte rushed back the way she'd come, and rather than waiting for the oak men to open the massive golden doors, she threw all her weight into them and sent the oak men scattering as the doors groaned open.

"What in Lyra's name . . . ?" one of them asked, replacing the hat that had fallen from his head.

"Do you know where the dryad is?" Charlotte asked, her feet itching to run.

"She's not here," the tallest guard said.

"She's in your world," said another, and received dirty looks from his comrades. "What?" he whispered. "She's the Keeper—she should know."

"Thank you," Charlotte said. "If you see her, tell her I need to talk to her."

"Yes, miss," said the short guard, giving her a nod.

Charlotte sprinted down the path toward the forest, the tall grass that lined the way reaching out to touch her as she ran by. The standing stones rose up out of the greenery as she stepped into the forest, and she hurriedly grabbed her violin from its hiding spot and shoved it under her chin.

She drew her bow across the strings. The song of the dryad rang out from under her fingertips, and she squeezed her eyes closed as she played. This song felt like second nature to her now, something that she could play by heart but could probably never write down.

Unlike the other times she used the portal, there was no sensation of dizziness or spinning out of control. When Charlotte opened her eyes, she was back in the Greenwood. The only hint that she'd even been to the fairy realm was the smell that clung to her hair and clothes but would soon fade away in the cold autumn air.

Her violin case still sat in the dirt and leaves where she'd left it, and she rushed forward to put her violin away. But as she knelt there, a shadow fell over her and goose bumps rose up along her arms. Her fingers froze on the violin case, and slowly, she turned around.

What stood behind her was taller than any man, with twisted horns sprouting from his shaggy head. His eyes glowed in the dim light, and his nostrils flared wide as he exhaled a long stream of warmth across her face.

She knew all along that he would return to haunt her, but she could never have prepared herself for this.

"Phooka," she whispered.

CHAPTER TWENTY-NINE

The phooka stood hunched over her, his arms dangling by his sides. His goat head was covered in thick, black hair with a beard that hung down to his chest. The phooka had a man's body, but with gray skin covered in a thin layer of hair. He wore dirty brown trousers and nothing else—his feet were bare, and his toes curled into the soft forest floor.

Charlotte couldn't move or speak and found it hard to breathe. This was the creature that had haunted her dreams since she was a little girl, and now here he stood before her, larger and more intimidating than she had ever expected. He must have been at least seven feet tall, and the twisted horns added another foot to that. She felt small and vulnerable in his presence, and part of her wanted to cower away and hide her face in her hands until he went away. But by the looks of it, the phooka wasn't going anywhere.

His dimly glowing eyes stared right into hers, and neither one of them moved or said a word. The trees around the phooka started to move, and Charlotte let out a small whimper when goblins crept from the foliage. They had snapping jaws and sharp claws and leathery wings like bats. They hovered around the phooka like small fish around a great white shark, waiting for the leftovers after a kill. They bared their teeth and watched Charlotte with wide, unblinking eyes, their maniacal laughter bouncing off the trees in an eerie cacophony.

The phooka lifted one gray hand and the laughter stopped. Charlotte's heart beat hard against her ribs as she stared up at him, wondering if this was the end. Had the dryad sent him to kill her? Were the kidnappings not punishment enough?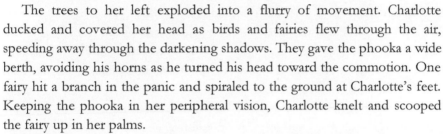

The phooka flicked his ears, moved his jaw, and then spoke.

"Shrine Keeper," he said in a deep, smooth voice. He reached one hand toward her.

Charlotte's eyes widened, and her breath came out as a croak.

The trees to her left exploded into a flurry of movement. Charlotte ducked and covered her head as birds and fairies flew through the air, speeding away through the darkening shadows. They gave the phooka a wide berth, avoiding his horns as he turned his head toward the commotion. One fairy hit a branch in the panic and spiraled to the ground at Charlotte's feet. Keeping the phooka in her peripheral vision, Charlotte knelt and scooped the fairy up in her palms.

"Are you okay?" she asked, and the fairy blinked up at her a few times before recognition crossed his face.

"Keeper," he cried, "you must go, quick!"

"Go where? What's happening?"

"They're taking our trees," he said, and tears began to stream down his cheeks. "Please, you must stop them." The fairy was down on his knees in Charlotte's palms, begging her between sobs.

"Okay, okay. I'll go. You just get out of here. Go somewhere safe." She lifted her hands, and the fairy flew away.

Charlotte turned and ran in the direction of the commotion, leaving her violin, and the phooka, behind. The goblin minions followed her, howling through the treetops overhead.

Leave me alone, leave me alone.

She sprinted through the trees as quickly as she could without twisting an ankle or running into any low-hanging branches. She had to duck and swerve to avoid the fairies, birds, and deer that ran in the opposite direction. She glanced over her shoulder, once, just to see if the phooka was following, but the goblin was nowhere to be found.

When she turned back around, a panicked deer was headed straight toward her, and she didn't jump out of the way fast enough. The doe clipped Charlotte's shoulder, throwing her to the ground, and she landed so hard on her back that it knocked the wind out of her lungs. She lay in the dirt and leaves, mouth wide open as she gasped and gasped for air but couldn't catch her breath. She had enough wits to drag herself away from the game trail she'd been running down, and then she was safe to crouch in the leaves until air finally returned to her lungs. Overhead, goblins still laughed in the trees and threw acorns at the panicked creatures fleeing past.

Charlotte turned, and not one hundred yards away was an eight-foot fence surrounding a section of the forest where machinery growled and chainsaws whirred.

"No," Charlotte whispered, using a tree to steady herself as she stood and stared at the destruction. She eased herself closer, using the trees to help her along, until she could clearly see the trucks driving back and forth and the men in hard hats using machinery to pull tree stumps out of the ground from their roots. And amidst it all was a tiny hedgehog pixie, crying beside a log that had been smashed to pieces.

"Oh, no," Charlotte whispered, her stomach falling to her feet. She gathered up enough energy to push off the tree and limp toward the fence, her arm outstretched. A truck screeched by, its tires so close to crushing the fairy that Charlotte screamed out, "Butternut!"

The pixie turned, startled, and then ran toward the fence when she recognized Charlotte. "Keeper!" the tiny pixie screamed, clinging to the chain-link fence.

Charlotte fell to her knees, putting her hand up to the fence so that Butternut could hold her finger.

"My family," Butternut cried, pointing one trembling paw at the remnants of her home. She tried to say something else, but it came out as a sob.

"I'm going to get you out of there," Charlotte said, trying hard not to cry. She looked up, but the fence was much too tall to climb. Maybe she could dig a hole under it that Butternut could escape through.

Just as she started to dig, the fence rattled overhead. Charlotte looked up and gasped. The phooka loomed over her, his gray fingers wrapped around the chain-link. He let out a mighty bellow, the muscles in his chest and arms bulged, and he ripped a hole right through the fence. With a huff, he glanced down at Charlotte and then climbed through the hole. Charlotte followed him and scooped tiny Butternut up off the ground just as a pair of headlights swung across her. The phooka stood beside her—watching, waiting.

The truck pulled to a stop, and the passenger door opened. Charlotte held up a hand to shield her eyes from the light, and only when the figure stepped closer did she recognize who it was.

"Mr. Nolan," she said, wondering why he was here instead of with his family. He had to have known Art was missing, so why was he at the job site instead of at home?

"Charlotte?" he asked, stepping in front of the headlights so that they illuminated him from behind, casting him into shadow with a hazy yellow silhouette. "What are you doing here? This is private property."

"You have to stop," Charlotte said.

Mr. Nolan let out one small, humorless laugh. "What?"

"These trees belong to the Greenwood. You have no business tearing them down."

"Actually, tearing them down *is* my business."

Some of the workers laughed in the dark. A guttural sound rumbled in the phooka's chest.

"I suggest you head home now," Mr. Nolan said.

"Art's life might depend on it," Charlotte said without thinking.

Mr. Nolan straightened. "Excuse me?" he said in a voice that was no longer friendly. "What do you know about Art?"

"I know that he's gone," Charlotte said, starting to wonder if this was a bad idea. "And I know that this forest is part of the reason, which is why—"

Before she could finish her sentence, Mr. Nolan lunged forward and grabbed her by the front of her jacket. "What do you know?" he asked, louder this time. Around them, the men stirred.

"N-Nothing," Charlotte said, trying to pull away from Mr. Nolan's grip.

"Tell me!" he screamed, shaking her hard enough that Butternut almost fell to the ground.

Before Charlotte could say another word, the phooka ripped Mr. Nolan's hands away and threw him hard enough that he flew a few feet before hitting the ground. He towered over Mr. Nolan and roared, but Charlotte was the only one who heard the sound.

"What the hell?" Mr. Nolan whispered, still lying in the dirt. Then he pointed one trembling finger at Charlotte. "Grab her!"

His men looked at each other, hesitant and confused.

"She knows where my son is!" Mr. Nolan yelled. "Don't let her get away!"

Charlotte ran. She bolted back to the hole in the fence and scrambled through, barely escaping the hands of a man who stood close by. She heard him start to climb through after her, but then the fence rattled, and she heard a loud *thud* as the man hit the ground. She risked one glance over her shoulder and saw the phooka standing over the man, his head tipped back as he laughed. Fear electrified Charlotte's body, forcing her legs to move faster.

Charlotte cradled Butternut against her chest as she ran, feeling the pixie's tiny paws against her collarbone. Tree limbs reached out to strike her across the face and tangle in her hair and clothing, and the more she had to fight, the slower she could run, and it was only a matter of time before more men were chasing her through the trees. Their feet, heavy in boots, pounded behind her.

She tried to push herself harder, but her lungs were already on fire and her heart felt like it was ready to burst through her chest. She didn't know how long she could keep this up. The men behind her didn't sound any better off, but they pursued her still.

There was a slight clearing up ahead, and Charlotte told herself to just make it that far.

You can do this, you can do this, she repeated to herself, forcing her legs to continue moving. The clearing was so close, just up ahead. She gritted her teeth against the pain and pushed a bit harder, straining to reach it.

Something suddenly gripped her beneath the arms, closing over her shoulders in an unshakable grip.

They've got me, Charlotte thought, losing her momentum. But then she was lifted, impossibly, off the ground. She flailed and screamed, kicking her legs as she was lifted higher and higher into the air. Butternut climbed into the collar of her jacket and clung to the straps of her tank top, huddled against her chest. Charlotte twisted, finally getting a look at the creature that had lifted her off the ground.

It looked like an eagle with sooty-black feathers, but it was bigger than any bird Charlotte had ever seen. At first, she wondered what this mutant bird was, but then it turned its head and she saw its glowing eyes.

Phooka had returned.

CHAPTER THIRTY

He carried her over the treetops, the powerful downstrokes of his wings causing the air to gust around Charlotte, tangling her hair and tossing it in her eyes. Butternut was safe inside her jacket, so her hands were free to cling to the phooka's mighty legs. She held on as tight as she could, trying not to look down at her feet dangling above the treetops. *Don't panic, don't panic,* she repeated to herself, trying to hold back the terrified tears that threatened to course down her cheeks.

She could hear the men in the Greenwood yelling to one another, trying to figure out where she went. She remembered what the brownie had said that first day she found him sweeping the porch—*one must believe in magic to see the things that magic touches.*

Charlotte tried to distract herself from her fear by looking out over the trees and watching the little black birds that flew alongside them. The sunset painted the horizon with strokes of red and orange, completely uninterrupted by buildings or trees or telephone wires. Goose bumps rose across her skin as they flew toward the horizon, and it felt like those watercolors may swallow her up and wrap her in the sun's warmth.

Before they could reach the light, the phooka began a slow, steady downward spiral. The trees rose up toward them, and Charlotte closed her eyes, thinking they were going to crash. She kicked her legs, panic overtaking her body as they spiraled closer and closer to the ground. The phooka tightened his grip on her arms, and one of his long talons punctured a hole in her jacket. She bit down on her lip and was thankful it had been the fabric and not her skin that tore open.

The phooka flapped his wings as they neared the ground, coming to hover just below the trees.

"Don't let go," Charlotte said, afraid she was still far too high off the ground.

The phooka lowered her a bit more and then dropped her. She let out a small cry and landed with an *oof* in the dirt and leaves. Butternut scrambled around inside Charlotte's coat and then poked her head out of the collar.

"Where are we?" she asked quietly as Charlotte got to her feet and looked around.

"The shrine," Charlotte said, brushing herself off. The phooka had dropped them right in the middle of the five standing stones.

Fairy creatures and forest animals had sought out refuge at the shrine, and some of them came forward when Charlotte arrived. Fairies landed on her shoulders and cried small tears into her hair. A fawn approached to nuzzle Charlotte's legs.

An old brownie, her back bent with age, held her arms up toward Charlotte. "Hand me the little one," she said softly, and Charlotte removed Butternut very carefully from her jacket and handed her over. The old brownie cradled Butternut against her chest and looked up at Charlotte with a frown. "I saw what happened to her family," she whispered, brushing gentle fingers over Butternut's head and eyes. "The poor dear is an orphan now."

Charlotte's throat tightened up and she fought back tears. She recalled Fiddleleaf's floppy cap and the gentle touch of Blue's paws as she held Charlotte's fingers. And Flora—tiny, curious Flora. Now they were all gone, and Butternut would grow up without them. A rogue tear slipped down Charlotte's cheek, and she bit her lip to keep from crying.

A gust of wind blasted Charlotte from behind, and she turned just in time to see the phooka land amongst the standing stones. He spread his great wings and shook his mighty head, and feathers floated down as he shivered and shifted back into his original form. Those glowing eyes stared out from his goat head, their gaze locked directly on Charlotte. The other fairies and forest creatures parted to make way for the phooka as he came forward. Charlotte wanted nothing more than to run screaming from him, but she held her ground.

He pointed one long, gray finger at Charlotte. "I know what you seek."

He exhaled a long breath, and his inky black nostrils fluttered.

"You know where the fifth stone is?" Charlotte asked, finding her voice. "Where?"

"It waits for you not far from here," the phooka said, turning his shaggy head and pointing toward the sky. He looked back to her, his eyes glowing in the deepening dark. "I will take you there."

Charlotte took a step back. She wanted nothing to do with the phooka. She didn't want to see him, she didn't want to talk to him, and she certainly didn't want to go anywhere with him. But how else was she supposed to find the stone? All around her were fairies in tears and animals trembling with wide, frightened eyes. They all looked at her, waiting for her response, waiting to discover whether their Shrine Keeper would abandon them again.

Charlotte took a deep breath and curled her fingers into fists.

"Can we go now?" she asked, and the phooka's lips pulled back in a smile.

He knelt on all fours, and Charlotte stepped forward. She reached out one hand to touch his gray skin, and he watched over his shoulder with glowing eyes. She had to do this—there was no other way. So, with a deep breath, she steeled herself and jumped up onto his back. His horns were tall and sharp and curled around her, and she was careful not to impale herself on them as she got settled. "Okay," she said, "I'm ready."

The phooka spread out his arms and began shifting beneath her. His gray skin became covered in soft feathers, and his horns shrunk away until they were tiny tufted ears on either side of his eagle head. He pumped his wings, and Charlotte leaned forward and wrapped her arms around his neck, burying her face in his feathers. The moment he kicked off the ground, she let out a whimper, her face still buried in his soft, warm neck.

It wasn't until they were soaring above the trees that Charlotte peeled her face away from the phooka's feathers.

The night air was cold but refreshing, and as she sat up and stared at the world around her, she couldn't help but smile. The evening sun had nearly set beyond the horizon and the watercolor sky was darkening with each passing minute. Below them, the city of Mapleton glowed in the lengthening shadows. Children must have been out trick-or-treating around this time, filling pillowcases with chocolates wrapped in foil and candy-apple suckers dipped in caramel.

The phooka carried her over Mapleton and toward the agricultural fields on the far edges of town. From up high, Charlotte could see the corn maze that changed every year and the patches everyone raided for the perfect carve-worthy pumpkin. The phooka shifted his wings and started a long, slow descent toward the corn field in the dark. Charlotte leaned forward and wrapped her arms around his neck again, hiding her face as they spiraled closer and closer to the ground. She knew he was about to land when he stretched his wings out wide and tilted them just slightly, catching the wind to slow their movement. It got rough after that, with all the flapping and crunching of the corn and then finally, the silence.

She peeked up from his feathers and found herself surrounded by tall stalks of corn that shifted gently in the evening breeze. She slid carefully off the phooka's back, weary of pulling out any of his feathers, and then watched as he shifted back into his original form.

"I've been taking pumpkins from these fields for years," he said. "An old farmer lives here, and he keeps the stone in his dwelling."

"How do you know for sure?" she whispered.

"I can feel it," he said, "just as I can feel a storm brewing or a shift in the air. I feel it here." He put a clawed hand to his chest and tilted his head. "Can't you?"

Charlotte took a long, slow breath and closed her eyes. The wind tugged on her hair and whistled through the corn, and somehow, just barely, she felt a thrumming in her chest like the distant beating of a drum. With her eyes still closed, she placed a hand on her heart and tapped out the rhythm that she felt.

"Yes," the phooka said softly, approvingly. "You are the Shrine Keeper, after all."

"Of course I am," Charlotte said, blinking her eyes open. "Now how do we get to that stone?"

The phooka smiled. "This way, Keeper." He led her through the corn, his tall horns poking out well above the stalks.

Charlotte moved as quietly as she could, though that was no easy task when shuffling through a field of dry corn. The wind was picking up, thankfully, so her footsteps and crunching through the stalks were somewhat masked by the sound of the wind through the fields.

The phooka paused at the edge of the corn field and snorted as he looked around. "The stone is there," he said, pointing at the farmhouse across the field. Lights glowed yellow in the windows, and smoke curled in tendrils from the chimney.

"How are we supposed to get in there without him noticing?" Charlotte asked, but the phooka did not respond. She looked up at him in the dark and felt a chill across her arms. With his eyes glowing and his goat's head silhouetted against the sky, he looked exactly like the creature that ran through her nightmares. She turned away and cleared her throat. "What's that building over there?" she asked, pointing out a dark shape to the west of the farmhouse.

"The barn," the phooka said. "He keeps horses inside." At this he snorted irritably, and Charlotte wondered if it upset him.

She didn't like the idea of horses, or any animal, being penned up. At the thought, an idea struck her. "I know what to do."

The phooka flicked his ears and turned his head slightly.

"You can take on the form of a horse, right?" she asked. He nodded and Charlotte smiled. She was suddenly very glad she'd read that chapter about the phooka in Art's fairy book. "I'll sneak into the barn and open all of the stalls, and you'll lead the horses out into the fields. The farmer will have to come out and get them back inside, and while he's busy we can sneak in and grab the stone." She expected the phooka to nod or agree with her, but he just stood there silently looking over the fields. "Well?" she asked. "Do you think it will work?"

He nodded slowly. "Yes, Keeper. I believe it will work." He turned his head toward her, and his glowing eyes met her gaze. "You are brave, and because of this I will help you."

The phooka let out a long, slow sigh and transformed into an old horse with a swayed back.

Charlotte was unimpressed. "Why are you so old?" she whispered as she climbed, with some struggle, onto his back.

He pinned his ears at her, and although she didn't know much about horses, she figured that was his way of telling her to shut up.

The phooka carried her across the field at a bouncy trot, and there were multiple times when Charlotte thought she would fall off. There was no saddle to hold onto, so she ended up entwining her fingers in his mane to keep from slipping off. Although the ride was short, it was rough, and she was thankful when they made it to the dark barn and she slid off his back.

"Wait here," she whispered, "and when the horses see you, lead them into the field." She crept closer and felt around in the dark for the latch on the barn door. She smiled to herself when she found it and then slowly pushed it open. The barn door squeaked on its hinges and Charlotte paused, her heart beating hard. She waited, expecting the farmer to run out and demand to know what she was doing, but nothing happened. No shadows moved in the windows of the house, so she pushed the door the rest of the way open.

The barn smelled like manure and hay, and the cracks in the roof overhead let silver moonlight slip inside to illuminate the horses in their stalls. They flicked their ears and watched her with wide eyes.

"Hi," she whispered to the horse in the first stall. "You wanna go outside?" She undid the latch on the horse's stall door and pulled it open, making sure to get out of the way so that he wouldn't trample her.

He stepped out, cautious at first, and then froze when he saw the phooka. The horse stood straight and tall, his nostrils fluttering as he inhaled the phooka's scent. He looked gorgeous standing there in the silver moonlight, with his head high and his tail lifted like a banner. The horse moved toward the phooka hesitantly, and Charlotte got back to work.

She continued to make her way through the barn, letting one horse out at a time. They all congregated in the aisle, touching noses and nickering to each other, all the while watching the phooka with curiosity and caution. But when the phooka tossed his head and galloped off into the field, all the horses ran after him. They kicked up their heels as they ran and whinnied to each other in joyous voices, their tails trailing behind them as they galloped away from the barn. Charlotte would have liked to stay and watch them, but the farmer would be coming out soon to see what the commotion was, so she hurried out of the barn and ran around the back to hide in the shadows.

From where she crouched she could see the front door of the house, and she held her breath when the old farmer came out on the porch to see what was going on. He threw his hat down when he saw the horses running free and then proceeded to pull on his boots and set off toward the field. He walked slow and the horses were a long way out, so Charlotte figured she'd have enough time to get into the house, find the stone, and get out without him noticing.

He walked over to the barn first, and Charlotte crouched down to hide in the shadows while he rummaged around inside. She saw a halter in his hand when he set back off across the field and exhaled a sigh of relief. She had just turned back toward the house to watch the windows when she felt something brush up behind her. She jumped and whipped around, but it was only the phooka.

"You scared me," she said, trying to calm her beating heart. "Does anyone else live here with him?"

"No," the phooka said. "He's been alone many years."

The outside of the farmhouse was illuminated in yellow light, a spotlight against the dark night. "What if he sees me?" Charlotte whispered.

"Run fast." He chuckled in the dark behind her.

She rolled her eyes. The books said the phooka was a mischievous trickster, but they didn't say anything about his sense of humor.

"Will you stay close behind me?"

"I'm with you, Keeper," he said, and for some reason, that made her feel a lot better.

"Okay, on the count of three," she said, still watching the farmer cross the far field. "One, two, three!" She sprinted out from behind the barn, heading straight for the house. The light washed over her and her skin prickled, but she kept running. She hit the porch, yanked the door open, and stepped into the front hallway. The screen door clicked closed a few seconds after she'd stepped inside and the phooka squished himself into the hallway beside her. His horns were so tall that he had to hunch over to keep them from hitting the ceiling.

"There," he said, pointing into the living room. Sure enough, the fairy stone, a big and beautiful black rock shot through with veins of shimmering purple, sat displayed on the mantel. It was concealed in a case of glass, like something someone would put a valuable baseball in.

Charlotte took a few steps into the room and then jolted to a stop. A dog was asleep on its bed by the couch, and when it saw her it lifted its head and snarled.

"Hi, handsome," she whispered to it in a high-pitched voice, but it wasn't fooled.

It stood slowly, the hair along its spine lifting. She took a step backward, reaching out for the phooka, but he wasn't there. The dog barked, and Charlotte took another few steps back, trying to figure out an escape route. She could go back out the screen door, but the dog could probably push it open. She glanced to her right down the hallway leading into the bedroom and thought she might be able to barricade herself inside. The dog snarled again and then lunged forward. Fear overtook her, freezing her to the spot, and all she could do was cover her eyes and wait. She imagined what it would feel like for the dog's teeth to sink into her skin, pull muscle from bone, and leave her bleeding for the farmer to find. But it never happened.

Vicious snarling and snapping filled the room, the sound of two dogs rather than one. Charlotte opened her eyes and found a large black dog drawing the farmer's dog away. He was the size of a gray wolf, and with his hackles raised and his teeth bared, he looked lethal. The farmer's dog didn't back down. The two canines growled at each other, and while they were distracted, Charlotte rushed into the living room and snatched the fairy stone off the mantel. It was heavy in her palm, and she felt its magic pulsing through the glass.

As she turned, the farmer's dog lunged at her. It grabbed her pant leg and shook its head viciously, knocking Charlotte to the ground. She dropped the stone when she fell, and the glass case shattered on the hardwood floor.

The phooka was on top of the farmer's dog before Charlotte could cry for help. He grabbed the dog by the scruff of the neck and yanked. The dog released Charlotte's pant leg, and she immediately scrambled to her feet, wincing at the glass that cut into her palms. She grabbed the fairy stone and ran toward the door.

"Come on!" she called back to the phooka, watching out over the field for the farmer. She didn't see him but she could see the horses running around, so he must have been having a tough time catching them.

The phooka snarled at the dog one more time and then backed away, and Charlotte pulled the front door closed so the dog wouldn't be able to follow them. She led the phooka around the side of the house and into the shadows. It was only then that she breathed a sigh of relief. The phooka transformed back into himself and knelt beside her to see the stone.

"Well done," he said, "but you are hurt."

"I'm fine," Charlotte said. "We have to go."

With a shrug, the phooka turned his back to her while she tucked the stone safely inside her jacket. Her hands were bleeding from the glass, but the adrenaline kept the pain at bay. She climbed onto the phooka's back and held on tight as he shifted into an eagle beneath her. She leaned forward and wrapped her arms around his neck, and this time she watched as he flapped his wings and lifted off into the night sky. He soared up and over the barn, and Charlotte saw the farmer down below still trying to catch the horses as they danced away from him.

The phooka circled back around, and before she could ask what he was doing, he dived toward the pumpkin patch, tearing a scream from Charlotte's lungs before he snatched up a pumpkin in his talons and lifted back toward the sky.

"You scared the crap out of me," she told him, but of course he said nothing in return. They soared through the night sky, the air cold on

Charlotte's face. She snuggled down into the phooka's soft feathers and wondered how things had come to be this way. Twelve hours ago, she'd been terrified of this creature, and yet he'd somehow become her protector and partner in crime, all in the course of one evening. Was that how all fear was? She felt like she'd wasted so many years of her life being controlled by it, only to discover that there was nothing to fear in the first place.

She remained quiet as they flew through the night, the only sound that of the wind in her ears and the air brushing over the phooka's wings. The air was cold but the phooka was warm, and despite everything she'd been through tonight, Charlotte felt calm. She could feel fairy magic radiating from the stone, still tucked safely inside her jacket. She'd done it—she'd retrieved the final stone.

The fairy shrine was still bustling with activity when the phooka landed softly amongst the stones. The gathered fairies stepped back, and the deer bounded off into the trees only to return later with ears flicking cautiously. Charlotte slid from the phooka's back and then waited as he shivered, dropping feathers to the ground as he regained his goat form.

"Thank you," Charlotte said, looking up into his glowing eyes.

He knelt, one knee upon the ground, and bowed his head. "Thank you, Shrine Keeper, for restoring magic to this world. We will remember this, always." He held a gray hand out toward the last standing stone, the niche in its belly waiting to be filled.

Charlotte unzipped her jacket to pull out the gently glowing fairy stone. At the sight of it, the assembled fairies began to whisper.

"Here you go," she whispered to the stones. "I give it back to you now." And with that she placed the fifth, and final, fairy stone in its place.

The air pulsed with such strong energy that it lifted Charlotte's hair and knocked fairies from the treetops like a sudden gust of wind. Energy crackled around them and tingled across Charlotte's skin. At first all was silent, but after it passed, the forest erupted into celebration. The forest came alive with song and dance. The phooka settled back against a tree to eat the pumpkin he'd snatched from the farmer's field, and it was only when Charlotte saw the stringy pumpkin flesh dribbling from his lips that she realized what exactly she'd seen on that night eight years ago. It wasn't a human head he'd been eating, despite the years she'd spent thinking so. The phooka had been eating a pumpkin on that night, and it was probably thanks to his frequent trips to the pumpkin patch that he had known the location of the fairy stone. Funny how things worked out.

Most of the deer had run off when the fairies began their celebrations, but one remained, and it walked quietly out of the forest and stepped up to Charlotte. It had beautiful antlers and wide brown eyes, and Charlotte recognized it as the deer that had been watching her for the past month.

"Who are you?" she asked, and in response the deer bowed its head.

A beam of light shot forth from the star on its forehead, so bright that Charlotte had to shield her eyes and turn away. When she turned back, the light was receding not into the deer's forehead, but into the dryad's.

"It's you," Charlotte whispered, realizing now that it should have been obvious all along. "You're the one that's been watching me."

"Yes," the dryad said, "and I am so proud of what I've seen. You've done all that I've asked, and have succeeded in not only restoring our magic to the Greenwood, but also in conquering your fears as well." She glanced at the phooka and gave Charlotte a small smile.

"Where's my mom?" Charlotte asked. "And where's Art?"

The smile slipped from the dryad's face. "You've done much for us, but there is one task you've yet to complete. Look around." She gestured to the assembled fairies and forest creatures. "These innocents are losing their homes." She looked at Butternut, still trembling in the old brownie's arms. "Some have even lost their lives." There was determination in her eyes. "You must put an end to the destruction of the Greenwood. I've seen the machines they use to rip down our sacred trees and have smelled the smoke and poison they spit into the air. You're our Shrine Keeper, and as such, our last hope. Please, save our trees." Then the dryad did something Charlotte never thought she'd do. She bowed.

Shocked into silence, the other fairies began to do the same, all except for the phooka. A shiver raced across Charlotte's skin.

The dryad was right. She was the Shrine Keeper, and it was her duty to protect the forest and its inhabitants from forces that would have rather seen it torn to the ground. Forces like Mr. Nolan.

"I'll stop them," Charlotte said. "And when I do, you'll return my mom and Art, and will swear *never* to take anyone from me again."

The dryad lifted her head and gave Charlotte a serious nod. "I'll do as you say. Now go, and stop this before it's too late."

CHAPTER THIRTY-ONE

She knew Mr. Nolan wouldn't listen to her—she'd already tried. The men at the work site would either laugh at her, kick her out, or worse. She couldn't risk going back there again, not until she had more leverage. There was only one person Charlotte knew that Mr. Nolan might listen to—his wife.

She ran through the trees, her feet sure on the forest floor as she jumped over rocks and made her way over tangles of roots impeding her way. She barely noticed the shadows between the trees now, and when she did, it wasn't with fear. She'd faced her worst fear and had come out of it alive—nothing could stop her now.

Once she emerged from the forest onto the dirt road that led up to her home, she sucked in a deep breath and ran. Her lungs burned and her legs ached, but she kept going. The sun had already set, and Mr. Nolan wouldn't be at the job site all night. Charlotte needed to get to his wife and tell her what was going on before Mr. Nolan arrived home. And in order to do that, she needed a ride.

"Dad!" she yelled as she burst through the front door. He was on the phone in the kitchen and was so startled that he dropped his cell and the screen cracked.

"Shit, Charlotte, you scared me." He picked up the broken cell and sighed. "What is it?"

"Can you help me? It's about Mom."

Dad abandoned his cell on the kitchen counter and grabbed his keys.

A few minutes later they were in his truck bouncing down the gravel drive. Charlotte hadn't explained everything, it would have taken too much time, but she told him enough to get him moving and get his keys in the ignition. She gave him directions to Art's house and chewed her nails anxiously whenever they hit a red light. Dad's knuckles were white on the steering wheel.

"It's that one up on the right," Charlotte told Dad as they drove under the skeletal oak trees that clattered in the wind.

Dad pulled over and Charlotte jumped out of the car.

"I'll be back," she told him, and then slammed the door and ran up the steps to the front porch. There were children trick-or-treating at all the houses on the street except this one. The porch light was off, and it looked anything but festive.

Charlotte rang the doorbell and waited. No one answered, so she rapped her knuckles against the wood. "Mrs. Nolan? It's Charlotte. I need to talk to you. It's about Art."

The door opened thirty seconds later, and there stood Mrs. Nolan, her eyes swollen, hair disheveled, and the home phone up against her ear. Charlotte could hear a man's voice coming through the speaker and held a finger up to her lips.

"Don't tell him it's me," she whispered, and Mrs. Nolan narrowed her eyes. "I'll tell you everything," Charlotte whispered again.

"I'll call you back," Mrs. Nolan said into the phone. "There are kids at the door. Yeah, yeah. I'll let you know. Okay, bye." She hung up the phone and stepped back. "Come in, please."

Charlotte stepped through the door and followed Mrs. Nolan into the kitchen. There were photos of Art spread across the kitchen table. Baby pictures, photos of his artwork, handsome shots that must have been senior photos.

"What do you know about Art?" Mrs. Nolan asked. "My husband said you were at the job site. Why?"

"Can we sit down?" Charlotte asked. "I have a lot to tell you."

A few minutes later they sat across the kitchen table from each other, steaming cups of tea in hand. Mrs. Nolan kept wiping at her puffy eyes, turning them an angry red in the process. Charlotte wasn't sure where to start, so she began by pulling Art's bracelet out of her pocket and handing it across the table. Mrs. Nolan's eyes went wide. She took the bracelet and held it against her chest.

"Where did you get this?" she asked.

"From Art. About an hour ago."

"An hour ago? I don't understand. Do you know where he is?"

Charlotte took a long, slow breath. "Just try to keep your mind open, okay?"

Mrs. Nolan nodded, and then Charlotte told her everything. She went all the way back to the day her mom went missing. She told Mrs. Nolan about the fairies and the dryad and the fairy stones. She came clean about the real purpose for the ritual at the lake, and about why Art had lent her all his books.

"Arthur knew about all of this?" Mrs. Nolan asked quietly, and Charlotte nodded.

"He's been helping me."

"Is that why they took him?" Mrs. Nolan asked, her voice wavering on the edge of anger.

Charlotte shook her head. "I don't think so. He's important to me, but I think the dryad took him because he's your husband's son."

"What does my husband have to do with this?"

Charlotte told her the rest of the story. She told her about the destruction in the Greenwood and the dead pixies and that the dryad would hold Art captive until Mr. Nolan halted the project in the woods and never lifted a finger against the trees there again.

"Art is leverage," Charlotte explained. She trailed off into silence and stared down into her mug of tea, which had gone cold.

"So why are you here?" Mrs. Nolan asked.

"Because your husband won't listen to me. You're the only one he'll hear, and if you don't convince him to stop building in the Greenwood, then I don't think Art or my mom will ever come home."

Mrs. Nolan didn't say anything. She looked down at Art's bracelet, and tears welled up along her lower lashes. Charlotte played with the sleeves of her jacket, anxiously waiting to hear what Mrs. Nolan would say.

"Mom?" came a small voice from the doorway, and Charlotte turned to see Tomas standing there. He seemed smaller than usual, and he still had his pajamas on.

"Come in, love," Mrs. Nolan said, and Tomas ran barefoot across the kitchen and jumped into her lap. He wrapped his arms around her neck, and she kissed the top of his head.

"Miss Charlotte is telling the truth," Tomas said quietly.

"What?"

"She's telling the truth." Tomas looked over at Charlotte, his eyes framed by dark lashes, just like Art's. "I saw her with a stone at the museum. It belonged to the fairies."

Mrs. Nolan looked at Charlotte and pursed her lips. She stroked her son's dark hair slowly, her eyes never leaving Charlotte's. Finally, she nodded.

"I searched everywhere for this bracelet this morning," she said, holding it up. "He never takes it off, and he'd never give it away." She slipped the bracelet onto her wrist and then kissed Tomas on the forehead. "I believe you. Now tell me what to do."

✖

Twenty minutes later, Dad's truck bounced down the dirt road toward the construction site. Mrs. Nolan sat next to Charlotte with Tomas on her lap. He had a puffy jacket on over his pajamas and stared out the window without saying a word. When Charlotte had thought about how to convince Mrs. Nolan of the fairies, she'd never thought to bring Tomas into it. He may very well have just saved his big brother.

Charlotte's heart pounded as the bright lights from the construction zone came into sight.

A man greeted them at the closed gate and inquired as to their business when Dad rolled the window down.

"I'm here to see my husband," Mrs. Nolan said, leaning across Charlotte to talk to the man in the hardhat.

"Evening, Claire," he said, and then opened the gate so Dad could drive through.

Dad parked the truck, and all four of them climbed out. Mr. Nolan saw them across the job site and headed their way as Charlotte slammed the truck door.

"Wait here," Mrs. Nolan said, and then went to meet her husband halfway.

"Who is this guy?" Dad asked, his arms crossed as he came around the front of the truck.

"Art's dad," Charlotte said, and then went on to explain that Art had been kidnapped by the same fairies that had taken Mom.

Dad's eyes softened, and he seemed to look at Mr. Nolan with gentler regard after that.

They watched from a distance as Mr. and Mrs. Nolan spoke. Neither one of them seemed happy, and Mrs. Nolan started waving her arms around at one point. Their voices carried, and Charlotte turned away as she heard what they said to each other.

"Do you know how much money we'll lose if I abandon this project?" Mr. Nolan asked.

"Are you *seriously* trying to put a price on your son's life?" Mrs. Nolan yelled back. She was so loud that some of the workers on the site paused what they were doing to watch the drama unfold. It wasn't until she pulled out Art's bracelet and held it up that the conversation settled down. Mr. Nolan took it and examined it carefully, and then he held it up to his chest like Mrs. Nolan had done earlier. After what looked like softer words were spoken between them, Mrs. Nolan waved Charlotte over.

Charlotte took a deep breath and set off across the job site. She could feel the eyes of the workers on her as she crossed under the beams of light shining from their trucks and stepped up to Mr. Nolan.

"You've seen my son?" Mr. Nolan asked, holding up the bracelet, and Charlotte nodded.

She could feel her dad hovering just behind her, ready and waiting.

"Then show me," he said. "Prove it."

Charlotte was trying to come up with something clever to say when she felt a warm, gentle hand on her shoulder.

"It is difficult for one so set in his ways to open his eyes to the other," the dryad said, tilting her head as she looked at the Nolans. "This flower will allow one a temporary peek into our world. Give it to him, and I will do the rest." The dryad placed a delicate flower in Charlotte's palm. It was soft yellow with heart-shaped leaves, and Charlotte recognized it as primrose. She'd planted it in the back garden with Mom on many summers past.

Charlotte held out her hand, the dainty yellow flower on her palm. "Eat this flower, and everything will make sense."

"What?" Mr. Nolan said, grimacing. "I'm not eating that."

"Eat it," Mrs. Nolan said. "For your son."

Mr. Nolan gave her a long, hard look. A tense moment passed between them before he picked up the flower and shoved it into his mouth. He chewed and chewed, staring all the while at his wife. He swallowed, hard, and then looked back at Charlotte. His mouth fell open.

"Holy shit," he muttered, his eyes flicking to the dryad. "Wha-What is that?" He looked either ready to faint or barf—Charlotte wasn't sure which.

"Mr. Nolan," the dryad said, and his face drained of color.

Right there, in the middle of the job site with his family and employees all watching, Mr. Nolan fainted. Dad jumped forward to catch him, and then he carefully lowered him to the forest floor. It only took a few seconds for his eyes to flicker back open, and when they did, the dryad was right there waiting.

"Welcome back," she said. "We've many things to talk about. Come." She offered him her hand but he scooted away, terrified.

"I'm not going anywhere with you," Mr. Nolan said as the onlookers exchanged confused glances.

"I'll go with you," Charlotte said. "You have to do this for Art."

Mr. Nolan still didn't look comfortable with the idea of following the woman with antlers into the forest, but he took Charlotte's hand when she offered it and got back to his feet. He brushed off his pants, straightened his jacket, and then gave Charlotte a small nod.

Together, the three of them walked further into the woods. They stopped at the fence, and the dryad reached up and slipped her fingers through the chain-link.

"Your fences have separated family members from one another," she said softly. "Innocents couldn't escape when your trucks came through, and now their family members mourn while we speak."

"What is she talking about?" Mr. Nolan whispered to Charlotte. "Is this some sort of Halloween prank? Because if it is—"

"I speak for the forest, Mr. Nolan," the dryad said, turning to face him with fire in her eyes. She was taller than him, even without her massive moss-covered antlers, and she looked beautiful and powerful standing there in the moonlight. "I speak for the flowers, for the trees, for the creatures that call this place home." She leaned forward, right up to his face, and her beautiful features folded into a snarl. "You will remove your machines from this sacred land. You will send your men home and instruct them never to return. You will make certain that humans never desecrate this place again, for if they do, it will be *you* I come for next." She grabbed him by the front of his jacket and, struggle as he may, he could not get free of her. "Do you understand me, Mr. Nolan?"

With wide eyes and a jaw slack with shock, Mr. Nolan gasped out an agreement. "Yes, yes, I understand. Now let me go!"

The dryad did just that, giving him a shove that sent him sprawling in the dirt. "I'll be watching," she said. "Do as I say, and your son will be returned to you. Fail to follow my orders, and you'll never see him again. Now *go*."

At her order, Mr. Nolan scrambled to his feet and took off across the job site. He waved his arms and yelled at his workers, who seemed frightened and confused by the change in their boss. Charlotte stood by the dryad, watching in amazement as the men removed their hardhats and packed up their belongings.

"Why didn't you do this before?" Charlotte asked, glancing up at the dryad.

"I could not have provided him the flower without your help, nor could I have forced him to eat it on his own. His mind was already beginning to open to us, or else the flower would have been powerless. Only those with the capacity to see the other can do so." She looked down at Charlotte and smiled. "Because of you, and the hope you gave him, he had the capacity to do so."

They stood longer still and watched as the machinery, driven by angry-looking men, rolled out of the forest and back down the dirt road the way it had come. One worker left a lunch bag behind, and Mr. Nolan picked it up and threw it at the man, yelling at him not to litter in the woods. The man held up his middle finger before climbing into his work truck and taking off down the dirt road.

"Get out!" Mr. Nolan yelled at the men who loitered, and a minute later the job site was abandoned. Only the damage that had already been done remained, including the crushed log that still pained Charlotte to look at.

"Happy now?" Mr. Nolan screamed, whipping around to look at the dryad. Although she was standing right beside Charlotte, his eyes couldn't seem to find her.

"The flower's magic has already worn off," the dryad explained, watching him with dignified disinterest.

"Now what?" Charlotte asked, turning to look up at her. "What else do I have to do to get my mom back?"

The dryad gave Charlotte a smile. "You've done it all," she said, taking Charlotte's hand. "And I believe it's time that I properly introduce myself." She turned to face Charlotte and dropped into a curtsy. "My name is Orrenda, but you may call me Ren. It is an honor to share my true name with you." She dipped her head so low that her antlers nearly touched the forest floor.

"Ren," Charlotte said softly, enjoying the sound of it on her tongue. "Thank you for trusting me. I know it's special to you."

"Yes," Ren whispered. "As are you, Charlotte Barclay." She leaned in and brushed her lips gently against Charlotte's.

Charlotte's eyes fluttered closed, only briefly, and then the touch on her lips was gone. When she opened her eyes, they filled with tears.

Mom and Art walked slowly out of the dark, stumbling and confused and looking like foreigners in a strange land.

"Mom!" Charlotte screamed, and then ran to crush her in a hug.

She felt Dad's arms around her next, and together they held Mom in a sandwich too tight to escape. Together they all sank to the forest floor, crying and laughing. Tears streamed down Dad's face as he covered Mom's cheeks and forehead and eyes in kisses. Across the way, the Nolans embraced Art, and Mrs. Nolan cried into her son's shoulder. Tomas wrapped his arms around Art's leg and didn't look like he would ever let go. From the corner of her eye, Charlotte saw a pale creature move in the dark, and when she glanced up she saw the white tail of a deer disappearing into the trees.

Although she doubted the dryad could hear her, Charlotte whispered a quiet "thank you" to the trees.

"Where are we?" Mom asked, looking around with sleepy eyes. "I don't remember how we got here."

Charlotte and Dad looked at each other and smiled.

"There's so much I have to tell you," Charlotte said, clinging to Mom's hand.

Dad ripped off his jacket and draped it across Mom's shoulders.

"Come on," he said, helping Mom to her feet. "Let's get you home."

"Wait!" Mrs. Nolan called before Charlotte could slide into the front seat with her parents.

"I'll be right back," she told them, but they were too busy kissing each other to hear her. She closed the passenger door and walked across the grass to where the Nolans stood. Mrs. Nolan was the first to embrace her.

"You are a blessing to us all," she whispered into Charlotte's ear, hugging her tight.

Tomas gave her a hug around the waist, and Charlotte laughed and ruffled his hair.

"I'm glad you're my violin teacher," he said, and Charlotte had to wipe away a happy tear.

"I'm glad, too," she said.

Mr. Nolan was next. His face was pale and his hair was disheveled, but he wrapped Charlotte in a hug and thanked her anyway. "I don't really know what happened here," he said, "but you were brave, and I respect you for that. Thank you." He gave her a shoulder squeeze and stepped back, wrapping an arm around his wife. "Tomas," he said. "Let's go home." The three of them walked off toward Mr. Nolan's truck, and that left Art.

Neither of them said anything at first. He stood there with his hands in his pockets and a smile on his face that made his beautiful green eyes crinkle in the corners. The moonlight illuminated the fly-aways from his dark, curly hair, and finally Charlotte couldn't stand it a moment longer. She stepped forward and slipped into the curve of his body, wrapping her arms around his waist and burying her face in his chest. He wrapped his arms around her and tucked his head down next to hers.

"What happened?" he asked, his voice muffled as he talked into her hair.

"She took you," Charlotte said.

"The dryad?" Art asked, and Charlotte nodded. A smile stretched slowly across his face, and Charlotte pulled back to look at him.

"What are you smiling at?" she asked.

"You know what that means, don't you?" he asked, slinging an arm over Charlotte's shoulders. "I guess you love me after all."

CHAPTER THIRTY-TWO

There were tears and embraces between Mom and Grandma when they arrived home, and then they all stayed up way past their bedtime to hear the stories Charlotte told Mom about the fairies and what had happened while she'd been gone. Charlotte slept better that night, cuddled up in her mom's embrace, than she had slept all month.

The old brownie that had watched after Butternut came by the house later that week to leave the young pixie in Charlotte's care. Charlotte accepted the responsibility with open arms, and the Barclay family grew by one.

Charlotte didn't return to school that week. The family needed time to heal, and they all abandoned their other responsibilities and to-do lists in order to spend their time together. By the time Saturday rolled around, almost a week after the chaos on Halloween, Charlotte felt almost back to normal.

She woke up to see snow covering the ground outside her window, and tears sprang to her eyes when she realized that Mom was home for the first snow. This was always their special day together, and it would be their day together again.

Dad went outside to chop wood and then started a fire in the old wood stove to keep Charlotte and Mom warm while they cuddled on the couch and knitted tiny sweaters for Butternut to wear. The hedgehog pixie sat on the couch between them, fast asleep on a ball of yarn. Charlotte had been surprised to find that Mom could see Butternut, as well as the other fairies that frequently visited the house. Her time in Lyra had given her the Sight, and Charlotte was overjoyed to know that she wasn't the only one who could see the fairies now.

Grandma made hot tea and brought the steaming mugs into the living room on a platter, and then the three of them knitted and sipped tea and talked of winters past and plans for Thanksgiving. They turned on the news to find out how severe this snow storm would be, and Charlotte pointed at the screen in excitement.

"Look! It's Mr. Nolan."

They all leaned forward in interest and listened as Mr. Nolan announced that he wouldn't be using the acreage in the Greenwood for a shopping center, as he'd originally intended, but had decided to donate it to a wildlife protection organization instead. Everyone in the crowd clapped and flashes lit up the screen as the whole Nolan family, Art included, smiled for photos with people wearing Mapleton Wildlife Organization sweatshirts.

"Well, would you look at that," Grandma said, clucking her tongue.

"Hey, Char," Dad said when he came in the front door. He stomped the snow off his boots and then removed them before walking into the living room. "This came in the mail today."

Charlotte took it and her cheeks heated up. It was a pamphlet for a college in Colorado, only about an hour from Mapleton.

"What about Bellini?" Grandma asked.

"I don't know if I want to go there," Charlotte said, hyperaware that Mom and Dad were listening in as well. "It's just that, I love it here. I love you guys, and I have the fairies to take care of now." She stroked Butternut gently and smiled when the pixie started to snore. "Besides, there are colleges in Colorado with amazing music programs. I don't *really* need to move to another continent to study music."

There was a pause, and then Mom leaned over and kissed Charlotte on the cheek. Dad ruffled her hair, and Grandma sat back in her chair and smiled knowingly.

"You're not disappointed in me?" Charlotte asked.

"Why would we be?" Mom pulled her in for a hug. "You're an adult. You have to make your own decisions."

"We'll support you either way," Dad said, leaning over the back of the couch to plant a kiss on Mom's cheek.

Just then Charlotte's phone rang, and she carefully untangled herself from the yarn and ran to her bedroom to answer it. "Hello?"

"Hey." It was Art, and he sounded like he was smiling. Charlotte could hear people talking behind him.

"I just saw you on TV," Charlotte said, plopping down on her bed. "It's amazing."

"Right? Who knew I could look so handsome in a suit?" They both laughed, and Charlotte rolled her eyes. "But in all seriousness," Art continued, "it's crazy. I never thought my dad would do something like this."

"Strange," Charlotte said. "It's like something changed his mind."

"Is that Arthur?" Mom asked from the doorway. Her blond hair hung loose around her shoulders, and Charlotte had to catch her breath at the sight of Mom standing there. She'd been gone for so long that Charlotte appreciated every moment they had together now. "Invite him for dinner, and call Melanie too. We're having chili."

"Chili?" Art asked, clearly having heard the invitation.

"We always make it on the night of the first snow," Charlotte explained.

"I'd love to come. See you tonight."

✼

Mom helped curl and style Charlotte's hair, and together they picked out a cute outfit for Charlotte to wear to dinner. They decided on a plush sweater, black leggings, and leg warmers. It wasn't something Charlotte ever would have picked for herself, but she had to admit that it looked great. She'd really missed Mom's fashion sense.

Art arrived right on time, and he even came bearing gifts. "Vegan pumpkin pie," he announced as he handed Charlotte the bag. "You'll love it." And then he stepped into the house and pressed a delicious kiss against her lips, his face still cold from the snow outside.

"Gross," came a voice from behind him, and then laughter filled the entryway as Melanie rushed in and wrapped Charlotte in a hug.

"Don't be rude," Marco said, giving Melanie a playful look before he reached out to shake Charlotte's hand. "Thank you so much for having us."

"No need to be so formal," Grandma called from the kitchen. "Get your butts in here. Dinner is ready!"

They ate around the kitchen table, which was too small for seven. Mom sat on Dad's lap, and they hugged and kissed throughout the entire dinner.

Art held Charlotte's hand under the table and she felt dizzy on his touch. She glanced over at him while they ate, unable to take her eyes off him. He was wearing a green sweater with a pressed collar poking out from underneath, and he looked schoolboy handsome. Even Grandma said so, which had made Art blush.

Melanie wanted to know the story behind Mom's miraculous return, and Charlotte promised to tell her everything later. *That* was bound to be an interesting conversation.

After dinner Charlotte and Art went out on the porch carrying steaming cups of coffee with spiced creamer. Before long the brownie came out of the woods and climbed up on the railing.

"Shrine Keeper," he said, removing his hat and bowing to her.

"It's good to see you, too," Charlotte said, smiling at him. Then she gestured between the brownie and Art. "Art, this is the brownie. He's the one that helped me with everything."

Although he'd only spent a day in the fairy realm, he too had come home with the Sight, and he'd been ecstatic to learn of his newfound gift.

"Actually," the brownie said, clearing his throat. "You can call me Thistleweed."

"Thistleweed?" Charlotte asked, a smile spreading across her face.

"Yes, yes," he said. "Don't wear it out."

"It's a fantastic name." Charlotte gave him a kiss on the cheek that made his cheeks turn red.

"What's that you've got there?" Thistleweed asked after wiping Charlotte's kiss from his cheek.

"Ever tried coffee before?" Art asked, holding out his mug.

Thistleweed gave the coffee a little sip, and a moment later he'd gulped it all down. Charlotte shook her head and laughed. Thistleweed burped and handed the mug back to Art.

"Hey," Art said, looking down into his empty mug, "wanna hear something crazy?" He looked up with a glimmer in his eye. "My mom's a *witch*."

Charlotte almost spit out her coffee. She swallowed, hard, and then smiled. "That's awesome. Maybe she could teach me something sometime."

"I should have known you wouldn't be surprised," Art said, shaking his head with a smile.

"Hey, I have something to tell you, too."

"Hmm?" He looked over at her, his eyes bright and his cheeks red, and

Charlotte knew she'd made the right decision—for many reasons.

"I've decided to stay here for college. I know I'm still a junior, but I'd been planning to go to this crazy prestigious school in Italy. And I've changed my mind."

"Why?" Art asked, his brow creasing.

"Because of my family. And the fairies. And this place." She waved a hand at the forest and smiled. "I found a few schools with really amazing music programs," she went on to explain. "They're a few hours from here, but at least I won't need to get on a plane."

"Are you sure about this?" Art asked, turning to put his hands on Charlotte's hips.

"Positive." She wrapped Art in a hug. She reached up to cup his face, prickly with the beginnings of a beard, and gave his bottom lip a gentle tug.

"Hey, love birds," Melanie called from the open window. They jumped apart and Melanie laughed. "Come inside. Time for a movie."

"Caught in the act," Charlotte mumbled, and then she and Art began to laugh. She picked up her mug of coffee, which Thistleweed had sneakily drank as well, and together she and Art walked back into the house to join everyone for a movie.

❦

The night was perfect and magical and ended all too soon. Melanie hugged each member of the family, lingering with Mom, and then leaned out of Marco's passenger seat window to wave as they drove away. Charlotte kissed Art goodbye at the door, watched him drive down the snowy drive, and then collapsed into bed still wearing her clothes. She could still feel his breath on her face and the touch of his hands on her hips, and she wondered what lay in store for them in the upcoming year.

Mom was home, Art was officially her boyfriend, and everything seemed to be falling into place. But, if Charlotte had learned anything over the past month, it was that the fairies had a way of changing everything.

She rolled over in bed and looked out her window. Unsurprisingly, a deer with beautiful antlers stood outside, its breath steaming out around its nostrils in the snowy air. Charlotte went to the window and yanked it open, then leaned outside to feel the cold on her face.

"Hello, Ren," she said to the deer. It flicked its ears and tipped its head at her. "What is it?"

The deer glanced into the trees, and then back at Charlotte.

A minute later, Charlotte crunched across the frozen yard in her boots. She was bundled up in her winter jacket, the big hood pulled up over her head.

The deer lingered at the edge of the Greenwood, and when Charlotte got close it bounded off.

"Slow down," Charlotte grumbled, following slowly as she weaved through the dense trees.

The deer led her deeper into the forest, slowing down each time Charlotte fell behind.

"Seriously," Charlotte said, planting her feet and refusing to move. "What's this about?"

The deer looked over its shoulder, and Charlotte followed its gaze.

A fairy stepped out of the shadows, his royal-blue skin glittering softly in the silver moonlight. He was tall and lean and dressed in a flowing tunic and tailored pants. Long black hair tumbled across his shoulders and tangled in the crown of leaves encircling his head.

"Thank you, Ren," he said. He smiled, his eyes and forehead wrinkling softly. "I've heard so much about you, Charlotte, and wanted to make your acquaintance. My name is Torin." He held out a hand, and Charlotte offered hers. Torin took it and kissed her knuckles gently.

"It's nice to meet you, too," Charlotte said, tucking her hand back into her pocket. A long, cold silence fell between them, and then Torin laughed. His breath steamed out around his lips.

"You must be wondering why I'm here," he said, and Charlotte nodded. "There's something I'd like to give you." He reached into a deep pocket on the inside of his tunic and pulled out a small, weathered journal. "I've had it much too long."

Charlotte took it and turned it over in her hands. It was warm and soft, and the pages were yellowed with age. "What is it?"

"A diary," Torin said, and he gave Charlotte a sad smile. "It belonged to someone I knew a long time ago."

"Can I read it?" Charlotte asked.

Torin nodded.

Charlotte undid the clasp and the journal fell open in her hands. The first page had nothing but a name, inked in a looping script.

Lillian Adair

Charlotte looked up at Torin. "Who is this?"

"I called her Lilli, but most of our kind called her Faer."

Charlotte narrowed her eyes. "I've heard of her," she said. "Who was she?"

Torin's lips turned up in a smile. "If I count the generations correctly," he said, "then she would be your great-great-grandmother."

Charlotte's eyes went wide. "My *grandmother*?"

"And that," Torin said, pointing at the journal, "is our story."

The End.

ACKNOWLEDGEMENTS

So much hard work went into this book, and I know I wouldn't have been able to persevere without the help of some very important people.

First and foremost, I want to thank the community of writers and readers on YouTube, Instagram, and Twitter. You all supported me and cheered for me and kept me honest. There was a time I thought it best to just abandon this book and move on, but I didn't, and you're one of the reasons why. I wanted to make you proud, and I wanted to make myself proud, and I have.

This book challenged me in so many ways. The plot holes were maddening, the research that went into filling those plot holes was tedious, and every word I wrote had to be combed over time and time again before being allowed to appear in this final draft. The first forty-nine thousand words of this story are still sitting in a trash folder somewhere, never to become anything more than a relic of what this story could have been: an afterthought.

So many of us allow our ideas to take hold and sweep us away, but then we let go and they flutter off without ever looking back. But when one of those ideas takes hold of you, don't just let it go. Hold onto it, cling to it for dear life, and eventually it'll settle in and take up permanent residence in your mind. That's what this book did for me. The idea was almost lost, nearly abandoned, and yet here we are, and I have all of you to thank for it.

A massive round of applause to each and every one of my beta readers. I trusted you with my book when no one else had ever seen it, and you were kind and thoughtful and encouraging and I am incredibly thankful for that. This story wouldn't be what it is today without you.

Thank you to my editor, who polished my manuscript to a shine and taught me valuable tips that I'll use when editing my books in the future.

Thank you to my cover designer and interior formatter, who took this mass of black words on white paper and turned them into a masterpiece.

A thank you to my mom, who snatched my proof copy off the coffee table and started reading it while I was walking the dogs. Your excitement for the novel made me even more excited to publish it.

Thank you to my dad, who is always willing to have lengthy discussions on the phone or over the kitchen table about publishing, business, and all my dreams.

Thank you to my sister, who isn't much of a reader, but supports me anyway. And thanks for helping me out with my videos – you've got the keen eye that I sometimes lack.

You've all listened to me go on and on about this book, and you've never let your eyes glaze over in boredom, even if you wanted to.

And a thank you to Greg, my love, who took me on that hike through the Enchanted Forest. We stood on that little wood bridge and I thought, "This is where fairies would live." I had no idea that two years later I'd be publishing this book about those exact fairies.

My heart is so full of love, and I can't wait to see where this journey takes me next.

Thank you.

ABOUT THE AUTHOR

Natalia Leigh graduated from Colorado State University with a bachelor's degree in English and a concentration in Creative Writing.

When not writing, Natalia can usually be found caring for her many pet-sitting clients, honing her practice on a yoga mat, or staring out a window at her favorite coffee shop.

Song of the Dryad is her third novel.

You can visit her at www.natalialeigh.com

CPSIA information can be obtained
at www.ICGtesting.com
Printed in the USA
LVHW111927011118
595631LV00009B/64/P